The SAVIOR

by MARVIN WERLIN
and MARK WERLIN

SIMON AND SCHUSTER   NEW YORK

ACKNOWLEDGMENTS

With thanks to Ron Adams, Philip Bruno and Don de Mesquita for their assistance, and with gratitude to Joan Sanger, our editor

For Jane Rotrosen, whose support, enthusiasm, care and concern made this book possible

The
SAVIOR

Prologue

The silver-gray Rolls-Royce glided silently past the luxurious homes of Philadelphia's most elegant Main Line suburbs. Narrow, sun-dappled streets bordered wide expanses of velvety green lawns that surrounded the stately Tudor, Edwardian, Colonial, and Victorian homes of wealthy, generations-old families. Private driveways were almost enclosed by great trees older than the houses they shadowed, trees that had been witnesses to history. Now they stood like massive sentinels, guarding the riches that lay behind them.

Driving west on Lancaster Pike, the Rolls left the suburbs behind and moved like an intruding phantom into the blazing Pennsylvania countryside. Autumn had swept a glory of red and gold foliage across the meadows, slashed with accents of slender white birches and vermilion-crowned dogwoods. As it flashed down the highway, the gleaming surface of the car reflected hues and tints in broad watercolor strokes; pockets of ground mist formed a multitude of tiny droplets on the gray metal, refracting the luminous saturation of color like cut glass.

Margaret Bradford stared out the window and shivered as if a chill had penetrated the enveloping warmth of her fur coat. She had a small oval face framed by fashionably cut short gray hair. The fine lines of middle age did not detract from her aristocratic beauty, but the vague, distant expression in her blue eyes seemed inconsistent with her bearing and apparent composure. With slender black-gloved hands, she lifted the cowl collar closer to her face and continued to watch the landscape streak by, her breath misting the glass. Gathering clouds passed before the late-afternoon sun, suddenly muting the fiery colors and giving promise of an early-evening drizzle.

"It's like a painting out of the Hudson River school, isn't it?" she murmured to the tall, white-haired man sitting beside her.

He patted her hand and she could hear the smile in his reply: "You say that every autumn, Maggie."

"Do I?" she asked vaguely.

In the touch of his fingers she sensed his tension and turned to look at him. The tired, worried expression in his eyes filled her with despair. He caught her look and smiled, revealing a flash of the spirited, vital handsomeness that she remembered so well. But the smile did little to relieve the lines of anxiety and grief that had, within the last year, so aged him. In those rare moments when she managed to forget her own pain, she saw what his anguish had done to him: the devastation of his spirit; his shoulders slumped in defeat; his eyes dulled, turned away from her, lost in thoughts he couldn't, or wouldn't, share.

He's so changed, she thought. And I, too? When he looks at me, does he see what it has done to me? Yes, he must. Bitterness and anger swept through her like a scalding heat as she thought of what had happened and what it had done to both of them.

And to Eric. God, what it had done to Eric!

"John, do you really think we're doing the right thing?" she asked, as she had so many times in the last few weeks.

He answered her patiently, trying to sound a conviction that he himself did not yet believe. "Yes, my dear, I'm sure it's right—for Eric and us. Now stop worrying." He smiled, hoping to reassure her. "Dr. Stevens said it will help Eric to stay with us for a while. It will give him a chance to—" he was about to say "recover" but finished instead "—get himself together, make plans for his future."

She saw the effort he was making to cheer her, and resentment flushed across her face, bringing spots of color to her pale cheeks. "And how do we get ourselves together? How do we go on?"

"Maggie, for God's sake," he sighed quietly.

"We're not much, are we, John?" She laughed harshly. "Money and all the goddamned breeding we could get from five generations of Main Line society, and here we are, cracked down our centers like cheap dinnerware!"

He bowed his head, his face set in a stoic expression, accepting her rage like a penance.

Leaning back against the deeply cushioned seat, she absently stroked the soft fur embracing her slim figure. "There was nothing to prepare us," she muttered in a tight voice. "Nothing to make us strong enough to—" Her words broke off and she fumbled in her purse for a handkerchief.

"Maggie, dear—" He touched her arm tentatively. "No one is ever prepared for that kind of tragedy. . . ."

She threw him a wild look and made a guttural sound of pain. "Tragedy! No, not a tragedy—a monstrous horror! An abomination!" She began to cry.

John put his arm around her shoulders, knowing how useless the gesture was, knowing that nothing could help now but time. She was right, of course. They were weak; protected all their lives by a cocoon of money insulating them in what was virtually a storybook world, positive that they were totally removed from the insanity that most people had accepted as a way of life.

They sat quietly as the car sped down the road and finally turned into a wide curving driveway bowered by tall stately elms. At the far end of the drive the Westvale Retreat appeared like an imposing country estate. With its noble columns and graceful veranda, wide windows and ornamental wrought iron, it looked as if it had been lifted bodily from somewhere in the Old South and transplanted to the rolling meadows of Pennsylvania.

The driver of the Rolls, a sturdy, pleasant-faced man in his early fifties, neatly dressed in a dark-blue suit and chauffeur's cap, turned to speak to them over his shoulder. "We're almost there, Mr. Bradford," he announced softly.

"Thank you, Michael." John pressed his wife to him. "Come, Maggie," he urged in a low voice. "We'll be with Eric in a few minutes. Let's do everything we can to make him comfortable."

"Yes, of course," she replied, taking out a compact to dab at her face with a powder puff. And then she added with uncharacteristic vulgarity, "The poor son of a bitch."

His bags were packed, books and records boxed. There was nothing else to do but wait. Eric sat down on the edge of the bed and looked around the room slowly. It was large and high-ceilinged, with pale-blue walls and white trim. Wide French doors opened onto a balcony that ran the length of the building, and opposite them, tall windows looked out over the ever-changing landscape. The furniture was antique and comfortable, a combination of English and Colonial that blended with almost no seams showing. The room had been his home for almost a year, and he'd grown used to it. But today he was leaving. He had expected to feel some sense of regret, or anticipation, or fear. He felt nothing, and wondered if that was all right.

Eric stood up, walked to the French windows and looked down at the curving drive that led from the road. He glanced at his watch. Margaret and John would be here soon to take him home. Home? No, not his home; to their house, the house that had been Jenny's home. He had no home. The apartment had been given up long since; other people were living there now.

He lit a cigarette and inhaled deeply, letting the smoke curl slowly out of his parted lips. Dr. Stevens had encouraged him to stay with Margaret and John, to be close to all the things Jenny had grown up with and so learn to live with his grief rather than deny its existence. "Remember everything," the doctor had counseled. Christ! As if he could forget. As if he would ever forget Jenny, with her long, dark hair like silk beneath his lips, the firm, full body that seemed made for his hands. And David, his son.

Eric leaned against the door, his blue eyes staring vacantly at the late-afternoon sun touching fire to the tops of the trees.

It had happened almost a year ago this month.

◆

Eric woke up before the alarm went off. He reached out and pushed in the alarm button on the clock, trying not to wake Jenny. She was curled up against his back with one arm flung around his chest and a leg nestled warmly between his thighs. It was the way she always fell asleep, her body pretzeled into his so that they formed a single solid shape under the covers. For Eric it was as if the whole of himself had slept, awakening to separate for the day, and then to be rejoined that night.

Enveloped by her warmth and her sweetly fragrant flesh, he watched the morning trickle through the drapes and lighten the night shadows in the room. Then he lifted his head slightly, straining to listen. Had the baby cried? No, just a deep sigh from the depths of the crib in the far corner of the bedroom. He smiled. The crib was an ornately carved, solidly made old-fashioned piece Jenny had found in one of the junk shops on Pine Street. During the last months of her pregnancy she had spent hours stripping away layers of dried, crusted paint and blackened varnish. Oiled and polished, the crib was reborn as a gleaming, lustrous walnut bed for their first child.

"A Wynters family heirloom!" Jenny had declared with satisfaction. "It will be the first bed for all our children. For David, then Andrew, then Kathleen, then—"

"Hey, wait!" Eric laughed. "How many kids are we going to have?"

"Who knows? I like the way you make babies!"

As Jenny had hoped, their firstborn was a boy, David. Six months old now, he was a wriggling bundle of energy and lopsided smiles, with his father's blue eyes and Jenny's dark hair.

Eric grinned with almost smug self-satisfaction; he had a son, a beautiful wife whom he adored, and a career that was moving into high gear, a career that had started two years before, when he was working as program director at John Bradford's WBTV, an independently owned television station. Eric had approached Bradford with the idea of letting him produce and host his own talk show, *Wynters at Large*. Eric wanted to interview everyone from visiting stage and screen stars to local politicians, resident celebrities in art, music, and literature, and victims of crimes on the streets; crackpots, cranks, and authorities on a wide variety of subjects that might excite the interest of people in Philadelphia and the Delaware Valley.

Bradford liked the idea. Eric had a strong background in public relations, a good education, an energetic approach to his work, and a salable appearance: six feet tall, athletically built, with light-brown hair, blue eyes, and an engaging smile. He would appeal to women and was rugged enough to encourage the respect and envy of men, a point in Eric's favor that Bradford was canny enough not to overlook.

The show was given a month's tryout. By the end of the third week the response from both public and press was strong and growing. Eric felt that he was on his way.

One night Bradford brought his daughter, Jennifer, to watch a show being taped, and he introduced her to Eric. At twenty-four, Jenny had the poise of Main Line breeding combined with the grace and striking beauty of a fashion model: dark hair that fell long and softly around her face, flawless skin, large brown, expressive eyes, and a wide, sensual mouth. She also possessed a candor that momentarily took Eric by surprise. When her father had moved off to talk with the director of the show, she stared at Eric frankly and said: "You're even better-looking in person."

His eyes swept over her svelte figure, trimly evident in a clinging red dress. "Thank you. So are you."

"What are you thinking?" she asked teasingly.

"You really want to know?"

"Uh-uh." Her eyes sparkled mischievously.

"That you look like a Vogue model with tits."

Jenny flushed slightly and laughed. "Direct and to the point, just as I had expected."

Eric continued to stare at her steadily.

"You're gawking," she said finally.

"No, I'm not. I always look like that when I'm hungry—for food," he added quickly. "I haven't had dinner yet. Have you?"

"No. But I will if you ask me nicely."

He grinned. "I just did. Now go sit in the back of the studio. We'll be finished here in about an hour."

"Why should I sit in the back?"

"Because I have a show to do and you're very distracting. You'll raise my blood pressure and lower my ratings. Now go do as you're told!"

"I think I like you," Jenny said bluntly.

Over dinner at Bookbinder's, he learned that she had been an art major in college, attended Pratt Institute in New York, and was currently designing graphics for a city magazine her father published, and newspaper ads for the station.

"As you can see, the Bradfords believe in nepotism." She laughed.

"I don't care what your religious beliefs are, I think you're wonderful," Eric replied, straight-faced.

She stared at him for a moment, then burst into a gale of laughter.

Eric shifted his body slightly and put an arm behind his head. He smiled to himself, remembering the weeks that had followed their first dinner together, the quick, comfortable way they started seeing each other almost every day, the long nights spent in discovery of mutual tastes, similar ideas, likes and dislikes. When they made love, Eric was surprised by her passion and abandonment, thrilled with her unhesitating sexuality. They were, he thought, perfect together.

The room was growing lighter. It was almost seven o'clock; he would have to get up soon. He could feel Jenny come awake behind him.

"Hi. You up long?" Her words were muffled against his back.

"A few minutes. It's early. Go back to sleep."

She stretched a little, nuzzling closer to him and moving her leg farther up between his. He felt her hand touch his chest, his nipples, then move down over his stomach in a silky, delicate exploration. He closed his eyes, his flesh responding with small tremors as her fingertips slipped to the insides of his thighs.

"Crazy girl, what are you doing?" he whispered, his cock quivering, springing into the warmth of her palm.

"Pretending I'm one of the blind men feeling the elephant. I just found the trunk." She giggled.

"Oh, God," Eric groaned, and turned to face her, his mouth covering her lips, his hands grasping the firm flesh of her buttocks. "Do we have enough time?" he teased.

"Christ, we'd better, or little David will have a very irritable mother today!"

Eric finished his coffee and grinned as the baby belched up some of his breakfast on Jenny's shoulder.

"The kid sounds like your father after a heavy meal."

"And he looks like you when he gets ready to pee." Jenny laughed. "Imagine getting erections at six months!"

"A chip off the old block."

"Chip, hell!" She gave the baby quick warm kisses and whispered into his ear: "You'll drive the girls crazy, you little lech."

Eric stood up, slipped on his suit jacket, and went into the living room to get some papers.

"You be home early tonight?" Jenny called from the kitchen.

"Maybe. Doing an interview with the father of the little boy who was murdered last month—the kid they found in the garbage dump.

And one with Vivian Lawrence. Her show opens in a couple of days."

Jenny put the baby down in his playpen and followed Eric into the foyer. "Honey, do me a favor?" she said, rubbing the back of his neck as she helped him with his topcoat.

"I just did, about an hour ago." He chuckled. "Now you owe me one."

She slapped him playfully on the rump. "No, seriously. That man —the boy's father you're going to interview. Take it easy with him?"

"What do you mean?" Eric asked, looking puzzled.

"Well—" She hesitated. "Don't come down too hard on him. The last couple of crime interviews you've done—that woman who was attacked, the man who was held up and beaten—sometimes the show sounds more like an interrogation than an interview."

Eric frowned. He had come under some attack from the press, and even a few members of his staff had criticized his interviews with people who had been victimized, either by crimes or by local political chicanery.

"Jenny, you know as well as I that the audience waits with bated breath to see someone break down, get confused or hysterical or defensive. It's a form of public sadism they've always indulged in. I have to get the people I interview to lower their guard, react spontaneously, no matter what that reaction is. What kind of ratings would the show get if I were one of those bland, commiserating, sympathetic hosts?"

"You don't have to explain the logistics of television ratings or the level of mass insensitivity to me!" Jenny flared angrily. "But do you have to attack your guests?"

"I don't attack!" Eric snapped.

"Eric, you can't always hear the way you sound or be aware of what you do—interrupting some poor inarticulate bastard who's groping for words with a witty put-down, suddenly changing the subject to disorient him—"

Eric stifled a groan and pulled open the front door. "That's what makes my show dynamic!" he almost shouted. "If I weren't forceful, I'd have to be all smiles, constantly avoiding controversy, rehearsing the interviews to make sure that nothing unpleasant is said! What the hell kind of show would that be?"

Jenny glared at him, her lips tightening. "I didn't mean to get into a fight with you about this. I just offered a suggestion! If you weren't so uncompromising, so insufferably dogmatic—"

"Dogmatic!" he exploded. "If I compromised myself at every turn there wouldn't be a show!"

Eric stormed out of the apartment, slamming the door behind him.

The rest of his day went badly. Eric hated himself for arguing with Jenny. During the morning staff meeting he gazed absently at his notes, castigating his cruelty and thoughtlessness, his insensitivity to her efforts to help him. By midafternoon he was wallowing in guilt and had categorized all his faults, enumerated every one of his short-comings. He began making elaborate plans to redeem himself with humble apologies and expensive gifts.

Just before the taping began, he called the apartment. There was no answer. She had probably taken the baby for a walk. His director signaled that the show was about to begin, and he walked onto the small, comfortable set of easy chairs around a large coffee table and took his place. His first guest was Robert Garson, the owner of a paint supply company in North Philadelphia, whose eight-year-old son had been kidnapped, sexually molested, and murdered. After the killer was captured, it was learned that he had been released recently from a state-operated institution for the mentally disturbed. Mr. Garson's reason for appearing on the show was to protest the irresponsibility of the doctors and state officials who had given the killer a premature release.

Eric gently led the still-shaken, grief-stricken man through the interview. When the distraught father broke down, Eric comforted him, added a terse plea of his own to the audience, and breathed a sigh of relief when the break came for a station commercial. His second guest, Vivian Lawrence, was the star of a new musical. Blond, brassy, and full of plugs for the show, she was a quick, easy interview, and then the show was finished. Relieved, Eric tried calling Jenny again. There was still no answer. It was almost five o'clock. He would go over the notes for tomorrow's show quickly and try to get home early. Maybe Jenny could get a baby-sitter and they'd go to dinner. He would make up for the fight over candlelight and wine.

As he started down the hall toward his office, his secretary came rushing up to him waving her note pad, oversized tinted glasses slightly askew on her short pug nose.

"What is it, Shelly?" He smiled. She'd been with him since the show started; a slightly overweight girl in her mid-twenties, always a little breathless, her short hair a shade more blond than it should be.

"Gore Vidal—his publicist just called. If we want to do an interview it will have to be tonight. His schedule's been changed; he has a booksellers' breakfast in the morning, a literary lunch he has to attend, and then a plane to catch for the Coast," she reeled off in a single breath.

"Oh, Christ! Did you tell Gary?"

"Yes, he's got the crew standing by. If we can do it, Vidal will be here in half an hour. He's waiting for my call." She beamed triumphantly. Getting Vidal to appear was Shelly's idea and personal project. Now it was going to happen, and Eric could see her quivering with anticipation.

"Call him—we'll do it," Eric sighed. And then he added: "It's a real coup for us, Shelly, and you did it. Thanks."

Her face flushed with success, she rushed back to the office. Eric frowned as he headed for the studio to talk with Gary Black, the director of the show. They had planned to do the entire show with Vidal as the only guest, which meant they'd be working very late. The romantic dinner with Jenny would have to wait.

It was almost midnight when Eric turned the corner of 14th Street and pulled up in front of the apartment house. He sighed wearily and looked up at the second-floor windows. There were no lights on. Jenny was probably asleep. He had tried calling her again before Gore Vidal had arrived, but there was still no answer. It worried him a little; she didn't usually keep the baby out so late.

Eric got out of the car and checked to see that all the doors were locked. He would have to clean out the junk they had stored in the garage to make room for the car. Parking on the street had become dangerous; in the last few months, vandals had slashed tires and broken windows all over the neighborhood. Even so, he and Jenny enjoyed living here in Center City. It was the closest residential neighborhood to the middle of town, running the width of Philadelphia from the Delaware to the Schuylkill. In the last few years the area had been reconstructed, blossoming with restored town houses, some of them dating back to the Colonial era. They had found the flat right after they were married. Although John and Margaret had offered to buy them a home close to theirs in the Main Line suburbs, Jenny insisted on living in town. It was convenient for Eric, being close to the studio, and they both liked being near all the city's cultural attractions. Using her own good taste and training as an artist, Jenny had done all the decorating herself, creating a warm and comfortable ambiance.

"It's our place," she had told her parents proudly. "If we ever want the Main Line, we'll get there on our own."

John had laughed, admiring his daughter's independence, while Margaret fumed and worried about the neighborhood being so close to downtown, a densely populated business area encroached on by slums.

Opening the front door, Eric saw that the hall light was out. Odd. Jenny usually left it on for him; there was only one switch, at the top of the stairs. He felt his way along the steps to the landing and flicked the light switch to see his key to the flat. Then he realized that the door was open, slightly ajar. Something was wrong. Jenny always made sure the door was locked when she was alone, especially since the first-floor apartment had been vacated recently.

He walked into the foyer, calling her name. There was no answer. The rooms were dark, and it suddenly seemed too quiet. His heart began to pound. He hurried into the living room and put on the lights. At first glance everything seemed normal. Then he noticed that a small table had been overturned and a ceramic lamp Jenny loved lay shattered on the floor.

Eric's throat went dry. "Jenny!" he yelled hoarsely.

A low moan from the bedroom made him break into a run, stumble against a chair in the hall, his breath coming in short gasps. The door was closed. He fumbled with the knob, his hands sweaty, and shoved into the room, searching for the light switch on the wall.

He saw the blood first. It seemed to be everywhere: on the floor, a spray of it on the white wall, but mostly soaking into the sheets bunched and snarled around her sprawled body on the bed. Her clothes were ripped, her arms slashed, her face a swollen discolored mass of bruised flesh.

Close to the bed, overturned and smashed in as if it had been kicked, was the baby's crib. It was empty.

The terrifying hours that followed were splintered into fragments of chilling reality and nightmare agony: the police swarming over the apartment, an ambulance siren shrieking a continuous echo of his pain as it raced through deserted streets, the swift flight down a yellow hospital corridor, a nurse barring the way as the stretcher bearing Jenny's torn body disappeared behind swinging doors.

Suddenly John and Margaret were beside him, their faces gray with shock and fear. They took him into the waiting room and they sat together, trying to comfort one another, but unable to speak. Pale, silent figures in the silent room, they accepted coffee from a young nurse, watched the large hands on the wall clock move slowly through the night hours, saw one another's faces grow haggard and drawn in the cold early light of dawn.

A doctor finally entered the room and stood by the door. Eric got to his feet, his body aching with dread. The doctor came to him and spoke softly, shaking his head, murmuring about extensive injuries and loss of blood.

Eric stood frozen. He heard Margaret cry out and John make a whimpering sound. The doctor was saying something to him, but Eric couldn't understand him. The man's face was changing shape, squeezing up into a puttylike distortion, enlarging like a misshapen balloon.

Eric began to scream.

The police had little to work with and only vague theories: the intent of the criminal was kidnapping; he must have known Jenny's parents were wealthy. She was beaten in the struggle to take the baby, but no clues were found in the apartment, and no one in the neighborhood had witnessed or heard the abduction. When no ransom demands were made, the police suspected that the kidnapper, fearing a murder charge, might have abandoned or murdered the baby. Weeks of intensive investigation proved fruitless, not a shred of evidence turned up.

Eric moved through the days like a sleepwalker, his grief and rage an unrelenting torment. Margaret and John were both under the care of their family doctor, and when Eric went to visit them, he came away shaking, close to collapse.

He moved into a hotel and avoided the calls of friends and members of his staff. Staying in his room most of the time, Eric was like a wounded animal hiding in a cave where he could nurse his grief and try to deaden his anguish. Eating little, drinking too much, he stared blankly at television for hours on end, desperately seeking some release. But when sleep finally came he was tortured with grotesque dreams of Jenny being savaged and David's tiny body lying broken in some foul grave. He would awake, drenched in the acrid smell of his own sweat, shouting hoarsely for his wife and son.

One morning the hotel maid, carrying fresh towels and linens, knocked at his door. Receiving no answer, she used her passkey to enter the room and found Eric lying on the floor, an empty bottle of barbiturates near his outflung arm.

◆

Eric watched the Rolls turn into the driveway and come to a stop. John and Margaret had arrived to take him home. He stubbed out his cigarette, slipped on a jacket, and picked up his bags. Without a backward glance, he left the room and walked down the hallway to the stairs with a brisk, determined step. He was well now; but more than that, he had a goal that filled him with a sense of purpose. During the months of recovery from his breakdown, Eric had become obsessed with the idea that his son was still alive. The police had never caught Jenny's killer, nor had they turned up any proof of the infant's death. Eric had decided that before discussing his feelings with Margaret and John, he would go to the police and ask them to reopen the case.

They were waiting in the foyer. At the doctor's suggestion, it had been almost six months since he had seen them last, although they had kept in touch by letter and telephone. They looked smaller than Eric remembered. Jenny's death has diminished them, he thought.

Margaret came into his arms and hugged him, her eyes bright with tears, covering her nervousness with quick, brittle laughter. John stood quietly, his smile not quite dispelling the haunted expression on his face.

While Michael took his bags and led the way to the car, they chatted, awkwardly trying to fill the gap of time and remembered sorrow. Eric put his arms around their shoulders, feeling a surge of love and concern for them. His own parents were dead; they were his family now, and they had carried the burden of Jenny's death and his breakdown alone. Now he was going to do something for them—he would find their grandchild!

A week later Eric drove into Philadelphia to see Lieutenant Charles Parker, the police officer who had headed up the investigation of Jenny's murder.

The day was clear and brisk, with the snap of approaching winter in the air. As he drove through the city streets, memories of Jenny tumbled before his eyes like a succession of snapshots: walking with her in Rittenhouse Square, long hours spent in the Rodin Museum, the laughter-filled lunches at the Automat, shopping sprees at Design Research and Gimbels to furnish their apartment. His hands tightened on the steering wheel and he guided the car carefully, nervously anticipating his meeting with Parker; he had to convince him to reopen the case.

The office was cramped and shabby, crowded with filing cabinets, a large metal desk covered with papers, and some hard, uncomfortable chairs. Eric blinked in the flat white fluorescent light and shook hands with Lieutenant Parker. He was a big man, more than six feet, with broad shoulders and a deep chest. Eric guessed he was in his early fifties.

"Sit down, Mr. Wynters," he said, his voice a deep, gravel rasp. "It's good to see you looking so well."

"Forgive me, Lieutenant," Eric said, lighting a cigarette, "but I'm afraid I don't remember you very well."

Parker made a sympathetic gesture. "I understand. The last time I saw you—well, you weren't in the best of shape."

"But I'm fine now—and I need your help."

The officer listened attentively while Eric explained the purpose of his visit. He nodded his head with understanding until Eric had finished. Then he leaned back in his chair and ran thick, strong fingers through an unruly shock of brown hair peppered with gray. When he spoke, his voice had the weary sound of a man who had fought in the jungle too long.

"I'm afraid I can't help you, Mr. Wynters. There's no new evidence to warrant reopening an investigation into your wife's death, and I simply haven't got enough men to spare to try to find your son." He pointed to the papers spread over the top of his desk. "They come in faster than we can record them: rapes, attacks, beatings, murders—it's as common as saying 'hello' to say 'bang, bang you're dead.'"

Eric's hands began to tremble and he clenched them tightly in his lap. "Then there's nothing that can be done?"

"There's nothing I can do, but—" The officer hesitated and Eric leaned forward.

"Please . . ."

"There is something you might do. It's a long shot, but it—"

"What is it, Lieutenant?" Eric pleaded.

"Two years ago a baby about eight months old was kidnapped. There were no ransom demands, no evidence of foul play, no clues. There was nothing we could do. The parents hired private investigators who uncovered a baby black-market ring. Incredible, isn't it? Kids bought from unwed mothers, stolen, or sold by people whose families are too large to sustain another child. Sometimes the sales are made through phony adoption agencies, or undercover, in back streets, like passing hot jewelry—and the criminals are that nice couple down the block."

Eric's face was pale. "What happened—to the parents looking for their child?" he asked, his throat suddenly dry.

"It took them two years and a lot of money, but a couple of weeks ago I learned that they had found him. The baby had been sold to a childless couple in Maine. The case is under investigation now."

Eric stood up quickly, his eyes glittering with excitement. "Thank you, Lieutenant—"

"Mr. Wynters, wait." Parker frowned, aware of what was going through Eric's mind. "If that did happen, your son could be anywhere in the United States—or even out of the country! These kids are transported from place to place to avoid being found."

Eric took his hand and gripped it tightly. "I understand that," he said. "But those people—they found their son! It's worth a try."

Parker nodded sympathetically. "I'll get you the name of the investigators who worked on the case. And if I get any information, any leads, no matter how slight, I'll call you."

Eric left Police Headquarters and walked down the street toward his car, oblivious to the noisy blare of traffic and crowds of people. In his coat pocket, like a key to a lock in an undiscovered door, was the business card of the investigating firm.

He felt strong and confident. The anguish he had been through was crystallized in a single, urgent conviction: somewhere his son was still alive and someday he would find him!

Part One

1

It was a cold, crisp day. Whitecaps glistened, a thousand tiny, dazzling reflections of the bright sun shining down on the harbor. Seagulls swooped and soared against the radiant blue sky, and heather-clad hills ringing the city looked down on green dells and glens and the flowing of the great Moray Firth.

The scene on the docks was one of frenzied activity; the air filled with shouts and curses of men loading and unloading cargo, the sound of waves beating against worn hulls and wood creaking as ships rocked in the icy waters. Winches and pulleys groaned with the weight of crates being lifted, and bells jangled, signaling an imminent departure.

Seaman Peter McKenzie hurried along the deck of the merchant steamer *Aurora*, his eyes searching anxiously through the crowd of men and women waiting on the dock below. Wind and sun had roughed high color into his cheeks and across the bridge of his long, straight nose, and although only twenty-four, the elements had creased the strong-jawed, handsome face with small lines that deepened when he laughed. Shaggy, sun-streaked blond hair escaped from under his woolen cap, and the solid bulk of his chest and strong arms strained against the coarse cloth of a dark-blue turtle-neck sweater. Broad shoulders easily supported his duffel bag, and his rangy figure moved with the light, rolling gait common to men who have lived at sea.

He stopped and leaned over the railing, his wide green eyes darting over the milling figures below. Then he saw her, a slim young girl standing at the edge of the crowd; Susan, his wife. Her long red hair was a halo of flame in the sunlight as she turned her face up to the ship looking for him. In her arms lay a tiny, blanket-wrapped bundle —the child he'd not yet seen.

Peter dropped his duffel bag and waved his arms wildly, calling her name. She started, turned her head and saw him. Laughing and waving her hand, she pushed closer to the gangplank, holding the tiny baby high against her cheek for him to see—Christopher, his son.

◆

They had met and fallen in love a little more than a year ago when Peter's ship had returned to Inverness for repairs. Although it was his home, he'd been away at sea since he was sixteen, and now felt as alien in the city as he did in the ports of the world he had seen. On his first day off the ship he had wandered the streets, dreading the weeks he would have to wait before the repairs were finished. Shy with women, and unassuming, he was most comfortable in the company of his shipmates, men who respected his great strength and good-naturedly accepted his quiet manner.

Suddenly wanting a sweet, Peter turned into a confectioner's on a side street and caught his first glimpse of Susan. She was standing behind the counter scooping candy into a paper bag for a customer. The afternoon sun pouring through the store windows seemed to bathe her in a golden glow, and for a moment he stood transfixed. While she finished the sale, he made an elaborate show of examining the trays filled with candies, stealing covert glances at her out of the corner of his eye. Finally he looked up and saw that she was watching him with an amused smile, her blue eyes sparkling mischievously. He shifted awkwardly under her steady gaze—and then grinned back.

It surprised both of them just a little that he was waiting for her when the shop closed that evening.

Over dinner at a nearby pub, Peter learned that Susan had left her native Ireland after the death of her parents in a railway accident. She had come to Inverness only a few months before when old family friends, the Donoghues, offered her a job in their candy store and a tiny apartment above the shop.

"You must feel as strange in the city as I do," Peter said.

Susan smiled. "I did—until tonight."

In the weeks that followed, Peter would wait every evening until the shop closed to take her to dinner and the cinema, or for long walks through the city. On Sundays, her day off, they wandered along the banks of Moray Firth and watched the townsmen fishing, or climbed the hills to picnic in deep, rippling fields of heather and talk about their hopes and dreams for the future. Peter was growing tired of the sea and wanted to settle down, perhaps buy a small farm and —he looked at her cautiously—marry and have a family. Susan had been raised in a rural area and felt a strong affinity for simple country life. It was her hope, she confided to him hesitantly, to find a strong, loving man to be her husband and father of her children.

From the ruins of Urquhart castle, they watched the sun set over the loch, saw the water turn to liquid gold and the sky fill with blazing reds and yellows against the approaching deep blue of the night. Peter took Susan in his arms. He had signed on for another voyage and would be gone almost a year. Would she wait for him?

The Donoghues and a few of Peter's shipmates attended the small wedding. In the few remaining weeks before Peter left, they made plans; Susan would continue to work and save their money, and when he came home, they would look for a small farm, begin to make their dreams a reality.

A few months after he had shipped out, Susan knew that part of their dream was going to come true. She was pregnant.

◆

In the kitchen of the tiny apartment they had rented after their wedding, Susan leaned forward, her arms resting on the table. She watched with amusement as Peter gently rocked the baby in his arms.

"He looks like you," she said. "Don't you think so?"

"He's so tiny," Peter whispered.

She laughed. "What do you expect? At three months do you want him to be a great lug of a man like you? And you don't have to whisper—once he's asleep, you could run a train through the apartment and he wouldn't wake up."

"Will he be tall, then?" Peter asked, smiling down at his son.

"Yes, love—tall and blond and handsome like you, a young Viking who will have all the girls chasing him down the street."

"You never chased me! It was I who chased after you." Peter grinned.

Susan stood up and took the baby from his arms. "That's what you think," she said dryly.

Peter chuckled and sat back, stretching his long legs. He stared up at his young wife, his eyes tracing over her long red hair framing her oval face, her wide blue eyes, short straight nose, and full, beautifully shaped lips.

"Is he down for the night?" he asked huskily.

"Yes," she answered in a low voice.

Peter followed her into the tiny cramped living room and watched as she tucked the infant into his crib, the gray wool dress she wore tightening over her slim hips as she bent down. He stepped up behind her, cupped her firm breasts in his large hands, and pressed himself into the softness of her buttocks. She straightened up against him, sighing as he kissed her throat.

"I don't have to chase you now, do I?" he murmured.

She turned in his arms, kissing him, her hands moving urgently over his body. "Oh, God, love, it's been so long," she moaned.

Moonlight filtered through the lace curtains at the windows, casting a silvery sheen over their bodies. Peter held Susan close to him and kissed her. His hands moved tenderly over her body, caressing the full breasts, teasing down her back. She made small impatient sounds deep in her throat and stroked his thighs and hips. Unable to restrain himself any longer, he moved between her legs and entered her with one swift movement. She cried out and tightened her arms around his neck, covered his lips with hers.

Suddenly he felt her body stiffen, go rigid beneath him. Her head fell back on the pillow and her eyes were wide and staring.

"Susan, what is it?" he whispered. "Did I hurt you?"

She lay quietly, without answering. Then, pushing him away, she stood up and turned to the door separating them from the living room. Her face was pale and expressionless, her body tensed, as if she were straining to listen to some sound being made far away.

Peter sat up, alarmed. "Susan, are you ill?"

Silently, she slipped on a dressing gown, opened the door, and hurried into the living room.

Peter followed, shivering as his feet touched the cold floor. He found her standing by the crib. "Is something wrong with the baby?" he asked anxiously, coming to her side. He leaned over and looked into the crib.

The infant lay on his back, his eyes wide open, staring at his mother with an emotionless, steady gaze.

"He's awake," Peter said, surprised. "I thought you said that when he slept nothing could—"

Seemingly oblivious to his words, Susan picked up the baby, opened her gown, and put him to her breast. She sat down in a chair, her face calm, immobile, waiting patiently until he had finished making tiny sucking sounds and was once more asleep. Then she put him back in his crib, covered him with the blanket, and walked back into the bedroom.

Never once had she uttered a single sound.

Peter followed her, bewildered. "I don't understand. He didn't cry, and you nursed him just a few hours ago . . . Susan?"

She was standing quietly by the bed, staring into space. He touched her shoulder, shook her gently. "Susan, love—what is it?"

Abruptly, she looked at him, her eyes blinking, focusing on his face. "Peter? What happened?"

She began to shiver and he drew her into his arms. "Are you all right?" he questioned anxiously.

"Why—of course, but what are we doing out of bed? My God, it's cold!" She huddled against him.

He lifted her into bed and got in beside her, holding her close to him until they were both warm.

"Is the baby all right?" she asked.

"He should be—you just fed him. Don't you remember?"

She lifted her head and stared at him, confused. "Did I? Why? Did he cry for me?"

"Not a peep. But I think your mother's instinct must have been working overtime. He was wide-awake, and very hungry," Peter said, smiling.

"The little devil," she murmured sleepily.

The months that followed were busy ones. With the money they had saved, Peter and Susan bought a small cottage on the outskirts of town. It stood a few hundred yards off the road on a grassy slope that rolled gently down to a wooded grove bordering a wide, rushing stream. Several acres of fertile land adjoined the property, and Peter hoped that with a good job he could earn enough money to buy them and begin the farm they had dreamed of. But he was a seaman, untrained for anything else, and jobs in the city that paid a decent wage were scarce for someone who was unskilled.

Susan watched him grow discouraged and restless. She had left the Donoghue's shop, and the money they had was beginning to dwindle away with the expenses of everyday living. To help out, Susan began to take in piecework sewing. She had always made her own clothes, and the women of the town who came to her thought she had a flair for dressmaking, improving on the patterns they brought her and even selecting materials and colors that better suited them. Peter reluctantly agreed, since she could do the work at home and keep an eye on Christopher. He was a good baby and would play quietly for hours on the floor, watching his mother cut patterns and pin material together, fascinated as she ran it through the sewing machine with calm, steady hands.

When Peter was approached by the shipping line to sign on for a voyage, this time as first mate, and at an increase in pay, it didn't surprise Susan that he was eager to do it. She agreed with his argument that they would have less of a struggle to save money, and a better guarantee for the baby's future. And he would be gone for only a few months, then home again.

It became the pattern of their lives for the next five years.

"It's not so bad," Susan told Mrs. McMillan as she pinned the hem of her skirt. "His voyages are short, and then he's home with us for a good while between."

"Well, I'm not sure I'd like the idea of Mr. McMillan traipsing around the world half the year," the woman declared, shifting her stout body to look in the mirror. "Don't you get lonely?"

"I don't have time," Susan answered sharply. Of all her customers, Mrs. McMillan was the one woman she disliked. Inquisitive and thoughtless, she spent most of her time eagerly seeking and spreading gossip. "Between my work and taking care of the house and little Chris," Susan went on, "there's too much to do."

"Well, you're a fine, understanding girl," the older woman replied, retreating from Susan's tone of voice. "And your little boy is darling! And so good! I never hear him yelling or crying like the other children. He's all right, isn't he? I mean, there's nothing wrong with him?" she asked with calculated sincerity.

"He's just well trained," Susan answered sweetly, smiling through clenched teeth.

"He certainly is!" Mrs. McMillan agreed with false heartiness. She gathered up her purse and gloves and walked to the front door, tugging at her girdle. "But you know, dear, good training in the home isn't really enough for any child. You should be taking him to church. Just the other day Father Gillian was asking me when you were going to join us. And there's a wonderful Bible story class for little Christopher."

Susan's face went grim. The woman was insufferable! But she was a customer, and paid well for her clothes.

"I'll certainly give it some serious thought," Susan replied, ushering her out of the house.

She waited until Mrs. McMillan had driven off before slamming the door and muttering: "The old bitch!"

The question of religious beliefs had plagued Susan many times. The daughter of lapsed Catholics, she had grown up seeing her parents endure the scorn of their neighbors rather than compromise their beliefs. They were Irish traditionalists, part of the movement founded by patriots, writers, and artists who attempted to promote a return to the Celtic origins of their country. Like the poet Yeats, they sought to bring pre-Christian lore and mythology back into the mainstream of Irish culture. For Susan, God was not to be found in the dogma of Christianity, but in nature and the beauty of His creations. Fiercely independent, she refused to be intimidated by the hypocritical piety of people like Mrs. McMillan and others in the town. She would live her life as she chose, and teach her son to do the same!

Susan turned back to her sewing, dismissing Mrs. McMillan's prying. Dollars-and-cents logic dictated that she would simply have to deal with the woman as long as she was a customer.

A few minutes later Christopher burst into the room, his thick blond hair blown in all directions by the wind.

"Our walk!" he cried breathlessly. "You promised a walk to the loch!"

Susan swung him up into her arms, delighted by the way he would suddenly appear like a wild, elemental sprite, exploding with childish energy. Now almost six years old, Christopher was growing into the image of Peter, with sparkling green eyes and sun-bleached hair that Susan lovingly referred to as "a crown of gold."

"Oh," she grunted jokingly, "what a great man you are becoming! I can hardly lift you. A walk to the loch, is it? And you say I promised?"

The child nodded solemnly, his large eyes imploring her to remember.

"Well, then, a walk it will be." She smiled, adding to herself: God knows, after a session with Mrs. McMillan I could use some fresh air!

The day was brilliant, the sky gleaming silver at the horizon and graduating to an intense blue that sharply defined billowing masses of white clouds. Wrapped in sweaters and scarves against the chilly fall breezes, Susan and Christopher walked through Glen Moriston and along the Highland roadsides. A herd of red deer ambled along the hilltops, and a flock of wild geese flew by overhead. They paused at the ruins of Urquhart castle and Susan remembered the moment when Peter had asked her to marry him. "Don't you get lonely?" Mrs. McMillan had asked.

You're damned right I do, Susan muttered to herself. He'd been away for three months and wasn't due back for another two.

Christopher tugged at her hand and they went on until they'd reached the grassy banks of Moray Firth where they sat down to rest. Susan smiled fondly at her son as he lay on his back, gazing at the ever-changing shapes of the clouds and giving each of them a name from the fairy tales and legends she had told him.

"Look, Mummy, look!" he cried, pointing to the sky. "The hound of Chulainn!" He laughed delightedly, then turned to her, pleading: "A story, a story—tell me a story!"

She laughed, remembering when she was a little girl in her grandfather's arms, listening as he spun out a treasure of tales like a true Irish *shanachie*, the storyteller who brought ancient heroes back to life. In his lilting voice he retold the wonders of their deeds, or whispered into her ear strange and eerie fancies he sometimes made up on the spot.

"No, it's your turn," she answered Christopher, ruffling his hair. "You tell me a story. You know them almost better than I do."

He sat up, creasing his brow with a grown-up frown. "Then I shall tell you the story of Cu Chulainn and his adventure with Aefa, the warrior goddess, and of his battle with the armies of Erc and Lewy."

Susan nodded, laughing to herself; those were his favorites.

When they returned to the cottage it was still early in the afternoon. Susan went to work at the sewing machine, cautioning Christopher to play close to the house and to come inside when it became too chilly. He waved and ran off into the fields to see a nest of birds perched in his favorite oak.

Clouds scudded across the lowering skies as the afternoon wore on. Christopher played in the tall grass, chasing imaginary beasts and fighting great wars. He heard the song of a bird and followed it into the thickly wooded grove that stood a few hundred feet behind the cottage. He wandered along meandering paths that led to the banks of a wide, rushing stream. It was only a tributary of the loch, but he imagined it a great harbor leading to the sea, bearing ships with black sails that voyaged to the other side of the earth.

Running along the bank of the stream, he imagined himself the hero Cu Chulainn, saving his people and defeating his enemies. Warring armies raged on the other side of the stream. He must ford the great river and engage them in battle. Christopher saw a path of flattened boulders and began to step from stone to stone, the water rushing rapidly between them, making white swirls of foam. The gaps between the rocks grew wider, challenging his bravery, and he jumped from one to the other, dangerously skidding on their wet surface.

Suddenly he lost his balance and tumbled into the swirling water. The swift rush of the rapids carried him downstream and slammed him into a log lying in a shallows. Stunned, he grasped the rotting bark and pulled himself up, clinging weakly to the log.

In the approaching dusk, Susan bent closer to the sewing machine and started a long piece of red wool under the needle, concentrating on the straight line of tiny stitches. Suddenly, she shuddered violently, as if an explosion had gone off inside her head. For one long moment she was unable to move, paralyzed by the icy sensation of tottering at the edge of an abyss. Then, without thinking what she was doing, she stood up quickly, overturning the chair, and began to run from the house.

She had no sense of where she was going, did not feel the cold mist against her face or the hard ground beneath her feet. She raced as one in a trance, dreamlike, flying through the fields faster and faster, as if some awesome force of nature were at her back, shoving her forward at a headlong, terrifying pace.

She tore into the woods, heedless of branches that ripped her clothes and slashed at her bare arms and throat. Trees and undergrowth shimmered, grew distorted, swirled around her body like fiendish, malevolent figures in a nightmare. At the bank of the stream, she turned without hesitation and ran to where Christopher had started across the boulders. Her body felt weightless as she flew lightly over the rocks and raced down the opposite bank.

A moaning wind surrounded her, whipping her hair before her eyes, stinging her face.

"Mummy!"

The piteous shriek cut through the ceaseless roaring in her ears and awoke Susan to a shocking awareness of where she was, what she was doing. Screaming Christopher's name like a madwoman, she searched the bank of the stream wildly and finally saw him clinging to the log. She threw herself into the water, struggling against the fast-moving current until at last he was in her arms, sobbing with fear and relief.

Dr. John McCallum softly closed the door to Christopher's room and walked into the kitchen where Susan sat huddled over a steaming mug of tea.

She looked up at the tall, portly man who had delivered Chris and taken care of him through a variety of childhood illnesses. "Is he all right?" she asked anxiously.

"Yes, he's fine," McCallum replied. "Do you have a cup of that Irish brew of yours for me?" He gestured to the tea, his eyebrows raised in a quizzical manner.

While Susan poured him a cup, he eased into the chair opposite her and said: "He's a bit bruised, and he may get the sniffles, but he's a strong lad. Just keep him in bed for a day or two—if you can." He chuckled at his bit of humor.

Susan shook her head with relief and ran trembling fingers over her brow. She had changed into a thick bathrobe of Peter's, wrapped almost double around her slim body, and her hair was still wet, lying in red strands across her forehead. She was pale, her face showing the strain of the last few hours.

Dr. McCallum sat forward and took her hand in his. "What about you, my girl?" he asked softly. "Are you all right?"

"Oh, yes, I'm fine," she answered with a distracted half smile. "Or at least I will be when my nerves stop dancing."

"You need a good night's sleep. I'll leave you something to help." He rose from the table and went into the hallway, where he had left his bag. Susan followed.

"Thank you, John," she said, helping him into his topcoat. "Thank you for coming so quickly. I was very frightened. . . ."

"I don't blame you," he said, rummaging in his bag. "The boy could have drowned, probably would have if you hadn't found him so quickly."

He pulled out a small bottle of pills and pressed it into her hands. "These will help you sleep." He shook his head wonderingly as he looked at her. "My God, the power of a mother's instinct. Amazing! That you knew he needed you—that he was in such peril. And to find him so quickly! It was a miracle, Susan, that's what it was."

"Yes," Susan replied after a moment's pause. "It was a miracle."

She opened the door for him and he bent to kiss her cheek. "Good night, dear. I'll come by in a day or two and check Chris out."

"Thank you, John. You're a good friend," Susan replied gratefully.

She closed the door after him and stood quietly in the hallway for a few minutes. Every bone and muscle in her body ached. She was tired and confused, and completely unable to remember exactly what happened.

In the living room she looked down at the sewing machine. The red wool she had been working on lay tangled under the needle. She stared at it, puzzled, searching her memory to fill the blank space of time between leaving the machine and finding her son. Then, slowly, the realization dawned on her. She had never actually known where Chris was or what had happened to him. She had run from the house, through the fields and into the woods, not instinctively, but *directed* by some force, some dominant will that had guided her to exactly where he was!

Susan sat down in a chair, her body trembling. It had happened before, she thought suddenly. When he was an infant—the first night Peter was home and they were making love; she had gotten up and gone to nurse Christopher without his making a sound or crying out for her. And there had been other times, other blank moments when she had found herself suddenly in his room because he had fallen or scratched himself while she had been working in another part of the house!

"I never hear him yelling or crying like the other children," Mrs. McMillan had said.

And it was true. Christopher had never cried for food or because he was wet and wanted to be changed or because he had hurt himself.

Whenever he had wanted or needed her, she had simply known and gone to him immediately!

Susan shivered and pulled the robe tighter. Had these things really happened or was she just so tired that her imagination was playing tricks? Suddenly she thought of her grandfather and the fanciful stories he had told her, stories that she told to Christopher and that he had memorized.

"Oh, Grandfather," she said aloud, laughing nervously, "what a wonderful tale you could have made up out of all this!"

Susan went into Christopher's room and looked down at him wonderingly. He was sound asleep, one arm flung outside his blankets. Yellow flames flickered and danced in the fireplace, casting a ripple of lights and shadows across his face. Quietly, so as not to wake him, she tucked his arm under the covers and pulled them up around his chin.

Dr. McCallum had called her rescue of Chris the power of a mother's instinct, she thought, gazing at her son tenderly. And that's what it had been, she decided. Nothing strange or mysterious, simply the miracle of her love for her child.

She started to leave the room and then something happened that she would never forget and never really understand.

As if seized by invisible arms, Susan was suddenly unable to move, gripped by a force that held her completely immobile. Then she felt a slow warmth spread through her, deep and comforting, like being lavished with a wave of love. Tears of joy came to her eyes as she stood overwhelmed by the sensation. Then, just as suddenly as she had been seized, she was released.

She staggered a little, stunned by what she had just experienced. Her face was wet with tears and she trembled, still in the grip of the extraordinary feeling of being absolutely loved.

Slowly, Susan turned to look at her son. In the pale amber light of the fire she saw that he was asleep, breathing evenly under the covers.

But he was smiling.

2

JANUARY, 1963

Heavy mists swept in from the sea, riding a bitterly cold wind that raced through the streets of the city. People hurried along the wet pavements, no more than vague shapes in the slate-gray light, pinched faces peering out of scarves and caps, and bodies that all but disappeared into bulky layers of sweaters and coats. By early evening the warm glow of streetlamps began to pierce the dense fog. A noisy clatter of dishes and shouts of laughter spilled from pubs and restaurants into the shrouded streets, offering an invitation to warm, cheery refuge from the chill of the oncoming night.

Susan pulled her coat tight and jammed her hands into the pockets, trying to keep warm. Her deliveries had taken more time than usual and now she was late getting home for dinner. She thought of stopping for a quick cup of hot tea, then decided against it, knowing that Christopher would be pressed up to the living-room window watching for her bus to come down the road. She smiled, thinking how dependable he was when she had to leave him alone to deliver the work she had finished. But in a few weeks Peter would be home, for a good long stretch this time, to be with his son—and with her.

And a good thing, too, she thought wryly; these marital vacations are hell!

Her bus pulled up and she got on quickly, grateful to escape the cold. On the road outside the city the fog had thinned to pale gossamer drifts that moved slowly across the Highlands and hovered over the dark waters of the Firth. Susan remembered that her grandfather had once called fog an enchantment of God, a silvery screen of magic that He would sweep across the face of the land to make the commonplace suddenly beautiful, serene.

But tonight, for some inexplicable reason, she felt uneasy, and found the fairy-tale loveliness ominous, a little frightening.

As she got off the bus and started across the field to the house, she saw a car parked in the lane by the front door. She wasn't expecting any customers, and the car looked unfamiliar. Had something happened to Chris?

Susan hurried up the porch steps and into the front hall, calling out: "Chris? I'm home—are you all right?"

In the living room a man in a dark-blue suit was sitting with his back to her, listening to Christopher tell a story. They turned at Susan's call and the man stood up while Chris ran to her arms.

"Hello, darling." She hugged her son, then looked up at the stranger.

"Mummy, this is Mr. Miles," Chris told her excitedly. "He's from the shipping line and knows Daddy!"

"Good evening, Mrs. McKenzie," the man said with a polite bow. He was middle-aged, with a smooth round face and thinning hair, and wore steel-rimmed glasses. The dark suit fit him snugly and the collar of his shirt was crisply white. His light-blue figured tie had a small, tight knot, and Susan thought he looked very official. The idea made her tremble slightly with anxiety.

She extended her hand and said: "Good evening, Mr. Miles. You're from the line?"

He hesitated, his eyes shifting to Chris nervously. Then, clearing his throat, he replied: "Yes, I am." There was a moment's silence and then he said, too heartily: "That's a fine lad you have, ma'am. He's been telling me some wonderful stories."

"Yes, Chris loves to tell stories," Susan answered softly. "Mr. Miles, why are you here? Is there something wrong?" she asked even more softly.

Mr. Miles fidgeted and adjusted his glasses. "Could we speak privately for a moment, Mrs. McKenzie?" he asked, glancing at Chris.

Susan felt a numbing tendril of fear start in her chest. She took a breath and said: "Whatever you have to tell me, Mr. Miles, my son can hear."

He looked at her uncomfortably and sighed. "Well—could we sit down?"

She nodded, and silently they sat down opposite each other. Chris came to his mother's side and took her hand. He knew that something was happening, something grown-up and not pleasant.

Mr. Miles leaned forward and his moon face took on a solemn expression. "Mrs. McKenzie," he began falteringly, "we've had word that the *Aurora* has met with an—accident. An explosion in the hold. . . ."

Susan's face drained of all color. She stared at Mr. Miles, examining his pale-gray eyes for some sign of hope. "Were there any survivors?" she asked finally.

He bowed his head, unable to face her. "No, ma'am. There were no survivors. All hands were lost."

"Oh, my God," Susan whispered, and then was silent.

Mr. Miles stood up and reached into his coat pocket. "I've some papers here to leave with you—insurance claims and a voucher for your husband's pay." He looked about helplessly and then put them on a table. "I'm very sorry, Mrs. McKenzie," he said in a low voice.

Susan sat without moving, her eyes wide and expressionless. Only her fingers holding Chris's hand moved convulsively.

"Thank you, Mr. Miles," she said finally, her voice strained. "I'll take care of those papers as soon as I can."

"No hurry, ma'am, no hurry. I'll be leaving you now." He picked up his topcoat and slipped it on quickly, relieved that his painful duty was over.

At the front door he turned to her. "If there's anything we can do, please call. . . ."

"Yes, I will. Thank you," Susan said tonelessly.

When he had left, she closed and locked the door and walked slowly back into the living room. Christopher came to her and took her hand. "Mummy, did something happen to Daddy?" he asked, looking up at her.

She stared at him, at the yellow silk of his hair and the large green eyes—Peter's hair and Peter's eyes. "Yes, darling," she answered huskily. "He's gone to join Cu Chulainn, and we shall not see him again."

Christopher frowned, looking puzzled for a moment. Then he asked: "But mightn't we see him in the clouds, then?"

A cry of pain wrenched from her throat and Susan fell to her knees, sweeping the boy into her arms and burying her face against his small chest.

◆

"Susan, are you absolutely sure that this is what you want to do?" John McCallum asked, his voice deep with concern.

She turned to him from the suitcase she was packing and replied: "Yes, John, I am. The last two months have been hell and I really can't stay here anymore. Inverness was my home only while Peter was alive to make it so. There's no one left in Ireland for me to go back to, and I need some place new, some place where"—her voice faltered and she bent over the suitcase—"where I won't have so many memories, so many reminders." She closed the suitcase, locked it, and straightened up. "There, that's the lot," she said with brisk finality.

John picked up the suitcase and two smaller bags sitting on the floor. "I'll put these in the car."

Susan took his arm. "Thank you, John, for being so good to us. I don't know what we would have done without you to help us."

"Nonsense, girl," he answered gruffly. "You've got a backbone made of pure steel. I just fussed around to keep you company and make sure that the boy was all right. Where is he, anyway?"

"Outside, playing in the fields. Here, let me help you with the bags."

"No, no—I can handle these. You lock up and we'll be off to the station. You don't want to miss your train."

Susan opened the front door for him and watched for a moment as he carried the luggage to his car. Then she turned for a last look at the house. In the gray overcast of morning the empty rooms appeared forlorn and desolate. She walked about slowly, lightly touching the walls and doors without thinking what she was doing. In the bedroom she imagined she could still smell a lingering trace of the pipe tobacco Peter had used, and tears welled up in her eyes.

Everything was gone, the last piece of furniture taken away this morning, bought and paid for, as was the cottage. There was nothing left here, nothing but memories. In less than an hour she and Chris would be on the train to London to start a new life. With the sale of the house, Peter's insurance, and the pay from his last voyage, she was sure they would be secure financially until she could get a job.

But she was worried about Christopher, how all these changes might affect him. Since Peter's death he had grown quiet and a little withdrawn, anguished as only a child can be over the mystery of life and death. She had done everything she could to comfort him. But there were moments when she thought of the incident at the stream, and later, those few seconds in his room that were so strange, and she would draw away, watching him, wondering what he was thinking. Then he would look at her, his eyes large and trusting, as if telling her without speaking that she was not to be afraid, that he loved her.

Susan went into the kitchen and opened the back door to call him. Christopher was standing in the middle of the field, his head tossed back, staring at the sky. The overcast had begun to lift and white clouds were slowly massing over the Highlands. He stood quietly, not moving, a tiny figure almost obscured by the tall rippling grass. He had taken off his cap and his blond hair caught the fresh light, moving in the breeze like fine strands of gold.

I will never see him quite like this again, Susan thought.

Then she called out to him to go to the car, that they were leaving now.

3

Mrs. Davis looked up from the manila folder on her desk, adjusted horn-rimmed glasses to sit more securely on her long, thin nose, and said: "So you've decided that London isn't what you want, after all." Her voice was slightly nasal and had a tone of carefully practiced refinement.

"Yes," Susan answered. "Oh, it's a friendly city. The people we've met have been very nice to us. But the expenses are high. We've lived here almost a year and it's been very difficult. I've gone through most of the money I had, and the saleswoman's job I have now doesn't really pay enough. You placed a girl I used to work with— Elspeth March—with an American family, and I thought perhaps—"

"Ah, yes, Elspeth," Mrs. Davis said. "She went to a family in California, some producer and his wife in Hollywood, I believe."

"That's right. She's written to me, and she's very happy there."

"I should think so," Mrs. Davis said disdainfully. "Those film people are very generous." She sighed. "I must admit, though, I do envy her the weather there." She gave Susan a wistful smile that revealed a great many teeth, and then said crisply: "Well, let's see what we can do for you."

"It doesn't have to be California or Hollywood or anything like that. A place in the country, perhaps?" Susan asked hopefully.

"Yes, yes," the woman murmured, opening the folder and shuffling through a few papers, stopping now and then to read something. Every so often she would pat her precisely set and sprayed blue-gray hair, as if to reassure herself that the lacquer was holding every strand in place.

"Well, it will be a bit difficult," she said finally. "You've worked as a seamstress and a salesgirl, and you have a child. A little boy, isn't it?"

"Yes, he's seven."

Mrs. Davis stared at her absently and rubbed her fingertips over creases of flesh under her chin. "Umm—yes. That's a bit touchy. And you've never worked as a domestic—"

"But I'm very strong and quick," Susan cut in.

"I'm sure you are, dear." She tapped a pencil against the desk and looked thoughtful. "I do have an American woman coming in shortly whom we might try. Let's see, I have her file here somewhere."

She got up from the desk, straightening a skirt that was too short for her skinny legs, and walked to a cabinet standing in the corner of the room.

"Ah, here it is," she said, pulling a large envelope out of a drawer. "Her name is Mrs. Stanwyck," she read aloud, "and she's looking for a woman to take back to the States with her." Pursing her lips, she stared at the sheet of paper in her hand. "Yes, we just might give this one a try. She'll be here in about half an hour. Do you want to wait?"

"Oh, yes," Susan agreed eagerly.

"Fine. I'll let you know when she arrives."

"My little boy is with me. He's out in the waiting room. Do you think that's all right? That she see him, I mean."

"Oh, I'm sure that if she's at all interested in you, she'd want to meet your son, too. Yes"—Mrs. Davis gestured grandly—"you may both wait."

"Thank you," Susan said. "May I ask where she is from?"

Mrs. Davis glanced back at the paper. "Pennsylvania. She and her husband live in a suburb of Philadelphia called Wynnewood— it's in a very elegant area known as the Main Line."

Charlotte Stanwyck swept into the office with a brisk, authoritative air. She appeared taller than she actually was due to the severe cut of her gray wool suit and the high crown of a large-brimmed felt hat. Everything about her suggested wealth, from the matching pearl earrings and single strand around her throat to the nonchalant way she carried a short cape trimmed in mink.

At her entrance, Susan looked up from the magazine she was reading and watched as she gave her name to the receptionist, a dowdy girl who was instantly intimidated by the woman's autocratic bearing.

"Would you tell Mrs. Davis that Mrs. Stanwyck is here. Mrs. Thomas J. Stanwyck." The tone of her voice was low but commanding, and, to Susan's surprise, contained the slight trace of an English accent.

The receptionist disappeared into Mrs. Davis' office in a flurry of clumsy movements while Mrs. Stanwyck stood imperiously by the desk.

Susan nudged Christopher, whose head was buried in a book of fairy tales he had brought along. He sat up straight and she fixed his hair, nodding over her shoulder toward Mrs. Stanwyck. He silently understood and smoothed his sweater and trousers to look neat.

Just before the receptionist returned, the American woman turned and gave them a casual glance. Susan returned the look evenly, noting the aristocratic, if somewhat fragile, beauty of her large dark eyes, the pale fine skin and cameo profile shadowed by the hat brim. Then Susan smiled and was pleased to see Mrs. Stanwyck smile back.

The girl opened the door to Mrs. Davis' office, uttering a faint: "Won't you come in, please?"

A few minutes later Susan was summoned.

"Do you mean that you made the dress you're wearing?" Mrs. Stanwyck asked dubiously.

"Oh, yes. I make all my own clothes, and my son's too," Susan replied.

Mrs. Davis nodded her head and smiled, affecting a familial pride in Susan's accomplishments.

"This is fine work," Mrs. Stanwyck said warmly, examining the stitching and the carefully placed darts, the cut of the dress. "You're really very good."

"Thank you," Susan said.

"I design a great part of my wardrobe myself, but I'm absolutely helpless with a needle or a sewing machine. And it's very frustrating trying to find someone who can translate one's ideas to the cloth."

Mrs. Davis stepped in smoothly, "I'm sure that Susan would be of great assistance to you. Possibly a real treasure!" she added too enthusiastically.

Mrs. Stanwyck ignored her effusiveness and continued to stare at Susan, a small frown lifting her eyebrows. Susan wondered what she was thinking. They had already discussed her references, her background, the fact that Mrs. Stanwyck was not looking for a domestic to work in the house but for someone to take care of her personal needs. The discovery of Susan's ability as a seamstress had apparently impressed her, and yet she was hesitating.

"I hadn't thought of someone quite so young," the woman said, looking at Susan doubtfully. "How old are you?"

"Twenty-seven."

"Twenty-seven," she repeated. A troubled expression crossed the fine planes of her face, and then, with blunt finality, she said: "No, I don't think it would work. But thank you, Mrs. McKenzie, for your—"

At that moment Christopher appeared in the doorway. He walked to his mother's side and took her hand, looking up at Mrs. Stanwyck curiously.

"Ah, this is your son?" she asked.

"Yes," Susan answered. "Christopher, this is Mrs. Stanwyck, from the United States."

He held out his hand and said: "How do you do, ma'am."

She knelt down and took his hand, saying softly: "How do you do, Christopher. What a handsome boy you are, and very well mannered, too."

He stared at her and murmured a small "Thank you."

Mrs. Stanwyck continued to hold Chris's hand. "Such beautiful green eyes," she remarked with a polite smile.

Susan started to say something about Chris having his father's eyes when she noticed that the woman's expression had changed while gazing at the boy. The polite smile had faded and a look of confusion appeared in her dark eyes, lasting only a moment. The grip of her fingers on Chris's hand tightened and then relaxed. She let go of him, touched his cheek lightly, and stood up. A flush of color suffused her face and her eyes glowed with excitement. Her whole manner seemed altered.

Abruptly, she told Susan: "I have a little girl named Nella. She's six years old."

"Oh?" Susan replied, puzzled by the difference in the woman's behavior.

"Nella had an accident a year ago," Mrs. Stanwyck went on. "She took a bad fall from her pony and hurt her back. The doctors don't hold out much hope for her ever getting off crutches."

"Oh, I'm so sorry," Susan said, trying to sound sympathetic. But she was bewildered; the woman spoke about her tragedy without a trace of sadness, but rather a strange agitation.

Mrs. Stanwyck turned and knelt once more before Christopher. "Would you like to meet my little girl?" she asked him. "Perhaps be her playmate? She has a tutor, but no children to play with."

Chris smiled and nodded enthusiastically. "I know lots of games and stories."

Mrs. Stanwyck gave him a quick hug and stood up, looking pleased. "It's settled, then." Her voice was excited. "You'll both come back to the States with me."

Susan stared at her in astonishment. "You mean you want us?" she asked, incredulous.

"I'll make the arrangements for your tickets and let you know when we're leaving. It should be in about a week." She turned to Mrs. Davis. "As soon as I know what my plans are, I'll contact you."

Mrs. Davis looked as startled as Susan at the sudden shift in her client's attitude, but quickly regained her composure. "I'm very pleased, Mrs. Stanwyck," she trilled. "You won't regret—"

"I'm sure I won't," the woman interrupted. She pressed Susan's hand, leaned down to give Chris a quick kiss on the cheek, and left the office, calling out cheerily: "See you both at the airport."

The door closed behind her elegant figure and there was a long moment of silence in the room. Mrs. Davis and Susan stood staring at each other until Chris broke the quiet, saying: "She's very nice, Mummy."

Susan didn't answer, too surprised by what had happened to speak. Mrs. Davis was suddenly galvanized into action and began to propel them out of the office, exclaiming breathlessly: "I never expected it to go so well! Americans can be so—unpredictable! But she's not really an American, you know. She's English. Born and raised here, she told me. But she's been living in the United States so long, I do believe she's picked up a bit of that American change-ability! They're always changing their minds, aren't they!"

Susan gathered up her coat and helped Chris into his windbreaker, barely listening to the woman going on about getting their papers in order, what an absolutely marvelous opportunity it was for them, and that she would call as soon as she heard from Mrs. Stanwyck.

A few minutes later they were out of the office and walking down the steps of the building into the rush of London afternoon traffic. Susan stopped to bundle her son up in his scarf and mittens against the biting cold of the wintry day.

"Aren't you glad we're going to America, Mummy?" Chris asked, wondering why she was so quiet.

"Yes, darling, of course I am. It's the most wonderful thing that could happen for us," Susan answered. Then her voice grew thoughtful. "I just don't understand what made Mrs. Stanwyck change her mind so suddenly. She seemed quite sure that I wasn't right for the job before you came into the office—"

She paused and stared at her son. He stared back at her, his face at once sober and hopeful, as if he had done something to please her and now wasn't sure that he had.

Susan grew pale. Had he done this? Had some silent communication passed between him and Mrs. Stanwyck, a communication as strong as the one that had taken her from the cottage to rescue him when he'd fallen into the stream?

She tried to control the trembling of her voice as she asked: "Chris, when you met Mrs. Stanwyck, did you—did you—" She stopped, at a loss for words, unsure how to ask the question that burned in her mind.

"Did I what?" Christopher asked innocently.

4

Susan stood by the tall black iron gates at the entrance to the Stan-wyck estate and waved after the school bus. She watched Chris's hand fluttering to her from an open window until the bus disap-peared around a bend in the road, then turned and started back up the brick-paved driveway that led to the mansion. Pale sunlight filtered through a dismal, leaden sky in a feeble effort to brighten the early morning. A soft mist lay over the grounds, glistening like a sil-very blanket, and teardrops of water ran off gnarled trunks and bare limbs of the great oak trees lining the drive.

Approaching the house, she stopped and admired once more the graceful dignity of its Colonial elegance, the sloping roofs and high, wide windows. A thick web of ivy rambled up brick chimneys to or-nately carved shutters and ledges, and crept around the fretwork of the second-floor balconies. Stately French doors led to barren ter-raced gardens; but in the spring (Mrs. Stanwyck had promised) all would be a riotous profusion of color—velvety green lawns and a patchwork quilt of flowers shining in the sun.

The gray, overcast morning, swept by chill March winds and filled with floating mists, reminded Susan of the cottage beckoning warmly through the winter fogs and of the Highlands rising like ghosts above Moray Firth. She and Christopher had been here for more than two months, but somehow the distance from their home to this strange new country seemed the distance of years. A fleeting sense of loss and isolation passed through her. She dismissed it from her mind and walked quickly up the drive to the front door; it was almost eight o'clock, and Mrs. Stanwyck would be expecting her breakfast tray.

As Susan came through the swinging doors into the massive kitchen of gleaming white porcelain and stainless steel, Mrs. Gregory, the cook, looked up impatiently.

"You're late," she grumbled. "She's already called down for her tray."

A hefty woman in her fifties, with hair the color of rusting iron pulled into a severe topknot and a face that looked pinched despite its width, Mrs. Gregory had a crusty, no-nonsense manner and ruled the kitchen like a tyrant. She was still suspicious of "the Irish girl"—her reference to Susan when gossiping with the rest of the staff—who had so quickly become Mrs. Stanwyck's companion.

"The school bus was late," Susan answered pleasantly while hanging up her coat on a rack near the door; she had been trying for weeks to make a friend of the woman. "I suppose Chris is really big enough to go down to the road by himself to wait for it. What do you think?" She faced the cook with guileless eyes, innocently seeking her opinion.

"Of course he is. Don't baby him," Mrs. Gregory admonished her. "He's a very self-reliant boy."

Susan went to the large chopping-block table in the middle of the kitchen and picked up Mrs. Stanwyck's breakfast tray. "You're right, of course." She nodded seriously. "Starting tomorrow he does it alone." As she walked out with the tray, she smiled and said gratefully: "Thank you, Mrs. Gregory."

A look of approval spread across the woman's face, and Susan breathed a surprised sigh of relief—she had finally cracked that rigid exterior; perhaps it would go more easily between them now.

It didn't surprise her, however, that Chris had already gained the cook's approval. Everyone in the house had taken to him from the first day they arrived: the two maids, Sarah and Betty; William

Donaldson, the chauffeur and gardener; Mr. LeClair, the young college student who was employed as Nella's tutor. And Nella.

When Mrs. Stanwyck introduced her daughter to Christopher, the two children had eyed each other solemnly. Nella was a pale little girl with large dark eyes and curly black hair. The long, painful recovery from her accident the year before had left her thin and quiet, and she clung to her mother's hand timidly.

Chris, his cap in his hand, made a polite little bow, and then grinned at her and asked: "Would you like to hear the story of Cu Chulainn? He was a great hero and had lots of adventures."

Nella's eyes widened with surprise at his Scottish accent. She nodded her head shyly. Within the next few weeks he had charmed her into laughter and squeals of delight with his stories and games, and the first day he went to school she had waited by her window all afternoon for the bus to bring him home.

◆

Susan hurried up the wide staircase that flowed in a sweeping curve from the center hall to the second-floor gallery. She still felt out of place in the magnificent house with its spacious rooms and ornate furnishings. Mrs. Stanwyck had given them small adjoining rooms with their own bath on the second floor, and even these were furnished more grandly than anything Susan had ever expected.

What amazed her even more was how quickly Mrs. Stanwyck had discovered in her capabilities beyond her proficiency as a seamstress. Now she was helping her employer with a busy social schedule that included organizing a variety of functions for many civic and charity organizations. Working together as they were, the two women had begun to form a close association that bordered on friendship.

Susan knocked lightly on Mrs. Stanwyck's door and went in, calling out cheerfully: "Good morning. Sorry I'm late, but the school bus was delayed and—"

She stopped, abruptly aware of a tall, husky man leaning against the mantel of the fireplace in the sitting area of the bedroom.

"Oh, I'm sorry," Susan said. "I didn't know anyone else was here."

"Did you bring enough coffee for two?" he asked with a slow smile, his slate-gray eyes examining her with more than casual interest.

"Why—yes, I did. . . ."

At that moment Mrs. Stanwyck came out of the dressing room.

"Good morning, Susan," she greeted her. "We were just talking about you." She went to the man and took his arm. "This is my husband, Tom. He surprised us all by returning home from Europe late last night."

Susan stared at him dumbly. On the plane from London, Mrs. Stanwyck had said that he was staying on in Europe to conclude his business. Now she suddenly realized that in the two months they had been here, she had never once heard him mentioned.

Recovering herself, Susan said: "Good morning, sir. And welcome home."

Tom Stanwyck shrugged out of his wife's grasp and came forward to take the tray from Susan's hands.

"Charlotte has been telling me some very nice things about you and your son," he said. His voice had a rough, almost arrogant tone, the sound of a man used to getting his own way.

Susan stood quietly, feeling a little uncomfortable. He had a look of enormous physical power; even the careful tailoring of his blue suit couldn't disguise the bunched muscles in his shoulders and arms, the tight pack of his thighs when he moved. She guessed he was about forty-two or forty-three, a few years older than his wife. Dark-complexioned, with straight black hair and a square, strong-boned face, he had a kind of coarse handsomeness: heavy brows, a thickish nose, and a wide, fleshy mouth that betrayed a hint of brutality beneath the sensual features that she found disquieting.

He put the tray down on the coffee table and said to his wife: "You didn't tell me Susan was so pretty, Charlotte. She's a real Irish colleen, with that red hair and those blue eyes."

There was a teasing sound in his voice that Susan didn't understand. She saw a quick flush of color wash over Mrs. Stanwyck's face, and sensed that there was something wrong, some strain between them.

"Why don't I come back later, Mrs. Stanwyck? You and your husband will be having so much to talk about, and I have work to do on the blue gown." She paused uneasily, suddenly feeling embarrassed.

Mrs. Stanwyck replied stiffly: "Yes, that's a good idea, Susan. I'll come by the sewing room later and we can try another fitting."

As she left the room, Susan was aware of Tom Stanwyck's eyes following her. In the hallway she took a deep breath and was surprised to find herself trembling.

Charlotte poured a cup of coffee and handed it to her husband. She was silent for a moment and then said evenly: "Tom, I don't want any trouble over Susan."

He gave a short, harsh laugh and put his cup down on the table. "You know something, Charlotte? You're a pain in the ass!"

She flinched a little, but continued to stare at him, her eyes determined, her mouth set in a firm line. "I mean what I say, Tom. I like that girl, and I won't have you—"

"You won't have me *what?*" he asked sharply. Then, in a softer tone, he said: "We made our arrangements a long time ago, Charlotte. And I've kept my side of the bargain, haven't I?"

"There have been lapses," she reminded him dryly.

He chuckled and reached into his coat for a gold cigarette case. "Well, none of us are perfect, are we?" He took a cigarette out of the case and lit it, watching her with narrowed eyes.

"Tom," Charlotte began in a low, pleading voice, "please don't—"

He interrupted her coldly. "I have to get into town for a meeting. It may run late, so don't expect me for dinner."

Their discussion was over before it had begun. It was a tactic he had perfected; any confrontation between them was sidestepped and as always left safely unresolved. They were like tightrope walkers with a net, never chancing a fall that might injure or kill.

"Shall I have Mrs. Gregory leave a tray for you when you come home?" she asked quietly.

"No, don't bother. I may stay over if the meeting runs too late. Is there anything happening that I need to know about?"

Charlotte went to her desk and consulted a large leather-bound date book. "The Bradfords have invited us to dinner on the tenth."

"The Bradfords?"

"Yes, John and Margaret Bradford. He's in publishing and broadcasting, I think. She's been working with me on the child-welfare committee."

"I'll check my schedule and let you know. Anything else?" He spoke in a tone he might use with one of his secretaries.

She kept her voice calm. "No, not at the moment."

He walked to the door and opened it. "Is Nella in the playroom? I'd like to see her before I leave."

Charlotte's face brightened momentarily. "Oh, yes, do. She's been asking for you. She's so much better since I brought Susan and

Christopher back with me. He's a wonderful little boy, Tom, so full of stories and games that—"

He closed the door firmly behind him.

Charlotte stood frozen, her mouth slightly open, lips shaping a word. The silence in the room was suddenly thunderous. Rage and humiliation choked in her throat. She took a deep, shuddering breath, then slowly sat down in the chair at the desk, staring blindly into space.

◆

Twilight cast a pale-blue wash of color over the playroom. Almost imperceptibly, shadows darkened and grew long around the two children sitting on the floor in the center of the room. Near them a rocking horse grinned savagely under a wild mane and brightly painted trappings. A three-story dollhouse filled with perfect replicas of Victorian furniture stood in a corner, its tiny occupants frozen in place, seated on miniature chairs or standing by Lilliputian doorways and windows. A large, sad-faced clown flopped its cloth-stuffed body on a pillow between the children, a silent third figure, its head bent forward at an odd angle, black button eyes staring intently. Everything in the room seemed to be listening to the low, mesmeric sound of an ancient legend being told in the dying light of the late afternoon.

". . . and so, at the end of a month, Midhir appeared at the entrance of the castle. Eochaid made sure that his men guarded all the doors so that Midhir could not escape with Etain. Then Midhir drew his sword in his left hand, put his right hand around her, and kissed her, and they rose straight up through the roof and were turned into white swans joined by a golden chain!"

Christopher sighed deeply and stopped.

"What happened then?" Nella asked. "Is that the end of the story?"

"No, but I'll tell you the rest tomorrow," Christopher said.

"That's not fair! You're just like my daddy."

"No, I'm not!"

"Yes, you are. He never finishes the story. He always says he has to go someplace." She paused, looking puzzled. "Why does he do that?" she asked.

Christopher thought about it for a moment. "Maybe he doesn't like telling stories," he replied.

"He says fairy tales are for little babies."

"They're not!" Christopher stood up. "My mother says fairy tales are important. She says they tell us about people who lived a long time ago, and she says they teach us lessons about what's right and what's wrong and how we should be!"

Nella looked stricken. "I'm sorry, Christopher! I was only teasing."

She tried to stand up without her crutches but her frail legs began to buckle. Christopher caught her by the arm and helped her gently into a tiny chair by the play table.

"You shouldn't do that, Nella," he said gravely. "You don't want to hurt yourself."

She held on to his hand, looking up at him. "Sometimes I wake up when it's dark, and my legs hurt, and I hear Daddy yelling at Mommy, and I want them to stop. One time Mommy came into my room and I said, 'Mommy, my legs hurt,' and she came over and sat with me and she was crying. She said, 'My poor baby, my poor baby,' and she was crying."

Christopher nodded his head seriously and sat down beside her. "My mummy cries sometimes too. But that's because my father died."

They were quiet for a few minutes, and then Nella said crossly: "I hate my crutches! Christopher, do you think someday I can walk without them?"

He stared at her for a long time before answering. "I don't know," he said softly.

It was almost dark in the room. The sad-faced clown had fallen over and appeared to be sleeping. The rocking horse was now a dark silhouette, and shadows had fallen over the Victorian dollhouse, its family lost from view. The children sat, as inert as the toys around them, comforted by each other's presence with the touch of clasped hands.

"Time for dinner, you two!"

Susan's cheerful entrance ended the shared moment and they turned to her, smiling. As Chris helped Nella stand and adjust her crutches, they gave each other a quick glance of understanding, as if an unspoken secret existed between them.

5

The day was going badly.

A light April rain started falling early in the morning, and the house was gloomy, oppressive. Mrs. Stanwyck had been in New York for almost a week, and everyone was beginning to feel her absence. Mrs. Gregory's temper flared more than once; the maids, Betty and Sarah, bickered all day; and Nella was fretful and cross, causing her tutor to leave early.

When Chris came home from school, Susan sighed with relief. He took Nella into the playroom, stacked the furniture into a fort, became her hero-prince, and rescued her countless times from a variety of enemies until she was exhausted but happy. After dinner Susan let the children watch an hour of television, then tucked Nella into bed, and spent the rest of the evening going over Chris's homework with him. By nine o'clock his head began to nod; he was almost asleep before she got him into bed.

Leaving the door between their rooms slightly ajar in case he should wake and need her, Susan went into the bathroom, filled the tub, and allowed herself the luxury of a long, hot soak. She reviewed in her mind what had to be done the next day: Mrs. Stanwyck would be home sometime during the morning; a stack of mail and a list of phone messages waited on her desk to be answered; a fitting on the chiffon gown and a new pattern to be cut for Nella's dress. It would be a very hectic day. The thought was wearying.

After drying herself and brushing her hair, she slipped on a nightgown and turned off the lights. The house was quiet now. The members of the staff had settled into their rooms for the night, and only the light sound of rain still falling could be heard. Moonlight pierced the quickly shifting clouds, and rays of silvery light shimmered through the wide casement windows.

Susan sat down on the window seat, her arms clasped around her knees. An aching sense of loneliness came over her; memories of home and Peter had plagued her throughout the day. Whenever she had gone into the playroom to check on the children, she kept seeing glimpses of Peter in Christopher. More and more he was growing to look like his father, and she felt at once anguished and grateful; her husband would always be with her in the image of his son.

"But I'm going to be needing more than the memory of a man," she said to the rain-washed windows, then added with a rueful smile: "And soon."

In London there had been an occasional evening out with a man from the shop she worked in—no more than dinner and a film. But each time he called for her, she had felt Chris's silent disapproval. The memory of his father was still fresh in his mind, and too, she was wise enough to understand the natural jealousy of a boy who was close to his mother.

But it's been more than a year, my lad, she whispered to herself, and your mother is not a saint. . . .

The rain began to fall more heavily, and she watched the cloudburst pour in gusty sweeps over the grounds.

Suddenly the headlights of a car cut through the darkness and moved up the drive to the front of the house. When the car stopped, she saw that it was a taxicab.

It can't be Mrs. Stanwyck, Susan thought. She would have called.

Putting a robe on over her nightgown, she hurried down the stairs and reached the front door just as it opened.

"Mr. Stanwyck!" she exclaimed. "I thought you were in Chicago."

"I was, but the conference ended early. Christ, what a night!"

"Oh, your coat is soaked. Here, let me help you with it."

"Is Charlotte home?"

"No, she'll be back from New York tomorrow morning."

"Is there anything to eat? I'm starved."

"I'll go check in the kitchen and see what I can find. And I think there's a bit of fire left in the library fireplace. Go and get warm."

"Thank you, Susan." He glanced at her briefly. "Did I wake you?"

"Oh, no, I was up. I couldn't sleep. Now go and get warm before you catch a chill."

He laughed a little and she looked at him, puzzled. "Did I say something funny?"

"No, no. It's your accent. I've never really talked with you before. It's charming."

She smiled self-consciously. "Oh—well, thank you."

There was an awkward moment of silence. She saw his wet hair lying in dark tangles across his brow; tiny drops of water beaded over his face and ran down the thick column of his neck.

"I'll get you a towel," she said.

"Yes, please."

A few minutes later she entered the library with a tray of cold chicken and hot tea. Stanwyck was standing by the bar, a half-empty whiskey glass in his hand.

Susan put the tray down and said: "I'm sorry there's no hot food, but I thought this might do. Have a cup of tea. That will take the chill off."

He grinned and raised his glass. "I think this will work more quickly. But the fire needs a little help."

"Let me do it," Susan said. "Here"—she handed him the towel— "dry yourself and then sit down and eat something."

While she added a few sticks of kindling to the low embers in the grate, Stanwyck dried his face and hair, then picked up his glass and a decanter of whiskey and carried them to the low walnut game table that stood before the fireplace. Lamplight softly illuminated the large, comfortable room. Paintings of landscapes and flowers in rich gilt frames hung on one wall, and another was covered by floor-to-ceiling shelves filled with books. Deep leather armchairs were arranged casually around the fireplace, and on the polished floor the intricate design of an Oriental rug twisted and curved in faded tones of wine and gold.

Susan smiled with satisfaction. "There we are—and very cozy too," she said, watching the wood catch fire and leap up in small, dancing flames.

She glanced up at Stanwyck and saw that he had taken off his tie and loosened his collar. His hair was mussed and he looked to her quite boyish and young.

"This is my favorite room in the whole house," he murmured, almost to himself.

"It is lovely," she agreed. "Quiet and peaceful—time seems to stop in here."

"Yes," he said with a deep sigh, and sank into a chair near her. He filled his glass from the decanter, turned and offered it to her silently.

She shook her head. "You'd feel a lot better if you ate some food first," she said almost reprovingly.

Stanwyck scowled and answered brusquely: "You sound a lot like my wife."

Susan, still crouched by the fireplace, reddened with embarrassment. Without thinking, she had been treating him like a husband! The thought shocked her and she fumbled for an apology.

"I'm sorry, Mr. Stanwyck. I shouldn't have spoken to you like that." She paused and then stood up. "It's late, I must be going to bed."

"No, don't go!" He sounded angry. Then, more softly, he said: "I was rude. Please stay?"

Still uncertain, she hesitated. "Well—I'm not sure . . ."

"Stay . . ." he pleaded in a low voice.

Susan sat down opposite him. "Just long enough for a cup of tea. It is late, and I am tired."

He smiled and sat back in his chair. His large, powerful body seemed to fill his shirt and pants until he strained the cloth. She could see the shift of thick muscles when he moved, and at the opened collar of his shirt there was a glimpse of dark, wiry hair.

"I understand you're a widow," Stanwyck said.

"Yes. My husband was a merchant seaman. He died at sea more than a year ago."

"Nella talks about your son all the time. He's quite a boy."

"He is—and she's a sweet girl. I'm glad they get on so well together." Susan smiled at him politely.

Stanwyck took a long swallow of whiskey and stared at her intently. "You must miss him," he said finally in a low voice.

"What?"

"Your husband—you miss him?" he said pointedly. A smile played across his lips and his eyes moved over her figure in a swift, almost insolent appraisal.

Susan put her cup down on the table and looked at him directly. "Yes," she replied slowly, "I miss him terribly."

He sat forward, the glass in one hand, the other hand resting on the solid curve of his thigh. Firelight flickered a nervous movement of shadows across the arrogant expression on his face.

"A year is a long time. . . ." His voice was husky, the whiskey slurring his words.

Susan stood up, her face suddenly pale. "It's late, Mr. Stanwyck, and I have a lot of work to do tomorrow. Good night."

Without waiting for his reply she turned and started from the room, trying to control the trembling in her legs.

He was on his feet and beside her in one swift move. "Susan, wait!"

She turned to him angrily. "You're not very subtle, are you? What do you think I am, some simple girl who just got off the boat?"

Stanwyck gripped her arms and pulled her close to him. "I think you're a beautiful woman who's been without a man too long."

He kissed her hard, his mouth warm, demanding. Susan wrenched herself away from him, a little frightened now of his strength, his urgency. The pressure of his hands was painful; she could feel the heat of his body.

She tried to laugh. "Isn't this a bit of a cliché—the master trying to have his way with the maid? You've just been drinking too—"

He clamped his mouth over hers again, trying to force his tongue between her clenched lips.

She twisted her face away from his. "Stop it! You're drunk!"

He relaxed his hold for a moment. She broke free and began to run for the doorway. He lunged after her and grabbed the back of her robe, ripping it open. And then he had her. Locking one arm around her throat, he forced her jaws shut so that she couldn't scream. The other arm became a vise, pinning her body to his. He dragged her back into the library and bent her to the floor, savagely throwing his weight on top of her. With one arm locked across her chest, he clawed at her nightgown and tore it away from her body.

Her breath was choked into guttural sobs. "Don't—" she whimpered. "Oh, God, don't."

He shoved himself against her, grabbing at her breasts, running one hand up between her legs to her crotch. His breath came in hoarse gasps, and he growled: "Goddamnit, relax! I don't want to hurt you!"

Holding her tightly, he kissed her mouth and neck, his lips and tongue burning over her flesh. The weight of him spread her legs apart, and he ground his hips against her, forcing her to feel his erection. For one awful, shocking instant she realized that she was responding to him, that she wanted him to take her. He sensed her sudden weakening and began to fumble with his belt and to tear at his zipper. But an icy wave of panic swept over her, stabbed at the backs of her knees and into the pit of her stomach. Her arms came to life and she beat at him with her fists, trying to fight him off. He reared up and smashed his open palm across her face, tearing her lip. Her mouth filled with the taste of blood and an anguished scream burst from her throat.

Stanwyck crouched above her, startled out of his rage by her cry. His face was covered with sweat, his mouth open, his eyes blinking as if suddenly coming awake from a nightmare.

"Susan— Oh, Christ!" he groaned. "I'm sorry. I didn't mean to—"

She tried to sit up, wincing with pain. He reached down to help her when a voice from the doorway cried out: "Don't you touch her!"

Stanwyck looked up and saw a small figure silhouetted by the light in the foyer.

It was Christopher.

The dying light of the fire glimmered eerily over the three figures frozen in a bizarre tableau: the small boy standing rigidly in the doorway of the library; Stanwyck on his knees, his face glistening with sweat, eyes wide and staring blankly; and Susan, huddled against the table for support, stunned by the appearance of her son.

Stanwyck started to rise, stammering, "Christopher, listen—I didn't mean to—"

He stopped, suddenly overwhelmed by an enormous pressure holding him in a painful grip. It seemed to him that the room had darkened suddenly and he could see nothing except the fixed stare of Christopher's green eyes illuminated in the blackness, shining at him hard and unswerving. Then all at once he went numb, unable to move or feel, aware only of the boy slowly approaching.

Now Christopher stood directly in front of him; Stanwyck felt the boy's eyes burning into him like a searing flame. And then he saw something that made him want to gasp, to tear his eyes away from the small, expressionless face. In the corner of Christopher's left eye, clinging to his pale-blond lashes like a glittering jewel, was a single blood-red tear.

As if he were a giant marionette controlled by invisible strings, Stanwyck rose unsteadily to his feet, reeled slightly, turned, and walked a few steps to one of the solid oak beams that framed the bookshelves. He stopped, as though waiting for a command. Then, with a violent spasmodic jerk of his body, he began viciously slamming his head against the wood. In the deathly silence of the room there was only the sound of bone crunching against the thick beam.

Susan watched, dazed, soundless, as if in a dream. But the grotesque sight of Stanwyck battering his bloodied skull brought a scream to her lips.

"Stop it! Chris, for God's sake, stop!"

He whirled around to face her, and for one brief, horrifying second she saw the blood tear glinting in the firelight. Then, as suddenly as she had seen it, it disappeared.

At that moment Stanwyck collapsed to the floor, his big body crumpling as if it had been dropped from a great height.

Christopher flung himself into Susan's arms, sobbing now like a frightened child. She held him tight, trying to quiet him, her mind reeling from what she had just witnessed.

Stanwyck uttered a low moan of pain. Susan looked over at him and saw a dark pool of blood near his head. She turned back to Chris and held his face between her hands, saying with deliberate calm: "Go and wake Mrs. Gregory. Tell her to come here at once, but not to wake the others. Then bring me some cold wet towels from the kitchen. Can you do that for me?"

He nodded his head, wiping his tear-stained face with his fingers. "Yes, Mummy." His voice was fearful, quavering.

As he ran out of the library, Susan got to her feet, drawing the torn shreds of her robe around her body. Ashen-faced and shaking, she staggered to Stanwyck's body and knelt by his side. Blood ran in dark streams over his face, seeping steadily from a deep wound in the center of his forehead. To her terrified eyes, he appeared a bleeding Goliath. The idea brought a hysterical laugh that ended in a sobbing intake of breath.

Then Chris was next to her, holding the wet towels. She wrapped several gently around Stanwyck's head and took one to wipe his face.

"Is Mrs. Gregory coming?" she asked Christopher.

"Yes—in a minute. She was very sound asleep." He looked at her face and his eyes grew large. "Mummy, you're hurt! Your mouth is bleeding!"

"Is it? Oh, yes. . . ." She had forgotten that Stanwyck struck her, and now the pain began to throb. Gingerly, she touched the corner of her mouth and grimaced. It felt bruised, swollen, and was still bleeding slightly.

"Let me help," Christopher said, reaching toward her face.

Instinctively, she pulled away from him, the gesture surprising both of them. Christopher stared at her, puzzled.

"Mummy, what is it? Are you all right?"

The image of him standing before Stanwyck, his face a stony mask, eyes blazing with a strange intensity, flashed through her mind.

She shook her head and the image disappeared, leaving in its place the tiny figure of her son, barefoot, in rumpled pajamas, blond hair a tangle over his forehead. He looked at her anxiously.

"What? Oh, yes, dear," she answered uneasily, "I'm all right."

"He hurt you, didn't he?" Christopher said, on the verge of tears, and gently laid his fingertips over the wound.

"He didn't mean to, darling. Don't worry, I can fix it later."

Her voice faded to a whisper. A strange warmth had begun to spread from his fingers through the wound and over the surface of her face. It was a tangible sensation, like the flow of a soothing balm.

Susan closed her eyes, feeling the tension in her body ebb away, leaving her quiet and peaceful. The pain diminished, then was gone. She put her hand to her mouth. Although it still felt slightly swollen there was no bruise, no bleeding.

Opening her eyes, she saw Christopher watching her. An expression of love radiated from his face, and on his lips was a pleasant smile.

Then Mrs. Gregory came into the room, crying out at what she saw.

With brisk efficiency, Mrs. Gregory called the Stanwyck family doctor and hurried Chris off to his room. While Susan rested by the fire, she went to make some coffee.

Left to herself, Susan became frenzied; what would she say? She had to have an explanation of what had happened! How could she tell anyone what took place when she didn't understand it herself?

She would tell them that Stanwyck was drunk, that he had attacked her and— She looked around the room frantically. A heavy brass candlestick on the fireplace mantel caught her eye. She picked it up and ran to where Stanwyck lay unconscious. Cautiously, her heart thudding loudly, she touched the base of it to the blood on the floor, then dropped it on the floor near his body.

The doctor, a thin man in his mid-forties named Maxwell Jordan, arrived a few minutes later. After a brief examination of Stanwyck, he phoned for an ambulance from a private hospital close by.

"It's hard to tell how serious it is," he told Susan and Mrs. Gregory. "Certainly fractures, and he's in shock. What happened?"

Susan took a deep breath and told her story: Stanwyck was drunk, had attacked her, and she fought him off with a brass candlestick she'd grabbed from the mantelpiece during the struggle. She pointed to it lying on the floor. No further explanations were needed. Stanwyck's reputation for heavy drinking and womanizing was well known to both Mrs. Gregory and the doctor, and Susan's ripped gown and robe were mute evidence of what had happened.

The ambulance finally arrived and Stanwyck was taken out on a stretcher. Dr. Jordan left a few minutes later, cautioning Susan to get to bed and rest.

Mrs. Gregory insisted on helping Susan to her room, talking all the while about Stanwyck and how she knew this would happen to him, that he had gotten one of the former maids in trouble, and wasn't it a shame for his poor wife.

Susan nodded her head dully, half listening to the woman's discourse. All she could think of was Christopher and what he had done to Tom Stanwyck—and to herself.

At the door to Susan's room, Mrs. Gregory said: "Get some rest, dear. And don't worry about anything. I'll stand by you when you tell Mrs. Stanwyck."

Tears filled Susan's eyes and she gave the older woman a quick hug. "Thank you."

As Susan turned to go into her room, Mrs. Gregory suddenly asked: "Susan, what was Chris doing in the library?"

For a moment Susan froze, her hand trembling on the doorknob. Then she replied as steadily as she could: "He heard me cry out and ran down to see what was wrong. He thought I had fallen and hurt myself."

Mrs. Gregory smiled, accepting the lie. "He's a good boy."

"Yes, he is," Susan whispered.

Alone in her room, she began to whimper like a child seeking rescue in the midst of a disaster. Tears streaming from her eyes, her body aching, she dragged herself into the bathroom and bathed her face with cold water. The reflection in the mirror showed a woman without a single bruise or wound. It was as if Stanwyck had never touched her.

She lay awake for hours, staring into the darkness. The natural order of her world had changed as suddenly and dramatically as did the ever-changing universe of myths and legends she had learned as a child. Her son was capable of nightmarish violence and miraculous healing, vengeance and restoration.

He had been given the "gifts."

Wonder and pride surged through her. And a fierce determination: he must be cared for and protected always, kept safe from any who might bring him harm.

Reality no longer existed for them as it did for others; it had been shattered a few short hours ago. In its place a shadowy world was born, a world more fearful than her wildest imaginings.

6

"—and then Mrs. Gregory called Dr. Jordan. After he came and examined Mr. Stanwyck, he called the hospital."

Susan finished speaking in a low voice and clenched her hands together nervously. Mrs. Gregory, standing beside her, nodded in agreement. Arms folded across her solid bosom, her big body was turned slightly to Susan as if to protect her from any attack.

Charlotte sat behind her desk. Strain and tension were evident in the tight stretch of skin across her face and the lines around her eyes and mouth, etched like the thin strokes of a sharpened pencil. On the mantel above the fireplace the soft ticking of a Seth Thomas clock measured her shallow breathing.

Finally, she looked up and said: "Thank you, Mrs. Gregory, for your quick thinking in calling Dr. Jordan. I saw him at the hospital this morning, and he told me that Mr. Stanwyck will recover. Now, if you don't mind, I'd like to talk with Susan alone."

"Of course, ma'am," she replied. Then, her chin thrust a bit defensively, she said: "The girl told you the truth, Mrs. Stanwyck."

Charlotte smiled wanly. "I'm sure she did. You don't have to be concerned."

When the cook left the room, Charlotte stood up and came around the desk. She took Susan's arm. "I think we could both use a cup of coffee," she said gently. "Why don't you sit down and I'll pour."

Susan sat tentatively on the edge of her seat and watched as Charlotte filled a cup and handed it to her.

"I'm so sorry, Mrs. Stanwyck—" Her hands shook slightly and the cup rattled loudly in the saucer.

"No, please don't apologize. You did the only thing you could do," Charlotte said. "It's I who should apologize to you. I was afraid from the beginning that something like this might happen—even in London, the day we first met."

Susan remembered the moment in the placement agency office when Charlotte had been so sure that she was too young for the job . . . then Christopher had walked in. At the thought of her son and what he had done, a quick jab of fear caught in her chest. Would Mr. Stanwyck remember what had happened?

Charlotte put down her cup and leaned forward worriedly. "Susan, you're so pale! Are you sure you're all right?"

"Oh, yes," she struggled to answer calmly. "I just slept badly—"

"My dear, forgive me. You've been through a terrible experience, and what I'm about to say is not going to help much."

"You want me to leave. I understand. I thought about it all night and knew that we couldn't go on living here," Susan said quietly.

Charlotte stood up and began to pace the room, rubbing her temples with trembling fingers. "Tom and I—our marriage has been far from perfect. We're very different in so many ways; he's ambitious and stubborn, and I suppose I've never really been the kind of woman he needed to—to satisfy his . . ." Her voice broke and she turned to Susan, tears brimming in her eyes. "Oh, you do understand, don't you?" She began to cry, the composure she had tried so hard to sustain shattering like a piece of delicate china dropped to the floor.

"Mrs. Stanwyck, don't," Susan said, near tears herself. She went to Charlotte and held her tightly. "I understand, really I do," she murmured. "You've been a good friend. Please don't worry about us. Chris and I will be fine. I've put a little money away, and I'm sure we can find a place to live—or perhaps even return to Scotland."

Charlotte's body tensed and she looked at Susan with alarm. "I don't want you and Christopher so far away that we can't see you," she said fiercely. "You must stay close by—I insist!"

"But, Mrs. Stanwyck, I don't see how we can—"

"Susan, please," she pleaded. "For my sake, and Nella's! Christopher has been so good for her. She would be miserable, even ill—I know it!"

Seeing how distraught she was, Susan slowly nodded her head, too confused by the woman's outburst to argue, too tired to make a decision on her own.

"What can we do?" she asked helplessly.

Charlotte walked quickly to her desk, suddenly infused with energy. "I'll start looking for a place where you can live, perhaps where you can work. I want you to go on doing my clothes, and all of my friends have been asking if you could sew for them." She looked at Susan, her eyes bright. "You might start a little business. And if you're close enough, I can bring Nella over to play with Chris. I know we can work it out!"

Susan suddenly laughed. "Mrs. Stanwyck, you have the instincts of a tiger protecting its cubs!"

"You're right. That's how I feel about you and Chris," she replied seriously. Then, smiling, she said: "And don't call me Mrs. Stanwyck. We're friends. Now go and get some rest. I have a lot to do."

"Mrs. Stan— Charlotte," Susan said shyly, "thank you."

"Don't thank me," Charlotte admonished her. "I am in *your* debt —yours and Christopher's." She paused and then added quietly: "Your son is very dear to me."

Suddenly uneasy, Susan started from the room. At the door, she turned and tried to ask casually: "Mr. Stanwyck—did he say anything about—"

Charlotte smiled grimly. "I only spoke with him for a moment. He admitted that he had been drunk and tried to—hurt you." She laughed a little shakily. "He doesn't remember your hitting him, but said that you were much stronger than you look."

Susan felt weak from the sudden flood of relief that went through her. "I'm glad he will recover," she said, and left the room, closing the door softly behind her.

Charlotte found a house that was owned by friends of hers who now lived abroad. By phone they agreed to sell her the house and a half acre of land around it. Within a week the arrangements were made and she took Susan, Chris, and Nella to see it.

Standing at the end of a lane that curved off the main road, it was a small brick-and-white-frame Colonial surrounded by a stretch of lawns and gardens overrun with weeds and wild flowers. Behind the house rose a bower of oak and elm trees that cast a dusty shade. The air was filled with the lazy hum of insects and the echoing calls of birds, while the house seemed to be dozing, waiting for a touch of life to fill its empty rooms and wash away the years of disuse.

Chris and Nella explored the grounds, and the two women walked through the rooms, talking excitedly about what could be done with the place.

"—and there's a lot of furniture and household things stored in our basement that you can have," Charlotte was saying.

"But how can I ever repay you for all this?" Susan asked, bewildered. "You're doing so much for us!"

Charlotte went to the bank of windows in the living room that looked out over the gardens. "Come here, dear."

Susan joined her and saw the children sitting together under the leafy, spreading boughs of a huge old oak tree. Blurred by a fine layer of dust covering the panes of glass, the two small figures were a soft impression of color and movement, like a rapidly painted watercolor. Shafts of sunlight cut through the tangle of branches, gleaming over his blond head and tracing gold streaks along the length of her dark hair. Chris was talking animatedly while Nella stared at him, enraptured.

"That's payment enough for me," Charlotte said. "And I think you can be happy here."

Susan watched the children with mixed feelings. They were so beautiful together, but she was worried about Christopher. In the days following that explosive moment in the library, he'd behaved as if nothing had happened. Susan, still stunned by the extraordinary experience, could not bring herself to talk with him about it. When she explained that they were going to move into their own home so that she might start a little business, he readily accepted the story and never questioned why they were leaving the Stanwycks. She began to think that, like a bad dream forgotten on awakening, he did not even remember what had taken place.

"You do like the house, don't you, Susan?" Charlotte asked.

"Oh, yes, it's lovely."

Could they live here? It was a quiet place, a few miles from the nearest village, and with no neighbors in the immediate vicinity. They weren't isolated, but they could keep to themselves. Wouldn't that be the safest way to protect Chris? She wasn't sure. But the house was more than she had hoped for, and Charlotte was offering to do everything she could to help.

"Yes, I think we can be happy here," Susan said.

And safe, she prayed fervently to herself.

The next few days were filled with bustling activity. Charlotte hired a cleaning crew to go through the house and make it habitable. Then she took Susan on a tour of the Stanwyck mansion's storage rooms to select furniture, rugs, dishes, silverware, and even an assortment of garden tools.

"As you can see, we never throw anything away." Charlotte laughed. "I used to think my mother was mad for saving all these things. Now I'm glad she did."

Trying hard to maintain a hold on her independence, Susan insisted on taking only what she absolutely needed, and also made Charlotte agree to accept a monthly rent for the house.

"Oh, Susan," Charlotte pleaded, "don't make it so difficult for me to help you. It's very important to me. And besides," she added with a mischievous smile, "I've never had such a good time!"

As furnishings were moved in and the house began to take shape, Susan decided to use a small room just off the kitchen for sewing and fittings. Charlotte called all her friends to announce that very soon they could begin to go to Susan for their dressmaking.

"That's another reason I wanted you close by," Charlotte explained. "Just about everyone I know lives in Gladwyne, Wynnewood, and Bryn Mawr. Being near Ardmore puts you within just a few miles of a great many women with very bad figures who will desperately need your consummate craftsmanship!"

A few weeks after they had moved into their new home, a sudden rainstorm had Susan and Chris scurrying for pots and pans to catch the leaks from a roof that had not been fixed in years. Susan called a local repair company, and the next day, while Chris was at school, a small truck painted fiery red pulled up in front of the house. The words "ANDERSON HOME REPAIRS" were neatly lettered in white paint along the sides of the truck.

A tall, thickset man in his early thirties climbed out of the cab as Susan opened the front door to greet him. The first thing she noticed was his hair. It was almost as red as the color of his truck. When he saw her, he stopped in his tracks, staring in wonder at the fall of *her* thick red hair, deeper in shade than his, but glinting in the sun like burnished copper.

"My God!" he exclaimed in a deep, booming voice. "What a pair we'd make! Our kids would all come out looking like carrots!"

The man must be mad, Susan thought, trying to ignore his infectious grin and snapping blue eyes. "Can you fix a leaking roof?" she asked primly.

"Can I fix a roof, the lady asks!" He laughed, flashing white teeth in his ruddy, cheerful face. "Just watch me!"

During the next few weeks, in a bewildering display of versatility, Michael Anderson repaired everything that was out of order in the house: the roof, doors that stuck, leaky water taps, furniture legs that wobbled, loose windowpanes. He waved aside Susan's protestations of not being able to afford all the repairs, and showed up at the house several mornings a week to rebuild sagging shelves or vigorously brush fresh paint over the back porch.

"You cannot keep doing all this!" Susan objected helplessly. "I must owe you a fortune!"

"You owe me a good cup of coffee, a slab of your incredible apple pie, and the pleasure of taking you to dinner and a movie." He grinned at her, but his eyes were serious. He'd asked Susan to go out with him every time he had seen her, cheerfully accepting the excuses she offered, and then asking her again.

She was attracted to him from the first time she'd seen him. Robust, good-natured, and crackling with vitality, he was impossible to ignore. She began to anticipate his visits, excited about seeing him, yet trying to maintain a cool detachment when he was close by. Once he caught her watching him at work and gave her an outrageous wink that made her flush and turn quickly away. She finally had to admit to herself that he stirred feelings she had tried to bury since Peter's death.

As the weeks went by she learned more about him. Michael ran his own business, doing repairs and building. He had plans to expand into contracting and discussed them with her eagerly, pleased by her encouragement. But whenever the subject of Chris came up, Susan became quiet, distant. He was aware that she had contrived to have him at the house while Chris was in school, and when he mentioned wanting to meet him, she always made vague promises that some evening they would have dinner together.

"But what about the grownups?" he persisted. "Do they get to have an evening out on the town? Like tonight, for instance?"

Susan laughed. "You remind me of my father. He was a man with a mad rush for life, always wanting to move and do as the thought struck him."

"Give me half a chance and I'll make you forget the idea of comparing me to your father," Michael said in a low voice, moving close to her.

"Go back to your work, man, and leave me to mine," Susan answered, flustered.

He flashed a dazzling smile and touched her hair lightly with his fingertips. "It's your beautiful Irish accent and gorgeous red hair that's driving me crazy."

One morning Susan was at work in her sewing room. Michael was on the roof installing an antenna for a television set Charlotte had given them. Suddenly she heard a loud cry followed by a crash and Michael's howling curses. She rushed outside and found him lying on the ground and the ladder he'd been using toppled over a few feet away.

"The goddamned ladder slipped!" he cried out angrily.

"Michael, are you hurt?"

"Christ, no! I've just sprained my ankle and I'm fucking mad! Help me up."

Holding him around the waist while he hopped on one foot, Susan got him into the house and onto the living-room couch.

"Oh, God!" he groaned, "what a stupid thing to do, falling off a ladder! Jesus!"

"Let me get that boot off and look at your ankle. Easy now, this may hurt."

"Not as much as my pride—ow-w-w!"

"There, it's done. Now the sock. Oh, dear, it's beginning to swell. I'll get some cold water and make a compress. Just lie still."

Michael grinned up at her. "I wouldn't leave even if I could."

"You're hopeless." Susan laughed and hurried into the kitchen.

A few minutes later she returned with a pan of water and a cloth and a pillow for his head.

"So this is what I've been missing all these years alone." He smiled as she made him comfortable and began to apply the wet cloth to his ankle.

"This, and the bills, the arguments, and all the other problems," she said teasingly.

He sat up and took her arm, pulling her close to him. "There wouldn't be any problems with you, Susan," he said huskily. "Just joy."

She felt the strength of his arms, saw herself mirrored in his eyes, and then his lips covered hers. His hands moved over her back and down her hips, lifting her onto the couch beside him.

"Michael, don't," she whispered. "Your ankle—"

"It's not my ankle I'm worried about," he chuckled, and kissed her again, his mouth softly insistent.

Susan lay against him, trembling, feeling herself grow weak with the touch of his lips, the firm pressure of his body. For a moment, behind her closed eyelids, she saw Peter bending over her, clean-limbed and strong. Memory and desire rushed through her until she was limp and unprotesting as Michael's hands moved under clothes. At the touch of his fingers on her flesh, all restraints fell away and she responded with a fervor that surprised and excited him. In moments they were naked, their bodies clasped together in close embrace. With his entry, Susan moaned, and the long years of denial and anxiety faded into a deep and satisfying contentment.

◆

"Chris, this is Michael Anderson, the man who's been doing all the work on the house."

Susan watched her son nervously. Would they like each other? She had told Chris that she had invited Michael for dinner to thank him for all the extra work he had done. In that way she hoped to bring them together on an apparently casual basis.

"How do you do," Chris replied politely. "Thank you for putting those shelves up in my room."

"You're welcome," Michael said, smiling.

There was an awkward silence, then Michael took two boxes from under his arm and held one out to Chris. "I saw this in a store the other day and thought you might like it. It's a model plane. Have you ever put one together?"

Chris took the box and examined the colorful pictures on the cover. "No." He shook his head slowly. "I never have."

"Well, if you like, after supper I'll give you a hand," Michael said.

Chris stared up at the tall man for a few seconds, examining him guardedly. Then a smile lit up his face and he turned to Susan.

"May I, Mummy? After supper can Michael and I build the plane?"

"Of course, dear," she said, relieved and grateful to Michael for his thoughtfulness.

"And a present for you, too, Susan," Michael said, handing her the other box. He glanced down at Chris. "I wasn't sure how you two felt about chocolate fudge, but it's my favorite candy, and I thought—"

"But it's mine too!" Chris shouted with delight.

"I can see that I'll have to share my gift with both of you." Susan laughed. "Now you get the table ready, Chris, while Michael helps me in the kitchen."

When they were alone, Susan said: "What a charmer you are! You're not Irish, by any chance?"

"Only in my heart." He smiled, kissing her quickly on the cheek. "He's a beautiful boy, Susan. Do you think he likes me?"

"I'm sure he does. The fudge clinched it. However did you think of it?"

"I've never known a child yet who didn't have a sweet tooth, especially for chocolate fudge," he chuckled. "I think he and I will be great friends."

In the weeks that followed, Michael became a constant and eagerly welcomed visitor to the house. He and Chris spent hours building and painting a succession of model planes. In the late afternoons, they would fly a kite he had made for the boy, running and yelling to each other through summer fields of buttercups and daisies while Susan followed, cheering them on. A game of checkers became an after-dinner ritual, and then a television show to watch was solemnly chosen by vote. Weekends were spent in long drives through the Pennsylvania countryside or picnicking along the banks of the Perkiomen Creek near Valley Forge. Michael's passion was American history, and he traded Chris stories of George Washington and his army for tales of Cu Chulainn.

Whenever possible, Nella was taken along on the outings. Charlotte wisely refrained from accepting their invitations to join them.

"Are you sure?" Susan asked while packing a picnic basket. "Michael's planned a lovely day in Philadelphia. We're going to the Betsy Ross House and to Independence Square to see the Liberty Bell, and then spend the afternoon in Fairmount Park. If the children aren't too tired, we'll stay for the symphony concert at Robin Hood Dell. Do come with us, Charlotte."

"I'd love to, really I would. But there's a raft of things I must get done at the house, and I'm sure that Nella will tell me every detail."

"She's positively blooming, isn't she? I've never seen her look so well," Susan said, glancing out the window at the children, who were waiting impatiently for Michael to arrive.

"She's never been so happy," Charlotte said, and then, with a sly smile, added: "I've never seen you so happy, either."

Susan looked up from her work, her eyes bright. "He's asked me to marry him. And I've accepted."

"Susan, how wonderful!" Charlotte exclaimed. "He's a lovely man. Have you told Chris?"

"Not yet. But we will, soon. I think he knows already, and I think he loves Michael as much as I do."

"Oh, my dear, I'm very happy for you," Charlotte said. "You'll be a real family."

Susan heard the wistful note in her voice and saw tears glistening in her eyes. Impulsively she reached out and hugged Charlotte tightly.

"You've been our family, you and Nella," she said softly, "and you always will be."

◆

Summer melted away into a dazzling autumn. A glorious burst of color swept over the countryside, and the air was crisp with the chill of approaching winter. With Chris's enthusiastic approval, Michael and Susan set a date in early November for their wedding. They spent long evenings making plans, going over budgets, and dreaming out loud about the future. Susan had never been happier. The joy of Michael's love for her and his tender concern for Chris were like omens of good fortune. She felt assured that the troubles of the past were over, and that her son could grow up like any other child.

One afternoon late in October, the skies began to darken with a rush of large, rapidly moving gray clouds. By the time Chris got home from school a heavy, driving rain had started. When the early-evening news reports cautioned all drivers to be careful of flooded roads and dangerous driving conditions on the highways, Susan grew worried. Michael had called earlier to say he would be late for dinner because of a job he was doing some thirty miles away, but that he was sure he'd make it by eight o'clock. She had said that she would wait to eat with him.

The rain grew torrential, with flashes of lightning and distant rumbles of thunder. Susan sat with Chris while he did his homework, glancing at the clock on the wall every few minutes and giving a start each time she heard a car go by. It was almost nine thirty and Michael still hadn't appeared. To keep herself occupied, she took out a large bundle of clothes that needed mending and began to sew.

Chris closed his books with a deep sigh and said: "There, that's finished." He looked at the clock and saw that it was a little after ten. Susan was sitting on the couch, her fingers moving quickly with needle and thread over one of his socks stretched on a glass.

"May I stay up until Michael comes?" he asked. "I'm sure he'll be along soon," he added reassuringly.

Susan looked up at him with anxious eyes. "All right, sit with me for a little while," she replied, and went back to her sewing.

Chris flopped down on the couch beside her. "What's this?" he asked, picking up a garment.

"That's one of Michael's work shirts. He tore it last week and I said I'd mend it for him." She bit off the thread and removed the sock from the glass. "Here, give it to me and I'll do it now," she said.

As she reached for the shirt, Christopher's hand suddenly clutched it convulsively. He sat up, his back straight, his small body rigid.

"Chris, what is it?" Susan asked. "Are you feeling sick?"

His eyes opened wide and seemed to glaze over as he stared into space.

Susan's face went pale and she touched his shoulder. "Chris, what is it?"

"Michael . . . I see Michael!" His voice was tight, as if being squeezed out of his throat against his will, and his hands gripped the shirt until his knuckles were white.

Susan gasped a sharp intake of breath. "What are you saying?"

Chris's body began to shudder. "The truck—Mummy, the truck! It's overturned! On top of him! I see it! I see it!"

His face was white, drained of all color, and tears brimmed in his wide, staring eyes.

Susan's hands shook as she pulled him into her arms. "Chris, don't—you're frightening me! It's just your imagination."

His body remained stiff in her arms, his face working as he tried to force the words from his lips. "Mummy—there's blood! It's all over Michael's face." His voice rose to a shriek. "I can see the blood! And Michael—he's not moving!"

Like a fragile twig being snapped, he suddenly collapsed against her, sobbing. Susan held him with all her strength, rocking back and forth, not even aware that she was moaning over and over: "No, please God, no, no, no. . . ."

The police called a little after midnight to tell her that Michael had been killed when his truck overturned after skidding off the road outside Wynnewood. In his wallet they had found an identification card bearing her name and telephone number. He had listed Susan as his next of kin.

7

Margaret Bradford stood patiently in the center of the fitting room while Susan knelt and carefully added some pins to the hem of her gown.

"This is a good color for me, don't you think?" Margaret asked, examining herself critically in the mirrors that lined the walls.

"It's lovely," Susan murmured, taking the last pin from between her lips and fixing it to the blue peau de soie. "Just right for your complexion, and it accents the color of your eyes." She stood up and took a few steps back. "There now, that should do it. Turn slowly so we can see how it moves."

Margaret did a dance-step turn, watching her reflection in the mirrors. "Oh, yes, that's perfect!" she exclaimed delightedly. "You really are a marvel."

Susan smiled. "You're easy to work with. You have a wonderful figure and great style. Now let's get you out of the gown without pulling the pins and have a cup of tea. We could both use a bit of a lift—we've been at this for hours."

Susan drew the delicate lace curtains against the afternoon sun, softening the light in the wide, airy living room, while Margaret sat back in a roomy armchair and sipped her tea.

"Ah, that's very restful," she sighed. "My dear Susan, you've simply done wonders with this old place—it's charming. Coming here is the one peaceful moment of the week that I can look forward to."

Susan's face glowed with pride. "Thank you, Margaret. I must say, even after five years, I'm still a little surprised by how well everything has gone. And I have Charlotte to thank for all of it. She's been a great friend to Christopher and myself."

"How is that darling son of yours? The last time I saw him he'd shot up like a weed. And more beautiful than ever."

"Well, he's twelve—almost a man," Susan said. "And looking more like his father with each passing month."

"Don't short-change yourself, Susan," Margaret said reprovingly. "You're a very attractive woman. Why you've remained unmarried is a great mystery to me. Are the men around here blind? You are much too young to simply devote your life to working and raising Chris."

Margaret was on to her favorite subject and Susan sat bemused, letting her talk.

"I understand how you feel, losing your husband and then Michael. But that was years ago! And Chris needs a father, you know that. I saw Charlotte at the club just a few days ago, and we both agreed that you are much too reclusive. You really must get out and meet more people."

Susan smiled at her patiently. "You're quite right," she agreed, "and I'm very grateful for your concern."

From the tone of Susan's voice, Margaret knew that the subject was closed. She put down her cup and leaned forward. "Oh, Susan, I'm sorry for prattling at you like some old biddy. You know how women are, always trying to marry one another off."

"Well, you can stop worrying about me," Susan said firmly. "I'm really very content just the way I am."

"I don't believe that any more than you do," Margaret snorted, "but I promise to try to keep my mouth shut." She glanced at her watch. "Oh, Lord, look at the time! I must run. John is bringing some people home for dinner and Jenny said she'd drop by for drinks."

"How is she? It's been ages since I've seen her."

"More beautiful and willful than ever," Margaret replied, gathering up her purse and gloves. "She's decided to be an artist and is begging us to send her to Europe to study. Oh, how I wish she were still a child; life would be so much easier. But she's nineteen, and that's a bit old for a heavy parental hand. I guess we'll just have to let her go."

"She's a lovely girl, and I'm sure you'll have nothing to worry about," Susan said as they walked to Margaret's car. "See you next week?"

"Same time, same place," Margaret replied, getting behind the wheel. She leaned out the window and took Susan's hand. "Forgive me for playing mother with your personal life, dear, but do think about what I said."

"Margaret, you're incorrigible." Susan smiled. "You won't rest till you see me married. Now off with you!"

She waved after the car as it started down the lane to the road, then turned and wandered slowly back toward the house, thinking how tiresome Margaret could be. Margaret meant well—she and Charlotte and all the other women—they genuinely liked her and were concerned about her welfare.

But I wish they'd leave me the hell alone! she thought in a sudden flare of anger.

"What time will Nella be here?" Chris asked, downing his milk in one long gulp.

"About three thirty," Susan replied, pouring him another glass. "And don't drink so fast; it'll make you sick. Want some cake?"

Chris nodded, drinking more slowly. "Will they be here for a while?" he asked, wiping his mouth with the back of his hand.

Susan put a slice of cake in front of him and sat down at the kitchen table. "About two hours. Charlotte and I are working out a new pattern."

She watched him take a bite of the cake and smiled at his ecstatic groan of pleasure. How handsome he is becoming, she thought. Tall and rangy, with wide shoulders and a broad chest. His blond hair had darkened slightly through the years to an unruly mass of deep gold, curling in a shaggy length over his collar. The brilliant green eyes were wide and honest, and the shape of his nose and mouth always brought a sharp memory of Peter. But in his tennis shoes, jeans, and T-shirt, the little Scotch boy had been replaced by an American teen-ager. "Mummy" had become "Mom," and the lilt of his accent was barely discernible when he spoke.

"Did it go well in school today?" she asked.

"About the same. I got a B on my history paper; that was a surprise." He laughed.

"Still having trouble with the Stark boy?"

"I just ignore him," he said cheerfully. "He's a stupid jerk who has to tease everybody to get any attention."

"And Willie and Jim—you're still friends with them? Would you like to have them over for dinner some night? I could make a very tasty—"

Chris finished his cake without looking at her. "No, thanks, Mom. We're not really friends—just hang around together in school," he answered.

"Well, even so—"

"Mom, they're kids," Chris explained. "What I mean is— Well, I guess I just feel older somehow."

Susan looked at him pensively. "Don't you get a little lonely?" she asked after a moment's pause.

"Never think about it," he answered evasively. Then, with a bright smile, he said: "Nella's my best friend, and you! The kids are just— just kids," he finished lamely.

Susan stood up and took his dishes to the sink, trying to appear unconcerned; but she was worried. Since Michael's death Chris had grown closer to her than ever. They never talked about what had happened. She was convinced that he didn't remember his vision of Michael dying; positive that, as with all the other incidents that had taken place, he had no awareness of his part in them.

Now she wondered if her silence and the efforts she had made to protect him had been a mistake. More and more he was becoming withdrawn from other children, going to school because he had to, but much preferring, she knew, to stay close to her and home. He helped her around the house and worked in the gardens, looking forward only to playing with Nella whenever Charlotte brought her over. On weekends, if Susan wasn't working, they would take long walks in the country, just as they had in Inverness.

The sound of a car coming up the drive brought Chris to his feet. "They're here!" he sang out, and rushed from the house to greet Charlotte and Nella.

Susan wiped her hands on a kitchen towel and followed him to the front steps, waving to Charlotte as she got out of the car. Chris helped Nella down and slipped her crutches under her arms. Then they walked off to the back garden, chatting excitedly to each other.

"Hello!" Charlotte said, coming up the steps and embracing her warmly. "How is everything?"

"Just fine, as always," Susan said, smiling.

Chris looked up at the sky and laughed. "It's a camel!" he exclaimed.

"No, no—a dog with a hump on its back," Nella insisted, shaking her head.

They watched for a moment as the white cloud spread and shredded into drifting puffs.

"Now it's marshmallows," Chris said, laughing.

"Stop, you'll make me hungry." Nella rolled over in the soft green grass to face him and suddenly winced in pain.

"Are you okay?" Chris asked, sitting up.

"Yes, just a twitch from moving too fast. I had three therapy sessions this week and Mother is talking about having someone at the house to do it all the time."

"Does it hurt?"

"No, just exercise and massage so the muscles won't get weak. But it's very boring," she sighed.

"Does it still bother you—being lame?" Chris asked.

Nella stared at him for a moment with a curious expression. They were very close together, and she saw a small pulse beating at the base of his tanned throat.

"Not so much—except in school. Everybody's too polite. Do you know what I mean?" she asked in a low voice.

"Yes, I guess so." He suddenly realized that she was staring at him, and he stared back, noticing for the first time the sooty fringe of lashes around her dark eyes and the tender color of her lips. Something moved within him, a feeling of warmth and a slight excitement that he didn't understand.

"Nella, you're very pretty," he said, startled to find that he was stammering.

She smiled and said in a slightly superior tone: "I'll be twelve soon."

"Well, I'm still older than you!" A little embarrassed, he leaped to his feet. "Oh, look!" he cried out, and pointed to a bird that had perched on a low branch of a nearby tree. "What is it?"

Nella pushed herself up and looked at it. "That's a starling. We don't see too many of them here." Then she laughed and said teasingly: "It's like you."

"What do you mean?"

"Well, it's a European bird, and see—its plumage looks almost iridescent."

"Do I have iridescent plumage?" he demanded.

"Yes," she giggled. "Your hair! It shines in the sun!"

"But I'm not from Europe—I'm from Scotland!"

"Oh, well, it's the same thing!"

"It is not." He laughed. "You're just being silly! Let's go back to the house—Mom made a terrific cake."

As they walked slowly across the lawn, Nella said: "I heard my mother say that your mother is alone too much and that it isn't good for her. She hasn't gone out much since Michael died, has she?"

Chris shook his head. "No. Oh, there were a few guys she saw once or twice. Mr. Morton, who owns the yardage shop in Ardmore, and Will Carson—he teaches in that art studio outside Bryn Mawr. I think there was another one, but I don't remember his name."

"Did you like any of them?"

Chris frowned and his face tensed a little. "No, not much," he replied.

8

JUNE, 1972

Mr. Strathmore, a small man with graying hair and deep-set eyes, sat behind his desk and watched his American history class struggle with a short essay test he had devised seventeen years before.

"You have ten more minutes to finish the test," he said in a precise, dry voice devoid of any inflection.

He heard the expected groan, strained to hear the inevitable whispers of students attempting to share answers, then scrutinized their lowered heads for any sign of conspiracy. Finding none, he returned to correcting homework assignments.

"Pitiful," he muttered to himself, racing his red pencil across the wrinkled pages. A few minutes later he sat back in the gray, office-type swivel chair covered with ink stains, tapped the pencil against the tight nostrils of his thin nose, leaving small red freckle marks, and announced gravely: "Time's up."

Christopher made a face, sighed deeply, crossed out a bad answer, and handed his paper to the monitor who was collecting them. Then he smiled. In a few minutes the Stanwyck chauffeur was bringing Nella to have lunch with him. It was finals time and she had a half-day off. He decided to cut the rest of his classes and spend the afternoon with her.

Everyone began to gather up books and papers. When the bell rang, a torrent of shoving, pushing bodies emptied out of classrooms into hallways and flew out the doors into the balmy June afternoon like a swarm of bees being released from a hive.

Basketball teams were immediately formed.

"We'll take Chris, Jimmy, and Steve; you can have Gary, Robin, and Keith. That's even, isn't it?"

"It's never even with McKenzie on your team!" someone yelled good-naturedly.

Chris gave him the finger and laughed. His height and speed put him in demand for most sports, but basketball was his favorite. And it was the only time he really felt a part of a group. Because he was always calm and able to make decisions without hesitation, his team usually won.

The boys played a fast, unrelenting game, growing sweaty and short-tempered in the heat of the afternoon sun. Chris made a basket, was fouled by an opposing player, then successfully made a free-throw shot.

"That's the way, McKenzie!"

"Good hands, man!"

Chris's team was ahead, but by only a few points. There were two minutes left before recess ended.

"Come on, let's teach those mothers how the game is played!"

Whooping and hollering encouragements to one another, his team drove down the court, colliding with the other players. Chris made a shot, but elbowed one of the boys. The other team took its free throws and evened the score.

Johnny Stark, one of the members of Chris's team, began to swear. "Goddamnit! We can beat them! They're nothing but a bunch of pussies!"

"Knock it off!" Chris yelled. "If you played in your zone, we'd have a better chance."

"Fuck you!" Stark shouted. "I'm the only one on this team with any balls!"

Out of the corner of his eye Chris saw the Stanwyck Cadillac pull up at the school gate. Nella waved to him from the rear window. He gave her a quick smile and returned to the game. His team passed and dribbled the ball up and down the court, unable to find an opening. Whenever Chris went in for a shot, he was blocked. With time almost up, they were desperate to make a point. Amid the yelling and cheering, Chris sped back to midcourt to attempt a long shot, encouraged by his team and by Nella, who was standing by the school gate, shouting: "You can do it, Chris, you can do it!"

All the boys grew silent as they watched Chris attempt the shot. The ball flew into the air, hit the backboard, and bounced off the rim, away from the basket. A cry of despair went up as a player on the other team caught the rebound, ran the ball down the court, and scored a basket. The school bell rang, signaling the end of recess and the end of the game.

"You shithead!" Stark cried out, his beefy face red and running with sweat. "We almost had them!"

"Okay, okay—so I missed." Chris shrugged. "It's only a game." He turned away and started to walk toward Nella.

Stark grabbed him by the shoulder and spun him around. "If you hadn't tried to show off for your little cripple, we'd have won!" he roared in Chris's face.

Suddenly livid with anger, Chris lunged forward and threw the boy to the ground, falling on top of him. "You fucking pig! Don't you ever call her that again!" he hissed, hitting him in the face.

Bellowing with rage, Stark jerked his heavy body and toppled Chris over. Then he flung himself on top of Chris and began punching his chest and head.

A noisy circle of boys and girls quickly formed around them, shoving against one another and yelling: "Fight! Fight!"

In his classroom, Mr. Strathmore heard the commotion and rushed to an open window. "Stop that!" he shouted. "Stop that fighting this instant!"

Chris strained to free himself from the trap of Stark's weight, flailing wildly against the larger boy. His head throbbed, the hot concrete was scorching his back through the thin material of his T-shirt, and there was a taste of blood in his mouth.

Stark grabbed Chris by the throat with one hand, and with the other he clamped Chris's wrists together over his head. "She's a cripple!" he snarled in Chris's face. "A cripple! A cripple!"

Suddenly Chris's body went slack and he lay still, staring at Stark with hatred.

"Hey, McKenzie, don't give up!" someone yelled.

"Kick the bastard!"

"For Christ's sake, get him, Chris!"

Stark began to laugh, gloating at his victory. But in the next instant his laughter died to a short, hoarse gasp. His vision wavered and blurred, and the sound of jeering children became a hollow, echoing noise in his ears. The bright afternoon sun seemed to darken around him until all he could see were Christopher's eyes burning into his skull. Then his face drained of all color and his mouth went slack.

Slowly forming in the corner of Chris's left eye was a blood tear. Stark's body abruptly straightened up as if someone had pulled him sharply by the shoulders. He got to his feet, his face blank, eyes staring like someone suddenly blinded. He staggered drunkenly in a circle, and the children around him stepped back, thinking he was going to be sick. Then, with a shocking burst of speed, he began to run.

A taunting cry of "Yellow!" went up from the onlookers, and they ran after him. Mr. Strathmore appeared on the steps, waving his arms and shouting at them to stop.

Stark's feet were a blur as he flew over the ground, zigzagging through his classmates until he reached the steps of a black iron fire escape that clung to the side of the brick building. His legs moving like pistons, Stark ran up the stairs to the second-floor landing. There he stopped, looked around groggily, then tottered to the railing overlooking the school yard. Below him a mob of children yelled wildly, laughed savagely, urged him to run, to hide, screamed that he was a coward.

But Stark heard none of it. Beating against his ears was the high roar of a wind that didn't exist, a moaning gale that whipped him forward, pushed him to climb awkwardly onto the railing.

They saw him poised on the narrow handrail, and there was an instant of stunned silence in the yard. Then a shriek of surprise and horror went up as his body shot clumsily into the air and fell with a sickening crunch against the concrete.

Mr. Briggs, the principal of the school, closed his office door against the noise of students milling about in the hallway. He motioned to Mr. Strathmore to take a seat and walked quickly to his desk. Through the large windows facing the yard came the sound of small knots of boys and girls chattering excitedly. He leaned out one of the windows and crisply ordered them to return to their classes.

At the sound of his voice they fled, and in a moment the yard was silent. Then Mr. Briggs sat down behind his desk.

Susan sat next to Chris and Nella, her hands clasped tightly together. Chris's face was a mass of bruises and small cuts that had been cleaned by the school nurse and covered with Band-Aids. He was pale and his hair was matted with sweat and dirt. One sleeve of his shirt was torn and both knees of his jeans had been ripped. Nella held his hand and looked at him anxiously, her eyes red from crying.

As Mr. Briggs spoke, Susan listened intently, trying to understand what had happened.

"The boy was severely injured," he was saying gravely. "A broken leg, fractured collarbone, a concussion, and possibly some cracked ribs."

"But why should Christopher be held responsible because that boy fell from the fire escape?" she asked, bewildered.

"I saw it all happen," Mr. Strathmore interjected, "and John Stark did not fall—he jumped!" His thin nostrils flared and his mouth formed a hard, indignant line. Too many years of teaching had convinced him that students—and parents—were not to be trusted.

"I don't think we can conclude that Stark actually jumped," Mr. Briggs said sharply. "That remains for the police to decide."

"The police!" Susan exclaimed, her face going white. "What do the police have to do with this?"

The principal explained carefully. "The insurance company needs a police report on the facts of any school accidents. Since the school is held responsible in such incidents, the involvement of the authorities becomes an absolute necessity."

There was a moment of silence in the office, and then Nella said in a small voice: "It was the other boy who started the fight. He called me a cripple and Chris got mad."

Mr. Briggs smiled at her quick defense. "Yes, we know that," he said gently.

"Then why are you blaming Chris?" Susan asked tensely.

Mr. Briggs took off his horn-rimmed glasses and rubbed the pink indentation across the bridge of his nose. "We're not trying to lay blame on anyone yet, Mrs. McKenzie," he replied with a tired sigh. "What we don't understand is why John suddenly stopped fighting with Chris and ran up the fire escape." Looking puzzled, he turned to the boy. "Chris, did you say something to frighten him, or threaten him in any way?"

"I didn't say anything, Mr. Briggs," Chris answered in a low voice. "Maybe he saw Mr. Strathmore coming toward us and got scared. Maybe that's why he ran."

"He was already running when I got out to the yard," Mr. Strathmore said, glaring at Chris. "He flew right past me, looking absolutely terrified. You must have said or *done* something to him!"

Susan suddenly stood up. "Mr. Briggs, I'd like to take Chris home. He's been badly bruised and I doubt if he'd be much good in class."

"Yes, of course, Mrs. McKenzie." He took them to the door and said: "Thank you for coming here so promptly. I'll let you know if we need to speak with you again."

They shook hands and Susan and Nella started down the hall. Behind her Susan heard Mr. Briggs say to Chris: "You're quite sure that you didn't say anything to John to scare him? That he just suddenly stopped hitting you and ran?"

She whirled around and watched her son with frightened eyes as he replied: "Yes, sir, I'm sure."

But he wasn't looking at the principal. He was staring at Susan and frowning, as if he were trying to find the answer to a question that had just occurred to him.

Mr. Briggs patted Chris's shoulder and smiled. "I believe you, son."

Christopher nodded, and then said huskily: "I'm sorry about Stark. I wish there was something I could do."

"Chris!" Susan called out sharply. "We're waiting."

A few hours later, after a hot bath and a snack, Christopher lay on his bed with his arms behind his head. The humid afternoon was disappearing into a cool twilight, and a soft breeze fluttered the curtains at the windows. He stared thoughtfully at a row of model planes sitting on top of the bookcase. Their bright red-and-blue wings and sleek silver fuselages stirred a memory that was at once elusive, yet almost within his grasp. He narrowed his eyes and concentrated, knowing that the memory, once secured, would answer the questions that had nagged at him from the moment they had left the school.

Susan knocked lightly at the door and came in carrying a basin of water and a cloth.

"How are you feeling?" she asked.

He let his effort slide away to the back of his mind and smiled at her. "Okay," he replied. "My head aches a little and my face hurts."

"Let me put another cold compress on it for you."

She sat down on the edge of the bed, dipped the cloth in the water, and wrung it out. Then she folded it and laid it gently against his cheeks.

"Nella called and asked how you were feeling. And Charlotte, too. They'll be over tomorrow to see you."

He nodded and shifted against the pillows, his eyes straying to the model planes. Susan turned her head and followed his gaze. Then she looked back at him. His eyes had the same questioning expression she had seen earlier in the school hallway.

"What are you thinking about?" she asked uneasily.

"Michael," he answered her, still looking at the planes. "I was remembering Michael."

Susan sat quietly, hoping her face would not betray the wave of apprehension that went through her. The silence between them grew uncomfortable. The last rays of light were dying away, and night shadows began to gather in the corners of the room. She reached out to a lamp on his table, murmuring: "It's getting dark. . . ."

"No, don't," he said, and took the cloth from his face, crumpling it in his hands. He was quiet for a few minutes and then he spoke.

His words went through her like a knife.

"I did it, Mom. I made Stark jump off the fire escape; I know I did. And you know it too."

Tears started in Susan's eyes and she bowed her head. "Tell me what happened, Chris," she said.

"We were fighting. He was on top of me, holding me down and calling Nella a cripple. He called her that over and over." His voice rose with anger. "I hated him. I wanted to hurt him!"

He paused, startled at the rage he was feeling. His skin was clammy and his hands shook. He took a deep breath and went on.

"And then something happened that I can't figure out. I lay very still, and all of a sudden I imagined him running up the fire escape and jumping off. I don't know why I thought of that; I just saw it happening in my mind. It was like watching a movie without any sound." He looked at her wide-eyed, and his voice sank to a whisper. "And then he did it. He did exactly what I had imagined."

Susan buried her face in her hands and began to cry. Chris sat up and took her in his arms.

"Mom, don't cry. Help me, please. I don't understand any of it, except that I know it happened—and that other things have happened too."

As he held her, he stared at the model planes on the bookcase, lined up one after another as he and Michael had finished them. And the memory that had eluded him all afternoon wavered briefly in his mind, then suddenly was whole and clear before his eyes.

"Mom," he said urgently, "the night Michael was killed— I was only seven. But I saw it, didn't I? I saw the truck overturned and Michael lying there."

Susan's body stiffened in his arms. "Yes, yes." She wept against his shoulder. "You saw it hours before the police called me."

He held her tightly. "What does it mean? Tell me!" he demanded. "I didn't hurt Michael, did I? I couldn't have—I loved him!"

"Oh, no, darling. You didn't do anything to Michael."

"But I saw it! I saw his death!"

Susan pulled away from Chris and clasped his hands between hers. "Please, dear," she pleaded. "No more now. Get some rest and we'll talk about it later. Please?"

"No, You've got to tell me now!" he insisted. "What else have I done?"

He waited for her to answer, his eyes searching her face desperately. Susan let go of his hands and stood up. The moment she had feared for so many years was here. But how could she explain to him what she barely understood herself?

"Mom, please!" Chris's voice rose impatiently. "I've got to know!"

Susan nodded slowly. "Yes—I'll tell you."

And the memories she had tried to banish were relived: his near-drowning in the stream in Inverness and how he had summoned her, directed her to where he was; the terrifying night when he had saved her from being attacked by Tom Stanwyck, and what he had done to him.

"I remember that!" Chris cried out. "But there was something else! You were hurt. Your mouth was bleeding and I touched you and the bleeding stopped!"

Susan looked at her son sitting tensely upright on the bed, his face a pale mask in the nearly darkened room.

"Yes," she answered after a moment's pause. "You healed me."

For a few seconds Christopher stared at her wildly. Then he

leaped from the bed, turned on the lights, and rushed to the mirror over his dresser, his hands going to his face.

"No, don't!" Susan screamed.

"I've got to see for myself!" he said harshly.

She ran to him and grabbed his hands. "And if you do it, what will they say? Mr. Briggs and Mr. Strathmore and the children you know—what will they say when you walk in without a mark on you?"

Chris tore his hands from hers and reached once more to his face. Then he stopped, struck by the impact of what she was saying. He turned to her in a panic of confusion. "But—if it's—true—" he stammered. "Mom, if it's true that I can heal, then I could help people."

"Or hurt them!" she burst out vehemently. "Tom Stanwyck and John Stark—did you help them? They could have been killed!"

Chris's face drained of color and he began to tremble violently. Susan put her arms around him and led him to the bed. They sat down and she cradled him against her body.

"What does it mean? Am I some kind of freak?" he cried.

"No, darling boy, no," she crooned, rocking him slowly and stroking his hair.

He lifted his tear-stained face from her breast. "I'm like the stories you told me about the boy with second sight—and the powers of Cu Chulainn. I'm like they were!"

His voice shuddered with childish, fearful wonder, and Susan held him with all her strength. Those were just fairy tales! she wanted to cry out; stories told to a little girl by her grandfather to while away the hours of the night; heroes and demons who were nothing more than legend.

But she had witnessed her son's acts. She had lain awake nights tortured by the fear of what would happen to him if anyone knew. He might be hounded and scorned, ridiculed by people who were afraid of what they did not understand, or persecuted by the people he hurt. . . .

And then she thought of something that gave her hope for his future, his life.

No one had remembered what he had done.

Tom Stanwyck thought *she* had hit him, had fought off his attack. And just a few hours ago, Mr. Briggs had called to tell her that the Stark boy remembered only falling from the fire escape. When questioned about Chris, he admitted starting the fight, but remembered nothing else until he fell! And even with Charlotte! If he *had* done anything to change her thinking when they met in the agency office in London, she had never said a word about it.

A slow resolve and purpose grew within her, a certainty of how they might survive and live with a measure of peace.

"Chris, you must listen to me," she said urgently.

The boy stirred in her arms, sat up and stared at her. Susan was grim with determination, her eyes hard and bright.

"You must do exactly what I tell you." She waited for his agreement.

Christopher nodded his head, too exhausted to think or argue, relying now only on her strength, her wisdom.

"You must never do anything like this again," she said firmly, "and no one must know. No one! Promise me!"

He saw the pain and fear behind her eyes and knew that he must do as she asked.

"I promise," he said solemnly.

And the pact was made.

Part Two

9

"Eric—it's Gary. You'd better get down here. The light man is going crazy and the old bitch is threatening to walk out!"

"Dammit! Can't you and Shelly handle it? I've been trying to get ten minutes with John all day! Do I have to do everything?"

"I've only got two hands and one mouth!" Gary burst out angrily.

"All right, all right! I'll be right down!"

Eric slammed the receiver down and lit a cigarette. He inhaled deeply several times and then crushed it out in an ashtray overflowing with dead butts.

On his way to the sound stage he stopped in the men's room, splashed cold water over his face, combed his hair, and straightened his tie. The face in the mirror was not his own, he decided, and then wondered why he'd thought that.

He could hear the sounds of voices raised in argument before he entered the studio and shook his head wearily. Every show had its problems, but tonight's was unsurpassed for sheer absurdity. His guest was an elderly Frenchwoman, Stephane de la Chesnay, who had written literally hundreds of highly successful romantic novels.

Her American publishers had brought her to the United States for a cross-country tour to promote her latest best seller, *The Flame of Port Said*. A notorious eccentric, she had arrived at the station in a chauffeured pearl-pink limousine, accompanied by her personal secretary, a hairdresser, her own make-up man, and a flashily attractive young man who seemed attached to her by invisible strings that had been pulled tight; he was never more than a reach of her hand away.

As soon as he walked onto the set, Eric saw what the problem was. The overbearing and affectedly regal authoress was sitting in the guest chair wearing a black velvet gown trimmed in ermine, and arrayed in a stupefying collection of jewels: an enormous diamond tiara crowning the tower of blue-white lacquered hair, pendant earrings, a wide choker of rubies around her creped neck, equally wide diamond and emerald bracelets on both wrists, and rings on every finger. Whenever she moved, the glare lit up the entire studio.

Gary rushed to his side and frantically whispered: "Do something! If she gives the crew one more direction they'll kill her!"

Eric nodded and waved him off to the director's booth. His secretary took his arm but he brushed her aside.

"Eric—"

"It can wait, Shelly."

Stepping to the center of the stage, Eric stood easily, looked around smiling, and called out: "Quiet, please. Quiet!"

A hush fell over the group, and Madame de la Chesnay turned from whispering to her companion to look at Eric. He approached her smoothly, bowed, took her hand in his and kissed it lightly, trying to avoid the rings.

"*Madame de la Chesnay, je suis Eric Wynters. C'est un grand honneur pour moi de vous rencontre*," he said in his best college French.

Her pale-blue eyes traveled slowly over his face and down his body, then back up to his dazzling smile.

"*Enchantée, Monsieur Wynters*," she replied in a low, intimate voice.

With a quick gesture of scarlet-clawed fingers she dismissed her young man, and while the crew watched in disbelief, Eric chatted and laughed with her, and helped to remove most of the jewelry, handing it to Shelly, who had hurried to his side.

As they walked off, leaving the Frenchwoman wreathed in smiles,

Eric muttered to Shelly: "Tell Harry to set his lights and we'll start taping this octogenarian coquette!"

Two hours later Madame de la Chesnay gathered her retinue together and left the studio, blowing kisses to Eric and the crew and inviting them all to visit her château.

Eric slumped wearily in a chair and lit a cigarette. Gary came by and shook his hand.

"You were terrific—sorry about blowing up on the phone."

"Forget it." Eric nodded. "But for Christ's sake keep your head the next time!"

Gary's face darkened with anger, but before he could reply, Shelly called out to Eric that there was a long-distance phone call for him. He hurried out of the studio to his office, leaving Gary tight-lipped and fuming.

"Take it easy, Gary," Shelly said, handing him a cup of coffee. "He's just tired. You know Eric—he's a perfectionist."

"Perfectionist, hell! He's turning into a goddamned shit!"

Eric gripped the receiver and listened intently to the voice of the man on the other end.

"—so that's it, Mr. Wynters. Our last lead drew a blank. The couple in Cleveland went through an agency located in Sinaloa, Mexico, and now the local police are investigating. But the kid didn't fit the description anyway."

There was a pause and Eric heard a crackle on the line. The connection from Ohio was poor and the operator cut in for a moment, then reconnected them.

"Simpson," Eric said desperately, "don't you have anything?"

"Sorry, Mr. Wynters. There's no point in chasing down any more leads here. I'll be checking with our man in Georgia tomorrow—he may have something."

The line crackled again and Eric raised his voice. "All right—do what you can. Tell him to call me at the same time next week."

"Will do," the man's voice splintered back, and then the line went dead.

Eric hung up and sat at his desk, his body rigid, the muscles in his jaws working. He took a deep breath and tried to relax. It had been four months since he'd hired the investigating firm to find David, and so far nothing had happened but a succession of phone calls from disembodied voices telling him what he didn't want to hear.

He lit a cigarette and inhaled, grimacing at the stale taste. He was smoking too much. And not sleeping well. He suddenly felt shrunken and hollow and his shoulders slumped with fatigue.

John Bradford tapped on the open door and said, "Eric?" The tone of his voice was the same as it had been every week when the call came in: Did they find anything, learn anything? Is there any hope? All those questions in the single word: "Eric?"

"Sorry, John. Nothing," Eric said dully to his father-in-law.

The older man stood in the doorway and looked at him with concern. "Why don't you come home with me and spend the weekend? You haven't done that since you moved into town. Margaret misses you."

"It's tempting, but I've got work to do tonight and tomorrow. Tell her I might be out on Sunday."

"All right," Bradford sighed, getting ready to leave. "The show was good tonight, but I really think you're working too hard."

Eric smiled at him. "You're a worrier. Kiss Margaret for me. Good night, John."

A few minutes later Shelly walked in. "Nothing, huh?" she asked softly.

"No, nothing."

"I'm sorry." She paused for a moment and then asked: "Can I buy you a drink? Maybe dinner?"

Eric looked up at her, considering the offer. Shelly had been the first one to come back when he reorganized the show. She'd worked hard and never complained. He was grateful for her help, and aware of her feelings for him.

He stared at her coldly, trying to arouse in himself some interest. The blond hair was longer now, prettier. She'd lost weight and her figure was good. He tried to imagine what she'd be like in bed. Soft, willing, ready to give him whatever he wanted. But not exciting, not spirited or passionate. Not Jenny.

"Thanks, Shelly—maybe some other time," he said brusquely.

He slipped on his coat, and they left the building together. On the front steps, Shelly said tentatively: "My offer for a drink still holds."

Eric shook his head. "Give me a rain check, okay?"

"Sure. Some other time." She watched him walk off down the street, then called out: "Get some rest!"

He waved his arm without turning around and kept walking.

Eric wandered along Walnut Street toward Society Hill. He had moved into one of the new high-rise apartment buildings facing the river a few months ago. But his quarters still looked as if he had just moved in: crates and boxes as yet unpacked; clothing, linens, and kitchenware still not put away, but left casually where he had used them. At his insistence, all the furniture he and Jenny had owned was sold; he didn't want any reminders of how they had lived. But it was a useless gesture, and so far all he had bought for the apartment was a bed and a couch. Barren and disordered, the rooms looked to him like a place for transients, a flop for the night before moving on in the morning. A perfect reflection of how he felt.

The street was deserted, even though it was only eleven o'clock at night. Luca streetlamps touched a golden glow to the old cobblestones and cast a pale light over rows of restored brick and white-frame town houses with dark-green shutters at the windows and flower boxes enclosed by ornamental grilles of wrought iron.

Everywhere it was quiet; doors closed, windows darkened, and no one on the streets except for the occasional police car prowling like a cat through the night, its headlights a baleful pair of yellow eyes searching the darkness.

Eric slowed his pace, reluctant to go home and face the chaos of his apartment. The empty night was like an extension of his empty rooms, but at least there were no walls to give him the feeling of being trapped and alone with himself.

He turned right at Front Street and walked quickly to a small bar tucked into an alley between two warehouses. If he got too drunk, as he had on other nights, he was only a few blocks from home and could manage.

A wail of music and air thick with cigarette smoke greeted him as he opened the door. The room was crowded, but he found a place at the bar and ordered a drink. People stood in small clusters in the corners, and raucous laughter came from the booths. In the garish red and green lights everyone looked slightly ill, and the thought made him laugh aloud. A woman turned away from her companion and looked at him. He stopped laughing and concentrated on his drink. A few minutes later she slid onto the barstool beside him.

"What was so funny?" she asked.

"What?" He looked up at her.

"A minute ago you were laughing. Why?"

Her hair was brown and swept back off her face. About thirty, Eric guessed, attractive, little make-up and a good mouth, sly eyes that invited. His eyes slipped down over her figure. Small but neat, good tits and long legs. He'd never seen her in the bar before.

"Why were you laughing?" she asked again.

Her voice was high, light in tone. He didn't like it. Maybe she'd keep her mouth shut.

Eric gave her a slow smile. "I bet myself that the liquor in this place was rotten—and it is. Agreed?" His smile widened and he shifted slightly so that their shoulders touched.

"Agreed," the woman said. She leaned against him a little.

Eric dropped his hand to her thigh and let it rest there. "I've got better stuff at my place," he said softly. "But no music. I like it when it's quiet." He paused and looked at her intently. "Agreed?"

"Agreed," she answered. "I have to get rid of someone. I'll meet you outside in five minutes."

He waited at the end of the block for her, listening to the distant sounds of tugs and barges moving up the river. He would take her back to the apartment, to the empty rooms. They'd move like wraiths through the ritual of drinking and small talk, undressing and making love, and for a few moments he could imagine that he was alive.

10

Amanda Howard paced the floor of her office in College Hall. She was thinking, and Amanda always paced when she was thinking. Head up, eyes cast heavenward, hands clasped behind her back, she walked briskly back and forth. Then she noticed a wide area of paint chipping off the ceiling over her filing cabinets.

Indignant, she rushed to her desk and yelled into the intercom: "Jean! Come in here!"

Her secretary, Jean Bailey, was a student majoring in political science. Nineteen, blond, and bored with school, she entered the office prepared to deal with another of Amanda's frequent tirades or complaints. She found her standing beneath the chipping paint with one arm raised over her head, a finger pointing to the offense.

"Look at that!" Amanda cried. "This office was supposed to have been completely refurbished and instead it looks like a tenement! File a 7-B59 form with Maintenance and have it taken care of as soon as possible!"

"7-B58 to Maintenance," Jean repeated indifferently.

"7-B59!"

"Sorry—B-59."

"I have many important guests of the university here for discussions concerning endowments and grants," Amanda said through clenched teeth, "and I will not tolerate a deteriorating environment!"

You nit! she added to herself, then muttered: "That's all—for now."

Amanda watched the girl saunter out of the office to the anteroom.

Jesus Christ, with an ass like that she probably has to fight them off! she thought, envy hardening her eyes to narrow slits.

She dropped her five-foot-two-inch, unpleasantly plump body into an overstuffed antique chair, reached into the lower drawer of her desk, and withdrew a carefully hidden silver flask of ten-year-old Scotch. A deep swallow directly from the flask spread a current of alcoholic warmth into her ample chest and gave her cheeks a rosy flush.

"Where would I be without you, baby?" she sighed, then kissed the flask and returned it to its hiding place.

A stack of unfinished paper work cluttered her desk: letters, notes and memoranda, proposals and recommendations. She decided to leave it all for Monday. The traffic out of the city was sure to be maddening on a Friday night, and rain was expected. She glanced out the window and saw banks of gray and black storm clouds massing in the leaden sky.

Terrific, she muttered to herself, gathering up her purse and gloves. It's cold enough to freeze your orifice closed, there's snow on the ground, and now we add a heavy dash of rain—and bang! we've got ice! Christ, I hope the antifreeze is okay!

Then she spotted a book lying on her desk and remembered a phone call that had to be made. She dialed quickly and waited, tapping her foot impatiently.

"Cathy? It's Amanda! Thanks for the book, dear, I got it a few hours ago. When does it hit the stores? . . . Next week—good. Listen—the cover's terrific, and that picture of you—gorgeous, you bitch! How dare you be so bright and look like that? . . . What do you mean, like what? Like a Jewish madonna whose mother was a belly dancer! . . . Yes, I'm coming to the party. . . . Eight thirty—yes. I'm on my way home now to make myself glamorous. Stop laughing or I'll poison your Mogen David! Who's going to be there? . . . Oh, God! Well, I'll come anyway. . . . Right—see you tonight. Bye, love."

Walking out of the building and across the campus, Amanda lifted the thick hood of her white fur coat and settled it around her face, wincing at the bite of the February cold. Several students dressed in caps and scarves and heavy sweaters hurried past, their long legs tightly clad in jeans.

Amanda eyed the group of slim hips racing over the grounds and groaned to herself: Christ! I must look like a misplaced baby polar bear! She strode more quickly along Locust Walk toward the university garage.

Opening the door of her bright-yellow low-slung Ferrari, she heaved herself into the front seat and started the car, letting the engine warm up. The seat belt couldn't make it around the bundle of her coat. She let it snap back with a derisive snort and drove out into the early-evening traffic.

By the time she got to the Lancaster Pike it was raining and traffic was almost at a standstill. A truck had jackknifed, blocking three lanes. Amanda cursed the driver, the police who were trying to untangle traffic, and the motorists leaning on their horns with manic intensity. As she crept along, furiously wiping the inside of her windshield, she saw an exit coming up to a back road she had often used as a shortcut.

Maneuvering the car in a series of jerky starts and stops, Amanda cut across two lanes, ignored the frantic protests of indignant drivers, and drove down the incline of the offramp to the narrow two-lane road.

The last traces of light faded and suddenly it was dark. The rain had become a downpour of sleet and washed across the windshield faster than the wipers could work. Amanda felt the front tires skid on the icy surface and slowed to fifteen miles an hour. She followed the twists and turns of the road, peering through the drenched glass for street signs, but none were visible. In the powerful glare of the headlights she could see only the dark, winter-barren shapes of trees enclosing her on both sides.

"This was a mistake, my girl," she said grimly. "Let's hear what the newsman has to say."

She turned on the radio and almost lost control of the car rounding an unexpectedly tight turn.

"Shit!"

". . . you folks in the Delaware Valley are really in for it tonight!" the weatherman was announcing cheerfully. "The U.S. Weather Service predicts at least three inches of rain and sleet, and we have reports coming in of hailstones as big as baseballs—"

"Asshole!" Amanda shut the radio off with a furious gesture. "I'm fighting for my life in this goddamned hurricane, and he's chuckling about hailstones!"

The force of the downpour increased, becoming a continuous drumming, like the sound of fists beating on the roof of the car. All around her was blackness, and a feeling of panic rose in her throat. She was lost.

Then she thought she saw a light in the distance. Through the slam of water on the windshield it wavered and gleamed, distorted for a moment, then solid and glowing. It might be a house. She could stop and find out where the hell she was. The curving road straightened out abruptly, and without thinking, she pressed down on the gas pedal. Suddenly the ground under her dropped away and the car plunged down a hill. Amanda slammed on the brakes and they failed immediately. For one brief, horrifying moment she saw an enormous tree looming up out of the darkness.

"Oh, God! That fucking tree is going to hit me!"

She was leaning against the door at the moment of impact.

She felt the flow of blood from head wounds over her face and down her neck. One arm was painfully bent under her, and there was no feeling in her legs. She took a breath and almost screamed. Broken ribs. She opened her eyes. Was she conscious? Yes. She was half out the door, but it was bent and squeezed tight against the tree. She couldn't move. Sleet beat against her face but she couldn't feel it. The bitter cold and wet were fading into numbness.

If I don't die from loss of blood, I'll freeze to death! She met the thought with a shock of fear, then accepted it as inevitable. She was dying. In a few moments it would be over.

A sound penetrated the roar of the storm; a voice was calling out. Then a shadow, liquid and hazy, was nearby. It grew and took shape as it approached, became solid. Legs in rough work pants. Boots. A man carrying a lantern.

The figure knelt beside her, saying something she couldn't hear. She tried to answer but could not speak. Her mouth was full of blood. He wrenched at the door and she felt her body shift. A fiery pain went through her and she screamed.

Then two hands rested on either side of her head.

A honey warmth spiraled into her body, coursing along her arms and legs, bringing a return of sensation. She took a deep breath of cold air and did not feel any pain.

She felt herself being lifted and carried in strong arms, and then she slid away into a deep and comforting sleep.

A few hours later in a room at the Booth Memorial Hospital, Dr. Seymour Bergman looked up from his clipboard and shook his head with surprise.

"Miss Howard, God was smiling on you tonight. From the police report, your car was totaled, the tree you hit will never be the same, and here you are, alive and kicking. My dear lady, you should be dead!"

"Maybe this whale blubber I'm encased in saved my life?" Amanda said to him from under a swathe of bandages covering her face.

Dr. Bergman lifted heavy gray eyebrows and shrugged. "It really doesn't make a lot of sense. Your clothes indicated that you'd lost a great deal of blood, and yet all we've been able to find are superficial body cuts and bruises. No broken bones, severed arteries—nothing."

"When can I get out of here?" Amanda asked tensely.

"Well, believe it or not, you are still in a state of some shock, though why you aren't completely unconscious baffles me. However, I should think that by tomorrow afternoon you could go home. I'll have the nurse bring you a sedative and you can get a good night's sleep." As he was leaving, he turned from the door and asked: "Are you quite sure that you're not in any pain?"

"Yes, quite sure—thanks for asking," she said, trying to joke.

"Incredible," Dr. Bergman muttered. "I'm amazed that whoever carried you from the wreckage didn't kill you outright." He kept shaking his head as he left the room.

Alone, Amanda closed her eyes and tried to remember what had happened. The road dipped away, the brakes failed, and the car hit a tree; of that much she was certain. She was conscious after the accident and bleeding profusely—and in pain, especially when she breathed. Yet there were no broken ribs. No broken anything!

But she had seen a man; she knew that. At least she had seen his legs. And he had touched her. . . .

Before picking her up he had touched her! That was when the pain had stopped. A few seconds later she had fallen asleep and awakened here in the hospital, alive and virtually unscathed. How?

Amanda was not a religious woman. She didn't believe in miracles. Yet apparently one had occurred.

Or had it? Whoever had taken her from the car had touched her first, stopped the pain with his hands. . . .

She began to feel cold, but it wasn't from shock. A mad idea had struck her. Tears started in her eyes as she tried to deny it, to put it out of her mind. But it was strong, insistent, and could not be dismissed.

She sat up, no longer surprised that she could move so easily, so painlessly. The tears were flowing freely as she reached for the phone on the night table and dialed.

"Cathy . . . Cathy, it's Amanda. Sorry I'm late for your party." She giggled a little hysterically. "I've had an accident. I'm at Booth Memorial." Now she was crying, sobbing into the receiver. "Cathy—something's happened, and I'm alive! Oh, God! Please come to me—I need you!"

11

"I know what I experienced!" Amanda said shrilly. "I was conscious the whole time, and I know what I felt when he touched me."

Catherine sat down on the edge of the bed and took her friend's hand. "Amanda, dear, calm down. Accident victims often experience delusions of injuries far worse than those they actually receive. I spoke with Dr. Bergman and he said you had only superficial wounds and bruises—"

"And did he tell you that I should have been killed? Did he describe the amount of blood on my clothes, and yet I didn't need any transfusions? Did that schmuck explain any of that to you?" Amanda demanded.

"Well, yes, he did," Catherine answered, "but even so, freak things do occur sometimes in accidents."

"Freak things!" Amanda exclaimed. "The only freak thing about all of this is Dr. Bergman, and you're beginning to run him a close second! I tell you my ribs were broken, my legs too, or my back, for all I know—I was numb from the waist down! And my face was covered with blood—"

Catherine shook her head and smiled. "Don't you think you might be overdramatizing just a little?"

Amanda fell back against the pillows with a hard, indignant plop. "Some friend you are! After all the efforts I've made on your behalf, the grants, and arguments with staff, the time in hours alone—"

"All right, all right! You sound like my mother! I believe, I believe. As soon as you've had a few days' rest, we'll drive out to the scene of your miraculous healing and play detective. Okay?"

Amanda smiled. "There's nothing as effective as making a Jewish girl feel guilty. We'll get the police reports and find out where the hell I was and then go there tomorrow. Now will you please get me out of here? I think the night nurse has a thing for chubbies and is after my body!"

Snow and ice had turned the countryside into a crystal etching, gleaming in silver and frost-white. Giant trees stood in glacial dignity, and brightly clad children were sledding down hills that were as smooth as bone china. Skaters turned and glided over frozen ponds, and smoke rose in fragile wisps from snow-covered chimneys of houses dotting the white landscape.

"I love this time of year," Catherine said, holding the car steady on the slick surface of the road.

"You love every time of the year," Amanda replied absently.

The two women drove on in silence. At a crossing, Catherine slowed the car and stole a glance at her friend. Amanda's face was drawn and her mouth was set in a tense line. A bright-red scarf covered the soft mass of her blond hair, and she huddled inside a heavy black coat as if it offered more than just protection from the cold.

"We're almost there," Catherine told her.

"Yes, I know."

Making a left turn, they started down the road Amanda had driven on just a few nights before. Catherine went over the details of the police report in her mind. She had seen the photographs of the car, smashed up against the tree, completely wrecked. An ambulance had been called for from the home of a Mrs. McKenzie. Her son had carried Amanda into the house, afraid that she would freeze if left in the car. The attendants had reported only shock and bruises and some superficial cuts. And Dr. Bergman had verified that she was virtually unhurt. Yet her clothes had been drenched in blood. It didn't make any sense.

"You still don't believe me, do you?" Amanda asked abruptly.

"That's the trouble with knowing someone for too many years," Catherine said lightly. "They begin to think they can read your mind."

"I don't have to read your mind. I know. You think I hallucinated the whole thing."

Catherine nodded her head slowly. "It's possible. The police suggested that you might have been thrown clear of the car."

"I might have been, but I wasn't," Amanda said stonily. "Catherine, I've never been as convinced of anything in my life as strongly as I am about this. I was saved by someone with an extraordinary power to heal."

Catherine remained silent for a few minutes. Then she asked: "What exactly did Mrs. McKenzie say when you called her?"

"I told you—she was glad I was well, and saw no reason for me to come over to thank her in person, and that she was really very busy."

"And that's all?"

"Yes. She didn't sound at all happy about my calling her."

"And now we're going to barge right in—"

Amanda turned to face her, china-blue eyes snapping defiance. "Yes, we are! Listen, Cathy, I'm no fool—I'm forty-two, over-educated, overqualified, and overweight! I do my job well and I'm reasonably happy. I know who I am and what I am. Now I've got to know *why* I am still alive when I shouldn't be. I won't have a minute's rest until I know for sure just exactly what happened to me!"

Catherine was quickly apologetic. "Mandy, I'm sorry—sometimes I play skeptic too hard. I do believe that *you* believe what happened. We'll talk to Mrs. McKenzie and then take it from there. Okay?"

Amanda didn't answer, but stared straight ahead, eyes wide. "There it is," she said, her voice choked. "There's the tree."

They drew alongside a huge old oak. The weathered bark on its knotted and gnarled trunk was violently torn, leaving a raw gash of naked wood.

"That must be the house up there, at the end of the lane," Catherine said.

As they parked the car and walked up to the front door, Amanda shivered and muttered: "Christ, I need a drink."

Catherine took her arm and pressed it. "Steady, girl—I'm right beside you."

The woman who opened the door was dressed in a black wool skirt and sweater. Her red hair, lightly streaked with gray, was tied back, emphasizing the strong bones of her face. Her eyes were a cold blue, and stared at them with mistrust.

"Mrs. McKenzie?" Catherine asked.

"Yes—can I help you?"

Amanda pushed forward a little. "I'm Amanda Howard. I had the accident down on the road a few nights ago. May we come in?"

Susan paled slightly and hesitated, holding the door firmly. "Why, Miss Howard, we spoke on the phone and I told you—"

"Yes, I know. But I had to come and talk with you. This is my friend Catherine Marlowe. Please, may we come in?"

Reluctantly, Susan opened the door and ushered them into the living room. "It really wasn't necessary for you to come over, Miss Howard," she said almost harshly.

"I thought it was," Amanda answered frankly. "Something very strange happened to me that night, and I was hoping you could explain it."

"Something strange? I don't understand. You had an accident, my son carried you into the house, and we called the police. We told them everything." Susan's voice was agitated, and she kept glancing toward the kitchen nervously.

"I don't think you told them quite everything," Amanda said forcibly. "Not that I blame you—I hardly think they would have understood."

"Miss Howard, what *are* you talking about? I'm very glad to see that you weren't seriously hurt, but I really don't understand—"

There was a sudden commotion at the back door and a voice rang out from the kitchen: "Mom, I'm home!"

Catherine had been watching Susan, and at the sound of the voice, she saw her face drain of color. The woman looks terrified, she thought.

Just then a young man walked into the living room. He was tall, and the rough work clothes he wore could not disguise his lithe, muscular body. A shock of golden blond hair fell in a shaggy length around his face, framing his strong, handsome features.

Susan went quickly to his side. "This is my son Christopher."

He looked at the two women warily, and then recognizing

Amanda, he gave her a cautious smile. "Miss Howard—what are you doing here? How are you?"

"I'm well—and alive, thanks to you," she answered bluntly.

Chris was silent for a moment, his face reddening with embarrassment. "Well—I certainly couldn't let you lie out there in that freezing cold, could I? I'm glad you're okay. I guess your injuries weren't as serious as they looked."

Amanda stared at him hard. "We both know better than that, don't we?"

Susan cried out angrily: "Really, Miss Howard, I don't know why you've come barging in here with your mysterious—"

"Please, Mrs. McKenzie," Catherine interrupted, "could we discuss this calmly?" She turned to Christopher. "I'm Dr. Catherine Marlowe and a close friend of Amanda's. She's convinced that before you carried her into the house, you touched her and released her from a great deal of pain."

"You healed me, didn't you!" Amanda burst out. "I was conscious the whole time. You put your hands on my head and you healed me!"

"No!" Susan shouted. "My God, what are you saying!"

"Amanda, for Christ's sake, sit down and shut up!" Catherine commanded. She turned to Susan and took her hands. "Mrs. McKenzie, please sit down. We didn't mean to upset you so."

She led a white-faced, shaking Susan to a chair, then looked up at Chris. "I'm very sorry about this, Christopher. My friend is still somewhat shaken from the accident."

He didn't reply, but stared at Amanda, his eyes wide and unblinking. "What did the doctors say?" he asked in a low voice.

Catherine answered before Amanda could reply. In a quiet, steady voice, she described the police report of the accident and Dr. Bergman's findings and diagnosis. When she was finished, Christopher sank into a chair and hunched forward, his large hands hanging limply between his knees.

Catherine pulled a chair up beside him and sat down. When he looked at her, she saw that his eyes were wet with tears.

"Is what Miss Howard thinks—true?" she asked softly.

He hesitated for a few seconds, then nodded his head. "Yes, it's true," he whispered.

"Will you talk with me about it?" Catherine kept her voice calm despite the shock she felt at his admission. "I'm a professor of psychology at the University of Pennsylvania, and I've done a great deal of work in the field of parapsychology. You can trust me."

"Chris, please!" Susan gave an agonized cry. "You promised me!"

He got up and went to his mother and pulled her into his arms. "Mom, I can't," he said, trying to soothe her. "I just can't go on like this, not ever really knowing and always being afraid."

Susan held her son's face between her hands, her eyes imploring him frantically. "Chris—I'm afraid. What will happen to you?"

"Nothing bad, I think," he answered gently. "Maybe it will be easier for both of us, not having to hide it anymore."

Catherine spoke up. "I promise that without your full permission no one outside this room will know anything about whatever I learn."

Chris turned to her, his face reflecting both relief and a shade of fear of what the future might bring.

"All right, Dr. Marlowe," he said quietly. "What do you want to know?"

Catherine realized she'd been holding her breath. She let it out with a sigh and answered: "I want you to tell me everything."

12

Eric called a staff meeting to discuss the guests for a program on the occult that they had been planning for several weeks. He riffled through some papers on his desk and looked up at Edith Richards, the librarian at WBTV.

"Thanks for all these notes, Edith," he said. "They've answered several questions I've had about this so-called 'occult explosion' in the country."

Edith shifted her ample behind on her chair, pulled down her skirt, cleared her throat, and said: "The general field of inquiry in the psychic sciences is now called psi, Mr. Wynters. No one refers to it as 'occult' anymore—too much of a carnival connotation."

Edith was noted for her careful research and precise information. Eric had learned never to dispute her.

"Right," he said, making a note on his pad. "Shelly, whom have we got lined up so far?"

Shelly turned a page in her notes and read: "Lorraine Berk, a local astrologer and tarot reader. She also claims to be a psychic and has testimonials from satisfied customers."

"Terrific," Eric grunted. "Who else?"

"Are you ready?" Shelly grinned. "Lorenzo Diablo—"

"You're kidding!"

"Nope. He's head of a coven of black witches who, by the way, reside on the Main Line! Also Elza—with a z—Harkness, who leads a coven of white witches. And they live on the Main Line too."

Gary gave Shelly a look of disbelief. "Witches on the Main Line? Are you crazy?"

Edith cleared her throat again. "She's absolutely right. According to an article that appeared recently in *Philadelphia Magazine*, our countryside is rife with pagans!"

Eric burst into a howl of laughter. "Great! We'll do an X-rated show on paganism!"

"Don't scoff, Mr. Wynters," Edith said in her scholarly voice. "Paganism is flourishing all over the country."

"That may be, Edith," Eric said, still chuckling, "but I want to do a show on parapsychology, and all we have so far are two screwballs and a fortuneteller!"

"I called the universities," Shelly continued, "but got a very apathetic response from the people I talked to. There was one professor" —she stopped and rummaged in an oversized tote bag hanging on her chair—"I really wanted to get to. Ah, here it is." She handed Eric a book. "I called several times but couldn't get through to her. A secretary told me that she got my message but had no wish to discuss her work on a TV show."

Eric looked at the book. "'*PSI: A Contemporary View of the Psychic Sciences* by Dr. Catherine Marlowe,'" he read aloud. "When was this published?" he asked, turning the book over and looking at the dust-jacket photo.

"A few months ago. Good reviews, small sales. I have a file of notes on her—"

Eric held out his hand and Shelly gave him the file. "I'll read it over the weekend, then try to see her on Monday. She'd make an interesting contrast to the witches and the palm reader," Eric said.

"And provide a note of some authority," Edith added.

Gary took the book and looked at the picture on the back. "She's a good-looking woman."

"Yes, she is. Let's write her in for the show," Eric said.

"If you can get her." Shelly looked doubtful.

"I think I can manage it," Eric said confidently.

Monday morning he drove to the University of Pennsylvania campus. He found a parking place on Spruce Street and walked across the grounds to College Hall. A light early-morning shower had washed over the lawns and the thick ivy covering the old brick buildings. In the spring sunshine the campus looked as if it had slipped on a new dress of dazzling bright-green embroidered with the multicolored clothes of students rushing to their classes.

Eric went to the admissions office. The receptionist recognized him from the show and quickly gave him the information he wanted. He gave her his public-image smile and left the building.

The psychology department's offices were located in an ugly old brownstone on Walnut Street. Not content to leave bad enough alone, someone had decided to disguise the eyesore façade with a frame of brass mesh sheets, giving the whole building a hybrid look combining the worst of modern decorating and the ugliest of old architectural design.

Eric stopped at the small enclosed reception area and asked to see Dr. Catherine Marlowe.

"Is she expecting you?" a thin, bespectacled woman asked.

"Yes," Eric lied. "Tell her it's Eric Wynters of the *Wynters at Large* television show."

"Oh, Mr. Wynters! I've seen your show and enjoyed it very much," the receptionist said, beaming. She dialed a number on the phone, spoke briefly, and hung up, looking at Eric with a puzzled frown. "Dr. Marlowe said she did *not* have an appointment with you, but that she would see you anyway."

"Thank you. I was sure she would." Eric smiled.

She gave him a spinster's frown of disappointment at his little deceit and said: "It's the last door on the right, just down the hall."

Another idol smashed, Eric grinned to himself as he swung down the hall to Catherine's office. He knocked lightly at the door, opened it, and stuck his head inside.

"May I come in—even without an appointment?" he asked, smiling.

Catherine looked up from her desk with a cool, impersonal expression. "I thought you might be as brash in person as you are on your show," she said matter-of-factly. "And you are. Come in."

Eric closed the door and sat down in a chair near the desk. "Then you've watched my show?" he asked easily, ignoring her comment.

"Only if there isn't a good late movie on."

"Do I detect a note of criticism?" He tried to keep his smile fixed, but she was making it difficult.

"Mr. Wynters, if I had the time, you wouldn't hear a note—you'd get a lecture."

"Are you always so rude to your guests?" he snapped impatiently.

The question took her by surprise and she flushed. "You're right—I was being rude. I'm sorry. It's just that I told your secretary I didn't want to be on your show, and now you appear breathing clouds of charm—"

"Ah, ah, careful"—Eric waved a warning finger at her—"that almost borders on insult, and television personalities have very fragile egos."

Catherine laughed. "You're probably the least fragile man who's walked into this office in the last year."

"A compliment—much better, thank you. And may I say that the picture on the dust jacket of your book doesn't begin to do you justice."

"Thank you. If my mother were alive, she'd agree with you. But I still don't want to appear on your show."

"Why?" Eric asked simply. He could see that she would not tolerate breezy professional charm.

"Very simply, because I have a great deal of respect for my work and find your show glib and commercially exploitative."

Eric leaned forward across the desk with a thin smile. "Dr. Marlowe, I checked the sales figures on your book, and they were not staggering. I'm offering you the opportunity to express your viewpoint to a large audience who just might learn something from you, and even go out and buy your book."

Catherine glared at him angrily for a moment without replying. Then she said slowly: "You make a dirty sales pitch, Mr. Wynters."

Eric drew back, feeling slightly ashamed. "I'm sorry—I guess I was hitting below the belt."

"Not at all," she said. "You were being frank. Truthfully, I hadn't even thought of the possibility of plugging my book like actors plug their new films."

"Publishing's gone the way of the business world." Eric shrugged. "But aside from that, I'd be grateful to have a guest who had more to offer than just a plug for his or her product."

Catherine smiled. "Thank you—I believe that was almost sincere."

Eric sighed and shook his head. "Could we drop the hostilities? I'm sorry for barging in here like Mr. Television and being obnoxious."

"Apology accepted and hostilities cease," Catherine said.

"Then you'll consider being a guest on the show?"

"Yes—I'll consider it," she replied.

Eric hesitated for a moment and then asked: "Would you also consider having lunch with me—so that I can properly make up for my boorishness?"

Catherine looked at her watch. "Mr. Wynters, it's only eleven fifteen and I have some work to finish."

"If I may, I'll wait. I brought your book with me. I can sit here and read it until you're ready to go."

"All right, Mr. Wynters," Catherine said, laughing. "You read and I'll work. But be prepared for a little quiz during lunch!"

Eric had La Taresse, a small French restaurant on Sansom Street across from the Law School, in mind for lunch, but Catherine had other ideas. Soon after leaving the university they were heading downtown toward the Philadelphia Museum of Art.

"The food in the cafeteria isn't much, but the paintings make up for it. Are you sure you don't mind?" Catherine asked.

"Of course not. I haven't been there in years. Do you paint?"

"I used to. Every once in a while I take a day and go out into the countryside and try a watercolor. And you—what do you do besides interrogate hapless guests on your show?"

Eric frowned and looked uncomfortable.

"Did I say something wrong?"

"Oh, no—just your using the word 'interrogate.' My wife said that to me once."

"Your wife? I didn't know you were married."

"She's dead."

"Oh—I'm very sorry."

"Didn't you know?" Eric was genuinely surprised. "It was in all the papers. It happened about a year and a half ago. She was murdered—and our baby son was kidnapped." His voice was flat, emotionless.

Catherine stared at him, shocked.

"I didn't mean to upset you," Eric said, glancing at her. "I thought you knew. Most people remember it but don't say anything."

"I didn't know," she said unhappily. "I was in England then—it must have happened while I was away . . . Oh, Eric, how awful for you!"

"Sometimes I think of it as something that happened to someone else," he said in a distant tone. "But I'm fine now, really I am." He forced a smile. "Please, don't be concerned. Ah, there's the museum! Who's your favorite artist?" he asked, changing the subject.

The Philadelphia Museum of Art stood high on a hill overlooking the parkway. The Greek temple design of the building gave it an imposing dignity, and as Eric and Catherine walked up the wide concrete steps to the front entrance, they stopped to admire the graceful columns and intense colors of the bas-relief frieze of ancient gods that decorated the walls just under the roof.

There were not many other visitors, and a stately, reverent silence cloaked the marble halls and high-ceilinged rooms. They wandered through the galleries, commenting occasionally on the paintings, but being mostly silent.

In the museum bookstore Catherine exclaimed over a tiny lacquered Chinese box in the crafts section. Eric insisted on buying it for her as a peace offering, and she accepted on the condition that she buy lunch.

Later, in the cafeteria, they sat quietly over coffee, chatting comfortably with each other. Catherine had not questioned him about Jenny's death, and Eric was grateful for her tact. He liked her, admitting almost reluctantly to himself that he had been attracted to her from the moment he walked into her office. The realization made him uneasy; Catherine reminded him of Jenny: the long, dark hair and impudent brown eyes, the full sensual mouth and beautiful complexion. But where Jenny had been the bright, shining all-American girl, there was a slightly European cast to Catherine's features, as if time had created a careful and beautiful refinement of the sturdy peasant faces in her family background. Eric remembered her bio on the book jacket: of Russian parentage, she had been born and raised in Philadelphia and had taken her undergraduate and postgraduate degrees at the University of Pennsylvania; she had become a full professor at the age of twenty-eight, two years ago.

"Wasn't twenty-eight very young to get a full professorship?" he asked.

Catherine replied airily: "Well, I was very bright, worked very hard, played a mean game of university politics—and finally someone died, leaving a vacancy!"

"Clever girl!" Eric laughed. "And the work in psi—when did that start?"

"Oh, I've always been interested in paranormal psychology. The university doesn't have a program for it, but I've been working independently and with colleagues. Someday I may quit teaching and devote myself exclusively to the field, maybe even have my own lab." She paused abruptly and looked at her watch. "Eric, we've been here for hours! I've got to get back to work—my desk is loaded with papers to read."

On the way back to the university, Catherine sat watching Eric out of the corner of her eye; he had lapsed into a thoughtful silence and she wondered what he was thinking about.

Suddenly he said: "I was just wondering if you would have dinner with me tonight," as if in answer to the question in her mind.

"What?" she exclaimed in surprise.

He looked at her, puzzled. "Didn't you just ask me what I was thinking about?"

"No—I did not. I didn't say anything. But I was wondering what you were thinking!"

Eric began to laugh. "I do believe we've just had an ESP experience! I could have sworn I heard you ask me what I was thinking."

"Has that ever happened to you before?"

"No, not that I can remember. And you?"

"Oh—once or twice. With a man I knew."

"Was it serious—the man?"

"For a couple of years, but not anymore."

Eric smiled. "That's good. Now, back to my original thought: will you have dinner with me tonight?"

Catherine hesitated for a few seconds, then dug into her purse and pulled out a pencil and note pad.

"What are you doing?"

"Writing down my address and phone number. Is eight o'clock all right?"

Eric's smile widened. "That's fine. And thank you for the trip to the museum, the lunch—I really enjoyed it. And by the way, forget about appearing on the show. You were right about its being glib and exploitative."

Catherine made a face. "Oh, dear, I was hoping you'd forget I said that. I would like to be a guest, really I would. Everything you said was true, and to be completely honest"—she smiled mischievously—"I wouldn't be adverse to selling a few more copies of the book."

"You're on!" Eric said, laughing. "We'll talk about it at dinner."

He pulled the car up in front of her building. Before she got out, Catherine turned to him and asked tentatively: "Eric, what happened to your child? You said he was kidnapped."

Eric's expression turned grim. "They never found him. At least, not yet. But I'm convinced that he's alive. I have detectives searching for him now."

Catherine looked at him with eyes full of sympathy. She pressed his arm in an affectionate gesture and got out of the car. "Thank you for a lovely afternoon—and for my Chinese box. I'll keep it on my desk."

"Catherine . . ." Eric leaned across the seat and looked out the window at her.

"Yes?"

His eyes searched her face intently. "Do you think I'm foolish to go on looking for my son after all this time?"

She heard the desperate plea in his voice, the need for support and approval.

"Of course I don't think you're being foolish," she answered. "I'd do exactly the same thing."

The tense lines in his face relaxed into a grateful smile. "Thank you," he said huskily. "I'll see you tonight."

She watched him drive away and then went into her office, surprised to find herself on the verge of tears.

The phone rang and she answered it, making an effort to regain her composure. It was the receptionist with a message from Mrs. Susan McKenzie. Christopher couldn't make his four o'clock session but he would see her next week.

13

"I think we're in for more trouble than we bargained for," Shelly said to Eric.

They were in the director's booth watching the guests assemble for the taping of the psi show. The first sight of Lorenzo Diablo had produced an uncontrollable wave of giggling disbelief. A short, chubby man with full lips, a pink doughy face, and a shaved head ("In homage to La Vey," he explained reverently), Diablo was enveloped in a black robe and wore an enormous gold pentacle studded with rubies. Waddling into the studio, he suggested more an epicene Boy Scout master than a disciple of Satan.

Lorraine Berk, dressed in a flowered pants suit adorned with a counterful of junk jewelry, was feverishly writing down the birth dates of the crew and hustling them for astrological charts.

Elza Harkness, a thin, waspish woman in a white gown splashed with embroidered mystic symbols, had Gary backed into a corner and was lecturing him on the secret rites of the Druids.

"Where's the star of the show?" Shelly asked Eric.

"Who?"

"Dr. Marlowe. I still don't understand how you managed to get her on the show."

"I have an excessive amount of charm—and here comes the star now."

Eric went to greet Catherine as she walked into the studio. She was radiantly beautiful in a simply cut blazing red gown. A low murmur of approval went up from the crew while the other guests stared at her with icy disdain.

"Is it too much—the color, I mean?" she asked a little nervously.

"You look absolutely smashing!" Eric beamed.

"Who are those people in the Halloween costumes?"

Eric hesitated. "Your fellow panelists."

"Oh, my God!"

"I'll make it up to you, I promise," Eric said, hurrying her onto the set and into a chair.

"Not if you live to be a hundred!"

"This isn't network, just a small local show," he pleaded.

"But my friends are watching!"

"I'll write each of them a personal note of apology!"

From the director's booth Gary called out: "Places, everybody. Eric—ready when you are."

Elza, Lorraine, and Lorenzo took their seats around the glass-topped coffee table, sitting in front of a bas-relief mural of historic Philadelphia buildings that made up the backdrop of the set. Eric straightened his tie, mopped his brow, checked his fly, and shot his shirt cuffs, a ritual procedure before every taping. He threw Catherine a quick glance and saw that she was staring at him, trying to suppress a burst of laughter.

Gary gave him the signal from the booth and the show began. After a brief announcement on the subject of the show, Eric introduced the panelists.

"Our guests tonight are Lorraine Berk, noted astrologer and tarot reader, and author of *Astrology for Love and Other Related Matters*; Lorenzo Diablo, head of the First Satanic Congregation; Elza Harkness, leader of a coven of white witches and an ardent champion of witchcraft as a legitimate religion; and Dr. Catherine Marlowe, professor of psychology at the University of Pennsylvania and author of the best-selling book *PSI: A Contemporary View of the Psychic Sciences*." Eric looked quickly to Catherine for approval of his "best-selling" plug for the book. She gave him a gracious smile that was frosted with ice.

Turning to Elza Harkness, he said: "Miss Harkness, traditionally, witches were thought to have committed evil acts and were always associated with the darker, more base nature of man. Does the practice of invoking demons and casting spells still exist?"

"Mr. Wynters, witchcraft is the oldest religion in existence." Elza spoke in the manner of a grade-school teacher, placing a careful emphasis on each word. "Our practices and beliefs injure no one and never have. We are most concerned with spiritual matters, the harmony of man and nature, the aspiration toward higher consciousness of the Deity."

"Utter nonsense!" Diablo exploded, his pudgy face turning red.

"You disagree with Miss Harkness?" Eric asked.

"Fear, Mr. Wynters! Fear and timidity before the specter of demonic power! That is what prevents these dispirited fools from gaining a true understanding of the prodigious power available to those with the courage and daring to invoke it!"

"Exactly what is that power?" Eric was beginning to have some difficulty keeping a straight face.

"To live to the fullest, to experience the magnificence of power, one must trample on the icons and symbols of Christianity, dethrone God, and worship Satan!"

The little fat man was roaring with theatrical relish and Eric let him rant on.

"The power of the demon to fill the spirit with life," Lorenzo cried, "life and sexual energy, to defeat enemies and seduce the object of lust, this is the power of darkness that the Satanist alone can master!"

There was a moment of shocked silence. Elza gasped an audible "Oh, my!" and Lorraine played nervously with her jewelry.

Eric tried to keep the laughter out of his voice as he turned to Lorraine Berk, the astrologer, and asked: "Miss Berk, do you have a response to Mr. Diablo's assertions?"

"I certainly do!" she declared in a high, nasal voice. "The science of astrology is the only true revelation of information from the higher planes! It is a well-known fact that world leaders and many, many celebrities in New York and Hollywood consult their astrologers daily. Astrology is now being taught in major universities in

America *and* Europe. The truth, Mr. Wynters, will ultimately be accepted by all people!" she finished in a triumphant whine.

Eric could no longer avoid the moment. He turned to Catherine. "Dr. Marlowe—"

"Yes, Mr. Wynters?" she said brightly before he had a chance to continue.

"As a scientist, I'm sure your views on the subject must be—"

"As a scientist, Mr. Wynters, I feel somewhat out of place on this *august* panel," she said with a tight smile.

"All scientists are suppressive reactionaries!" Diablo broke in. "Your theorizing is impotent, useless. Science is lies, dried-up and sterile! The power belongs to those who worship Satan!"

"Please, Mr. Diablo, allow Dr. Marlowe to finish," Eric snapped.

"Thank you, Mr. Wynters." Catherine smiled at Eric sweetly and turned to Lorenzo.

"Mr. Diablo, two of my students attended a meeting of your congregation and made notes. They found your sermon entirely devoid of mysticism and concerned more with advice to your members on how to improve their sexual performance! In fact, what you operate is not a true Satanic church but an unlicensed sex therapy center. Yours is a commercially acceptable Satanism, bland and ultimately inoffensive."

"Lies! Slander!" The little man's face wobbled in fiery indignation.

"You're a bluff, Mr. Diablo," Catherine said, laughing. "True Satanism demands a priest who has abandoned his faith; you're just a little showman trying to make some money!"

Diablo began to sputter furiously and Elza Harkness exclaimed: "Really, Dr. Marlowe! You're being most unfair! We are, all of us, trying to find our way to a greater understanding, a higher consciousness—"

Eric jumped in, trying to regain control of the show. "I'm sure that Dr. Marlowe meant—"

"And furthermore," Lorraine Berk joined in, "I fully concur with Miss Harkness' argument for a return to pre-Christian worship."

"Ladies, if you'll allow Dr. Marlowe to continue—" Eric said weakly, but Catherine cut him off.

"That's only appropriate, Miss Berk," she said smoothly, "since you and Miss Harkness are collaborating on a line of so-called pagan jewelry and ritual clothing to be sold in a shop that you own in Center City. I read about it in a little magazine Miss Harkness publishes, which, I might add, has a rather steep subscription rate!"

Eric groaned inwardly as Lorraine and Elza began a furious babble of protestations that ended with the astrologer crying out: "Dr. Marlowe, I'd like to ask you a question!"

"Yes, Miss Berk?"

"What's your sign?" she demanded angrily.

A burst of hilarity broke out in the studio as soon as Lorraine, Elza, and Lorenzo stormed out the door. John Bradford, wiping tears of laughter from his eyes, shook Catherine's hand warmly and said: "My dear, I've never enjoyed a show of ours so much! Eric, you really must do an entire segment with just Dr. Marlowe."

"I don't think I'll ever be able to talk her into coming to this studio again," Eric said, wiping his brow.

"Oh, I don't know," Catherine said slyly, "I rather enjoyed the whole thing. If you twist my arm, I just might come back."

Eric took her arm. "We'll discuss your terms over dinner." He looked up at the director's booth and called out: "Shelly, can you and Gary wrap it up? I've had enough of this place for one night."

Shelly smiled and waved him off. She turned to Gary. "I think our führer has met his Eva Braun."

"Don't be bitter, kid. With his problems, she'll have her hands full."

Eric took Catherine to La Camargue, a small French restaurant on Walnut Street not too far from the studio. With its white plaster walls crossed by dark beams, big hothouse hanging plants, and beautifully set tables, the dining room had a Continental ambiance.

When they had finished the main course, a busboy quickly cleared away the dinner dishes, and a waiter appeared with a tray of coffee and thin crystal cups of chocolate mousse.

Eric lit a cigarette and leaned back in his chair with a satisfied sigh. He stared across the table at Catherine. In the low amber light her dark hair looked almost black and her skin glowed against the red tones of her gown.

"You're staring at me," she said a little self-consciously.

"You're right, I am," he replied with a slow smile. "You're a beautiful woman."

"Malarkey! You just want to get me back in that studio for another chance to prove you can handle your own show!"

He began to laugh. "I sure as hell lost control of it tonight! But you were wonderful—you really were."

"I was rude and bitchy," she said, sipping her coffee. "I'm ashamed of myself. But that trio of dummies was too much!"

"Tell me more about your work," Eric asked.

"No, not tonight." She lowered her eyes from the intensity of his glance. "I want to hear more about you. We've known each other for two weeks, had dinner together three times, two very quick coffee breaks at the university, and talked on the phone a half-dozen times—"

"You've been keeping track—how very nice," Eric said.

Catherine flushed. "Just my statistical mind at work. At any rate, I still don't really know very much about you."

He reached across the table and took her hand. "I'll tell you whatever you want to know—but not here," he said.

Catherine felt the warmth of his fingers, the unspoken message that was transmitted with his touch. She withdrew her hand and picked up her purse.

"All right," she said in a soft voice. "I've been saving a bottle of good French burgundy for just such an occasion."

Her apartment was in one of a row of converted brownstones in University City. High-ceilinged and with a small tiled fireplace, it was neat and comfortable, with the stamp of her taste and personality: rich brown walls and white woodwork trim, a mix of furniture styles that blended easily, and bright splashes of spring flowers in bowls and vases.

While Catherine went to the kitchen to get the wine, Eric wandered around the room feeling suddenly nervous and uncertain. The easy confidence he had in bars had totally deserted him; Catherine was no nameless, faceless woman he'd picked up for the night. He examined some prints and drawings on the walls, read the titles of books in a long, low bookcase behind the couch, and glanced at the magazines lying on the coffee table. Memories of the apartment he and Jenny had lived in flashed through his mind, and he suddenly felt cold and afraid to stay.

Catherine came out of the kitchen carrying a tray of wine and glasses. Seeing how pale he was, she asked: "Are you all right?"

"What? Oh, yes, of course." He took the tray from her hands and set it down.

"Eric, are you sure?"

"Yes. It's just that—for a minute I was reminded of the home I had with . . ."

He saw the look of concern and caring in her dark eyes and held out his arms. She moved into them, her body fitting against his in one fluid movement.

Eric sat up and reached to the night table for his cigarettes. He fumbled in the dark, found the pack, and pulled one out. His finger-tips continued searching and closed over his lighter. In the flame his face was illuminated in a quick flare of light and harsh shadows.

"I'm sorry," he said under his breath. "I seem to have lost more tonight than just the control of my show."

Catherine lifted herself on one arm and lay her cheek against his naked back. "Don't you dare apologize to me," she said softly. "I haven't been this nervous since I was a teen-ager. We just didn't get to the wine when we should have. Would you like some now? I would."

"Yes—some wine," Eric agreed absently.

Catherine slipped on a robe and went into the living room. Through the open door he saw her turn on a lamp and go to the coffee table to get the tray. A moment later the lamp was turned off and she came back into the bedroom. On the tray, in glass holders, were two candles casting a soft, mysterious glow that barely reached her face.

"Candlelight and wine," she said with a smile, and put the tray down between them.

Eric lifted his glass. "Very romantic. Do you think it will help, Doctor?" he said with a slight edge in his voice.

Catherine ignored the barb and laughed lightly. "Eric, this isn't therapy—and it seems a bit ludicrous to call me 'Doctor' here; you're naked and I'm wearing a very flimsy robe. The candles are simply to protect my vanity. My make-up is gone, and this light is supposed to be flattering for a woman. Is it?"

Eric smiled. "You don't need candlelight to be beautiful. And I'm sorry for snapping at you. That was just *my* vanity, or crushed ego, speaking."

Catherine put her glass down and reached to touch his face. "Eric, not with me—no fears of ego or vanity with me."

He moved his face in her hands to kiss her palms. She put the tray aside and drew him down beside her so that he lay with his head against her breasts.

When he spoke, the words came slowly and with effort. "After Jenny died, I was ill. I had a kind of nervous breakdown."

"You don't have to tell me this."

"I want to." He was silent for a few minutes, and then said: "I tried to kill myself. I took sleeping pills. Jenny and David had been my whole life—" His voice broke and he began to cry in hard, racking sobs.

Catherine held him tightly, stroking his hair and murmuring to him until the sobs subsided. She slipped off her robe and touched it to the tears on his face. He turned so that she was lying in his arms, and he kissed her, softly at first, then more urgently, so that her mouth opened beneath his lips. His fingertips traced down the curve of her throat to the hard tips of her breasts and over the firm stretch of ribs to the taut smooth skin of her hips. Catherine moved her hands across his back and slid them firmly down to cup the rhythmic clutch of his buttocks. They fluttered into the soft flesh of his inner thighs and met at the center of his body, stroking and caressing until he moaned with impatience. Shifting under him, she opened her legs and gathered him into her body with a faint cry.

Eric opened his eyes. Catherine was lying next to him, against the pillows. In the guttering light of the candles her face became a series of images; lights and shadows moved across her features, revealing at once an expression of burning intensity and then a sculptured look of enigmatic passivity.

"I like waking up to find you looking at me," he whispered. "The next time I wake up, I'll be afraid."

"Afraid of what?"

"Afraid that the next time I wake up you won't be there."

She smiled and gently caressed his body, then moved close to him, her lips at his ear. "It was marvelous," she breathed.

"It was? Really fantastic?"

She pinched his nipple lightly. "Marvelous, yes. Fantastic, no."

"Oh?" He began to chuckle. "Then we have something to look forward to: fantastic, sensational, gigantic, stupendous . . ."

She flung herself across his chest and stopped him with her lips, turning his laughter into a throaty growl as her tongue filled his mouth and her hand stroked him erect. She pulled her mouth away and curled up with her head resting on his stomach, her fingers still moving slowly over his cock.

"I feel like Connie in *Lady Chatterley's Lover*."

"Why?"

"I want to gather daisies and decorate this beautiful thing with garlands."

"You're mad, dotty."

"No—just poetic. Men and women don't make tributes to each other the way they should. They're too selfish. They read all the books, learn all the right moves, and turn sex into a game of who can give the most pleasure."

"Do you think they keep score?" Eric asked, smiling.

Catherine laughed. "Probably. Sometimes I'm convinced that people have become insulated against feeling anything more than just desire and a craving for satisfaction. They're afraid and grow careful."

"If you're not careful with that 'beautiful thing,' I'm going to have a very serious problem in a minute," Eric said thickly, his cock throbbing in her hand.

Catherine looked up at him. Eric's head was thrown back, his eyes closed, lips parted slightly. For a moment she stared in wonder at the clean, sweeping lines of his shoulders and chest, the narrow tapering to his waist. Then she turned and her lips went seeking through the tangle and curl of his pubic hair to the broad base in her hand. His body moved convulsively, and she felt a surge of power over him. The feeling startled her momentarily, and then she gave in to it, teasing her mouth slowly upward to cover and envelop the flamingly blooded head. Eric gasped and jerked his hips, forcing himself into her mouth. She paused and held him until his body relaxed, then began again.

He raised himself up to watch her, his eyes following the curves of her body from the nape of her neck to the flaring fullness of her buttocks. He had a sense of floating beneath her lips and the touch of her fingers, a lingering between gratitude and ecstasy. Suddenly his moment was upon him.

"Cathy, wait . . ." he moaned.

She raised her head and swiftly moved to straddle him. Leaning forward on her arms, her eyes held his with a glazed, opaque intensity. She lowered herself, and his penetration was quick and smooth. Her hips began a slow grind, gripping him in a velvet vise. He lay back, shudderingly content to follow her quickening thrusts, his legs stretched tight, muscles straining for control. Then he cried out, and they came together in a final aching spasm that flowered into a white, blinding universe.

14

Christopher stood at the edge of the terraced gardens in back of the Stanwyck house and smiled with satisfaction. The smooth green lawns were clipped to a fine edge around the vivid color of spring flowers, like a frame for an Impressionist painting. He gathered up the spade and shovel, hooked his fingers into the handles of the garden shears, and carried them to the small tool shed near the garages. With everything put away, he was finished for the afternoon. He glanced at his watch; enough time to clean up and get into town for his session with Dr. Marlowe.

On the way to the house, he stopped for a few minutes and looked over the gardens once again. Overhead an azure sky and bright sun intensified the subtle tints and hues of the flowers, so that they ran together in a shimmering blur like a fresh mix of paint on an artist's canvas.

Mrs. Gregory's booming voice called out from the back door of the kitchen: "Chris, there's a slice of fresh cake and a glass of milk for you before you leave!"

"Be right there," he called back, and started up the path.

A car turned into the driveway and he saw Charlotte behind the wheel. He waved to her and waited until she drew alongside him.

"Chris, how are you? I've missed seeing you!" she exclaimed.

"I'm fine, Aunt Charlotte," he said, smiling. "Mom was asking for you just this morning."

"Oh, I've got to get down and see her—it's been ages. I've just been so busy. Is she well?"

"Sure, you know Mom, never resting for a minute, always on the go. Have you heard from Nella?"

"Yes, and there's a letter for you." She opened her purse and took it out. "She'll be home soon, and we'll have her again for the rest of the summer!" she said, handing it to him.

"That's terriffic! God, I've missed her."

"I know you have," Charlotte said sympathetically. "But I really think going to school in Switzerland has been very good for her. And she's been under the care of the best doctors."

"Has she made any improvement?"

Charlotte frowned and answered: "Well, not really. But they're trying. Chris, I've got to get into a hot tub—I'm a wreck and there's a dinner at the club tonight. Give Susan my love and tell her I'll come by first chance."

He waved her off and continued on his way to the kitchen. Mrs. Gregory looked up and beamed when he walked in. "It's on the table, Chris, but get those hands clean first!"

He threw his arms around her stout waist and gave her a bear hug, lifting her off the floor. "You are what every boy needs—a bossy grandmother who makes the best chocolate cake in the world! Give us a kiss!"

"Oh, stop it!" she cried out, flustered. "Save that nonsense for the girls. Now have your cake!"

"Aunt Charlotte just drove in," he said, sitting down at the table. "She looks beat."

"She's been working very hard and not getting enough rest. Why she felt she had to take over after Mr. Stanwyck died makes no sense to me. She never had a head for business!"

Chris nodded his head and dug into the cake, letting her ramble on; gossiping was her favorite pastime. Finally, he broke in: "Nella's coming home for the summer, she just told me!"

"Is she? How wonderful! She's probably as thin as a rail. I'll fix all her favorite foods and try to fatten her up a bit."

Chris put his milk down and laughed. "You haven't changed since I first came here! Still the old fusspot!"

"You're right!" she said with a mock-fierce expression. And then, more warmly: "God, how the time goes by. I can remember the first time I saw you, a bit of a thing with the manners of a Lord Fauntleroy. And look at you now! A big, tall handsome man who drives our girls crazy!"

"I haven't touched your girls!" he protested. "You know I wouldn't fool around with any of the maids."

"That's not to say they wouldn't want you to!" Mrs. Gregory said with a sly twinkle in her eyes.

"That's enough of that," he muttered, looking at his watch. "I've got to go—I'll be late."

"Some more 'errands' for your mother?" the housekeeper asked archly, always curious when he left the estate early.

"That's right," Chris answered curtly. He stood up, anxious to escape the questions he knew were coming. "Thanks for the cake. See you tomorrow. I've got to put a retaining wall in at the south end of the gardens, so I'll be along early."

"Give Susan a hug for me. Tell her to come by on Sunday for lunch."

"I will," he answered, going out the door.

He hurried to his vintage Volkswagen parked at the end of the drive and opened the door. Stripping off his shirt, he wiped his chest and arms with it and threw it in the back of the car, then took a fresh shirt from the seat and slipped it on. Suddenly a voice called out from a second-floor balcony. He looked up and saw Janet, one of the maids. She beckoned to him, and he walked a few steps until he stood under her.

"Are we still on for tonight?" she called down to him softly.

"Sure, but for Christ's sake, be careful. I think the old lady's on to us. She's got ears like a hawk!"

She blew him a kiss and disappeared into the house. Chris went back to the car, turned it around, and rolled down the driveway to the road. If he hurried he'd just make it to Dr. Marlowe's office by four.

The afternoon traffic on Lancaster Pike was light, and Chris did some quick lane changing to make up for lost time, something he wouldn't dare if Susan were in the car. He liked driving fast and a little dangerously; it made him feel free. And freedom was something he was beginning to long for. I'm getting boxed in, he thought; everything's confused and nothing makes any sense. There had been another argument with Susan that morning; it was getting to be a regular thing. A few nights before, they had watched Dr. Marlowe on a talk show. Susan became agitated and started in on her favorite theme: his being used or exposed to the world by Dr. Marlowe. Ever since he'd helped Miss Howard, this was all Susan talked about, how "they" would use him or exploit him because of what he could do. Christ!

A station wagon loaded with schoolgirls drew alongside him and one of them called out, interrupting his thoughts. He looked over, scowling. A girl called out: "You're cute!" The other girls giggled wildly, and he laughed, winking at them. Then he gunned the car and pulled ahead of them without looking back.

Girls and their games, he sighed to himself. He could never understand what they were doing. In high school he had been teased and led on, but when he tried to get down to business, he was put off. If Charlotte hadn't given him the job of gardener on the estate when Mr. Donaldson died, he wouldn't have met Janet. She didn't play games. They'd been getting it on once or twice a week for almost a year. Remembering the last time they were together made him smile. She did anything he wanted. She made him feel like a man.

Then he thought of Charlotte's news about Nella coming home. Her letter was still in his pocket, unread. Maybe he'd have a minute before talking to Dr. Marlowe. Nella. He hadn't seen her for more than a year. She had sent him some pictures, blurred or a little out of focus, with snow-covered mountains in the background and the laughing faces of strangers around her. What was she like? Had she changed much? Would she think he'd changed? Home in a couple of months . . . God, what would he do about Janet?

He swung the car off the pike and into city streets, racing a red light. He didn't want to be late. He liked Dr. Marlowe, enjoyed talking with her. The tests she had been giving him were interesting, even a little frightening. He was learning more about himself and that's what he wanted. All he had now was his mother, more troubled and afraid with every passing day, and making him afraid too. That was the truth; he had to admit it. He *was* afraid—to leave home, to try to make it on his own. And afraid of what he could do, what he was yet to learn from Dr. Marlowe. He'd been so careful these last years, tried so hard never to lose his temper, like he had with the Stark boy. The sight of that kid lying on the concrete, bleeding . . . Christ, he'd never forget it! And his mother would never let him forget it, either. He felt trapped by guilt and fear.

"You look a little tense this afternoon," Catherine said. "Anything wrong?"

"No," Chris sighed. "Just the same thing—another argument with my mother. We saw you on that show a couple of nights ago, and she's been at me ever since. She didn't understand how different you were from those other people on the program."

"Oh, Chris, I'm sorry. And I'm sorry about appearing on the show, too," she said with a laugh. "Would it help any if I went out to talk with her again? We didn't get very far the last time we spoke."

"Thanks, but don't bother, Dr. Marlowe. I really think she's afraid of you. I'm beginning to think she's afraid of the whole world."

Catherine looked at him, surprised. With each visit he had grown more relaxed, more comfortable with her. And more observant about himself and people around him. This was the first time he had expressed some understanding about his mother, and she was pleased.

"Well, let's get started," Catherine said, standing up. "We don't have too much time."

"Where are we going?" Chris asked, following her out the door.

"To the physical sciences building. One of the professors has left us something to play with."

"Oh? What is it?"

"A rabbit."

As they crossed the campus, Catherine couldn't help noticing the glances Chris was getting from some of the girls they passed. One of them stared at him boldly and said "Hi." Chris nodded but kept his head lowered as they went on. Catherine smiled to herself. The boy was very handsome, with his shaggy blond hair and beautiful eyes. He moved his lithe body with the grace of an athlete, and working outdoors had given him a deep tan. He had a look of radiant good health and easy charm, an almost irresistible combination in a young man. She wondered how long it would be before he realized it himself, began to use it for his own ends?

In the science building, they walked down a long corridor of laboratories in the basement. A few students were still at work, even though it was almost the end of the day. Otherwise the building was quiet, and Catherine breathed a sigh of relief. She didn't know what might happen with this test, and she didn't want any people around being inquisitive.

They entered a lab at the end of the hallway. A worktable stood in the middle of the room, covered with equipment and notes left behind by students working on projects. Around the walls stood a group of cages containing laboratory rats and rabbits. One of the cages had been left at the end of the table. A note was stuck to the top. It was from Don Graham, a biologist and one of Catherine's closest friends at the university.

"Dear Cathy—this rabbit has had it (forgive the bad poetry). It's dying from an experimental virus infection. What exactly do you want with it??? Nothing kinky, I hope!! Let me know what happens —Don"

Catherine laughed and put the note aside. She looked in the cage at the rabbit. It was lying on its side, its frail body trembling with labored breathing, its white fur the color of putty. Its large brown eyes were glazed in a look of imminent death.

Chris stood behind her, staring into the cage. He loved animals, and this pitiful sight made him long to reach in and touch it. He moved around the table to face Catherine. "Is this the test?" he asked. "Do you want me to heal it?" he asked hopefully.

"Have you healed animals before?"

"Oh, yes," he answered quickly. "But Mom doesn't know. I was afraid to tell her. There was a horse Mr. Daly owned, a fine bay. He went lame, and nobody knew why. They were going to shoot him. I healed him, and an old dog, too, that was going blind—belonged to Mrs. Carlson, a neighbor." He smiled. "They all think I have a way with animals."

"Well, then, let's see what you can do for this rabbit," Catherine said.

Her throat tensed as she watched him open the cage. "Let me put on the light. It's getting dark in here."

"No, not yet, please," Chris said, almost in a whisper.

He reached into the cage and touched the rabbit's chest with his fingertips. Catherine leaned close, peering intently at the small animal. It gave a tiny jerk and quivered and for a moment she thought it was dead. Then something happened that brought a cry to her lips: "My God, Chris!"

The rabbit's body began to glow a luminescent white in the semidarkened room, a light that seemed to pulsate in time with its breathing. The little body shook as if surprised, and suddenly the rabbit sat up.

Catherine paced Amanda's office, her hands jammed in her skirt pockets, her shoulders hunched as if she were cold.

"A rabbit? That's all you made him do—heal a rabbit?" Amanda asked.

"What did you expect me to do, take him into the nearest hospital emergency room and say 'Heal'?"

"But, Cathy, after what he did for me—"

"Mandy, nobody was there to see it!"

"I did! I experienced it!"

"But that's not enough. These things take time, and I've had only a few opportunities to work with him. I think he gets into town on the sly; his mother's been opposed to the tests since the first day we talked to her."

"She's a very frightened woman."

"Yes, and I think Chris is a little worried about all this too. He's very evasive sometimes."

Catherine stopped pacing and threw herself into a chair. "God, I wish I smoked! Watching that rabbit come back to life really shook me."

"Where's Chris now?"

"He left a few minutes ago, smiling and happy, like a Boy Scout who's just done a good deed."

"Some Boy Scout!" Amanda said. "For him I'd lose forty pounds!"

Catherine laughed. "God, what a lech you are. But you're right—he's beautiful. And still a nice boy. He's very concerned about his mother, and really a little shy."

"I doubt if that will last long," Amanda said cynically. "Have you discussed the results of any of the tests with him?"

"Just superficially. He's very interested, but I don't think he understands all the ramifications of what his powers mean. He scored almost fifty percent in the ESP symbol-card test, but that didn't seem to mean much to him."

"What about the Kirlian photography?"

"He was a little nervous at first. We did the usual thing with a leaf from a dying plant. When I asked him if he could heal the leaf, he laughed and said he was the best gardener on the Main Line." Catherine sat up, excited. "Mandy, it was really amazing. He touched the plant and at first the energy radiating from his hand diminished significantly. Then a single ray began to shoot out of his fingertips directly into the leaf. It lasted only a few seconds, and the leaf's image actually grew larger as the stream of energy flowed into the stem and through the plant."

"Well, that and the rabbit prove I was right!"

"No"—Catherine shook her head—"it's going to take awhile before anything more conclusive can be said. I need more time. And as much as he's interested in what we're doing, I think this is difficult for Chris. He's a very simple person, really, with just average intelligence. His mother went overboard trying to protect him and keep his gifts a secret. I think that's one of the reasons she never remarried."

"Are you having any trouble finding enough time for this research? I might be able to dig up a small grant—"

"Oh, no. I don't want that. Too many people would have to know, and I promised Chris and his mother absolute secrecy. I can manage."

"You certainly managed very well on the *Wynters at Large* show the other night," Amanda said, smiling. "I haven't laughed so much since my last date! And you looked gorgeous!"

"Oh, God, weren't those people awful?" Catherine laughed.

"Uh, uh." Amanda looked at her with a sly expression. "But not Eric Wynters. There's nothing awful about him."

Catherine grew quiet. "No, there isn't. He's—very nice."

"Nice! Nice, you say! He's fabulous!" Amanda roared. "And he likes you, *very much!*"

"Okay, who's been talking?" Catherine demanded.

"Everybody! Well, mostly Miss Bedpan, your receptionist. The woman has a mouth like Niagara Falls!"

"Oh, God!" Catherine groaned.

"C'mon, tell Aunty Amanda—do you like him?"

Catherine stood up and headed for the door. "Telling *you* anything would be like giving a news item to Associated Press!"

"Catherine! I'm your friend!" Amanda shouted.

"Okay, friend, I like him," she called over her shoulder before she slammed the door.

15

The phone rang. Catherine stirred a little and continued to watch Eric interview a city councilman who was growing more evasive and nervous under Eric's barrage of questions. The phone rang again and she reached across the couch to answer it.

"What are you doing?" Eric's voice came out of the receiver just as he fired another question at his helpless guest on the screen.

"Listening to you in stereo," Catherine replied. "One ear on the phone and the other pitched to my TV set. I look very peculiar."

"Do you like having me there when I'm not there?"

"It's nice, but not quite the same," she answered, smiling. "Would you like me to find you a good lawyer? After what you've done to poor Councilman Davis, I expect I'll have to visit you with a cake baked around a file."

"Poor Councilman Davis is a dangerous son of a bitch and should be run out of town!"

"You're making your feelings quite clear on the show—just a minute, I want to listen. . . . Jesus! You really know how to hurt a guy!"

"Forget my journalistic savagery and invite me over—I'm lonely."

"I'm not sure I want to see you. Are you still in that same mood?"

"No, that was taped two days ago. Now I'm worse. I have strong urges to bite and slap and do brutal animal things."

"Oh, well then, come right over!"

"Can I bring anything? Some wine, cake, or whatever?"

"Just your urges. I'll get out the whip and the boots."

"What a considerate girl you are. I'll be there in ten minutes."

Catherine hurried around the apartment, straightening it up, then went into the kitchen to put on some coffee. While it was perking, she brushed her hair and applied a little fresh make-up. It was just like Eric to call without any warning, but she was beginning to get used to it. She stared at herself in the mirror. Her face was flushed and her eyes were bright, excited.

"Jesus, you're even breathing hard," she muttered. "So that's what Pavlov was all about!" The thought was disturbing.

She and Eric had been seeing each other two or three times a week, and she was beginning to wonder where they were going. She had tried to keep a perspective on her feelings for him, playing that cautious game men and women engage in during the first months of a relationship. Sometimes she felt that he had come to her with just an overwhelming need to be comforted in his aching loneliness and reassured about his obsession to find his son.

Catherine had been reluctant to use that term—"obsessed"—where his feelings about the child were concerned. But she had to admit, finally, that it was accurate. There were times when his life seemed to hang on the report that he received once a week from the investigators. In the two months they had known each other, she'd watched him come alive with hope on a clue that turned out to be false, or fall into black despair when a trail that might lead to the whereabouts of his son died. He was like a drowning man clinging to a frayed rope, losing one strand at a time, yet still holding on with fierce determination.

And she knew, too, that the image of Jenny haunted his search, floated at the back of his mind with a spectral hold on him that she couldn't fight.

The doorbell rang and she hurried to answer it, trying to dismiss her troubled thoughts.

She opened the door to find Eric with his arms wrapped around dozens of red and white carnations that covered his face.

"This better be the right apartment, or I'm in a lot of trouble," his voice came from behind the stalks of flowers.

"This is the right apartment and you're in a lot of trouble," Catherine said, laughing. "Where the hell am I going to put all of them?"

He lowered the flowers, peered at her owlishly over the top of the huge bouquet, and said with a burlesqued English accent: "We of The Little Flower Shop Around the Corner come fully prepared. If madame will lead me into her abode and relieve me of a tote bag hanging painfully in the crook of my arm, she will find a ghastly assortment of bowls, vases, and cheap bric-a-brac containers!"

"You're potty in the head!" Catherine cried through her laughter as brightly colored ceramics tumbled from the bag. "These are without a doubt the ugliest vases I've ever seen! And I love every one of them!"

He opened his arms and let the flowers fall to the floor in a heap. "A woman with taste!" he exclaimed. "Come, kiss me quick; I'm overcome with excitement!"

"You fool," Catherine said, holding him tightly.

The kiss grew in intensity, and he picked her up and carried her to the couch, where hands and lips sought out the warm, secret places of each other's body. When Eric reached to turn off the light, Catherine stopped his hand.

"No, leave it on," she whispered, "I want to see you."

Catherine opened her eyes and saw bowls of carnations covering the top of the coffee table. Eric was sitting beside her, smoking a cigarette. She took his hand and put it against her face.

"You delivery boys really know how to take care of your customers," she sighed.

He smiled. "We aim to please, ma'am. Want some coffee?"

"Um, lovely idea."

While he was in the kitchen she leaned over and buried her face in the fragrant blossoms. "I feel like Theda Bara. Next time bring orchids."

Eric came through the door with a tray of coffee and cups. "What a lovely sight that is, a naked you amidst all those flowers."

Catherine sat up and looked at him. She whistled appreciatively. "You're the best-looking waiter I've ever seen. I love your uniform."

Eric bowed. "Thank you, madame. It's the latest thing in bare skin."

He put the tray down and settled himself next to her while she poured the coffee. Catherine was filled with a rich contentment and satisfaction, a feeling of closeness with Eric that was almost domestic.

"You've been in a very jolly state this evening," she said. "Dare I attribute that to my fatal allure and all-around terrific personality?"

She instantly regretted the question, hating herself for asking it, yet unable to resist wanting to know what his feelings for her were.

He gave her a cheerful smile and replied: "You dare ask, and yes to all the aforementioned qualities. Also, I heard some good news tonight."

For a moment she felt a small disappointment; it wasn't just seeing and being with her that had inspired his romantic lunacy.

"Oh? And what was that?" she asked, knowing the answer.

"Simpson, one of my investigators, called. He stumbled on to a ring of baby black-market operators working the Midwest and felt very confident about finding some trace of David there."

His voice had taken on an excitement she heard only when he received this kind of news, and despite herself a flash of jealousy swept through her.

"There are no details yet," Eric went on, "just that the ring had operators working on the East Coast, and that they transferred the infants to the Midwest in order to avoid detection. Simpson said he'd keep me posted daily; he felt that sure of something turning up."

"Eric, that's very encouraging news," Catherine said with enthusiasm.

But she couldn't help wondering how long this would go on. Every disappointment had been so hard on him. What would happen when he learned that there weren't any more leads to follow down, or some evidence turned up to prove that the baby was dead? She had never dared to discuss that eventuality with him. All she could do was to go on giving him the support he needed.

Eric turned her face up to his and kissed her lips. "Cathy, if I haven't mentioned it before—thank you."

"For what, dear?"

"For being here to share with, for your patience and caring. I'm very grateful."

Catherine smiled and held him close, knowing that she loved him. That had become a fact of her life. How long it might take before she became a fact of his life no longer concerned her.

A few days later Catherine was in her office when Christopher walked in unexpectedly early.

"I just got a little fed up with working this morning and decided to cut out early," he explained. "Is it okay?"

"Of course it is," Catherine answered. "But won't you be missed?"

Chris grinned. "I'll make up some excuse . . . tell them I've been going to a shrink to find out who and what I am."

"Do you think of me that way?" Catherine asked, a little surprised.

"Sometimes," Chris admitted. "I've learned so much about myself in the last few months. You know, I think that's what scares my mother—that I'm too young to handle it." He laughed a little contemptuously.

Catherine frowned. She had hoped he would gain, through their work together, a perspective on his gift less frightening than the one his mother had imposed. But she was worried now about his increasing unrest and dissatisfaction. At their last session she had recalled his desire to buy a farm for himself and Susan. He had smiled cynically and asked: "Do you think I could do that, now?"

"Well, Chris, your mother may be right to some degree," Catherine had said thoughtfully. "What you've learned so far is important, although not conclusive. We have a long way to go; you'll have to be patient with her—and yourself."

"Yeah, I know," he had agreed reluctantly. "It's just that for the first time in my life I feel like I'm really beginning to do something."

Catherine had laughed. "I know the feeling," she said warmly.

Now, looking at her watch, she asked: "How 'bout some lunch before we start working? I missed my coffee break and I'm starved."

Chris's face brightened. "Terrific, but I'll buy, okay?"

They left the building and walked to the campus cafeteria. A noisy group of students was in line at the sandwich counter. Catherine spotted a boy she wanted to talk to getting some coffee. Chris said he would pick up the sandwiches. A few minutes later he caught up with her. The boy was sitting at a table and Catherine stood by his side, talking.

"—it's not that you can't do the work," she was saying. "We both know you can."

The boy slowly raised his head and looked at her. Catherine recognized the blank expression, the glazed, distant stare. He was on something—Quaaludes, or whatever was going around the campus. Frank Pearson was a short-tempered but quite often brilliant student. Catherine had been doing her best to help him straighten out.

"Frank, I'm sorry. All I could give you on your paper was a D, but you still have time to make it up."

The boy stared at her, his pallid face turning sullen. "You gave me a D?" he questioned her stupidly. "A D?"

"Yes, but, Frank, if you just get yourself together, you can make up for it."

He shook his head, dazed, and picked up his coffee, watching the steam rising from the cup. Catherine was about to turn away when he began uttering a stream of invective at her that rose to a shout: "You bitch! Goddamned bitch!"

A shocked silence fell over nearby students who were watching the scene.

Catherine tried to quiet him. "Frank, stop it. You're not well—"

"I don't give a fuck about your class! Or you either, cunt!" he yelled.

Suddenly he raised the cup of coffee as if he were going to throw it at her. Then, so quickly she couldn't be sure what happened, Frank's body snapped rigid. His arm made a convulsive movement and he threw the coffee violently into his face. He screamed and fell off the chair, clutching at his face and neck.

"My face! Oh fucking Christ, my face!" he shrieked.

An overwhelming impulse made Catherine whirl around. Chris was standing behind her, his face livid with anger. His eyes were wide and burning with fury at the boy writhing on the floor.

Several students rushed to help, yelling at one another to get him to the dispensary. Catherine stood mute, too shocked to speak. A sudden nausea churned at her and she bent forward, gripping her stomach. Chris grabbed her arm and led her to an empty table. Catherine put her head down. She felt chilled; a light film of sweat covered her brow.

"Dr. Marlowe, are you all right?" Chris asked anxiously.

She took several deep breaths and raised her head. Chris was pale. He looks frightened, she thought. Behind him she saw Frank being hurried out of the cafeteria, his howls of anguish echoing over the excited jabber of the students. Her eyes came back to Christopher. The terrifying rage she had seen in his face was gone. Now the handsome features registered only concern for her.

"Chris, what happened?" she asked, watching him closely.

"That kid was really out of it—he was gone! For a minute I

thought he was going to throw the coffee at you!" His answer was given too quickly, almost defensively.

Catherine sensed his fear. "He *was* going to throw it at me—I saw that," she said with deliberate emphasis. "I also saw him go rigid, as if he'd been struck. I saw him deliberately throw the coffee in his own face. Why did he do that?" she demanded.

Chris turned away from the accusation in her eyes. "I don't know," he said weakly.

"I think you do."

He caught his breath in a choked, guttural sound. "I'm sorry, Dr. Marlowe. God, I'm sorry," he said in a hoarse whisper. Tears started in his eyes. "I did it for you. I was afraid he'd hurt you. I did it for you!"

Chris followed Catherine back to her office, shamefaced and miserable. They stopped at the dispensary and the nurse told them that Frank had received minor burns on his face and neck, and that he remembered only throwing the coffee at himself, attributing his action to being so stoned that he didn't know what he was doing.

Chris sprawled on the small couch in the office and wearily closed his eyes. Catherine sat down at her desk and took out his file. She read through her notes; nowhere was there anything about his ability to mind-pressure. Still stunned by what had happened and by his admission that he had done it, she found her fingers shaking as she quickly wrote down the details of the incident.

Looking up from her papers, she studied Chris for a few minutes. His face was still pale, but calmer now, the lines of anxiety smoothed out as he dozed. Catherine's mind was in a turmoil; the boy had the sweet look of innocence, and yet, during that awful moment when she had faced him, she had seen a shocking expression of pure vengeance contorting his features.

"Chris," she said softly, rousing him.

He sat up and rubbed his eyes. "Yes, Dr. Marlowe?"

"I want you to tell me as simply as you can if you've ever done this to anyone before, and what happened."

His eyes grew wide with fear. "Oh, please, I can't . . . I just can't!"

Catherine's voice was gentle but firm. "Chris, do you trust me?"

He nodded his head slowly.

"Whatever it is that's frightening you—you've lived with it in silence. If I'm to help you at all, you must believe that I will never do or say anything to hurt you, and you must confide in me."

He nodded his head again and slumped back on the couch. Hesitantly at first, then more quickly, as if to speak before he lost his confidence, he recounted the moment in the Stanwyck library with Tom Stanwyck and then the incident in the school yard with John Stark. He also described what Susan had told him about his making her rescue him from the stream in Inverness.

Catherine listened intently as he spoke, her well-trained mind taking over and keeping under control the emotional response she felt to what he was telling her.

Keeping her face and voice impassive, she asked: "And were there any other incidents where you made someone do something?"

"No, just those—and what happened today."

"And no one remembered afterward that you had anything to do with how they had behaved?"

"Only my mother, after rescuing me from the stream. I was very close to her; we shared so much together while my father was at sea. I think that's why she knew."

Catherine finished making her notes and then said: "Chris, I'd like to try some simple tests of your ability to mind-pressure—but under controlled conditions. Will you do them?"

She saw the struggle taking place within him as he considered her request, and added: "I promise you that nothing will happen to hurt anyone."

He drew a deep breath and sighed. "All right. I'll do it."

"Can you come in tomorrow afternoon? I need the time to set up the tests, but I want to do them while all this is still fresh."

"Yes, I'll come in tomorrow." He stood up and started for the door. "Dr. Marlowe," he said, turning to her, "will we ever find out why I can do these things?"

Catherine stared at him, wondering how to answer his question. Scientists all over the world had been proving and disproving theories for years, and new breakthroughs in understanding psychic power occurred regularly. But as yet there was no final answer, and there might never be one.

"Chris, I honestly don't know," she said finally. "Maybe by working together we'll find out."

His eyes clouded with disappointment and he sighed: "Well, I guess we just do what we can, then."

Catherine watched him walk out of the room, his back bent slightly, as if he were carrying a burden that nothing in the world would ever be able to relieve.

That night, unable to sleep, Catherine went over the incident with Frank Pearson, replaying it in her mind like a film run at slow speed. She saw again the jerky, convulsive movement of his body suddenly stiffening, the quick, violent action of his arm as he threw the coffee into his face. And Chris, staring at him with a rage that burned from within, his eyes like hard turquoise stones.

There was something else about his eyes—What was it? A subliminal image, it flickered in her mind, appearing and disappearing before she could grasp it, see it clearly. A spot of color? A birthmark that had flared with his anger? No, that wasn't it. But something, noticed so quickly as to be almost not seen at all.

A spot of color, she said to herself. Red.

Like blood.

16

Catherine arranged to use a behavioral science lab for Chris's mind-pressure tests. There were two adjoining rooms with the unique feature of a window-sized two-way mirror, permitting them to observe subjects without being seen themselves.

"I've asked two students from my lecture class to come here, one at a time," she told Chris. "Neither of them knows about the test. They think I have some notes for them."

"What do you want me to do to them?" Chris asked.

"I'd rather not explain until just before we do the test. That way you can't think about it in advance."

Christopher was nervous as he sat down at the mirrored window. He wished he had never started any of these tests. His palms were sweating and his throat was dry. He wanted to tell Catherine that he didn't know how to make it happen, that he couldn't do it.

"You know this has worked only when I've been angry, when I lost my temper," he blurted out to her.

Catherine patted his arm. "I know that. Don't worry about these tests. They aren't like the ones you took in school." She smiled reassuringly. "No matter what happens, you can't fail them. However, all of it is important to me, so try to relax."

Just then the door to the other room opened and they saw a boy, about nineteen, dressed in sweater and slacks, walk in. He looked around the room and then sat down, putting the books he was carrying on the seat beside him. He opened one and began to read.

"That's Bill Stevens," Catherine said. "He's a good student, a very quiet boy."

Chris stared at the young man. Bill had a puzzled expression that seemed built into his features: his brow was creased in a permanent frown and his eyes shifted rapidly over his book as if in a frantic search for an answer to some question. His mouth was half open in a fixed look of surprise.

"What do you want me to do to him?" Chris asked in a shaky voice.

"Something really very simple," Catherine replied calmly. "Make Bill get up and march the length of the room."

"Now?"

"Whenever you're ready."

She turned back to the window and watched her student. A minute or two passed in strained silence. The boy continued to read his book.

Catherine began to think nothing was going to happen when, abruptly, Bill set the book aside. She stared intently as his face underwent a change. It seemed to drain of all personality: his mouth closed into a firm line, his frown cleared into a smooth brow, and his eyes went blank, devoid of all expression. He rose from his seat in a mechanically precise motion and turned slowly, like an animated corpse. Then he raised one leg and began to march, turning carefully at one end of the room and proceeding to the other end.

Catherine looked quickly at Christopher. He was sweating, but his eyes were calm, impassive as they followed the boy's movements.

"Chris, can you hear me and keep your hold on Bill at the same time?" Catherine asked quietly.

"Yes," he replied in a distant tone.

"Return him to his seat, sitting just as he was before."

Chris did as she asked, and the boy settled back into an eerie facsimile of his original pose, a mannequin artfully posed to appear lifelike.

"Now release him," Catherine said.

The boy suddenly relaxed, his shoulders slumped, his face resumed its perplexed expression, and he picked up his book and continued reading as if nothing had happened.

The second test with Bill was more difficult. Catherine gave Chris a simple line drawing of a house on a hill, with a tree standing next to it and the sun in the background.

"Can you make Bill draw this?" she asked.

"I think I can." Chris's voice was steady with confidence. He stared at the drawing for a few seconds and then looked up at Bill. Almost immediately, the boy dropped his book and went to a large blackboard on the wall behind him. He picked up a piece of chalk and drew the picture in Chris's hand with near perfect accuracy. This time his movements were less sluggish than before, but again his face had become a blank mask. He finished the drawing, then Chris made him erase it, wipe the chalk from his hands, return to his seat, and assume his former position.

He turned to Catherine. "I'm getting good at this!" he said with boyish enthusiasm, excited by the growing knowledge of his power.

Catherine had to laugh. "Okay, Svengali, take a rest while I talk to Bill." She glanced at her watch. "Sarah should be here in a minute. She's the other student I asked to come by."

Chris watched her walk into the outer room, chat with the student for a moment, and then usher him out the door. A moment later a young girl appeared, and Catherine spoke to her briefly, then left her alone.

Chris examined the girl with interest. She held her books protectively against her breast and looked around the room nervously. Her listless brown hair was tied back so severely it gave her face a look of being suddenly exposed. Pale, with no make-up, and an expression of such timidity in her small dark eyes that Chris thought she looked like a nun.

Catherine rejoined him and began to say: "Now, Chris, what I'd like you to do is—" She stopped in mid-sentence.

Christopher was not listening to her. He was focused on the girl.

"Chris, wait. I haven't explained—"

He was ignoring her. Catherine turned quickly to look through the window at Sarah.

The young girl's manner was changing dramatically. She had untied her hair, letting it fall to her shoulders. Her body was relaxing in a smooth transition from the rigid position she'd been sitting in to a pose that rapidly grew provocative. Legs crossed like a fashion model's, she threw back her head and arched her small breasts. One hand trailed down her throat to the top of her blouse. With a teasing sensuality, she began to unbutton it. Her fingers played for a moment with the tiny gold cross she was wearing on a thin chain, then slipped inside her bra and began to caress and knead a breast. Her eyes were closed and her lips parted slightly in an expression of longing.

Catherine turned from the shocking transformation. "Stop it!" she said to Chris in a low, forceful tone.

"What, and leave her like that?" Chris asked with a remote, amused smile.

Catherine raged inwardly. "Return her to herself, at once!"

Within a few minutes Sarah was once more enclosed in her protective shell of timidity. Catherine went to her and they talked, then the girl left.

Catherine came back to Chris, trying to keep her anger under control. "I don't want to hear any excuses," she said quietly. "You exploited that girl. I don't care that she'll never remember it; it was a selfish and adolescent thing to do!"

In the months they'd been working together, this was the first time Chris had seen Catherine lose her temper. He looked away from her outburst, ashamed.

Catherine took a moment to control herself. There were too many things happening all at once for her to deal with. She didn't want to alienate Chris by using Susan's tactic of making him feel guilty; on the other hand, his self-confidence had asserted itself so quickly that she was suddenly afraid of what he might do.

The thought was instantly sobering. Chris's power was like an untapped well of oil. Once fully released, it might surge out of him with uncontrollable force.

"I know it was just a prank," she went on more calmly, "and I can understand the impulse that made you do it. But, Chris, we must be very careful. Every day we are learning more about the range of your gifts, and with that knowledge must come the understanding of how best to use them."

"I know," he said under his breath. "I guess I just got carried away."

"Well, this time you're forgiven," she said, smiling. "I know it's a little like having a terrific new toy, but just remember how fragile it is. Now let's get out of here—it's late." She picked up her notes. "I'd better check the other room just to make sure everything is in order."

They walked into the outer room and Chris saw a book lying on the floor.

"What's this?" he asked her.

Catherine opened the cover. "Oh, dear, it's Bill's text for my class. I know him, he'll be in a panic without it, and he's probably long gone by now. Well, there's nothing I can do about it now. I'll give it to him tomorrow."

She held out her hand, but Chris didn't move. His hands caressed the covers of the book, his fingertips feeling the cloth binding. He closed his eyes.

"Chris, what is it?" Catherine asked.

He was silent for a moment and then answered with a deliberate certainty: "He's here, on campus. In a room, a big room. There's a man and some students talking together."

Catherine swallowed hard, staring at him in disbelief. "Where?" she questioned thickly. "Where is Bill?"

"In the room. He's looking for something."

"What room?"

"The door is open. There's a number on it—204."

Catherine felt herself go pale. She stared at Chris, incredulous. "That's my classroom," she whispered huskily. "Is he there now?"

"Yes." Chris opened his eyes. "I saw him," he said simply.

Moments later they were hurrying through the hallway to the lecture hall where Catherine taught her class. A professor, his assistant, and a few students were standing by the open door talking.

Catherine went past them quickly, nodding, and Chris followed. She looked around the room. It was empty.

"Bill," she called out.

There was a scuffling sound, and a figure suddenly rose up from between a row of seats.

Bill Stevens got up from where he had been crouched on his hands and knees and came toward Catherine, dusting off his hands. A smile of relief broke out on his face at the sight of the book in her hands.

"You found my book!" he exclaimed. "I've been looking all over for it."

17

Susan poured Christopher a second cup of coffee and sat back, watching as he finished his dinner.

"You haven't eaten very much tonight," he said. "You on one of those new diets?"

Susan smiled. "Do I look like I need to lose some weight?"

"Not to me, you don't." His eyes twinkled. "I think you're a fine figure of a woman," he said, aping her Irish accent.

"Indeed, now? And would you be takin' me out to a pub for a laugh and a pint if you were me young man?"

"Aye, that I would, woman." Chris laughed. "Except for one thing."

"And what's that?"

"Why, you're old enough to be me mother, you are!"

They laughed together at the exchange, and then Susan began to clear the table while Chris helped himself to a second piece of pie, making contented sounds and rolling his eyes in exaggerated delight.

"You still make the best apple pie in Lower Merion," he mumbled through a mouthful.

"Lower Merion, you say? It happens to be the best west of County Cork!"

"Aye, it is that, and you're in a very good mood tonight. Have a good day?"

Susan's face darkened slightly. "Good enough," she said. "Charlotte came by for a visit. Did you know that Nella will be home soon?"

"Yes, I got a letter from her."

"Oh? You didn't tell me." The accusation in her voice hung in the air between them.

"Well, I've been busy—" Chris hesitated. "It must have slipped my mind."

"I know how *busy* you've been," Susan said with an edge of sarcasm. "Mrs. Gregory called this afternoon to ask where you were. Seems you slipped away early."

Chris looked at her defiantly. "That's right, I did. Dr. Marlowe had set up some tests that took longer than usual, so I went in early."

Susan's back stiffened slightly and her eyes grew hard. "And for how long will you be going in to see Dr. Marlowe? When will she be finished with all of her tests and experiments?"

"You make her sound like one of those crazy doctors in the old horror films!" Chris said angrily.

"Well how do I know what she's been doing to you?" Susan cried. "You haven't told me a single thing about what's been going on!"

"Only because you've been so damned set against the whole thing from the beginning!" he exploded.

Susan caught her breath and remained silent for a moment. Then, with an effort to control herself, she said: "I'm sorry. I'm just that worried about you, I don't know what to do."

Her voice broke in spite of her effort and she began to cry. Chris got up and went to her. He put his arm around her shoulders. "Mom, please. Try to understand how important this is to me. Dr. Marlowe wants to do a long-term project with me. I don't understand all of it, but she believes that studying people like me will someday help a lot of people in many different ways. The work she does is very important. She's a respected scientist, not some quack. You've heard about her book—"

"And will she be putting you in a book, too? For everyone to read about?" Susan asked scornfully.

"No! That's not what she's doing at all. She's trying to help me understand about myself so that I don't have to live the way you've been living—with fear and shame!"

Susan drew away from him, furious. "Is that what she thinks? That you'll be able to live like any other man once you and she know what it's all about? Well, I don't think so! She doesn't know any more about the world and the people in it than you do!"

"She's a damned sight better educated than the two of us, and knows a lot more—"

"She knows nothing!" Susan shouted. "I watched my parents being insulted, humiliated, even spat on because they thought differently from other people. What do you think they'll do to you?"

"That was forty years ago, in another country! Things have changed; people know more now."

"You think that because of what she's told you, but you're just a boy! You don't know what the world is like!"

"Dammit, I'm a man! When will you realize that?"

"When you begin to act like one!"

"I will if you'll just bloody well give me a chance to!"

In a burst of rage, Susan slapped him hard across the face. Chris stared at her, breathing heavily, his eyes hard with anger. Then he grabbed his jacket off the coatrack and slammed out of the house.

Driving furiously through the dark countryside, the sting of Susan's slap still burning across his face, Christopher's mind was filled with a rush of chaotic thoughts. Events of the past months tumbled before his eyes in quick, frozen images: the dying rabbit glowing white in the semidark lab, Frank Pearson's scream of pain when he scalded himself with the coffee, the mind-pressure tests with Catherine's students. He saw Bill Stevens marching like a robot, back and forth, and timid little Sarah turn sexy.

Taking a sharp turn in the road with a savage twist of the wheel, Chris laughed to himself, feeling as if his body could not contain the energy he was beginning to master. He cursed the years wasted in fear and restraint. A dynamic force surged through him, exhilarating and powerful, and he felt a little drunk. His mind went back to the sight of Sarah arching her body and running her hand over her breasts. He had made her do that, had held her with his mind! He felt a throb of excitement between his legs and took one hand off the wheel to rub himself. She hadn't remembered it; *no one* remembered what they had done. He could do it again, at any time—he could do it now! For a moment he heard Catherine warning him to be careful with his power, and he hesitated. But no, for once he had to do something on his own, something *he* wanted to do! He pressed down on the accelerator and the car leaped ahead into the night.

The shopping center in Wynnewood was just closing as he turned the car into the main street and cruised along. A small crowd of people was drifting out of the movie house; the early show had just ended. A few couples were hurrying to their cars in the parking lot, and several girls were walking toward a nearby coffee shop. Chris recognized two of them as girls he'd gone to school with. He averted his head before they saw him and waited until they had gone into the shop before turning to look along the street. Then he saw her.

She was standing at the curb, waiting for the light to change. He drove up to her. She was plain, maybe twenty-eight or thirty, he guessed. Not unattractive, but no raving beauty. She reminded him of Sarah, and the thought increased his excitement.

When he pulled up beside her, she looked a little startled and turned away. He leaned forward, staring at her as she started walking rapidly along the sidewalk. His consciousness filled with the single urge to bring her to him. Then she stopped walking, as if she had just thought of something she'd forgotten. Christopher watched her carefully, and she turned and came slowly up to the car. He leaned across the seat and opened the door. She got in beside him. He made her turn and face him. Her face was blank, vacant-eyed. He thought she looked as if she was waiting for something to happen, for *him* to make something happen. The idea was powerful and erotic in its implications. Then he suddenly thought of something that frightened him: would he lose his hold on her by looking away? He turned and stared at the street. She sat quietly, her soft breathing the only sound in the car. He made her move closer to him, his eyes still fixed on the shadowy street, not moving until he felt her body firm against his.

Then he started the car and drove into the country, taking twisting and unlighted roads.

18

Eric had just left the studio and was walking to his office when he saw Catherine standing in the hallway.

"Hey, what are you doing here?" he called out. "I was just going to call you. Are we having another flash of ESP between us?" He took her in his arms and kissed her lightly. "I'm glad to see you," he murmured against her cheek.

"Am I catching you in the middle of anything?" she asked.

"Nope. Just finished screening tomorrow's show, was getting strange rumbling sounds of hunger in my stomach, and thought of you."

"That's nice—an intimate association of ideas," she said, laughing. "Will you take me to dinner?"

"Of course. That was my plan: fill you with food, ply you with wine, then carry you off to my bed!"

"I'm for all of that, but could we talk first?"

He saw the troubled look in her eyes, the tense lines of strain in her face. "Cathy, is something wrong?"

She shook her head. "No, not really. At least I don't think so."

168

He took her arm and they started for the front door. "C'mon, we'll go someplace quiet and have something to eat, then you can tell me all about it."

A half hour later they were settled into a booth at a small restaurant. Eric ordered drinks and lit a cigarette.

"Okay, I'm ready," he said, taking her hand. "Tell me all."

Catherine gave him a faint smile. "You know, you're really very nice."

"Wait till you get my bill." He smiled. "What's wrong, Cathy?"

For the next hour he listened intently as she told him about Chris. Once or twice he interrupted with a question, but otherwise remained silent. Catherine described what had been happening since her first meeting with Chris.

"—I'm beginning to feel as though I've opened a Pandora's box," she said.

"Haven't you come across anyone like him before in your studies? Your book covered such a wide area—"

"My book!" Catherine laughed. "He's made my book obsolete! When I wrote it, it was from the point of view of a smug graduate student. With the glut of paperbacks on reincarnation, psychic phenomena, healing, and other voices from other worlds, I thought the important issues in psi were being overlooked in favor of a fast sale, a quick buck." She sipped her drink and sat back with a wry smile. "I wanted to shake up the psi establishment with a scathing critique. If the tone of the book hadn't been so vitriolic, it probably wouldn't have been published at all."

"Are you absolutely certain of everything this boy has done?" Eric asked.

"At the moment I'm not certain of anything," Catherine admitted. "His powers make most of the standard tests useless. His abilities lie outside the structure of study I've been working on."

"Can you call in someone else to verify your findings, someone who's worked longer in the field than you have?"

"I've wanted to, several times. But I made him and his mother a promise of absolute secrecy about these tests. I've even been reluctant to mention them to you. His mother is terrified that something will happen to Chris, that he'll be exploited or harmed."

"She's probably right," Eric said. "If he's as gifted as you think he is—"

"It isn't just a matter of what *I* think," Catherine said earnestly.

"If I can establish the empirical validity of his power, there would be important ramifications in other disciplines, like medicine, biology, physiology, even psychology—as well as psi."

"Cathy, how can I help? Is there anything I can do?"

"You've been doing it, just by letting me sit here and babble," she said. "I feel much better. I was really shook up after what happened this afternoon."

"Oh, what was that?"

"When we finished the mind-pressure tests, we found a book belonging to the boy we had worked with. It had fallen on the floor under his chair. I assumed he had gone home and I was going to give it to him tomorrow."

"What happened?"

"Chris picked the book up and sighted the boy. He was in my classroom looking for the book. I couldn't believe it! We rushed to the room, and there he was, down on his hands and knees looking for the book!"

Eric stared at her. "What do you mean 'sighted'?"

"Well, technically, it's called psychometry. What it means is getting a picture in your mind of a person or place by holding an object belonging to that person or associated with that place. Chris told me he had done it only once before, when he was a little boy. A man his mother was going to marry had left a shirt at the house for her to mend. He was due there for dinner one night during a heavy storm. Chris picked the shirt up and saw the man lying under his overturned truck. He had died in a crash."

"Jesus!" Eric breathed slowly. "That's incredible."

"But not uncommon," Catherine went on. "There have been many reports and articles written about people with the same gift. What I have to do is test Chris's ability under controlled conditions, set up a situation that I can study and verify. The thing this afternoon might have just been a fluke—the boy is a mass of surprises!"

Eric lowered his eyes from hers and studied his drink. "What kind of situation would you set up?" he asked finally.

"Oh, I don't know. I thought I'd send Amanda out into the country somewhere and see if he could sight her by holding her watch or a scarf she owns. I'm not sure right now," she sighed. "I feel a bit drained by everything that's happened. My head isn't functioning too well." She smiled at him, then realized he was caught up in some thought of his own. "Am I putting you into a state of total boredom with my ramblings?"

He looked up at her seriously. "Cathy, could I be the test for Chris's sighting?"

"What?" she asked, surprised by the request. "I don't understand. Why do you want to—" A slow realization of what he was asking, and why, dawned on her. "Oh, Eric, you can't be serious!"

"I have a christening blanket that David slept with all the time. Jenny had it in the laundry hamper to wash the day she was—"

"Oh, Eric, don't," Cathy cried out. "Don't even think about it! We have no way of knowing what Chris can do—not on the basis of this incident with my student—or even what happened when he was a child."

Eric's voice was pleading. "Cathy, please. Try to understand how I feel. I'm not a fool. I remember that couple, a year or so ago, whose child was kidnapped. They went to some psychic who was sure the baby was in some village in South America. And when they got there, nothing. But at this point, what have I got to lose? My investigators haven't turned up a thing."

Cathy searched his face, moved by the pain he felt and afraid of the hope she saw glimmering behind his eyes. "Eric, I couldn't bear to see you have another disappointment, they hurt you so." Her voice broke and tears filled her eyes.

He looked at her for a few minutes, the expression on his face changing to a look of wonder and surprise. Then he took both her hands in his and kissed them softly.

"I'm the idiot of the world," he murmured. "I just realized that you love me."

"Of course I do, you fool. That's why I couldn't let you—"

He held her hands in his and leaned over the table to kiss her. "Don't you understand," he said. "I love you too. I feel strong with you, and knowing you'll be there, nothing we find out will hurt me."

Catherine lowered her head and rested her cheek against his hands. "I feel as if I've just stepped off the edge of the world," she whispered to him. "It's probably the drinks and you, and Chris—" She closed her eyes for a moment. "All right," she said, raising her head and looking at him. "We'll do what you want. I'll call Chris and set it up. But I think we should do it at my place, not the university."

"When?" Eric asked, trying to control his excitement.

◆

In the hushed silence of the late afternoon, Christopher sat on the couch in Cathy's living room running his hands over a small blue blanket. His large, square-tipped fingers caressed and touched the soft material in an easy stroking motion, stopping occasionally to search out a fold or wrinkle, almost as if he were examining it fiber by fiber.

Catherine sat across from him, silent, a clipboard on her lap, a pen resting between her fingers. Eric had brought a small tape recorder, and it was on a table by her side, waiting to be turned on as soon as Chris began to speak.

Eric was in a chair nearby. Now that the test had actually begun, he felt impatient and apprehensive. Would it work? What if the boy saw nothing? He watched Christopher closely, not certain now that he hadn't let his hopes run away with his logic. When Chris had arrived an hour or so before, Eric had been impressed with his openness, his youthful sincerity. They had talked only a little about the search for David, Catherine being especially careful not to mention any of the states or cities that had been covered by the team of investigators.

Chris had surprised Eric when he said that he knew Margaret Bradford, Eric's mother-in-law.

"My mother made dresses for her and her daughter Jenny—" Chris stopped, seeing the expression on Eric's face. "Oh, I'm sorry. I wasn't thinking. Jenny was your wife."

"Yes, she was," Eric said with some difficulty. He gave Chris a wry smile. "Funny, isn't it, the ironies of life. You knew Jenny before I did."

And now, Eric thought, this same boy is holding my baby son's blanket in his hands and trying, by some miracle of a gift that almost no one understands, to find him for me. Christ! The whole idea was foolish. He shouldn't have talked Cathy into doing this.

Eric looked over at Catherine and caught her eye. She smiled at him, her eyes warm and loving. He knew that she didn't really think anything would come of this. She had done it, out of her love for him. And now they were sitting here, waiting . . . for what? He lit another cigarette and tried to relax.

Sunlight slanted in long rays through the casement windows. Chris sat with his head slumped forward on his chest, almost as if he were asleep. Catherine observed him with unwavering eyes. A few more minutes, she thought, then I'll put a stop to this. Chris looks ready to pass out from his concentration, and Eric is sitting in the corner like a time bomb ready to explode. It's foolish to go on. . . .

Suddenly Chris straightened up. His eyes were wide-open, his face expressionless. He stood and, taking the little blanket with him, walked to the windows. Rays of sunlight bathed his head, setting a white glow around his thick blond hair. He pressed the blanket to his cheek and turned to face them before speaking.

"I see a child," he said in a flat, unemotional voice.

Eric started, dropping his cigarette and picking it up quickly, brushing bits of glowing ash from his shirt. Catherine reached out and touched a button on the tape recorder.

"The child is being held in a woman's arms," Chris went on. "She's rocking him, crooning to him. She loves him very much."

Eric sat in petrified silence, his eyes wide, heart pounding. Catherine gently asked Chris where the woman and child were.

"I'm not sure," he replied slowly. "A room, I think. It's—" He stopped and swallowed hard, pressing the blanket against his cheek in a quick, wiping motion. "It's a pretty room. There are figures on the wall—from stories. . . ." His voice grew distant. "Snow White, I think, and the dwarfs, in a funny line behind her."

"Are they in a house?" Catherine asked.

"Yes."

"Can you describe it?"

"No—all I see is the room."

She took a deep breath. "Can you describe the child?"

"Yes. He has dark hair. Blue eyes. He's laughing. There's something on his chin . . ." Chris's voice grew faint.

Eric stood up, his face white. "What is there on his chin?" he asked hoarsely.

Chris's body was beginning to tremble. His hands clutched the blanket violently. "On his chin—a mark, something small, dark."

The tension in the room crackled like volts of electricity. Chris was weaving slightly, his body moving back and forth.

"Is it dirt?" Catherine asked. "A stain? Is that what you see on his chin?" Her eyes swung wildly from Chris to Eric, her breath caught in her throat.

"No—not dirt." Chris's voice was agonized. "A mole, I think; a small dark mole."

Eric let out a cry. "Where is he?"

Chris's body froze absolutely still. His head fell forward onto his chest, burying his face in the blanket.

"Chris, for God's sake, where is he? Where's David?" Eric shouted.

Catherine leaped to her feet. "Eric, don't!"

Chris raised his head from the blanket. His face was wet with tears. "I don't know!" he cried out. "I can't see where—" Suddenly he bent forward as if seized by a cramp. His knees buckled and he began to fall.

Eric was across the room in seconds and caught Chris as he collapsed. He lowered him gently to the floor. "Get some brandy!" he called out to Catherine.

She rushed into the kitchen and seconds later was kneeling by the two men. Eric slipped his arm under Chris's shoulders and raised his head. The boy took a few sips from a glass Catherine held, then looked up at Eric and whispered: "Your son is alive, Mr. Wynters . . . he's alive!"

Part Three

19

For the next few weeks Chris, Eric, and Catherine spent long hours in her apartment doing one sighting test after another. Only a few hazy details emerged from each session, but despite the strain and frustration, Eric was driven to continue, clinging to the conviction that Chris might find his son.

Catherine did her best to maintain her objectivity and to keep Eric's excitement under control, but he grew increasingly anxious. When he stayed with her overnight, their lovemaking was feverish, almost desperate. Several times she awoke to find him sitting in the dark or restlessly pacing the living room.

His work began to suffer. Flare-ups of anger caused scenes in the studio with outraged guests and delays in taping shows. A member of the crew quit one night after an argument. John Bradford did what he could to cover for Eric, but many times even John's patience snapped and they had words. Eric made excuses and apologies for his behavior, and drove himself harder, until by the end of a workday he was drained. Only his anticipation of what the next session with Chris might bring kept him going. He seized each new detail that

Chris sighted, racking his brain to give it meaning, as if he were trying to put together a giant jigsaw puzzle while being handed a single piece at a time.

Early one evening he and Catherine were having dinner before Chris arrived for another series of tests. Eric was tense and moody. Catherine tried to cheer him with a light, easy flow of conversation, but getting little response, she finally lapsed into silence.

They ate quietly for a while until Eric asked: "Cathy, are we really getting anywhere?"

"Yes, darling, I think so. I've made notes on every session and my guess is—"

"Your *guess*?" Eric snapped.

"That's right, my guess," Catherine went on calmly. "Eric, try to understand. I have no one to compare Chris to. I've read every available report, paper, and book I could find on sighting and no two people do it the same way. One responds to holding an object, as Chris does, but sees symbols that have to be interpreted. Another reacts to geographical coordinates; given the latitude and longitude of a place, he sees it—a desert, a lake, a city. . . ."

"And Chris? How is he different?"

"My theory is that he sees the child, wherever he may be, at precisely the same moment in time that he's sighting."

"I'm not sure I understand."

"When we have a late session, as we did the other night, and once last week—remember?—well, Chris only sees the child asleep. But when we do the tests in the afternoon, he sees the boy playing in a garden, or on a swing, sitting on a woman's lap. It's my guess that wherever the boy is, there's either no difference in the time zones or very little difference, perhaps just an hour or so."

"That might make it someplace in the Midwest; they're about an hour earlier than we are." Eric's voice brightened.

"Possibly, but don't start thinking about that now. With each session Chris has grown more confident, relaxed. And each time he sees a little more than just the child. The first time he saw the room, and the Snow White figures on the wall. Last week he saw the front of a house, the porch, and part of a garden. I think that soon he'll be able to see everything around the child."

"I understand what you're saying. If the boy is taken anywhere, to a town or a place where Chris might see street signs, or a name, even the countryside, it would help begin to pinpoint the location."

"That's it exactly. That's what I'm hoping for," Cathy said.

"But it could take months!" Eric exploded.

Catherine looked down at her plate, not wanting to see the anguish in his face. "I know that, darling," she said quietly. "You simply have to be patient. We can't work any faster at this point."

"All right, all right," Eric muttered, pushing away from the table and standing up. "I'll do my best."

He went into the living room and sat down on the wide sill of the windows, staring out at the street. The sun was low in the sky, and a few gray clouds were edging into view, threatening a light shower. He sighed and lit a cigarette, trying to quiet his nerves.

"What time is it?" he called out.

"About five thirty," Cathy answered from the kitchen.

Wherever David is it might be about four thirty, he thought. The idea made his son seem somehow closer, but where? Dear God, where was he?

Chris entered the apartment a few minutes later. "Sorry I'm late," he said. "Mom was upset. She doesn't understand why I'm coming into town so often. I've put her off as best I can, but I think we're going to have to tell her something pretty soon."

"Maybe I should talk with her," Eric suggested.

"No, I'll do it," Cathy said. "We've talked before, she knows me. I'm sure I can explain it to her. Chris, do you want some coffee before we begin?"

"No, thanks." He looked at a box of toys sitting on the floor by the couch. "Are those David's?" he asked Eric.

"Yes. I had them packed away. Catherine thought they might help."

Chris sat down and reached into the box. He picked up a stuffed clown with black button eyes and a red-and-white-striped suit. Turning it over in his hands, he ran his fingertips over the grinning face and floppy ruff.

"Was this a favorite toy?" he asked.

Before Eric could answer, Chris leaned back on the couch, holding the clown tightly. A strange expression came over his face and his eyes grew distant. Catherine was startled at Chris's reaction to the clown; it was the first time he had gone into his trancelike state so quickly. She motioned to Eric to sit down, then started the tape recorder and took up her note pad and pen.

Chris was still for a few minutes, then suddenly became a little agitated. "Christ, it's hot!" he said loudly.

Catherine looked at him, puzzled. The apartment was air-conditioned, cool. But a film of perspiration had formed on Chris's brow.

"What is it?" Eric whispered.

"I'm not sure. It's as though he is having a physical response to whatever he's seeing."

Chris shifted uncomfortably on the couch and looked irritated.

"Where are you, Chris?" Catherine asked gently. "What do you see?"

"Sun. A big yellow sun. Hot." He paused, then: "Fields. Big fields. Wheat, maybe, but dry."

Eric sat up straight, staring at him wide-eyed.

"Is the child in the fields?" Cathy asked.

Chris was silent for a few seconds. "No. With the woman, sitting on her lap."

"Where?"

"In a truck." His body began swaying slightly. "Riding in a truck. On a dusty road."

Eric leaned forward, gripping his hands together until the knuckles were white.

Catherine's voice was low and she spoke very carefully: "Chris, try to describe everything you see, every detail."

"He's in a truck. Looking out the window. Fields . . ." His voice faded.

Eric started up from his chair, but Catherine held up a warning hand.

"Can you see the road?" she asked. "Are there any signs on the road?"

"No—wait, yes . . . a crossing. Two signposts."

"Can you read them?"

"No. Letters faded, blurred," Chris took a deep, shuddering breath. Sweat was running down his neck and stains appeared on his shirt, under his arms.

"Chris, do you want to rest for a moment?"

"No. The truck is slowing down, turning into a lane. I see a house. Big, white, like in children's books—"

"A farmhouse?"

"Yes. And a tree—and the swing I saw before, it's hanging from the tree, near the house."

Chris's eyes were glazed, fixed in a sightless stare. Abruptly he leaned over and plunged his hands into the toy box, filling them, letting a few slip from his fingers, clutching others for a moment, and then reaching for more. His fingers closed around a tiny pillow and his body stiffened.

Catherine watched with alarm, ready to stop the session. But then he sat back, holding the pillow against his chest and smiling.

"Chris, what is it? What's happening?" Cathy asked.

"The little boy is running around the garden. He's chasing a butterfly and laughing."

"Do you see anything else?"

"No. Just the boy. Now he's stopped. He's going away—"

"Can you follow him?"

"Yes. He's going up the lane. He's so little." Chris's voice grew tender. "He runs and stops, with his arms out to balance himself."

"Where is he going? Chris—where's he going?"

"Up the lane—near the truck. . . ." Chris's breathing became rapid. His eyes were squeezed shut and his hands kneaded the tiny pillow. "Be careful," he half whispered. "Don't run too fast—you'll fall down. . . . Oh, look out, look out!"

"What happened?" Eric said hoarsely.

"He fell. He's crying. He's near the bumper of the truck and he's crying. Don't cry, baby."

Catherine's eyes widened as she listened to him. She got up quickly and went to Chris, kneeling on the floor by his side.

"Chris, can you see the bumper of the truck?" she asked, trying to keep her voice under control.

"Yes. Oh, he's scratched his leg. He's crying hard."

"Chris, listen to me. Look at the bumper of the truck. Is there a license plate on it?"

Eric stood up, suddenly realizing what she was asking. His face was white.

"The license plate, Chris—can you see the license plate?" Cathy asked again.

"Yes. Numbers—all covered with dust. . . ."

"Not the numbers, Chris. The state. Can you see the name of the state?"

The silence in the room was like a deafening roar in Eric's ears as he stood paralyzed, watching Chris. The boy was straining to answer, his body rigid with the effort he was making. When he finally spoke, his voice was guttural, croaking: "N—E—B—" he said slowly.

"Are you sure?" Catherine asked. "Be absolutely sure."

"Yes—Nebraska."

"Oh, my God!" Eric breathed in a choked whisper.

Catherine remained kneeling by Chris, her eyes focused hard on his face. "What's happening now?" she asked firmly. "Chris—are you still there? What's happening?"

"Yes—he's all right. The woman has him in her arms. He's laughing and she's kissing him. They're walking—"

"Where are they walking to?"

"Down the lane . . ."

"To the house?"

"No, away from the house—to the road. To a box. A mailbox . . ."

Eric's legs trembled as he moved across the room to crouch on the floor by Catherine. He knew what her next question would be and was terrified that there might not be an answer.

"Chris, take your time now," Catherine said in a calm, steady voice. "Is there a name on the mailbox?"

Eric held his breath. Chris's head was nodding from side to side as if he might collapse at any moment. His large hands clutched and kneaded the pillow until the fabric began to tear.

"Chris, please—is there a name on the mailbox?" Catherine pleaded.

Chris threw his head back, the muscles of his neck straining like taut ropes. There was no color in his face and sweat poured freely, soaking his shirt.

Suddenly the pillow ripped in his hands, and he opened his mouth, releasing the name as if it had been imprisoned in his throat.

"HARKIN!" he cried out.

20

Eric waited impatiently for Simpson to get back on the line. He stubbed out his cigarette, lit another one, and swore softly at the delay.

Finally Simpson was on, saying: "Okay, Mr. Wynters, here's what we have on Nebraska. . . ." He went on to describe the reports he and his men had accumulated on the baby black-market activities in the state, concluding with ". . . so, in the last couple of years, there have been sales made in Omaha, possibly in Springfield."

"Thanks, Simpson, that's what I wanted to know. I'll get back to you."

"What's up, Mr. Wynters? You got a line on something?"

"I'll let you know in a few days," Eric said brusquely, and hung up.

He waited for a moment, then dialed Lieutenant Parker at Police Headquarters. Since October they had kept in touch intermittently; Parker had always been encouraging about the possibility of finding the baby.

As soon as the officer came on the line, Eric told him that his investigators had turned up a couple named Harkin who lived in Omaha or Springfield and had adopted a child soon after Jenny's death. Being purposely vague about his information, Eric asked if Parker could check them out, get their location or address through the Omaha police. And once that was verified, could he clear it with the police for Eric to go to see them?

Parker was skeptical. "That's not much to go on, Mr. Wynters. Are you sure this isn't just another false lead? You've had a lot of them."

"I'm not sure of anything," Eric said wearily, "but whatever it is, I think it's worth a try. Will you help me?"

"Get back to you within the hour," Parker said.

Eric hung up and sat back in his chair, rubbing his temples to ease the nervous throbbing in his head. Now all he had to do was wait; all he had to know was whether the Harkins really existed. In the hard glare of morning light flooding his office, the sighting sessions with Christopher took on the aspect of a wildly fantastic dream, an indulgence he had pursued with childish tenacity. The facts of his existence were here, in his office, on his desk piled high with memos, production sheets, schedules; not in the phantom visions of a young man with mysterious, inexplicable gifts.

Eric shook his head in a vain attempt to clear the confusion and doubt from his mind. He had to try—anything was worth the effort. If there was a family named Harkin living in Nebraska, then what Chris saw was real enough to follow through on, certainly as real as his own belief that David was still alive.

While he waited for Parker to call back, Eric roughed out a plan of action: he'd book seats on the first plane out for himself, Chris, and Catherine. There were four shows in the can; he could take a few days off and give John some excuse—a visit to an old school friend, getting away for a rest . . . For a moment he thought about John and Margaret, how they would feel if he came back with their grandson in his arms. The dream became painful and he put it out of his mind.

He had David's birth certificate; they'd have to get a fingerprint expert from the Omaha police—could Parker fix that? Would there be any legal difficulties? He should call his lawyer—but how could he? What would he tell him? Eric grew angry with himself; what the hell was he doing, thinking like this, making these plans?

He got up and paced the office nervously. The phone rang. It was

Shelly, asking about the staff meeting scheduled for that afternoon. He put her off rudely, then apologized and said he'd get back to her. He glanced at the clock on his desk. It had been only thirty minutes since he'd talked to Parker. He lit another cigarette and walked to the windows, stared out at the city, trying to silence the frantic voices of his thoughts.

The phone rang again. It was Parker.

"Mr. Wynters, I don't know what you've got going, but there is a family named Harkin living just outside Springfield. . . ."

Eric almost shouted with joy. Barely able to contain himself, he listened as Parker went on.

". . . I spoke to Police Chief Ned Forbes, explained the case to him, and he said he'd do whatever he could to help. He made a couple of phone calls and found out that the Harkins have a child about two years old—a boy."

Susan poured tea from a silver service and handed a cup to Eric and another to Catherine. Chris sat next to his mother on the couch, silent and a little apprehensive. All he had told her was that Catherine wanted to see her immediately and that she was bringing a friend with her.

"It's very kind of you to see us on such short notice, Mrs. McKenzie," Catherine said, sensing Susan's impatience with the unexpected visit.

"Chris said it was very important, Dr. Marlowe," Susan replied crisply.

"Yes, it is. . . ." Catherine hesitated, then went on: "I'll begin by explaining why Mr. Wynters is here. I understand you knew his wife, Jenny."

"I met Jenny only a few times, when she was a girl. I know her mother very well; she's been a client of mine for years."

"Then you remember what happened to Jenny?"

"Of course." She turned to Eric, her expression softening. "It must have been a horrible experience for you, Mr. Wynters, losing your wife and child like that. I'm so sorry," she said sympathetically.

"Thank you, Mrs. McKenzie," Eric said. "Why we're here has to do with what happened to Jenny—and our son, David."

"I'm afraid I don't understand." Susan looked at Catherine and then glanced at her son. "Does this have to do with Chris?" she asked her.

"Yes, in a way it does," Catherine answered. She took a deep breath and began to explain what had happened, starting with Eric's conviction that his son was still alive, hiring investigators to search for him, and finally the events of the last few weeks involving Christopher.

When Catherine was finished, Susan sat quietly for a few minutes before turning to Eric and asking: "Do you really believe that Chris saw your son?"

Eric answered cautiously. "I believe only what we've learned so far: that a family named Harkin lives in Nebraska, and that they have a child, a boy. That he might be my son is what we want to find out; that's why we're going to Omaha and want to take Chris with us."

Susan said to Catherine: "I can understand why you told Mr. Wynters about Chris, Dr. Marlowe, even though you promised me that no one else would know." She sighed deeply. "I probably would have done the same. All I ask is this—if you do find that the boy is Mr. Wynters' son, will you keep Chris out of it?"

"We understand your fears, Mrs. McKenzie," Eric said, "and we respect them. I assure you that if anything happens, there'll be no mention of Chris to anyone, not even the Bradfords."

Susan nodded her thanks and looked at her son. "Chris, are you quite sure of what you saw?" she asked gravely.

"Yes, Mom, I am," he replied.

"Well, then, of course you must go," she said.

Eric gave an audible sigh of relief and said: "Thank you, Mrs. McKenzie. I'm very grateful for your understanding."

Susan smiled and for a moment the years of fear and anxiety were washed away, revealing her still-attractive, spirited beauty. "I'm really not an ogre, Mr. Wynters, although at times it may appear so. I've lived with the knowledge of my son's gifts for many years and have simply done my best to protect him from harm."

"We understand that," Catherine said warmly, "and appreciate your feelings. I promise that we, too, will do our best to take care of Chris."

For the first time since they had met, there was a sense of communication, almost friendship, between the two women. They shared for an instant a burden of responsibility for Chris's welfare, and quite possibly the welfare of other lives he might touch.

"What time will you be leaving?" Susan asked Eric.

"We've booked seats on a plane to Omaha for tomorrow morning at eight," he replied.

"I'll have to wash and iron some things for you, Chris," Susan said.

Catherine and Eric rose. "Thank you, again," Eric said.

"All that I ask is that you keep your promise about Chris," Susan repeated as they walked to the door. Then, looking up at Eric, she took his hand and pressed it tightly. "And I pray that the child is yours."

As Eric and Catherine drove off, Chris stood with his arm around his mother, watching until the car disappeared. His eyes were filled with the promise of excitement that tomorrow might bring.

"You remind me of your father," Susan said quietly, looking at him, "just before he was about to leave for a voyage. Face shining and eyes twinkling like stars."

Christopher smiled. "It is a voyage for me, Mom. My first time away from home! And just think what it will mean if the child I saw is Eric's son." He saw the troubled look in her eyes and gave her a hug. "It'll be all right, Mom, I promise. Nothing will happen to me, and I'll come back to you."

Susan held him, and remembered the many farewells she had said to Peter and his promises to return to her. But she had finally lost him to the sea. Now she was certain that Chris, too, would be taken from her, but by something much stronger than a force of nature.

21

Ned Forbes was a tall man, slender and lithe, in his early fifties but appearing younger. There was almost a touch of the dandy about him, belying his position as head of the Omaha police force. He welcomed Eric and Chris into his office with a surprisingly hearty handshake and bowed to Catherine in a courtly, old-fashioned manner.

Once they were seated he got quickly to the point. "I spoke with Lieutenant Parker in Philadelphia again last night and went over the details of the case," he said in a light, slightly nasal voice. "We've had some instances of baby purchases throughout the state, and a few right here in Omaha, so your investigators might be on to something with the Harkin family."

"How soon can we go out to their place?" Eric asked, his voice tight with fatigue. He had slept fitfully the night before, and his face was drawn, his eyes hollowed by dark shadows.

"Right away, if you like," Forbes answered. "I have a fingerprint man, Detective Lew O'Brian, standing by to go with you. He can take the child's prints there and compare them with the ones on the birth certificate for an immediate identification. If they match, then you can bring the child back. We'll have blood tests made, and if everything checks out, the boy is yours."

"What will happen to the Harkins?" Catherine asked.

"Hard to say, ma'am. They'll be brought in for questioning, but if they've been victimized by some phony adoption agency, they can't really be held responsible. It's always a hard thing, though, whenever we recover a child like this."

Eric stood up. "I've rented a car. Could we go now?" he asked.

Forbes took a sheet of paper from his desk. "Here's the address. I'll get O'Brian for you," he said, lifting the phone and dialing.

Eric turned the car off the highway onto an unpaved road, raising clouds of dust that floated slowly in the still air. Farmland stretched away for miles in a flat, unbroken plain. The vast sweep of land had the harsh, primitive look of a country that had been laid to waste, scorched raw by some awesome act of nature.

Catherine looked out the streaked windows as they drove through the monotonous landscape. Despite the air conditioning in the car, her light summer dress was heat-soaked and sticky. She shifted uncomfortably and patted a handkerchief at the film of perspiration on her face and throat.

Chris sat beside her, silent, staring ahead as if he were asleep with his eyes wide open. He had not said a word since they left Omaha. No one had. In the front seat, Eric drove with his hands gripping the wheel tightly, his body tense, rigid, as if he were holding his breath. Detective O'Brian sat next to him with the quiet, official air of a man doing his job, unaware of the mounting tension in the people he was riding with.

Suddenly a crossroads appeared ahead of them, marked by two signs mounted on posts. Chris came to life and leaned forward, his eyes narrowed slightly and focused in a hard, intense gaze.

He whispered to Catherine: "The signs—those are the signs I saw!"

She put her hand over his in a restraining gesture. "Eric," she called out in a casual tone, "those road signs up ahead—"

"Yes, I see them," he answered. His voice was thick with the effort to control his excitement.

O'Brian said: "The Harkin place is to your left and just down the lane off the road. You can't miss it; it's the only house around for a mile or two."

Eric made a turn at the signposts, and a few minutes later O'Brian said: "There it is, down at the end of that dirt road."

Catherine gave Eric a quick glance in the rearview mirror. A small nervous tic was jumping in his jaw, and his eyes searched rapidly over the area as they turned into the road. It was there, just as Chris had described it: a large, old-fashioned white-frame farmhouse, sitting in the shade of a big elm tree. A small, neat garden extended from the wide front porch to the edge of the road. A homemade swing hung from one of the lower branches of the tree, and on the porch a collection of toys spilled out of a cardboard box. Near the turned-post railing sat an old wicker rocking chair, moving slowly, as if someone had gotten up from it a few minutes before. And out by the edge of the road stood the mailbox with HARKIN lettered on it.

Eric stopped the car, and the road dust settled around the tires in lazy puffs. They sat in silence until Eric said to the detective: "Will you wait here until I call you? We'd like to speak to the Harkins alone first."

O'Brian nodded, and Catherine, Eric, and Chris got out of the car. As they started down a path through the garden, the screen door opened and a woman stepped out onto the porch.

"Hello," she called out hesitantly. "You folks lost?"

"Are you Mrs. Harkin?" Eric asked.

"Yes, I am," she said with a shy smile. At first glance she appeared to be about forty or so, but with the smile, Eric saw that she was younger, maybe in her early to middle thirties. She was thin and dressed in an ill-fitting housedress that might have been bought from a Sears catalog. Her blond hair, drawn back and tied with a pale-pink ribbon, hung limply to her bony shoulders, and her eyes, a light sky-blue, observed them with a soft, tired expression.

"Mrs. Harkin," Eric began nervously, "my name is Eric Wynters. Does that mean anything to you?"

She looked at him, puzzled. "Why, no—should it?" Her gaze wandered questioningly to Catherine and Chris. Then she saw O'Brian sitting in the car. He had taken off his cap, but she could see the dark shirt of his uniform, and for a moment her eyes flickered with concern.

She looked back at them and said: "Why don't you folks come up on the porch and get out of the sun? Would you like something cold to drink? I got a batch of lemonade I just put up. Won't take but a minute to bring it out."

Eric began to shake his head no, but Catherine said quickly: "Thank you, that would be lovely. It's very warm."

The woman laughed. "Warm? Why it's the hottest summer we've had in years! There's some chairs down there at the end of the porch. You sit down and get comfortable. I'll be right out."

As she disappeared into the house, Eric took a step to follow her. Catherine put her hand on his arm and held him back. "Darling, take it easy," she whispered. "I know how you feel, but you can't just spring it on her."

Eric nodded and wiped his face with a handkerchief. "Christ, I've never been so scared in my life!" he muttered.

Chris brought the chairs and they sat down. His face was flushed with excitement and disbelief. They were here, sitting on the porch of a house he had seen in his mind! That vague image was now distinct, real. It could be touched!

A few minutes later Mrs. Harkin returned with a tray of glasses and a pitcher of lemonade clinking with ice cubes. "Here we are," she said cheerfully.

Eric took the tray from her hands and set it down on a nearby table. The small courtesy brought a surprised smile and a faint blush to her pale face.

"Thank you," she murmured, pouring the glasses full and handing one to each of them.

Catherine introduced herself and Christopher, and the woman smiled and shook hands with a polite formality. Then she turned to Eric.

"Should I know you, Mr. Wynters?" she asked.

"Well, no—not really," Eric stammered. He cleared his throat self-consciously and began to explain why they were there. He spoke slowly, making a careful effort not to say anything too abruptly that would frighten her. But as soon as he mentioned the baby black market, Mrs. Harkin's face went pale. As Eric continued, she became more agitated. When he told her that his investigators had received information that his son was somewhere in this area, she stood up, her hands clenched stiffly at her sides.

"I don't understand what any of this has to do with me," she said in a frightened voice.

"You have a son, don't you, Mrs. Harkin?" Eric asked gently.

"Yes, I do, but what has that—"

"Is he yours? That is, did you bear him?"

O'Brian had gotten out of the car and was leaning against the door, watching them. The woman's eyes swung to him and then back to Eric.

"Why, no. He's my sister's child. She died in Omaha, and my husband and I took him—"

"May we see him?" Eric's voice was hard.

"No, you may not! I don't know who you are or why you're here, Mr. Wynters, but I'm not going to listen to any more of this!"

"Mrs. Harkin," Catherine interjected, "please try to understand."

"Why should I?" Her voice rose. "He's my son!"

Eric turned impatiently and called out to O'Brian. As the detective started toward the house, a man drove up in a small open truck and pulled in behind the car. He swung down from the cab, tall and rawboned, in a work shirt and dusty overalls. A sweat-stained, faded old hat shadowed the hard planes of his face.

Mrs. Harkin ran to him, crying out: "Seth!"

"Nancy, what is it?" He took her in his arms. "What's happening here? Who are you people?"

O'Brian took over and explained the situation to him with a quiet but firm authority.

"—and these other folks are friends of Mr. Wynters," he concluded, introducing Catherine and Chris. "Now, Seth, Mr. Wynters is here to see your boy, and I'm here to see that he does and verify the child's fingerprints. If the boy isn't his, we'll be on our way with apologies for botherin' you folks."

"Do we have to do this?" Harkin asked angrily.

O'Brian shrugged. "If you ain't got nothin' to hide, why not?" he answered. His gray eyes were steady, calm. He had the couple backed into a corner, and he knew it by the defeated slump of Harkin's shoulders.

Nancy looked at her husband, her eyes wild with fear. "Seth, we can't. He's—" she searched for some excuse. "He's asleep—takin' his nap," she said desperately.

Harkin kept his arm around her protectively. "You'll have to wake him up, honey." His voice was low and filled with emotion.

They waited in the small living room while Nancy went off to the back of the house. The blinds had been drawn against the afternoon sun, and the room was dark and stifling, burdened with overlarge pieces of furniture. A few family photographs hung on walls papered with a fading print of roses and jonquils. One of them showed

Nancy and Seth at a school dance, dreamy-eyed and youthful, standing under a paper cutout of a harvest moon.

There was little resemblance between the gawky youth in the picture and the man standing silently in the center of the room. Seth had taken off his hat. His short, dark hair lay in sweat-soaked strands across his forehead. Large hands hung limply out of the frayed shirt sleeves, the fingers worn and nubbed with calluses, and his long back was bent with resignation.

Catherine moved to Eric's side and took his hand, while Chris and O'Brian stood awkwardly near the couch. It seemed an eternity before Nancy appeared in the doorway.

"You can come in now," she said in a husky, tear-filled voice. "He's awake."

Eric started forward stiffly and stumbled against an ottoman. Cathy grabbed his arm and held it as they followed Nancy down a hallway. Chris and O'Brian were close behind, and Harkin walked heavily after them. They turned into a room that was flooded with sunlight. The walls gleamed in bright white, and were hung with cutout figures from fairy tales. Chris saw a colorfully painted Snow White, trailing a line of tiny dwarfs that wiggled across the wall. He gasped a quick intake of breath and turned to Catherine. She was staring at Eric and then following his gaze to the little boy sitting up in a small bed.

"Oh, God!" Eric cried under his breath.

The shape of Jenny's chin and nose, her dark hair, and his own blue eyes were in the tiny face that peered up at the strange group around his bed.

Nancy picked up the boy and cradled him against her breasts. "His name is Alan," she said, weeping. "He's our son, not yours!"

O'Brian came forward and gently took the child from her grasp. "I'll take some prints, ma'am. Then we'll be sure."

Harkin led his wife out of the room, murmuring to her. Sobbing, she kept repeating: "He's our son, Seth. Alan is our son."

Catherine and Chris followed them into the dark, stuffy living room. Harkin sat on the couch, holding his wife in his arms. He looked up at them with hollowed, dead eyes.

"Nancy had a miscarriage with our first baby," he said painfully. "The doctor told her she couldn't have any more. There was a woman in the hospital, worked there part time cleaning up. She said she could help us."

"Please, Mr. Harkin, you don't have to explain," Catherine said, moved almost to tears.

He shook his head and went on. "She told us we might have to wait a long time by going to an adoption agency, and Nancy, she was miserable, losing the baby and knowing she couldn't have another. So we borrowed some money and the woman made the arrangements and brought us our boy, little Alan. She said his momma had died and that his daddy was long gone before he was even born. And we believed her."

Catherine could not speak, her feelings and emotions torn between her love for Eric and the simple dignity of Seth Harkin trying to face a situation over which he had no control. She looked at Christopher and wondered what he felt, knowing that with his gift he had brought both joy and pain, had wrenched apart the lives of two people who were complete strangers to him.

Just then Eric and O'Brian walked into the room. Eric was holding the boy in his arms, and his face was wet with tears. Seth and Nancy stood up, clinging to each other, their faces drawn and white. They stared at O'Brian, waiting for him to destroy them.

"We'll have to take these prints in and enlarge them, just to be sure," he said as gently as he could. "And we'll take a blood test of the boy too. But as far as I can see, my prints and the ones on his birth certificate are a perfect match. I'm pretty certain that the boy is Mr. Wynters'."

Nancy Harkin gave a short, sharp scream, and then she fainted.

22

Christopher leaned back in his seat and watched white clouds move slowly past the plane window. Every once in a while the tip of the wing caught a ray of sun, flashing a blinding light that refracted into a rainbow of colors. He moved his head to one side and glanced at Catherine and Eric, sitting across the aisle. David was curled up on his father's lap, wrapped in a light blanket and fast asleep. Catherine looked up, caught Christopher's eye, and smiled. Chris nodded and turned back to the window, frowning. He felt confused and vaguely unhappy. All the excitement was over and now they were going home, back to Philadelphia. And he was going back to—what? Being a gardener for Charlotte Stanwyck? Back to living within the tight confines of his mother's fears and apprehensions?

For Chris the last few days had been a breaking out from that monotonous routine, a thrilling revelation of himself and his effect on other people. Some of it still bewildered him: the agony of Seth and Nancy Harkin saying goodbye to the child was a scene he would not soon forget. But his remorse and sympathy had been swept aside by Eric's joy. After the fingerprints and the blood tests taken at the police lab in Omaha had proved conclusively that the boy was David Wynters, there had been a delirious celebration. Eric called the Bradfords from the hotel, laughing and crying as he told them what had happened. Then there had been an early dinner in the hotel dining room so that David could be put to bed. And after that he and Catherine and Eric had sat up drinking wine and talking. They had been almost like a family, Chris thought. Alone in their room, Eric had embraced him like a father, swearing that he would do whatever he could to help him, that as soon as all the excitement had died down, they would have a long talk about his future.

His future? Chris wondered to himself. Catherine had said they would go on with her tests and studies, and Eric had talked of college or trade school, or a down payment on the farm Chris had spoken of once.

But Chris knew that would never be enough for him—not now. *He* had found Eric's son, when no one else could! And yet everyone seemed to want him to go on just as he had before, as if nothing had happened. But something *had* happened—to him! He knew what he could do, what he was capable of. He wasn't sure yet exactly what it meant in terms of his own life, but he did know that nothing could ever be the same for him.

The captain announced over the loudspeakers that they would be landing in a few minutes. Catherine crossed the aisle, sat down next to Chris, and took his hand.

"How do you feel?" she asked.

"Okay—a little tired. Is David all right?"

"Yes. He slept most of the way. Poor darling, he's so confused. It will take time for him to forget Nancy and Seth. Eric will have to be very patient."

"Well, he's lucky," Chris said, grinning. "He has you to help him."

Catherine smiled. "Thank you, Chris. That's a lovely compliment." She glanced at her watch. "We'd better get ready; we'll be landing soon. Remember, you and I will leave the plane after Eric gets to the arrival lounge with David. He'll go with the Bradfords, and you and I can slip out of the airport with the other passengers."

"It's a little like a spy movie, isn't it?" Chris said somewhat cynically.

"A little." Catherine laughed. "But we can't risk having the Bradfords see you—or me, for that matter. Margaret Bradford knows you so well, and I think John would remember meeting me at the studio the night I did the show."

"Isn't Eric ever going to tell them what really happened?" Chris asked.

There was a hard, almost angry edge in his voice that disturbed Catherine. Ever since he had sighted David, they had all agreed to keep Chris's efforts a secret, knowing full well the kind of sensational publicity the real story would attract. Susan was the only other person who knew the truth, and there was no concern that she would ever tell anyone or *want* anyone to know what her son had done.

But now Catherine wondered about Chris. With all the healthy ego of a twenty-one-year-old, he was bursting with the importance of his accomplishment, and they were forcing him to keep a low profile, fade into the background. It was bound to upset him. And yet they really had no other choice. As soon as she could, she would talk with him, Catherine decided.

The sign to fasten their seat belts came on, and Catherine went back to her seat. Chris looked out the window at the lights of the city below, scattered like silver-white pinpoints against the velvet darkness, growing larger, more luminous as the plane descended. As he stared at the abstract design of life and movement rushing past, Chris fell into a strange dreamlike state of confusion; he couldn't tell whether he was seeing the city or sighting it in his mind.

When Eric stepped off the passageway from the plane into the arrival lounge, a crowd of people surged forward, surrounding him and David. Reporters and newsmen were shouting questions as flash bulbs went off, and TV men carrying cameras pressed close. John and Margaret pushed their way through the mob and embraced him. David began to cry, and Eric put the child in Margaret's arms.

"Your grandson is home," Eric whispered to her and she held the boy close to her and sobbed with joy and relief.

John shouldered his way past a reporter and hugged Eric as microphones were thrust into his face and a babble of questions was asked.

"How did you find the boy, Mr. Wynters?"

"When did you receive word that the baby was alive?"

"How does it feel to be reunited with your son?"

Eric turned to his father-in-law. "What the hell is this, John?" he asked, shocked.

"Word got out as soon as I told the crew at the studio what had happened. The newspapers have been all over us since you called."

An aggressive young woman pushed in front of them and held a mike up to Eric's face. "Mr. Wynters, just exactly how did you find your son?" she demanded.

John muttered in his ear: "Make a statement so we can get out of here! They've got Maggie and the baby cornered over there. I'll go help her."

Eric faced the confusion, blinking his eyes in the glare of lights mounted on reflectors. Cameramen shifted to get a better view of him, and TV men talked into headsets. Other passengers mingled with waiting friends and pushed into the group to see what was happening. Eric wondered whether Catherine and Chris had managed to slip through the crowd.

The woman in front of him barked her question again: "How did you find your son?"

"All I can tell you is that my investigators traced the location of my son to a small town near Omaha. With the help of the Philadelphia police department and the police in Omaha, we were able to verify the identity of David."

"Are you going to do a show about the recovery of the boy?" someone called out.

"Who were the investigators?" another voice asked.

Eric held up his hands in a futile effort to quiet the chaos. Finally he grabbed the nearest microphone and, putting on his TV-personality smile, announced: "That's it for now, ladies and gentlemen. You'd better get to your studios and newspapers. There are only a few hours left before the late news goes on the air, and we know what it's like to miss a deadline!"

There was a burst of laughter and the crowd began to give way before him as he walked quickly to John and Margaret and they started to leave the lounge.

In a far corner of the room Catherine stood with Chris, watching the scene. As the newsmen began to disperse, Catherine said: "We'd better take a side exit and catch a cab into town."

Chris didn't move for a few seconds, his eyes hungrily absorbing the flow of excitement around Eric and the Bradfords.

Catherine tugged his arm gently. "C'mon, Chris—we've got to get out of here."

By the time they got to Catherine's apartment it was midnight. Chris had been silent in the cab, and when they arrived at her door he mumbled a sullen good night and drove off in his car. Catherine knew he was upset, but she was too tired to do any more than fall into bed. All Chris needed was some rest, she thought. They could put this whole incident behind them and go on as they had. But even while thinking it, she knew it wasn't true, knew that what had happened and its effect on Christopher would have to be dealt with —and soon.

Susan was waiting for Chris at the door when he drove up to the house. She embraced him warmly and led him into the kitchen.

"I saw it all on the late news," she said. "It was wonderful, and I'm proud of you. Dear Margaret, she looked so happy."

"Yeah, it was pretty exciting," Chris replied, sitting down at the table wearily.

"Are you hungry? I can whip up some dinner or a sandwich and some milk. . . ." Susan looked at him anxiously; he was so drawn, so pale.

"No, thanks, Mom. I had dinner on the plane."

"Was it a hard thing, taking the child from those people?"

He looked up at her with a frown. "Yes, it was. But you should have seen Eric's face when he saw David. I thought he'd burst from happiness."

"I'm sure he is happy." She smiled at him. "And I have some news for you that will make you happy too. Nella's home!"

Chris's face brightened. "She is! How is she? Do you think I could call her? Did she ask for me?"

Susan laughed. "Yes, she asked for you. I told her you'd call her in the morning, that you were doing a couple of days' work over at a farm near Rocky Hill, just like you told Charlotte."

"God, I can't believe she's back. It's been more than a year since I've seen her." He got up and stretched. "I'd better get to bed. I'm bushed."

"I'll lock up and bring you a glass of warm milk to help you sleep well," Susan said, giving him a hug.

In his room, Chris stripped off his clothes and crawled under the covers of his bed. When Susan came in a few minutes later, he was lying with his arms behind his head, staring into space.

Susan sat down on the edge of the bed, and he sat up and took the mug of milk from her hand.

"I was half afraid I'd be seeing your face on the television tonight," she admitted.

"No, they kept me out of it—and Dr. Marlowe, too. We slipped past the news people with the other passengers."

"They kept their word to me, and I'm that grateful," Susan said. "When you see them, please tell them for me, will you?"

"Sure, Mom. I told you—they're good people, the best."

"And you were right."

Chris drank the milk and gave her the mug, then slid down to the pillows. "Good night, Mom," he murmured sleepily.

Susan leaned over, kissed his cheek, and stood up. As she turned off the small lamp by his bed, she asked in a hesitant voice: "Chris, is it over now? I mean the tests with Dr. Marlowe—and anything else, like finding the Wynters child?"

Chris was silent. Susan wondered what he was thinking. With his gift he had made one man happy and scarred the lives of two other people. Did he realize now why she had been so afraid for him? Why she wanted so desperately to keep his power a secret from the world?

"Chris? Please tell me that it's over," she whispered into the darkness of the room.

There was no answer except for the sound of his breathing.

◆

The following morning Chris left the house after a hurried breakfast and headed for the Stanwyck mansion. He drove through the gates and up the driveway just as Charlotte came out of the front door. With a screech of tires he brought the car to a stop and bounded across the gravel and up the stairs to her side.

"Where is she?" he asked breathlessly.

"In the old playroom," Charlotte answered, laughing. "She's been waiting there since you phoned."

Chris flung open the door and started to run across the foyer as Charlotte called out: "Stay for dinner—I'll be back around five!"

He waved his hand in answer and raced up the wide, curving staircase, taking the steps two at a time. At the door of the playroom he stopped to catch his breath, suddenly nervous about seeing Nella again. Had she changed? Would she think he had changed? He opened the door slowly and stepped into the room.

Nella was sitting on the floor, her white chiffon peignoir spread in softly folded masses around her like the fragile petals of a flower.

The morning sun slanted shafts of light through the half-opened shutters at the windows, and motes of dust floated in the air, a fine spray of golden powder drifting in lazy motion. She looked up at him as he stood in the doorway, and he saw how beautiful she had become: dark shining eyes in a delicate oval face; a generous, full mouth, lips half parted in surprise; and flowing around her shoulders, a fall of dark hair that accented her flawless complexion.

"Hello," he said in a half whisper. "My name is Christopher McKenzie. I know lots of stories about heroes and princes, the mighty Cu Chulainn, and Cathbad, the Druid. Would you like to be hearin' a few?"

With a slow smile, Nella answered, trying to match his accent: "Sure and you're a darlin' boy to come and keep me company and tell me your stories. Will you be stayin' long?"

He crossed the room and knelt down beside her. "I'll stay as long as you wish," he murmured, cupping her face in his hands, "but only if you'll give us a kiss."

"Ah, but you are a fast one," Nella said as her lips touched his.

Chris's hands slipped to her waist and he stood up, bringing her with him, holding her slender body close to his as his mouth moved over hers with a fervor that surprised them both.

She pulled away from him and said huskily: "If you let me go, I'll be back on the floor—and not because I'm a cripple, but because you're making me weak as a kitten."

He laughed and picked her up. "Oh, Nella, it's so good to be with you again!" He carried her to the wide cushioned window seat and sat down, cradling her in his arms.

"You missed me, then?" she asked, sitting up and looking at him closely.

"I did that—and I didn't know how much till I walked through that door. And you? Did you miss this poor lad while you were larkin' about the world with your rich friends?"

Nella's face sobered as she stared at him. She touched her fingers to his face, over his lips and eyes, and through the silky ripple of his hair. "Yes, I missed you, Chris," she said seriously. "And I didn't know how much until you walked through the door."

"Didn't you like the people you met, the other kids at the school?"

"Oh, they were all right—very nice to me. Too nice. You know, too polite, too considerate, always going out of their way to help me.

God, sometimes it drove me crazy! It was the same with the doctors."

"Did they help you any?"

"Not really. They helped themselves mostly, to Mother's money. They must have cost her a fortune!"

"Then you're glad you're back?"

"Oh, yes! And I'm staying—I told Mother that. We had a few words, but I think she sees it my way. And you? Are you glad that I'm back?"

"You know I am," he answered, smiling. "It's like old times."

"Well, not quite, judging by that kiss you gave me," Nella said with a mischievous glint in her eye. "I think we've outgrown our playmate stage—"

"And thank God for it!" Chris said, kissing her again.

"Chris, wait," Nella murmured, drawing away from him. "Let's not outgrow the playmate stage too fast."

"Do I frighten you?" he asked jokingly.

"Just a little—but not for long, I promise. Just give me a chance to get used to you."

"Have I changed that much?" His voice was suddenly sober.

She leaned back and examined him with mock seriousness. "Well, let's see . . . you're no longer a boy, that's for sure."

He laughed and reached for her again, but she ducked out of his arms.

"Ah, ah—I'm not finished yet. You're a very handsome man, and I'll bet a lot of girls are after you!"

He grinned a bit smugly. "Not a lot . . ."

"Oh? Well, I'll skip that point for the moment. But there is something different—"

"What?"

Her dark eyes searched his face carefully. "I'm not sure," she said slowly. Then, more excitedly, she asked: "What's been happening to you?"

Chris saw the eager light in her eyes, the wanting to share secrets as they had when they were children. But what could he tell her? Never once had he mentioned anything about his gifts, always afraid that Susan might find out, or that Nella might think differently of him, be afraid of him. It was the only secret he had ever kept from her, and now that secret had become the pattern of his life. How could he explain it to her?

"Oh, come on, it can't be that bad," she chided him for hesitating. "You're not into a life of crime, are you?" she kidded.

Chris smiled weakly. "No, I'm not into a life of anything." He stood up and walked slowly around the room, touching the toys they used to play with, as if trying to find a link between the time they were children and the present. "I'm your mother's gardener, and I work for farmers when they need me. I'm good with growing things and with animals," he said, laughing cynically at his private joke. He turned and gave her a look at once hopeless and apologetic. "I'm a clod, a great lump of a clod."

"Chris, don't talk about yourself that way!" Nella struggled to sit up and began to slip off the window seat. He rushed to her side and caught her in his arms. She started to laugh and pressed her face against his.

"The clod and the cripple—I think we make a terrific team."

He held her close to him, feeling emotions he was afraid to name but knowing that having her near was what he needed to bring some order into the confusion of his life.

"Let's get out of this room," he whispered thickly. "There are too many memories here. Come, I'll take you for a walk. Where are your crutches?"

"To hell with my crutches," she breathed against his ear. "Carry me—I want to be in your arms."

"You're a shameless hussy," he said, picking her up.

Mrs. Gregory was in the foyer as they came down the stairs. She looked up at them with a wide smile and said: "Now there's a pretty picture, I must say! But be careful—"

"Not a word out of you, you old fussbudget," Chris said, scowling at her, "or I'll put Nella down, throw you over my shoulder, and lock you in the garden shed!"

"I'd like to see you try!" the housekeeper replied, planting her hands on her solid hips.

"I bet you would, too," Nella giggled.

"You watch your mouth, Miss Nella. You're not so big I can't put you over my knee!"

Nella waved at her airily as Chris carried her out the front door. "You do and I'll have my prince cast a spell on you," she called back.

Chris began to laugh softly to himself as he ran across the grounds holding Nella tightly in his arms.

23

The Bradford house stood on a hill above Mount Pleasant Road in Gladwyne, overlooking tree-lined streets that wound past the elegant homes of Lower Merion Township. In startling contrast to its more ostentatious Georgian and Tudor neighbors, the house was relatively small, having only six bedrooms, and was distinguished by an almost storybook appearance. Set a mile or so back off the road and surrounded by the quiet shade of huge old oak trees, it was Normandy styled, with a peaked roof and leaded windows. Dark beams crossed the white plaster walls, and brick walkways threaded through a wild English garden that was bordered by a rolling expanse of green lawns.

Catherine parked her car in the driveway and walked up the steps to the entrance. A handsome, elderly black man wearing a white jacket that was matched by the woolly cap of his hair opened the door at her ring and ushered her through the house and out onto a flagstone terrace.

Eric was sitting with John and Margaret at a glass-topped white wrought-iron table. In a high chair placed between his grandparents,

David was waving a spoon wildly in the air, laughing with childish glee.

"Cathy!" Eric cried, jumping up and coming to her. "We were afraid you had gotten lost." He put his arm around her and led her to the table.

"I did, just a little," she said. "Main Line roads still confuse me." She turned to the Bradfords. "Mr. Bradford, it's nice to see you again. And Mrs. Bradford—Eric has told me so much about you."

Margaret smiled at her cordially. "Do sit down, my dear. We were just about to have some iced tea. The heat has been killing, hasn't it?"

Another white-jacketed servant appeared as if on cue, wheeling a tea cart of glasses, a tall pitcher of tea, and an assortment of ornate pastries on small glass plates.

"Is the timing always so perfect here?" Catherine murmured to Eric.

"Shhh," Eric said under his breath. "This is gracious living on the Main Line. Remember *Philadelphia Story?*"

"Oh, yes. I felt a little like Katharine Hepburn just by walking into the house."

"Dr. Marlowe," Margaret said, "Eric has spoken of you so highly, and you handled yourself just beautifully on his show."

"We really should have Catherine back," John said. "Let her talk more about her work. There's a lot of interest in— What do you call it—psi?"

"Thank you, but at the moment I'd much rather talk about David. He's a beautiful child."

"I can't tell you how we feel, having him home again. It's like a miracle, finding him after all this time," Margaret said, smiling at the little boy.

"It is a miracle," Eric said, glancing at Catherine out of the corner of his eye.

"And he's in perfect health," Margaret went on. "The Harkins obviously took very good care of him. I've written them a letter expressing my gratitude."

Catherine smiled and nodded, wondering what Seth and Nancy Harkin would think if they saw the child they had so adored sitting here, now probably an heir to a fortune, being cared for by this chic, graceful woman in her flowery summer dress and light sprinkling of diamonds.

John spoke up, adding: "I had my attorney draw up a letter offering them remuneration for their care of David." He sighed and his voice filled with emotion as he went on: "There's no way to set a value on a child, or repay them for the heartache they've been through. But I hope they accept my offer of fifty thousand dollars. And I also said I'd do whatever possible to help expedite the adoption of another child."

"That's very generous of you, Mr. Bradford," Catherine said sincerely.

"Oh, please, you must call us John and Margaret. We really feel as if we know you very well, Eric has talked about you so."

Margaret smiled in agreement. "And may we call you Catherine? Ever since the show, we've gathered that Eric has seen a great deal of you. And I must say, I don't blame him. You're lovely, my dear."

Catherine's teeth began to ache at the woman's effusiveness. Eric had told her how kind they had been to him, their consideration during his illness and their efforts to help him afterward. She genuinely liked John, but suspected that Margaret was getting concerned about Eric's feelings for her.

"Having Eric stay with us has been so wonderful," Margaret said. "Watching him play with David, and just being here, well—we're a family again. But I do hope we haven't been taking him away from you too much."

Suspicion confirmed and on target, Catherine thought to herself. Aloud, she said: "I think it's perfect that David is here with you. This is a lovely place for a child to grow up in. As for Eric and myself—" she caught a warning glance from him, and finished smoothly "—we've found time to see each other."

John made harrumphing noises and said: "Margaret, why don't we go inside and let Eric show Catherine the grounds? This heat is beginning to get to me."

"Of course, dear," Margaret said. She reached to pick up David.

"Leave David with us, Margaret," Eric said. "We'll take him for a little walk."

"Well, all right—but don't keep him out too long, dear. He's due for his nap soon."

John took her arm and muttered: "Stop fussing, Maggie . . ." as they walked into the house.

Catherine let out a deep breath as soon as they were gone. "Christ, I feel like I've just played a scene out of a forties movie!"

Eric laughed. "That's where Margaret lives—graciously, of course. She'll be easier to take once she gets to know you."

He stood up and swung David out of his high chair, settling him comfortably in his arms. The little blue-eyed boy held on to his spoon and waved it around, hitting Eric on the nose.

"Hey! No fair," Eric cried, kissing him. "I'm your daddy!"

Catherine smiled as they started to walk. "How does it feel, being a father again?"

"I love it. He's a big boy, isn't he? And he can talk, too!"

"Really?" She laughed. "Intelligently, I hope."

"Sure! He says 'no' and 'yes' and 'I want' and best of all—'dada.'"

"Positively brilliant!"

They strolled through the garden of brightly colored wild flowers and dark-green shrubs, following a path that curved out to the wide expanse of lawns. Eric put David down and let him toddle off into the grass, watching him proudly.

"It's nice seeing you like this, so paternal and loving," Catherine said, taking his arm. "And so relaxed! I've been so used to seeing you on the edge of a breakdown, I'll have to get to know you all over again."

"And won't that be fun," Eric said, taking her in his arms and kissing her.

Catherine pressed herself to him and felt his hands slip down her back to her hips, his lips and tongue teasing her until she pulled away to catch her breath.

"Is there a haystack nearby? You're making me feel very bucolic," she sighed.

"Just a peasant wench at heart," Eric said, smiling.

"Your son is watching every move we make," Catherine said, looking over his shoulder.

"Obviously he's a chip off the old block. I used to watch too when I was his age."

"Oh? Who?"

"Never mind. Let's walk—there's a gazebo over there behind the trees, with an old-fashioned glider swing."

He picked David up and planted him on his shoulders. "No kicking and no pulling hair!" he warned him.

David laughed, grabbed a chunk of Eric's hair in each hand, and swung his little legs wildly.

"That's what I like," Eric muttered over Catherine's laughter, "a kid who listens!"

A few minutes later, with David getting sleepy in his father's lap, Eric and Catherine sat, moving the swing slowly back and forth. A soft breeze stirred through the treetops, warm and sultry, offering no relief from the penetrating heat of the afternoon. Catherine touched a handkerchief to her brow and patted her throat.

"I think we're in for one of those deadly summers," she murmured.

"It's the happiest summer I've known for years," Eric said.

"I can see that." She smiled at him. Then, after a moment's silence, she asked: "Eric, what are you going to do now?"

"You mean now that my obsession is over, now that my main goal in life has been accomplished?" he said with a smile.

"You're getting good at reading my mind," she said. "I'll have to be very careful with you."

"Don't be careful with me. I like you just the way you are, with no pretenses, no being careful, just being you."

Catherine leaned over and kissed him softly. "I may read that back to you at a future date, like the fine print in a contract."

"Speaking of contracts, do you consider a marriage license binding?"

She stared at him, taken by surprise for a moment, before answering: "Only after the ceremony has been performed."

He nodded his head solemnly. "A small point, but well taken. How do you feel about ready-made families?"

"Only if it's a boy about two years old with a penchant for pulling his father's hair. Are you asking me to marry you?"

He looked at her with mock surprise. "I thought I did that just a minute ago."

"I thought you did, too—I just wasn't sure. . . ."

"Well, be sure." Eric's voice dropped and his manner was suddenly serious. "Is the idea too surprising? You know how I feel about you."

"Yes, darling, of course I do. I guess I'm just more concerned with how you feel about yourself right now." He made a face and she laughed. "Am I sounding a lot like a psychology professor? Sorry. But it's true, Eric. I am concerned. Your whole life has been focused on finding your son. It's all you thought about, dreamed about—and now you have him. It's bound to be a bit anticlimactic for you. Sure you don't want to marry me just to fill the void? It would give you a whole new set of things to think about, worry about."

"Hey, will you stop for a minute?" Eric shifted the sleeping child in his arms and faced her. "Okay, most of what you say is true. I have been thinking a lot about my life. David means the world to me, but he can't ever *be* my world, I know that. But the three of us could make a small world together until he grows up and makes one of his own. Then there would be the two of us, and I think we could manage to get along, somehow, don't you?"

Catherine couldn't keep from smiling at his earnest, almost angry declaration. "I love it when you talk in paragraphs," she said. "You get so impassioned."

"Oh, woman, for Christ's sake, will you marry me?"

"Darling, of course I will," she replied laughing.

"Thank God that's settled. Kiss me."

She did, long and lovingly.

"Thank you. I'll pick up on that kiss when I go home with you tonight," he said with a lecherous wink.

"And what will John and Margaret say about your going home with me?"

"Nothing. They'll still be reeling from the news of our impending union."

"Eric, seriously, do you think they'll mind? After what they've been through, and just getting David back—let's wait to tell them. Besides, I've never been engaged."

"An old-fashioned girl, huh? I'll bet you want a ring and everything, candlelight dinners, hand-holding . . ."

"You can skip the hand-holding." She laughed. "But do let's wait to tell anyone, all right?"

"Whatever you want is all right with me. I'm feeling very benevolent these days."

Catherine kissed him again, careful not to disturb the sleeping child in his lap. Then she sat back and laughed lightly.

"I'm a little breathless!" she sighed happily.

"Good! I'll do my best to keep you that way." Eric smiled. He looked down at his son and touched a fingertip to the fine curly hair.

Catherine knew he was thinking of Jenny, but remained silent. She and Eric would have a lifetime together, and through his son, Jenny would always be part of it. That was as it should be and she could accept it.

"We'd better get back and put him to bed or Margaret will have my scalp," Eric said, standing up. "Shall we stay for dinner or go into town?"

"Let's stay. I'll have to start getting to know John and Margaret and I want them to like me."

As they walked toward the house Eric seemed preoccupied. Finally he turned to Catherine and asked: "What's going to happen to Chris? He's done so much for me that anything I do hardly seems enough to repay him."

"We haven't really talked since we came back from Omaha. His mother called and wanted to know if our sessions were over, if I was going to do any more tests. She told me he's been very upset— moody and restless."

"I wish I could help him. With his gifts there's so much he could do. I must admit it's been very difficult not to tell anyone what he did for me. He's a wonderful kid, and it seems unfair to keep him under wraps like this."

"I know how you feel. But in a way, I think Mrs. McKenzie is right. We both know what would happen if anyone ever found out about his capabilities. Can't you just see what the public response would be?"

"That's true, of course. But if there was some way to manage him, control the use of his powers. Besides being able to help people, why —he could make a fortune."

Catherine looked at him with surprise, then smiled. "You show biz folk are all alike—can't resist the idea of promoting a talent, no matter what it is."

"No, I mean it, Cathy," Eric said seriously. "It just doesn't seem right to let him waste away doing something menial when he could be—"

"Be what?" Catherine asked sharply. "Eric, what are you thinking?"

The tone of her voice made him hesitate. He knew how deeply she felt about her promise to protect Christopher from exploitation. And she was probably right. Any revelation of what he had done, what he could do, would bring the whole country into their back yards.

"Don't look so worried," he said lightly. "It's just the old agency man in me thinking out loud. I wouldn't do anything to hurt Chris. You know that."

The look of concern in Catherine's eyes faded. She took his arm and pressed it against her side. "I know. I'm as worried about him as you are. But we have to be careful. He's young and impressionable—and a little overcome by what he's done. But after all, he's only twenty-one years old. There's enough time to guide him through this period in his life and help him make plans for his future."

Eric nodded in agreement, but the thought of Christopher and his powers settled into the back of his mind like fine dust in a hidden corner, present but unseen.

24

August heat descended on the city like an act of retribution. A cruel sun burned relentlessly through the days, leaving an oven warmth to stifle the nights. Humidity rose with the dawn, and by midday the streets were sweltering. People grew unnaturally lethargic, eyes burning from glare and throats choked by the heavy layer of pollution from factory smoke and auto exhausts. The elderly went about with handkerchiefs over their mouths or sat on benches holding newspapers to shade their heads. Children's faces looked middle-aged and weary, and infants cried fretfully.

Catherine took her second shower of the day, even though it was only midafternoon. The air conditioning in her apartment had, with inevitable timing, gone on the fritz. It was Friday, which meant getting a repair man was like trying to find your doctor on a weekend.

Drying herself quickly, she began to get dressed. Chris had called and insisted on coming to see her, saying that he had to talk with her about something very important. She tried to put him off, too enervated by the heat for a visit. But the urgency in his voice made her acquiesce.

The doorbell rang as she was brushing her hair. It was Chris.

"Sorry to bust in on you like this, but I really had to see you," he said as they went into the living room. His white T-shirt clung damply to the muscles across his broad back and sweat poured in rivulets down his tanned neck.

"You need a towel and some ice water," Catherine said, smiling. "Sit down and relax. It's the only way to survive in this kind of heat."

"It's even worse out on the Main Line," Chris said. "I had to quit working in the Stanwyck gardens; the mosquitoes were making breakfast, lunch, and dinner out of me."

Catherine came out of the kitchen with a pitcher of ice water, some glasses, and a hand towel. "Here, this may help," she said, putting everything down on the coffee table.

Chris took an ice cube and ran it over his face and throat, then patted himself dry with the towel. His eyes were bloodshot from the foul air, and his thick blond hair lay limp and matted. Lines of anxiety creased his face, and he sat on the edge of his chair, tense and agitated.

"Chris, what's the matter?" Catherine asked. "You look awful, and not just from the heat."

"Something's happened to me," he said nervously. "Something I didn't expect. . . ."

"Well, why don't you just take it easy and tell me about it. Maybe I can help."

He looked up at her with an expression of anguish. "I'm in love," he said softly.

Catherine began to laugh and then stopped herself, seeing the pain in his face. "But that's wonderful. Who's the lucky girl?"

"Nella Stanwyck. We've known each other since we were kids. We were always very close, playmates at first, then good friends. About a year ago, she went to Switzerland to go to school. We wrote to each other, a lot, at first, then just occasionally." He faltered in his rush of words and then went on hesitantly: "I—I met a few other girls, but I always thought about her. I mean, I didn't forget her just because she was away."

He stopped and sipped some water while Catherine watched him, amused. "So—what happened?" she asked gently.

"Nella came home while we were in Omaha. I went to see her as soon as we got back, and—it happened, just like that. I mean, she was suddenly more beautiful than I remembered, and wonderful—"

"But, Chris, I don't understand. Why are you so upset?"

He sat up and clasped his large hands, squeezing his fingers together tightly. "Because she's crippled. She's been crippled since she was five years old," he answered in a harsh voice.

Catherine was silent as she realized what he was telling her. She stood up and walked to the windows, trying to think of what to say to him.

"Had you thought about healing her before, when you were children?" she asked, finally turning to him.

"I didn't know about it—my power to heal—until I was fifteen. Remember, I told you about it?"

"Oh, yes—the night of the incident with that boy in school. That was when your mother told you. Nella was the little girl in the house you first lived in when you came to this country. Yes, I remember now."

"Well, after that, Mom was so afraid for me that I didn't do anything. There were a lot of times when I thought about it—"

"But she was afraid of what people would think, what they would say," Catherine interrupted.

"Yes—she was always afraid," Chris replied bitterly.

"But, Chris, surely you understand that that same situation exists now. So many people know Nella, know that her condition has been called incurable."

"But I did it for Miss Howard," he flared angrily. "And I don't care what people think! I only care about Nella."

"I can understand that, but there are problems that have to be faced," Catherine said. "We don't know how seriously Amanda was injured. We'll never know to what extent you really healed her."

"But couldn't I try?" he pleaded. "You saw what happened in the lab with the rabbit."

Catherine went over to him and sat down. "Yes, I saw what happened. But that was a rabbit. Suppose it didn't work with Nella? Suppose that in some way you hurt her? We don't know all the ramifications of your power to heal. It might be dangerous, can't you see that?"

Just then the phone rang. Catherine picked it up, irritated at the jarring interruption.

"Hello? . . . Yes, this is Dr. Marlowe. . . . Oh, Mr. Deardon, how are you? . . . Yes. . . . You did? Oh, good! . . . You mean now? . . . Oh, I see. Yes, I'll come right over. See you in a few minutes."

She hung up and said to Chris: "That was Sam Deardon; he's a friend of mine and a book dealer. He just received a monograph I've been waiting for from England. I have to go pick it up. He's taking off for a month's vacation tomorrow morning."

Chris stood up to leave, but Catherine stopped him. "Why don't you come with me? We can talk in the car, and we'll be more comfortable. It's got air conditioning."

In the car, Chris countered Catherine's argument. "I don't understand why I can't try to help Nella. If I hadn't tried to sight Eric's son, he'd never have found him. And when I saw Miss Howard lying in her wrecked car, all I thought was 'that woman is going to die if you don't do something!' I didn't stop to worry if it was right or wrong, I just did it! I help people I don't even know, and I can't do anything for someone I love."

"Chris, I'm not trying to tell you what you should or shouldn't do. I'm just asking you to consider the consequences of such an act. How could it be explained if it were successful?"

"Why couldn't it be kept a secret? Eric managed it. Maybe we could take her out of the country. Charlotte Stanwyck is rich; she could always say she found some fantastic doctor in South America or someplace. Hell, I don't care! I just want to do it for Nella."

Catherine turned off the expressway and into a business district a few miles south of Center City. A heavy pall lay over the streets, darkening the air, as if a storm threatened to break at any moment. Catherine pulled the car into a parking space in front of the dusty window of a book store.

"Stay in the car and keep cool. I'll only be a minute," she told Chris.

He slumped in the seat and watched her disappear into the store. Anger and depression settled over him, and he stared out the window glumly. When she got back in the car, Catherine looked at him and smiled.

"Hey, it's not that bad. Why don't you stay and have dinner with me instead of driving back this afternoon? Eric is coming over, and maybe between the three of us we can come up with some answers."

"Sure—okay," Chris replied dully.

It was almost four thirty by the time they got back on the expressway. Traffic had increased, and in the scorching late-afternoon heat, cars began to stall. Drivers leaned on their horns or opened windows to call out, swearing hoarsely at the delay.

"Christ, I hate creeping along like this," Catherine said. "I'll have to turn off the air conditioning, otherwise we'll overheat and join that army of stalled cars."

They rolled down their windows, choking slightly from the fumes.

"Maybe we'd do better to get off at the next ramp and take—"

Suddenly a thunderous explosion split the air.

"My God, what was that?" Catherine exclaimed.

A pillar of black smoke rose from a two-story building a few hundred yards off the expressway. Another violent explosion followed within seconds of the first.

Chris leaned out the window as brakes were slammed and traffic came to a standstill. "That building is on fire!" he cried out.

"Oh, Jesus, there are oil refineries all over this area!" Catherine said anxiously.

Traffic began to move cautiously, then stopped again at the sound of fire-truck sirens.

"What's happening?" Catherine asked Chris. "The fire engines can't get through this mess!"

"They're coming in from the other side, on surface streets," Chris answered.

Several people got out of their cars and ran to the low wire fence at the edge of the expressway to see what was happening. Chris leaned farther out the window and called to one of them: "What is it? What is that place?"

"A chemical and dye plant!" one of the men yelled back.

Fire burst out of the windows, engulfing the entire structure in a spectacular display of multicolored flames from the burning chemicals. Through the haze and smoke, people could be seen staggering out of doorways, gasping and choking. A single figure, on fire, leaped from an upper window, jerking like a crazed puppet as it hit the ground.

Traffic had begun to move slowly again when Chris abruptly opened the door and jumped out of the car.

Startled, Catherine hit the brakes and yelled: "What are you doing?"

"I'm going to help!" Chris cried.

"Chris! For God's sake, don't! Come back!" Catherine shouted over blaring horns.

"I know what I'm doing!" Chris called as he darted through the line of slow-moving cars. He reached the wire fence and climbed over it, then began to run toward the burning building.

Catherine forced her way through the paralyzed traffic and finally got off the expressway a quarter of a mile past the site of the explosion. The street at the bottom of the off ramp was blocked with police cars, and an officer was pointing traffic away from the yard surrounding the burning plant. She parked the car and hurried toward an open field that led to the disaster area.

"You can't go through there, lady!" the officer yelled.

"I'm a doctor!" Catherine shouted back and began to run.

The air grew thick and her eyes started to burn as she struggled over the rough ground. The entire area alongside the Schuylkill Expressway was a series of yards enclosing pastel-colored storage tanks, refinery pipes, and gas flaming towers. Through tear-blurred eyes, the landscape appeared surreal, familiar shapes melting into nightmarish forms. Giant pieces of machinery, trucks, loaders, and cranes stood abandoned in mid-operation. Black smokestacks emitted streams of yellowish-gray fog, and electrical towers stood like skeletal giants with arms outstretched.

The heat grew more intense, and billows of smoke darkened the sky overhead. Catherine saw that her way was barred by tanks and storage sheds. Then she spotted a scattering of workmen and ran up to one.

"How do I get through?" she cried, gasping hoarsely from the foul air and smoke. "I'm a doctor."

"There's a road just past those tanks. It'll take you straight into the yard," the man said. "But be careful, miss. This whole area could go up any minute!"

Catherine ran on, her lungs bursting, arms and face covered with streaks of drifting soot. Once on the road, she was slowed by crowds of onlookers and policemen. She pushed her way into the yard and followed a procession of ambulances to the center of the chaotic scene. The air was filled with the screams of sirens and the cries of people. Paramedics rushed to aid victims while firemen, their uniforms charred with ash, turned hoses on the flames. Ambulance attendants lifted and carried stretchers of wounded as doctors administered to the burned and bruised.

In the midst of the turmoil Catherine saw Christopher kneeling by a group of people who had been stretched out on the ground. His hands moved rapidly over their chests, arms, and legs, then he rose and ran to another victim being brought out of the burning building.

Catherine shoved past the crowds, trying to reach him, but was held back by a line of firemen. She ran past them and around a truck and came up a few yards behind Chris. Stopping to catch her breath, she watched, dumbfounded, as men coughing from smoke inhalation became quiet when he touched their throats, bleeding stopped under his fingers, and wounds and bruises disappeared. The people he touched struggled to sit up, rose to their feet and looked about, stunned to find themselves without pain.

Chris ran from stretcher to stretcher, touching smoke-blinded eyes and torn limbs. His body seemed to glow with an extraordinary light, a visible outpouring of energy. At one point, he stopped and reeled dizzily.

Catherine started forward and screamed: "Chris! Chris, stop!"

He straightened up and searched the ring of people who had begun to gather around him. When he saw her, he shouted: "I can't! I have to finish what I started!"

His eyes were burning with an iridescent fervor, and his face was set in an expression of intense concentration. He had finally made a choice of his own.

At that moment local TV vans drove into the area, spilling cameramen with portable cameras on their shoulders and newsmen with battery-pack microphones. One of the paramedics was stopped, and he began to talk quickly gesturing toward Christopher. The newsman frowned in disbelief, then another medic joined them and described what he had seen. Within minutes the word spread among the newscasters, and they started to converge on the group of people milling around Chris. A path was cleared, and cameramen began filming what was taking place. An excited commentator led the way, his voice incredulous as he described the scene: "Something almost beyond belief is happening here; a young, unidentified man is healing the burned and wounded with his hands!"

He pushed past an ambulance attendant and knelt by a stretcher where an injured man was sitting up.

"Sir, can you tell us what happened?" the reporter asked.

The man touched his face and arms gingerly, his eyes staring in astonishment. "I don't know. I don't understand . . ."

"The young man who was with you a minute ago— What did he do?"

"I fell . . . the explosion knocked the wind out of me. I got burned trying to get out; then I must have passed out. The next thing, I see this kid and he's touching my face. His hands were hot, hotter than the fire; but when he took them away, the pain was gone!"

He lay back on the stretcher, and the attendants picked him up and put him into an ambulance while the newscaster scanned the crowd to find Chris. He finally saw him and beckoned to a cameraman to follow as he shoved his way to the boy's side.

Chris was holding a middle-aged woman in his arms, covering a gaping wound in her head with one hand. In moments it stopped bleeding. He moved his hand swiftly down her body to where her leg lay bent at a grotesque angle. Gently, he touched it, then firmly straightened it out. She screamed once, then her face cleared of pain, and she opened her eyes, lids fluttering to focus.

"Oh, God," she whispered tearfully, "thank you—thank you."

The newscaster was speechless. He turned dumbly to the cameraman, who nodded and muttered: "If what I saw really happened, I've got it all on film!"

Christopher picked the woman up and carried her to an ambulance, followed by the two men, trying to ignore the newsman's excited questions. Catherine finally managed to reach him just as the reporter was insisting: "Will you tell us your name? Who are you?"

Chris handed the woman over to a waiting attendant and turned to the reporter. His face was white, drawn with exhaustion and smeared with sweat and soot. His eyes glowed feverishly, and his body was trembling from strain. He saw Catherine watching him with a frightened expression as the reporter asked him once more: "Who are you? What's your name?"

Catherine shook her head quickly, motioning him not to answer. He gave her a helpless smile, as if to reassure her that he knew what he was doing and was not afraid.

"My name is Christopher McKenzie," he replied to the man. "I saw the explosion from the expressway and ran over to . . ."

Before he could finish speaking, a surprised look came over his face and he staggered slightly.

Catherine pushed past the newsman and cried: "Chris! Are you all right?"

He started toward her, his arms outstretched, when abruptly his knees buckled and his body crumpled slowly to the ground.

25

As the ambulance raced through the city streets, Catherine crouched beside Chris, watching anxiously while the attendant gave him oxygen until he revived. She leaned close and whispered: "Chris, I'm here. You're all right now."

He smiled weakly. "I did it, didn't I?" he asked. "I healed—"

"Yes, dear, you did. Now rest—"

"I proved I could do it," he sighed, closing his eyes. "Now I can heal Nella."

At the hospital, Catherine followed as Chris was wheeled into the emergency room. Around them were the fire victims. Some were sitting up on their stretchers, and others were standing, waiting to be released. She heard one doctor say: "What the hell is going on here? Most of these people aren't even hurt!"

"I don't understand it," another said, shaking his head in confusion. "There are a few cases of mild shock and some bruises, but no serious injuries!"

While Chris was being examined, Catherine called Eric at the studio and quickly explained what had happened.

"Oh Christ!" he exclaimed. "We've got to get him out of there. Reporters will be crawling all over the hospital within minutes! Don't let anyone near him. I'll be right there!"

"Eric, call Mrs. McKenzie first. She may have heard about it on the radio."

Twenty minutes later she saw Eric coming down the corridor and ran to his arms. He held her tightly as she cried with relief.

"Cathy, listen to me," Eric said firmly. "Mrs. McKenzie called the woman Chris works for, Charlotte Stanwyck, as soon as she heard the news on the radio. Mrs. Stanwyck sent a car for her and they're coming here. I told them to stay in the car at the back of the hospital until I came for them. Is Chris well enough to be moved?"

"I think so. The doctor said he was suffering from exhaustion, that all he needed was rest. He pushed himself to heal, Eric; I saw it. He used all of his energy. He wanted to prove that he could do it, to make me believe in his power."

"The important thing is to get him out of here before the story hits the evening news on television and every patient in the hospital is knocking down his door!"

They found Chris's doctor talking with one of the floor nurses, and after a hasty conference, he agreed that Chris could leave, and that he would help them take him out the back entrance.

"I don't know what it is that boy can do," the doctor said as they hurried to Chris's room, "but if what I've heard is true, there are going to be a lot of questions and damned few answers." He turned to Catherine, his eyes worried. "You were there? You saw it?"

"Yes—I saw it," she answered quietly.

"Christ, how did he do it? No—don't tell me. I probably wouldn't believe it, even if I knew. Let's just get him out of here, fast, before the whole building goes crazy."

Chris was groggy but awake when they entered his room. Eric and Catherine wrapped him in a light blanket while the doctor had a nurse bring a wheelchair. A few minutes later they were at the service entrance just as the Stanwyck limousine drove into the parking lot.

That night the story was featured as a local Special Report on television, preempting a half-hour comedy show. The dark-haired, usually exuberant anchor man forced his blunt features into a semblance of seriousness and reported on the explosion and fire.

"At four thirty-five this afternoon, the Ridgeway Chemical and Dye plant in South Philadelphia was ripped by two explosions, said to have been caused by escaping gas and a defective unit in the processing equipment. Fire units responded to the four-alarm fire that followed the explosions. . . ."

His voice continued over helicopter views of the fire, showing the burning building and then efforts of firemen and paramedics to help victims of the disaster. At that point the ground-crew cameramen had picked up Chris's figure running from stretcher to stretcher.

". . . and this, ladies and gentlemen, is where tonight's story takes an extraordinary turn," the newsman went on. "While doctors and paramedics administered to the injured, a young man was seen going from one burned and bleeding person to another, apparently healing them with the touch of his hands."

Now the film, jumpy and at times out of focus, began to narrow in on Christopher, with zoom close-ups of him stopping the flow of blood from severe wounds, restoring badly burned limbs and faces. Around him was clearly registered the stunned disbelief of attending doctors and paramedics.

". . . reporter Jim Sprauge and cameraman Bill Dean are to be credited with the astonishing film record of this strange event," the anchor man continued. "They were finally able to question the young man . . ."

The segment went on, showing a close-up of Chris as the reporter, Jim Sprauge, was asking his name and Chris answered: "My name is Christopher McKenzie. I saw the explosion from the expressway and ran over to . . ."

The film showed Chris's startled look and his collapse, then blacked out. The anchor man once more appeared on the screen.

"At that point, the young man collapsed. He was taken to General Hospital and was subsequently released. We talked with several of the survivors of the fire who had been treated by McKenzie . . ."

Two interviews were shown, and several paramedics were questioned about what had taken place. All of them expressed their shock and confusion over what they had witnessed. The woman whose broken leg Chris had healed was weeping, saying over and over: "It was a miracle. He just touched me and took away the pain! It was a miracle. . . ."

The anchor man turned from the monitor behind him and faced the TV audience, his face solemn, his voice dramatically hushed.

"The whereabouts of Christopher McKenzie is, for the moment, unknown. But we have with us in the studio Dr. Gerhard Hauser of the staff at General Hospital. Dr. Hauser was an eyewitness to the so-called healings, and examined many of the victims after they had been touched by young McKenzie."

The camera pulled away to reveal a middle-aged man sitting beside the commentator. He looked uncomfortable as he was asked: "In your opinion, Doctor, did this young man actually heal these people?"

Hauser replied gravely. "We cannot answer that question. What we can say is that many injuries were significantly relieved by Mr. McKenzie."

"But how is that possible, sir? Can you offer any explanation of what caused those burns and injuries to disappear?"

Dr. Hauser shifted in his chair and offered another evasive reply: "Such explanations would, at this time, be entirely conjectural." He hesitated, searching for words. "Hysteria and hallucination quite often play a large part in what we think of as 'healings,' however—"

"But, Doctor, we've just seen proof of this amazing young man's gift," the anchor man reminded him soberly.

"Yes. Well, it is my hope that the young man will come forward to be examined, tested by—"

Eric leaned forward and switched off the television set. He turned to the others and said: "That's it. Now everybody knows."

For a few minutes there was silence in the Stanwyck library. Charlotte sat close to Susan, her face a study in astonishment, her eyes still focused on the now-silent TV set.

Susan turned to Catherine, sitting across from her. "I know that you aren't responsible for any of this, Dr. Marlowe."

"If I could have done anything to prevent it, Mrs. McKenzie, I would have."

"I know that. If anyone is to blame, it's myself, for trying so hard and for so long to make myself believe that this would never happen."

Charlotte faced Catherine and said: "I must admit, Dr. Marlowe, that when Susan confided to me, on the way to the hospital, what has been happening, I didn't know what to think. And I was very skeptical when you told me earlier this evening about your tests with Chris. But now, with these films—" she paused, as if seeing them again in her mind, before finishing "—I believe completely in Christopher's extraordinary gifts."

Eric looked at her and said: "I'm glad to hear that, Mrs. Stanwyck, because we need your help."

"Mr. Wynters—may I call you Eric? You probably don't remember, but I was a guest at your wedding. Margaret Bradford and I have been friends for a long time, and I knew Jenny."

"I do remember, Mrs. Stanwyck," Eric said. "You were a great comfort to my mother-in-law after Jenny's death."

"And I shall do whatever I can to help now." Charlotte put her arm around Susan's shoulders. "I brought Susan and Chris to this country, to my home. They are like family to me. Tell me how I can help you."

"I think Chris and Mrs. McKenzie should stay here for a few days, perhaps longer," Eric said. "By now reporters have undoubtedly checked at the hospital and have their home address."

"Oh, God, I didn't even think of that when I signed him in!" Catherine exclaimed.

"Well, I'm sure they did. But no one knows he's here, and we have the weekend to figure something out before they get to us."

"Chris and Susan can stay with me as long as they like," Charlotte said.

The phone rang and she went to answer it. "Yes? . . . Oh, hello Margaret. . . . Yes, I did see the news report. . . . Yes, it was quite astonishing. . . . No, I had no idea. . . ."

Charlotte glanced at Eric, silently asking him what to say. He motioned that he would talk with Margaret.

"Margaret, could you hold on for a moment?" She handed the phone to Eric.

"Margaret, it's Eric. . . . No. Listen, get John on the extension and I'll talk with both of you. . . ."

He carried the phone to a corner of the room, his voice a low murmur as he began to explain what had happened.

Mrs. Gregory came in with a service of coffee and a report on Christopher.

"He's sound asleep, and Nella is right there by his side, watching over him like a nurse."

"Oh, that's good," Charlotte said. "When he wakes up, she can ring for some supper for him."

The cook's face was drawn up in a puzzled frown. "Mrs. Stanwyck, I don't understand. I just saw the news program, and our Chris, healing all those people. What does it mean?"

Susan went to her. "I'll come into the kitchen later, dear, and tell you about it. We'll talk over a cup of tea, like we used to."

"But is he all right?"

"Yes, he's fine—just tired," Susan replied, walking her to the door.

When the elderly woman had left the room, Susan turned back to the others. Charlotte was talking with Catherine, and Eric was still on the phone. She looked around the library and thought of that night, so many years ago, when Chris had stood in the doorway, his eyes blazing with anger. And then his gentle child's touch on her bruised mouth. So much had happened, so many things had changed. She walked to the windows and stared out into the night. Then she saw her reflection in the glass, made visible by the lamplight behind her. For a moment she thought she was seeing someone else, a face darkly shadowed, creased with lines of anxiety, tense from sleepless nights, worn from years of fear. She sighed bitterly, aware that this was herself, the result of twenty years of sacrifice, rendered meaningless by the events of a single afternoon.

Charlotte approached her with a cup of coffee, and she took it gratefully.

"You shouldn't have carried this burden alone all these years," Charlotte said gently.

"I know that now," Susan replied. "I did what I thought was right for Chris."

"Of course you did, dear. And whatever happens, I shall see you through it, you know that, don't you?"

Susan nodded and grew tearful. "Oh, Charlotte, there's so much I have to tell you—that I've not told anyone. . . ." She began to cry, letting the pent-up strain of the day be released in a flood of tears.

A few minutes later Eric hung up the phone and announced: "A few developments I hadn't expected have come up. Seems that I was recognized in the hospital, and John has been getting calls asking what my connection is with Chris. He's been fending off the press with whatever excuse he could think of."

"Did you tell him about Chris finding David?" Catherine asked.

"I had to. There can't be any more secrets among us now. He and Margaret are in a small state of shock, but I told them we'd come out tomorrow and explain the whole thing to them."

He took Catherine's hand. "You must be exhausted. I'll take you home. I think we've all had as much as we can handle tonight."

As Catherine prepared to leave, Eric said to Charlotte and Susan: "We'll stop by on our way to Margaret and John's tomorrow and see how Chris is doing."

"Mr. Wynters, thank you for all you help," Susan said.

He smiled at her. "Please, call me Eric. We've just been through a lot together, and I have a feeling there's more to come."

He kissed her cheek, and she said shyly: "It's a lovely man you are, Eric."

Catherine took his arm and smiled. "I agree. I don't know what we would have done without him."

There occurred among the four of them one of those rare moments of warmth and friendship, the intimacy of a common bond. Susan felt suddenly stronger than she had in years, knowing that she was no longer alone with her fears for Christopher's welfare. There were friends here who cared for him as she did.

As Catherine and Eric began to leave, Charlotte asked: "Dr. Marlowe, there's one thing I don't understand. Why did Chris do it? Why did he make a public demonstration of his power instead of continuing to work in secrecy with you?"

Catherine looked at the poised, attractive woman standing so securely in the solid comfort of her home, so generously offering her help. She hesitated for a moment, took a long, deep breath, and answered: "He did it this way to prove he could heal. Prove it to you, I think."

"To me?" Charlotte questioned. Then the realization of what Catherine meant struck her. She gave a low, almost inaudible gasp.

Catherine nodded her head and said: "Yes, it's exactly what you're thinking. Christopher wants to heal Nella."

In the guest room at the end of the gallery on the second floor, Nella reached from her chair and turned off the small television set as the Special Report on the explosion and Chris's part in it ended. She leaned back and stared at the boy lying asleep in front of her. The low light of the night-table lamp traced fine lines over the tousled spread of his blond hair on the pillow. Deep shadows covered the wide set of his eyes and hollowed the strong bones in his face and jaw. Her eyes moved slowly over his features, as if seeing him for the first time: the straight line of his nose, ending in small, delicate nostrils, and the full, shapely curve of his lips, the color of dark-red wine in this half-light. Under the light covering of a sheet, she saw the shape of his body, long and powerfully muscled from all his work outdoors. His hands lay by his side, and her eyes rested on them, studied them almost as something apart from the rest of him. They are beautiful hands, she thought, as beautiful as he is. For a moment she was stirred to tears, remembering what she had just seen: his hands moving, touching burned flesh and torn bodies, healing. And she thought of their childhood, the hours they had spent together, the stories and legends he had filled her days with. She could see those children in her mind, the ruddy-faced, golden-haired little boy with the thick accent, and herself, pale and thin, swinging alongside him through the grass on her crutches.

Chris sighed in his sleep and then opened his eyes and saw her. They looked at each other for a long time before he spoke.

"You know, don't you?" he asked in a whisper.

"Yes, I know," she answered quietly.

He half sat up and reached out to take her hand. Instinctively, without thinking why, she drew back for a second, then tentatively touched his fingers, feeling them beneath hers before slipping her hand into his.

"Are you frightened of me now? Does it make that much difference?" he asked, his eyes searching hers anxiously.

"It makes a difference," she admitted. "I still don't know quite how. I was just thinking of the stories you used to tell me, and now—"

"Now you think of me as—as something freakish, someone strange, like in the legends."

"Oh, no, Chris—no!" She leaned forward and took his arm to help slip herself from the chair to his side on the bed. He lay back on the pillow, staring up at her.

"I did it for you. You know that, don't you? I was afraid, before, to say anything, do anything. I wasn't really sure, and my mother was so frightened that I might hurt someone in some way."

"I know, Chris, I know," Nella murmured. "As soon as I heard about it, I realized what it meant. I knew why you had done it; I knew that it was for me."

Tears filled her eyes, and with a cry, she threw herself into his arms, her face pressed tightly to his. His lips touched her throat, her cheek, and she turned her head to feel his lips cover hers.

"Will you let me do it?" he asked, pulling away from her. "Will you let me try to heal you?"

Nella hesitated. "Chris, I don't know. I'm a little frightened. . . ."

He put her head against his chest and stroked her hair. "I love you, you know that," he said huskily.

"Yes, and I love you too," she answered.

"It makes no difference to me, your being crippled," he said. "I love you the way you are. It's for you that I want to do it."

She sat up and looked at him, her eyes shining. "Do you mean that? It makes no difference to you? You love me the way I am?"

"Of course I do."

Nella looked over at her crutches leaning against the chair. "Those two pieces of wood have been like an extension of my body," she said. "But I don't think I'll miss them." With a sudden cry of laughter, she turned to Chris and flung her arms around his neck.

"You'll let me do it?" he asked excitedly.

"Oh, yes!" she cried.

Hours later Chris awoke out of a restless, disturbed sleep. He turned on the lamp and saw that it was a little after two, turned off the light, and tried to lull himself back to sleep. But he felt strangely agitated and tense. The room was warm, almost stifling from the humid night air, and the sheet clung damply to his body. He flung it aside and sprawled on his back.

He began to think about Nella and the way she had said she loved him. The taste of her lips lingered on his mouth, and he remembered the fragile yielding of her body under his hands. He became aroused and automatically caressed his erection, a little surprised that he was thinking of her like this. In all their moments alone, they had both been shy of intimacies, responding to each other with only fervent tenderness. Now he grew more excited as he imagined what it would be like to make love to her.

But his excitement turned into an angry impatience that he couldn't understand. He let go of himself and tried once more to sleep, turning from side to side. His uneasiness grew stronger, and with each twist of his body, he became more aware of a craving need to be relieved of his tension. Suddenly he thought of Janet, the Stanwyck maid he'd been seeing. His mind filled with images of what they had done together, their frantic, thrilling sex. He had not been with her since Nella had come home from Switzerland. The few times he had seen her while working around the grounds, she had glared at him angrily. Once he had caught her alone, tried to explain how he felt about Nella, but she had pushed him away and run off crying.

Chris sat up in bed. Janet was here; she had one of the small servants' rooms on the ground floor at the back of the house. There was a private entrance off the garden—no one would hear him. Without thinking, acting only on his compulsive need, he slipped on a robe and left his room.

The large house was dark and silent as he hurried down the stairs and slipped through a side door to the garden. Moonlight flooded the grounds and he ran, staying within the long shadows of trees and high shrubs. At the back of the house he skirted the windows of the other servants, crouching low in case one of them was still awake. Finally he reached Janet's door and knocked softly, urgently. There was no answer. He tried the knob and the door opened. Noiselessly, he slipped inside and closed the door, breathing quickly. In the pale light of the moon streaming through the window, he saw Janet in bed, asleep. She was naked, lying on her side with one arm curled up under the pillow. The curve of her hips and thighs was silvery in the dim light, and Chris felt himself grow hard with desire. He tiptoed to the bed and eased himself down beside her.

"Janet, wake up," he whispered, leaning close.

The girl stirred and opened her eyes. She started violently at seeing him, but he clamped a hand over her mouth before she could cry out.

"Don't scream—it's me, Chris," he said in a low voice.

As soon as she had relaxed, he took his hand away.

"What the hell are you doing here?" she demanded, covering herself with the sheet.

"I've missed you," he answered, trying to pull her into his arms.

She tore herself away from him, sat up, and turned on a small reading light over the bed. Her dark curly hair was disheveled, her eyes blazing.

"Are you crazy?" She stared at him, confused and angry. "Why are you dressed like that, in a robe? Where are your clothes?"

"Don't you know what happened?" he asked her.

"What do you mean? I was out all evening— I just got in about a half hour ago. What are you talking about?"

Chris smiled; she hadn't seen the Special Report or heard the news of the explosion. She didn't know what he had done.

"What happened?" she asked. "Why are you here?"

"Oh, well—Mrs. Stanwyck wasn't feeling well and Nella asked me to stay over," he lied.

Janet picked up a cigarette from the night table, lit it, and drew deeply. "So you decided that as long as you were here, you'd sneak down to visit me." She let out a breath of smoke and laughed. "Well, forget it. Get out. I haven't seen you for weeks, and now you think you can just bust in and pick up where we left off!"

"Janet, I'm sorry, but I tried to explain it to you," he said.

"Explain what? That you were just balling me until the little princess came home?"

"Nella and I grew up together. We have something very special between us."

"Bullshit! What are you after anyway, her money?"

"Oh, Christ, Jan, knock that shit off," he burst out angrily. Then, contrite, and aroused more than ever by her closeness, he smiled and touched her bare shoulder with teasing fingers.

"We had some pretty wild scenes," he murmured huskily. "And I've really missed you." His hand moved over her breasts, outside the sheet, and he felt the buds of her nipples grow hard. When she tried to stop him, he pulled her close and kissed her, his tongue moving inside her mouth. Suddenly she relaxed against him and slipped her hand inside his robe, ran it lightly up his thighs, and stroked his cock. He began to move his hips and tried to slip the sheet away from her body. She pulled out of his grasp and laughed.

"Okay, that's it! Now get out of here!" she said sharply.

Chris half sat up, staring at her furiously. "You bitch!" he muttered, breathing hard.

"Screw you!" she snarled. "You get horny and think that all you have to do is walk in and we'll fuck. Well, to hell with you! Go fuck the cripple!"

Her face was only inches from his, her eyes mocking and insolent. Chris stared at her, dark with rage. She tried to look away, but was held by the strange, intense light burning in his eyes.

"Stop looking at me like that," she whispered uneasily. "What's the matter with you?"

The words caught in her throat and changed to a low, frightened moan. She felt herself losing all control, as if her will had suddenly drained away. It seemed to her that the light on Chris's face was changing, darkening into odd shadows until all she could see were his eyes staring at her. Then an icy chill of fear swept through her body.

Forming in the corner of Chris's left eye was a tear. A blood-red tear.

She watched it slip out of his eye, as tiny as a pinpoint. It swelled and caught on his lashes, growing larger and gleaming in the light, iridescent, blinding.

Then all sensation dropped away and she went limp. Chris slipped off his robe and bent over her, his mind forcing her to respond to him.

26

Early Monday morning Eric slipped into the building by a service entrance to avoid being seen by a group of newsmen gathered on the front steps.

Shelly was in his office trying to organize a stack of messages covering his desk. She looked up as he walked in and said: "Have you been nominated for Man of the Year? *Time* and *Newsweek* have called, and *The New York Times*, the *Washington Post*, and the *Chicago Tribune*, not to mention our own papers, and all three networks and their local stations! I'm going deaf in one ear, and my left arm is permanently bent at a right angle!"

Her breathless delivery made Eric laugh. "Thanks, Shelly. I'll take over now."

"What's all the mystery?" she asked. "What do you have to do with Christopher McKenzie?"

"Not now, Shelly. I'll tell you about it later," he replied. "Screen any further incoming calls, will you?"

"Okay, but I'm dying to know what's going on!"

"Later, I promise. Right now I want to get to these messages."

Shelly went to her office and closed the door as Eric began to leaf through the notes. A few minutes later she buzzed him on the intercom.

"It's the *Times* on line one. What shall I tell them?"

"Tell them I'll call back later this morning. And hold the rest of the incoming calls. I'll be dialing out for the next hour or so."

The "next hour or so" became almost four hours as Eric returned calls to magazines, papers, and television stations promising a complete statement about Christopher in the near future.

"But we have a deadline to meet!" one editor complained.

Eric answered, explaining his "obligation to the McKenzie family" and "the need for restrained, responsible reporting" about Chris's part in the rescue of the plant workers. In a tireless display of public relations maneuvering and side-stepping, Eric managed to placate the press's hunger for immediate information. Hanging up on his last phone call, he felt as if he had won the battle, but only temporarily.

He buzzed Shelly and asked: "Is John in? . . . Good, tell him I'm on the way up and to get the drinks ready. I'll need three, at least!"

Eric took the stairs to the second floor, swung down the corridor and into John's office, falling with a groan onto an overstuffed plush velvet couch, one of Margaret's decorative inspirations.

John smiled at his collapse and brought him a drink. "Shelly said you've been on the phone for hours. Do you have any voice left?"

Eric took the drink down in one long gulp and sank back into the couch. "I was on the debating team at college, and notoriously long-winded even then. Christ, what a morning this has been! I'm still not quite sure how it happened, but I appear to have become Chris's spokesman."

"Have you seen the papers?" John asked. "The letters to the editor are very interesting." He picked up a newspaper and turned to the editorial section. "Listen to this: 'Whoever Christopher McKenzie is, he is surely touched by God's own hand. My husband was one of the workers he healed, and we both recognize the Spirit in him. . . .'"

Eric sat up as John went on: "Here's a contrasting point of view: 'This boy is obviously the Devil's tool on Earth!' And a more scholarly opinion: 'We witnessed several healings in the Philippines, ten years ago, similar to those performed by Christopher McKenzie. It is our profound hope that this young man uses his great gift for the benefit of all mankind.'" John set the paper aside and looked at Eric gravely. "We can't keep this boy in hiding much longer. I've used up all the excuses in my extensive repertoire with everyone who's called me, but excuses aren't going to be enough."

"I know, I know," Eric said, lighting a cigarette. "I think I have an answer. At this moment Chris is one of the hottest news stories in the country. By keeping him under cover, even for another week, the mystery of who and what he is will only add fuel to the fire."

"I don't understand. What's the point?"

"He wants to heal Nella Stanwyck."

"But the girl's been crippled since she was a child; I remember when the accident happened."

Eric smiled and shook his head in amusement. "That's a funny reaction, John—but understandable. Chris sighted and found your grandson, you saw the films of his healing, listened to what Catherine told you about her tests with him, and yet you respond to the idea of his healing Nella as though it couldn't happen."

"God, you're right," John muttered. "I guess I still can't get used to the idea of anyone having such capabilities, such power."

"That's my point exactly. What happened last Friday has been so distorted by conflicting accounts, the hemming and hawing of the medical profession, and the free-swinging purple prose of newspaper writers and TV's so-called journalists, that the public has no clear picture of Chris's ability."

"How does his healing Nella change any of that?"

"I think we should tape it."

John stared at him, stunned by the idea. "You're not kidding, are you?"

"Not even a little bit. Think about it for a minute; Chris heals her and our crew captures the event on film. Let's say it's done in the presence of Charlotte Stanwyck, one of the wealthiest society women on the Main Line; Nella's doctor, an eminent orthopedic specialist; you and I, representing the media, especially with the dignity of your position and background; and Catherine, a psychologist with a published work on paranormal studies."

"It's a hell of an idea," John said admiringly. "When did you dream all this up?"

"I've been thinking about it all weekend. Now listen to the rest of it. We interview the doctor *after* the healing, film a brief documentary on Chris's background and his tests with Catherine, and then we drop a last bombshell—we do a story on how David was found and reveal that in addition to his power to heal, Chris can sight."

John sat silent for a moment, regarding Eric with surprise. He had always admired his son-in-law's ambition and shrewdness but was a little taken aback by the audacity of his proposal.

"Don't you think this whole idea is a bit exploitative?" he asked tentatively.

"Not at all," Eric replied firmly. "I'm convinced that it's the only way Chris can be presented with dignity, without sensationalism. Do you think that after what he's done for me, finding my son, that I would do anything to hurt him?"

"No, of course not," John said hastily. "But we can't ignore the fact that a program of this nature would be a bonanza for the station. The ratings would be spectacular, advertising rates could be increased, and we'd probably have the publicity coverage of the entire country."

"I'm aware of all that, but the fact is that the cat's out of the bag; everybody has heard about what Chris has done. If we don't direct his public presentation, then I'm afraid he will be exploited as some kind of freak sideshow performer."

John stood up and walked to the large windows behind his desk. He clasped his hands behind his back, thinking about what Eric had said. He looked down at the street below and smiled.

"Did you see the reporters out there this morning when you came in?" he asked.

"Yes. I slipped in the service entrance to avoid them."

"I spoke to them when I arrived. They wanted to talk to you. I said I didn't know what time you'd get in, and they said they'd wait. They're gone now."

Eric came to John's side. "They'll be back, you know that," he said softly.

John faced him, nodding his head slowly in agreement. "How soon will Chris attempt—that is, heal Nella?"

"Within the next few days, I think."

"Do you think everyone will go along with your idea? Charlotte, his mother—even Chris and Nella?"

"I can handle them," Eric said confidently.

"Are you out of your mind?" Catherine asked in astonishment.

"Cathy, please hear me out."

"It's a betrayal of everything we promised Susan and Chris! It's exploitative and cruel, and can only hurt Chris. And what about Nella? Being a public show couldn't possibly be what she and Charlotte would want!"

"They've already agreed to it!" Eric said angrily.

"They what?"

"They've already agreed to it," he repeated more quietly.

Catherine looked at him scornfully. "So you talked them into it," she said caustically. "The smooth-talking agency man strikes again!"

"Now you listen to me!" Eric said fiercely. "You don't seem to understand the situation. Chris has already betrayed any promises we made to keep him out of the spotlight. Public response to that Special Report has been overwhelming. I spent all day dealing with newsmen who were frantic for more information. So what do we do? Let a lot of ambitious investigative reporters hound all of us, maybe try to steal your files or bribe witnesses for details? Or do we present him in a sober, unsensational manner? Don't you see? Healing Nella, under controlled conditions, with Charlotte, Susan, Nella's doctor, and you present at the time, will mean legitimacy for Christopher, and for your work with him. People all over the country will be seeing a dignified presentation, not a piece of film that was made under grueling and hysterical conditions and underscored by the foolish commentary of a sensation-seeking journalist!"

Catherine sat staring at him, silenced by his outburst. Finally, she took his hand and pressed it to her cheek. "As my mother would say, you've got some mouth on you," she murmured. "I'm sorry I yelled. The whole idea just took me by surprise."

Eric began to laugh and pulled her into his arms. "Then you do understand?"

"Not really," she sighed. "It's all moving too fast for me. But I guess you understand the public and its strange behavior better than I. If Charlotte and Nella have agreed, that means they trust you."

"And you do too, don't you?"

"More than that—I love you."

"Cathy, I promise you that I'll never betray your love or your trust."

"Oh, Christ, Eric—don't make any promises," she said seriously.

"Is that the cautious voice of the psychologist talking?"

"No, darling. The cautious voice of a woman who knows better than to think that promises can be kept."

He smiled and held her tight. "Don't be such a cynic."

◆

Chris and Nella sat close to each other on the delicately shaped French Provincial couch in Charlotte's study. Sitting across from them, Charlotte studied their faces as they finished having coffee and croissants.

"Absolutely delicious," Nella sighed, licking some crumbs from her fingertips. Catching her mother's quick smile, she asked: "And what are you grinning at?"

"You, dear," Charlotte replied. "Licking your fingers like a little girl." She turned to Christopher. "More coffee, Chris?"

"Thank you, no. I'm stuffed. Amazing how filling these little things are."

"Only when you eat a half dozen of them," Nella kidded him. Then, looking at her mother with an amused smile, she said: "Are you going to tell us why you asked us for breakfast, or do you want us to guess?"

"All right," Charlotte said. "I'll stop playing this social scene and get to the point. I thought it only fair to tell Chris that I've consented to this—this healing at your insistence." She looked at Chris soberly and went on: "Despite my awe at the evidence of your gift, Christopher, I must tell you that I'm quite prepared for the possibility of failure, and I hope that both of you are too."

"I appreciate your honesty," Chris responded quietly. "But I believe that I can heal Nella. I still don't understand how I do these things, or where my power to do them comes from. That's something Dr. Marlowe and I are still working on. And I guess at this time I just don't question it. It happens; that's all I know. But I'm absolutely sure it will happen with Nella."

"I believe you are," Charlotte said, moved by the intensity of his words.

"I've talked with Eric about the tape he's going to make," Chris said, "and he's agreed that if there is anything in it that embarrasses you or that you do not like, we'll erase it."

"That's very considerate of you, Chris," Charlotte said gratefully.

"Hey," Nella cut in, "don't I have anything to say about it?"

Chris laughed and hugged her. "You don't have to say a word. All you have to do is walk." He looked at his watch and exclaimed: "It's late! I've got to get to work. The whole south end of the garden needs pruning."

Charlotte began to stop him. "Chris, you don't have to do that. I really feel a little foolish having you work in my garden, what with all the—"

"Please, Aunt Charlotte," he interjected. "I enjoy it, and for the moment, I still want to go on earning my keep."

He kissed them both on the cheek and left, telling Nella he would see her later.

Nella poured herself another cup of coffee and looked at her mother in a slightly superior way. "He's full of surprises, isn't he?"

"To say the very least," Charlotte responded. She grew quiet, thinking about Chris and Susan and the years she had known them, the ties of their shared experiences.

"What are you thinking about, Mother?" Nella asked.

Charlotte looked up at her daughter, frowning. "I was just wondering why, in all these years, Susan was so *afraid* of letting anyone know what extraordinary gifts Chris possesses."

27

The solarium was a large Victorian-style room that curved in a wide arc of windows and white gingerbread molding. It rose to a high, domed ceiling made of glass and fretted woodwork, and was shaded by the spreading branches of huge oak and elm trees that stood just outside, like guardians of a precious jewel. White wrought-iron and wicker furniture was arranged on the flagstone floor amid bowers of lush green plants grouped on fluted pedestals and dripping over the sides of intricately woven baskets. A peaceful quiet pervaded the room, a stillness that suggested another, more gracious era.

It was Nella's favorite room in the house, and at her request, it had been agreed to tape the healing there. The crew arrived early to set up, and Eric and Chris conferred with the director of Eric's show, Gary Black, on how best to proceed with the taping.

Catherine was in the library with Charlotte, Nella, and Susan, doing her best to keep them calm. Charlotte was trying to maintain her composure but giving away her nervousness with distracted answers and quick, worried glances at Nella. Susan was silent, sipping her coffee quietly, making little or no comment on what was said.

She appeared almost removed from the group, her eyes distant and thoughtful. Only Nella seemed herself. Dressed in a pale-yellow blouse and a long, pleated skirt, she radiated excitement and an anticipation of what was going to happen.

"Mother, you look so nervous," she said. "Please, don't worry."

"Darling, are you sure you want to do this?" Charlotte asked, as she had so many times in the last few days.

"Of course I'm sure," Nella answered positively. "I trust Chris completely, and I believe in him."

Just then Dr. Ernest Thayer entered the room with a dramatic flourish. He was an orthopedic specialist and had taken care of Nella since her childhood accident. Tall, stout, with thinning white hair, delicate hands, and a strong profile that suggested old European nobility, he directed his opening remarks to Charlotte as if they had been in the middle of a conversation.

"I'm not in favor of this, Charlotte, not at all! I've agreed to be present because I'm your friend and Nella's doctor, but I want it clearly understood that I do not share your enthusiasm for this—this experiment!"

Nella smiled at his outburst and said: "Dr. Thayer, don't start badgering Mother; this is my idea. Now stop being such a bear. Sit down and have some coffee."

He tried to give her a severe, professional glare, but broke into a grin and sat down beside her, shaking his head in resignation. "All right, all right," he sighed. "Two lumps, no cream. You always were an unpredictable little pest, Nella." He kissed her cheek affectionately.

Charlotte said: "Now that we've tamed you, Ernest, I'd like you to meet Mrs. Susan McKenzie and Dr. Catherine Marlowe."

He glanced at Susan and Catherine. "Ah, the mother of the young man and his—what shall I say, mentor? Charlotte tells me you've been working with Christopher for some time," he said to Catherine. "Can you tell me more about him and his so-called gifts?"

"Really, Dr. Thayer, your skepticism is a bit grating at this particular time," Catherine said sharply. "After what occurred a few days ago at the Ridgeway explosion, I should think you might be less inclined to be so absolute in your judgment of Chris's gifts."

"My dear Dr. Marlowe, I do not consider what happened at the explosion under conditions of extreme pressure and hysteria, to be scientifically acceptable," he said loftily.

"I can appreciate that, Doctor. But a little more reserve in your opinions and behavior would, under the present circumstances, be very welcome," Catherine snapped.

Charlotte intervened with a pleading look to both of them. "Ernest, please. This is hardly the time for an argument."

"Or your old-fashioned high-handedness," Nella added dryly. "Why don't you just wait until it's over and then expound on your theories?"

Not in the least chagrined by their reprimands, Thayer raised a hand in a conciliatory gesture and bowed his head, saying: "Agreed, ladies. I shall do exactly that—I shall wait." He turned to Susan and said: "I hope I've not offended you too, Mrs. McKenzie."

"Not at all, Doctor," Susan replied quietly. "You remind me of a neighbor we had in Ireland when I was a little girl."

"Oh? In what way?"

"He too was a very strong man, unshakable in his convictions. But my parents had beliefs that were different from his; not opposed to his, but different. However, our neighbor was a very self-righteous man; and in his righteousness, he led a group of other neighbors and they burned down my father's house."

Dr. Thayer frowned, then smiled and nodded his head in understanding. "You make your point softly, but very directly, Mrs. McKenzie. May we speak together again, later?"

"If you wish," Susan replied indifferently.

Eric and Chris came into the room. Charlotte looked up with a nervous start, then recovered herself and introduced them to Dr. Thayer.

He rose and shook hands with Eric, then with Chris, regarding him with a curious, inquisitive expression. Chris returned his look calmly, waiting for him to speak, to make some objection about what was going to happen. But Thayer simply said: "I wish you great luck, my boy."

Chris smiled and replied: "I don't think luck has anything to do with it, sir."

Catherine laughed to herself at the exchange, observing with satisfaction Chris's growing ability to handle himself maturely. When he glanced at her she gave him a smile of approval, and he returned it with an audacious wink.

Just then John Bradford came rushing into the library, breathless and apologetic. "Sorry I'm late. Margaret made me change ties four times! Isn't that ridiculous?"

Charlotte stood up and took his arm. "You look very handsome, John," she said, smiling.

"Well, I think we'd better get started," Eric announced.

Chris lifted Nella in his arms. "Ready, darling?" he whispered.

She put her arms around his neck, her face close to his. "I love you, Chris," she said so that only he could hear.

Eric gave Catherine his hand.

"Sit with me, please?" Catherine asked.

"Of course, dear," he replied.

Dr. Thayer offered Susan his arm and they all left the library, walking across the foyer to the solarium in a procession that suddenly grew quiet. Charlotte had given the staff the day off and the house was unnaturally silent. Their footsteps echoed on the tile floor and their faces grew solemn, as if they were about to attend a religious ceremony.

At the door to the solarium, Charlotte saw Mrs. Gregory standing off to one side and beckoning to her. Leaving the others to enter the solarium, Charlotte went to her cook.

"Mrs. Gregory, why haven't you taken the day off with the others?"

"Please, Mrs. Stanwyck, let me be there with you when it happens." The elderly woman's eyes were moist and pleading. "Nella told me what Chris is—is going to do. They're like my own, and I want to be with them. Please?"

"Of course you can be with us, dear. I didn't mean to exclude you. I just thought it would be better—"

"I know, ma'am, I know. But I'll stay out of the way, I promise."

"Nonsense. You will sit with me," Charlotte said warmly, taking her arm. "Come now, they're waiting."

Chairs for everyone had been grouped in a half circle around the center of the room where Nella sat on a white wicker love seat. The two cameramen with porta-packs checked their zoom lenses and were framing shots while the light man arranged quartz lamps under Gary's direction.

"Are you ready for my close-up, Mr. De Mille?" Nella kidded with Gary. "Can I use this as an audition film for Hollywood?"

"You know you're very unnerving?" Gary said, laughing a little shakily. "Aren't you nervous?"

"Now I am, but only because of the cameras. Do I look all right?"

Chris walked up in front of her and replied: "You're absolutely beautiful."

"That's what I wanted to hear." She grinned. "Ready when you are." She glanced over her shoulder and smiled at Charlotte, sitting with John and Mrs. Gregory. Eric and Catherine were to her right; and in a corner, Susan with Dr. Thayer. As she turned back, the lamps were turned on. She saw Chris standing before her in a blaze of light, his skin and hair frost-white in the glare. For a moment he appeared larger than life, almost unreal. A vision of the prince he had described to her so many times in their childhood flashed before her eyes, taking his form—legendary, mythic.

"Okay, let's go," Gary said, shattering her momentary illusion.

Chris reached down to help her stand with her crutches. In the hot light she looked tiny and fragile. She stared at Chris like a quiet child, defenseless and vulnerable. He touched her cheek lovingly and then moved behind her, resting his hands lightly on her shoulders.

She was suddenly nervous and wanted to giggle as his fingertips began to trace the delicate shape of her back to her waist. His hands grew warm as they moved slowly over her small buttocks and down the upper part of her thighs. She sighed and closed her eyes, relaxed now in the warmth of his touch.

"Do you feel anything?" he asked in a low voice.

"Yes, but don't ask me what—my mother's sitting right over there and I—" She paused as her body suddenly stiffened. Her eyes flew open and she made a small moaning sound.

Dr. Thayer sat forward abruptly, and Charlotte half rose from her seat, her face white.

Chris's hands moved firmly down Nella's legs. "What do you feel?" he asked. "Tell me what you feel."

"A shock—and heat from your hands, burning like fire!" she cried out.

Thayer got to his feet, his face red with anger, ready to protest.

"Chris! My legs!" Nella's voice was choked.

"How do they feel?" he asked tensely.

"Like they were solid, heavy, made of stone!"

"I insist these proceedings stop at once!" Thayer declared furiously.

Charlotte moved quickly to his side, ready to agree with him,

while Eric and Catherine, now on their feet, hesitated, torn by indecision.

Chris ignored Thayer's outburst and continued to run his hands
over Nella's back and legs feverishly.

"Chris, stop, please. It hurts!" Nella cried.

Instantly he withdrew his hands and stepped in front of her.
"Nella, are you all right?" he asked, his face strained, lips white.

Charlotte had started toward her. "Nella, darling, no more,
please."

"Mother, wait!" Nella called out. "The pain is gone." She stood
absolutely still, clutching her crutches, beads of sweat covering her
brow and across her upper lip.

"Nella, let go of your crutches," Chris said softly. "Give them to
me."

She stared at him, her eyes frightened and confused. "I'm afraid
to," she said, her voice verging on tears.

Chris stepped back from her. "Drop your crutches and walk to
me," he said in a ringing command.

Without taking her eyes from his face, Nella slowly let the
crutches slide out from under her arms and slip to the floor. Everyone in the room stood paralyzed, not breathing, watching her slim
figure totter slightly, then become still. Tears began to flow down her
cheeks as she took one hesitant step, then another. A low cry escaped
from Charlotte's lips, and one of the cameramen swore softly.

Chris held out his hand and Nella took her first unaided steps
since she was a child. He held her hand firmly, keeping her still a few
steps from him, and said: "Now, walk to your mother, darling."

A slow, sweet smile spread across his face, and Nella let go of his
hand and began to move toward Charlotte.

"Oh, my God!" Charlotte cried, weeping unashamedly as her
daughter came into her outstretched arms.

A cheer went up from the crew. Dr. Thayer sat back in his chair,
aghast, and the others crowded around Nella and Charlotte, shouting and crying.

Only Susan stood to one side, tears running down her face as she
stared at her son. Chris was standing where Nella had left him,
watching the joyous group. In the harsh radiance of the lights she
saw a man, strong and self-assured, no longer the child in need of her
protection. What he had done filled her with pride, and with the
sorrow of knowing that at this moment, he had, once and for all, left

her. Chris turned as she approached, and in his eyes she saw that she was right; they had made their farewell without ever uttering a word.

Susan held him tightly for a moment, then stepped aside as the others closed in around him.

Part Four

28

Eric glanced at the clock on the studio wall. In a few minutes the program he had assembled on Christopher would begin. He patted his forehead with a handkerchief, checked the knot in his tie, ran a cautious finger along his zipper, then took his seat on the set. Just outside camera range Catherine sat with Chris, Nella, Charlotte, and Amanda. Eric threw them a quick smile and looked to the control booth where John was talking with Gary and Shelly. Gary turned to him and held up his hand. It was almost time. Eric knew that major network representatives would be watching the show tonight, as well as members of the press and national magazines. The knowledge made him tense with anticipation; what would their reaction be to the program?

Gary gave him the signal and he was on.

"Good evening, ladies and gentlemen. Tonight we are departing from our usual format of taped interviews. What we are going to discuss is of such an extraordinary nature that we felt it was important that you see and hear our guests live, to avoid any possible doubts about their veracity." He paused for a moment and then went on.

"A few weeks ago, the piece of film you are about to see was shown on every newscast in the city and across the nation."

Footage of the Ridgeway explosion and fire came on while Eric narrated the event and Chris's part in it. When the film was over, he continued.

"Hundreds of letters have come in asking about Christopher McKenzie, wanting to know who he is, where he's from, and more about the nature of his gift of healing. Tonight we shall try to answer some of those questions."

For the next few minutes Eric gave a brief summary of Christopher's childhood and youth. He introduced the subject of Chris's gift to heal by recounting Amanda's automobile accident and then interviewed Amanda. Catherine followed and talked about her studies with Chris and the events that led up to the afternoon of the explosion.

When she was finished, Eric went on, telling of Charlotte's consent to the healing of Nella and their decision to tape it. Then Eric introduced the film. While it was being shown, he left the set to talk with the group.

"It's going beautifully, darling," Catherine whispered.

Charlotte murmured: "I'm very pleased with the way you're handling this, Eric."

Chris and Nella smiled in agreement, while Amanda stared intently at the monitor; this was the first time she had seen the tape. As it drew to a close, she leaned over and said to Catherine: "It's incredible, but I'm not really surprised; he only made her walk—he saved my whole life! I wonder if anybody from Hollywood is watching this?"

"Why?" Catherine asked.

"Because if they don't accept him as a healer, they'll be offering him movie contracts. He's gorgeous!"

Catherine laughed, then grew quiet as Eric returned to the set and introduced Charlotte and Nella. The camera swung to where they were sitting. Nella rose gracefully to her feet, offering Charlotte her hand. The camera followed them as they walked to the set and took seats next to Eric. Nella's movements were slow, but sure, with no hint that she had ever been crippled. She spoke first, describing the accident that had occurred when she was five, the years spent with specialists, and finally what the healing meant to her.

"Chris has given me my life," she said softly in conclusion.

Charlotte said: "My daughter and I agreed to appear on this program to add validity to what you've already seen and heard. There are no words to describe how deeply I feel about this, or how grateful I am to Christopher McKenzie. It is our hope that everyone who is watching tonight will learn and profit from the experience as much as we have. Shakespeare wrote: 'There are more things in heaven and earth . . . than are dreamt of in your philosophy . . .' It would be wise of us all to consider those words carefully."

The camera followed them as they left the set, then closed in on Eric.

"Before I introduce Christopher McKenzie, I want to answer a question that I've been asked many times in the last few weeks concerning my relationship to this extraordinary young man. Many of you remember the tragedy that struck my family almost two years ago."

Eric related the circumstances of his meeting Chris, and proceeded to detail the sighting tests, pausing in his narrative to play some of Catherine's tapes.

Amanda, unaware of these events, was astonished and angry. She glared furiously at Catherine, who whispered quickly: "Don't blow a fuse, we're in public! I couldn't tell you about it; we promised Susan to say nothing."

Just then Eric brought John on. He spoke for a few minutes, concluding: "In a world full of bizarre coincidences, it seems no less strange to me that the finding of my grandson and the healing of Nella Stanwyck was accomplished by a young man who grew up in our midst and was known to all of us. I can only add my own wish to Mrs. Stanwyck's that we all make a greater effort to learn more about ourselves and others."

In the control booth Gary smiled and said to Shelly: "This show has the calculated dignity of a High Mass!"

She glared at his flippancy and replied: "I think it's splendid, the best thing Eric has ever done. No moralizing or conjecture, just a presentation of the facts."

"Okay, okay," Gary muttered. "Here comes the star." He cued a camera to pick up Chris as Eric introduced him. Dressed in light summer slacks, a soft shirt, and a pullover sweater, Chris looked like an advertisement for the American college student. His blond hair gleamed under the lights, and his face was set in an earnest, sincere expression.

Shelly watched him closely as he talked about his hopes for the further study of his gifts and the knowledge such study might bring to the rest of the world.

"What do you think of him?" Gary asked.

"He's beautiful," she replied softly. "He could make American women forget Robert Redford."

"You think so? Well, one woman seems to have forgotten *him* tonight."

"What do you mean?"

"Don't you think it's strange that his mother isn't on the show?"

Susan reached out, turned off the television set, and sat back in her chair. She stared at the blank screen for a few minutes, her face expressionless, hands resting quietly in her lap. Then she got up and went through the house, turning off lights and locking up. The door to Chris's room was open; he had left a small lamp near his bed turned on. She went in, straightened the covers on the bed, turned off the lamp, and left the room, closing the door softly behind her. A few minutes later she sat down at her sewing machine and began running a deep-scarlet material under the needle, concentrating on the tiny stitches flowing past her hands.

Charlotte had planned a late dinner for everyone, and an hour or so after the program was over, they all assembled at the Stanwyck mansion. John stopped off on the way to pick up Margaret, and soon after they arrived, Mrs. Gregory announced that dinner was being served.

Nella took Chris's arm as they walked across the foyer to the dining hall. "This room is used only for very special occasions," she told him.

"And this is the most special of occasions," Charlotte said. "I only wish Susan were here. Is she feeling better?" she asked Chris.

"Oh, yes," he replied. "I called her from the studio after the show, and she sent you her love and regrets about not being here tonight."

He looked away from her sympathetic glance, remembering his mother's steadfast refusal to appear on the program. Eric and Catherine had both tried to change her mind, but she had remained adamant. It was probably for the best, he thought. He felt some regret for the way their life together was changing, but it was inevitable, he reasoned. He was no longer a child; he had to make his own decisions, choose his own path. And so far, everything had gone better than he'd expected; he was gaining more control of his own future. He looked at Nella, walking beside him, and he smiled. She was supremely happy, the full skirt of her gown swirling around her slender legs as she delighted in every move she made. And he had done this for her, he thought proudly.

In the dining room they took their seats at a long table covered with gleaming silver and china. Chris looked around the richly appointed room that was bathed in a soft glow cast by crystal lamps and candelabra. He admired the antique English furniture and the delicate French wallpaper, the rosewood sideboard and the gilt-framed paintings. And for the first time since he had entered the house so many years ago, he felt that he belonged here.

Wine was served and Charlotte proposed a toast to Chris. Everyone stood and lifted their glasses. Eyes shining, his face filled with happiness, he returned the toast, thanking all of them for what they had done for him.

Amanda whispered to Catherine: "If that boy ever goes into politics, he'll get my vote!"

"Oh, you'd vote for anybody who saved your life," Catherine commented dryly.

"Ah, then you finally believe me about that." Amanda smiled victoriously.

Catherine nodded her head slowly. "Yes, I finally believe," she sighed.

Amanda looked at her, puzzled. "What's the matter? You don't sound happy. Is something wrong?"

"No, of course not," she replied.

But as the dinner progressed, she found herself watching Chris and wondering why she felt so uneasy about him. Nagging at the back of her mind was the sullen disappointment he had expressed at the airport when denied credit for finding Eric's son, and his question: *Isn't Eric ever going to tell them what really happened?* And the day of the explosion, when they had argued about healing Nella, and then his impulsive act of running to the disaster. Or was it impulsive? He'd not only performed acts of healing, but he had readily told the newsman his name before collapsing. And finally his words to her in the ambulance: "I healed— I proved I could do it."

Had he done it all purposely, even healing Nella? Was this what he had wanted all along—the notoriety and acclaim? The idea was disturbing; but then she thought, wasn't it perfectly normal? He was young, and had been cloistered for years by a promise of secrecy to his mother. Catherine had seen the strain he was under trying to keep that promise. It made sense for him to want to be recognized. And yet . . .

Her thoughts were interrupted by Charlotte calling for everyone's attention.

"Thank you," she said as the chatter at the table quieted down. "I have something very important to say that concerns all of us." She paused and looked directly at Chris. Then she went on. "What Christopher has done for my daughter and for me cannot be expressed in words. Therefore, I intend to express my gratitude in a way that may be beneficial to many other people. I'm going to endow a foundation for the research and study of parapsychic phenomena. And I intend to call it the Christopher Foundation, in Chris's honor."

There was a moment of surprised silence from everyone at the table, then Margaret Bradford exclaimed: "Charlotte, that's an absolutely splendid idea!"

"And we insist on being the founding members," John stated. "Our debt to Chris can never be repaid."

Charlotte turned to Catherine and said: "From our conversations in the last few weeks, I know that such a foundation has long been a dream of yours. I'd very much like to have you direct the research and studies. There'll be a salary, of course, more than equivalent to your teaching contract at the university. Will you do it?"

Catherine stared at her, speechless. Then she stammered: "Mrs. Stanwyck, I'm a little overwhelmed. I never expected . . . but— Oh, yes! Of course I'll do it!"

Amanda's face was wreathed in smiles. "Oh, Cathy, it's what you've always wanted!"

Charlotte looked at Amanda and said: "We could use an expert on organizing fund raisings and grants, Miss Howard. Would you be available to us?"

It was Amanda's turn to be dumbstruck. Tears started in her eyes and she turned to face Chris. "I could never find a way to thank you until now." She dabbed at her eyes and said to Charlotte: "I'll do everything I can for the foundation."

Charlotte's face was radiant. "I can't tell you how happy I am at the way this is working out. I believe the foundation will be a way of giving something in return for the gifts we've received. With Chris as our symbol and spokesman, I feel that for the first time in my life, I shall be engaged in something very, very worthwhile."

"Charlotte, is there anything I can do, anything I can contribute?" Eric asked.

"A great deal, I think," she answered, smiling. "Probably more than any of us, in a way. We'll need a liaison to the media and the public, a public relations director, but in an executive capacity. If your contract with John isn't too binding, I can't think of anyone more qualified to represent the foundation."

Eric was a little startled. "That's quite an offer, Charlotte," he said slowly.

John said: "I think we can work something out, Eric, as far as your show is concerned."

Eric smiled. "In that case, I'd be delighted to take the job!"

Suddenly the impact of Charlotte's proposal hit everyone and they all began talking at once. Chris was on his feet, shaking hands with Eric and hugging Catherine. He went to Charlotte and kissed her shyly, while Nella exclaimed excitedly and insisted on working with Catherine and Amanda as an assistant.

"This is the most incredible night of my life!" Chris declared.

"I have a feeling there are a lot more to come!" Amanda stated.

"It's all very exciting," Margaret said to Charlotte. "I shall organize every club we belong to!"

John pumped Eric's hand and said: "Don't worry about the show. You'd probably never be able to top tonight's program anyway!"

At Charlotte's suggestion they all moved into the living room for coffee and further discussion of the foundation. Eric drew Cathy away from the others and led her to the solarium. Once they were out of sight, he took her in his arms and kissed her fervently.

"Darling, isn't it wonderful?" he asked happily.

"I don't know what to say—everything is happening so quickly," she answered, a trace of uncertainty in her voice.

"What are you worried about? C'mon, tell me. I can see it in your eyes."

She moved out of his arms and walked through the darkened room to the glass walls, staring out at the night-shrouded grounds. From the living room she could hear the excited chatter of the others. Eric came up behind her, and she looked at his reflection in the glass.

"Tell me what's worrying you," he said, putting his arms around her.

"I'm not sure," she replied hesitantly. "I'm thrilled about Charlotte's idea and"—she smiled—"the prospect of our working together. But I'm afraid of what may happen to Chris. When the announcement is made about the foundation, on the heels of the program we did tonight, he'll be in for a lot more publicity."

"Cathy, you mustn't judge the public prematurely," Eric said. "We don't know how people will respond to the show. If the reaction is supportive, then the foundation would be the most sheltered atmosphere for you and Chris to continue your studies in."

"That's true, of course," she admitted reluctantly.

He turned her around so that she faced him. "You know, you worry too much."

"It's only natural—I'm a psychologist and I'm Jewish," she sighed, moving into his arms.

He laughed and kissed her tenderly. "I think that's a hell of a combination. Now stop worrying. I promise you from my gentile heart that I'll do everything I can to protect Chris and his gifts. Any healing and sighting he does will be performed under the watchful eyes of the foundation and yours truly."

Abruptly, Catherine was aware of what had been disturbing her all evening. She had almost forgotten another of Christopher's gifts—his ability to mind-pressure! So had Eric, obviously. She had mentioned it to him once, but caught up in the search for his son, and then the explosion and the healing of Nella, they had both been too preoccupied to remember it.

Now Chris's power to command others was suddenly vivid in her mind: how he had made Frank Pearson throw scalding coffee into his own face; and later, during her tests, his playfulness with her student, Sarah, making her alter her behavior so radically; and what he had told her about the scene that had taken place here in this house with Tom Stanwyck. She knew so little about this ability; she had never had the opportunity to question him further and they had made so few tests. As soon as the furor surrounding him died down, they would get into an extensive study of mind-pressure, she decided. If she mentioned it now, to Eric or the others, with no real facts or information to substantiate her brief tests, it would only cause confusion. Eric was right; she worried too much. Chris had done those things out of fear and anger.

But for the rest of the evening, despite the gaiety and excitement over Charlotte's project, Catherine couldn't shake off her feeling of apprehension.

29

Over the weekend, following the Friday-night airing of Eric's show, news clips were picked up, shown, and discussed on every major newscast in the country. By Monday morning the station was flooded with phone calls and telegrams, many of them from the same people who had called right after the Ridgeway coverage. Only now they were more demanding: national magazines insisted on interviews with Chris, newspapers wanted to do feature articles, NBC suggested a program where Chris would be questioned by a panel of eminent scientists and theologians, CBS said it wanted to do a special on his background and home life, ABC put out feelers on the possibility of a half hour with Barbara Walters and even a cameo appearance on one of its dramatic series as a special guest star.

Eric was canny enough to release a statement about the organization of the Christopher Foundation before answering any of the requests from the press and the networks, knowing that it would only increase their interest in Chris.

During the week, John had the phone company install extra lines to relieve the jammed switchboard and hired a small staff to take care of the increasing number of letters that were beginning to overflow the mail room. Almost all of them were from people asking for Chris's help in healing or sighting.

"Did you expect all of this?" John demanded, waving a sheaf of letters at Eric as he paced his office.

"I expected a response, but not quite this overwhelming," Eric admitted. "After all, other psychics have appeared on television and have been interviewed in magazines."

"Yes, but they didn't have the immediacy of what Chris has done, healing those people at the explosion, and then Nella, the daughter of one of the wealthiest and most prestigious families on the East Coast! Nor did they have tapes made of their healings, and testimonials to support their accomplishments."

"That's true, of course," Eric agreed. "But why are you upset? The show had the highest ratings of any we've ever done, and I understand you've been deluged by new advertisers wanting to buy time."

John sat down at his desk and nervously drummed his fingers. "I have meetings set up with potential buyers for the next three weeks."

"So—what's the problem?"

"Every one of them wants to buy time on a show featuring Chris, preferably a weekly show."

"You mean like the one Kathryn Kuhlman used to do?"

John nodded. "They want to know if we plan a program of healings and sightings."

Eric whistled softly in surprise. Then he began to laugh. "Christ, what an idea! But you know," he added thoughtfully, "it's a good one."

"Jesus, Eric, use your head! We're not equipped to do anything like that!"

"But we could be," Eric said slowly, warming to the idea.

"What do you mean?"

"If we formed our own production company to do the show, we could syndicate it, not just in Philadelphia, but all over the country."

John was shocked. "Are you joking? Do you realize what an undertaking that would be?"

"Of course I do," Eric answered easily, "but think about it for a minute. It hasn't been a week since the show aired and there are hundreds of letters downstairs from people begging Chris to help them, letters not only from here on the East Coast, but from people all over the country. And a great many of them are saying that they'll come to Philadelphia, do whatever they can to get to Chris."

John's eyes became sharp with interest as Eric pulled a chair up to his desk, sat down, and continued.

"Think about it, John. I've got messages on my desk from media people all over the country. Every network wants to do some kind of special program with him. And you know why as well as I do. He's salable. Chris is twenty-one, as handsome as a movie star, and as sincere as an altar boy—the perfect commercial property. Do you think half as much attention would be paid to him if he were some homely middle-aged man or an eccentric fanatic? There are a lot of healers in the world, but few of them have his youth or charisma."

"If you propose to merchandise that boy into a cult idol, like some rock star, I hardly think you'll get an approval from Charlotte or Catherine," John commented tensely.

Eric turned on him angrily. "What the hell do you think I am? I wouldn't hurt Chris for anything in the world! But you've been in this business long enough to know that if the networks and agency men get ahold of him, he'll be wined and dined into a deal that will burn him out in a year and wreck his life! Look what happened to that Olympic swimming champion with all the gold medals. He ended up being plastered around the country on a cheap poster and selling milk on TV! At least with us Chris has a chance to do something meaningful. We'll own the show, have complete control over it. That way he has nothing to fear!"

For a few minutes John sat silent, considering everything Eric had said. Finally he replied: "I think you're right, and I'm willing to go along with you. What's the first step?"

Eric stood up, his eyes bright with excitement, his voice crisp. "A meeting with Charlotte, Chris, and Catherine. They have to be made completely aware of the situation. And I want the foundation behind us all the way."

"I can help you there. I've known Charlotte a long time and she respects my opinion. Since Tom Stanwyck died and she took over the control of Stanwyck industries, she's become a very knowledgeable businesswoman. She'll understand what we're proposing and why. Do you think Christopher will agree to your ideas?"

"I'm sure he will—the boy trusts me. He knows I want only the best for him."

"And Catherine?" John questioned.

"No problem there," Eric replied positively. "If we work under the auspices of the foundation, she'll be part of it and have a say in what we do."

"You're serious about her, aren't you?" John asked unexpectedly.

Eric paused, looking at his father-in-law for some sign of disapproval or objection. "Yes, I am," he answered quietly. "Is that all right with you and Margaret?"

John smiled. "Of course it is. We rather suspected you two were in love, and we're very happy for you. Is there a wedding in the near future?"

Eric laughed and shook his head. "First things first. I have a feeling the Christopher Foundation is going to keep us all hopping for the next few months. And we'd better get started now, before they start knocking down the studio doors."

"After we have the meeting, what are you going to do?" John asked as they left his office.

"I'm going to call the biggest press conference this town has ever seen!"

◆

The ballroom in the Hilton Hotel that Eric had booked for the conference, was jammed with people. Bellboys hastily brought folding chairs to accommodate the large crowd, while newscasters stood to one side describing the proceedings and crews manning video tape recorders scanned the audience.

Eric waited near the podium, his eyes sweeping through the crowd. The turnout was even greater than he'd expected. There were reporters from the Philadelphia offices of *The New York Times*, *Chicago Tribune*, *Washington Post*, *Los Angeles Times*, and other major newspapers. Men from AP, UPI, and Reuters sat with representatives of *Time*, *Newsweek*, and *People*; and ABC, NBC, and CBS news persons were busily exchanging the latest network gossip.

A few feet away from the dais, Catherine sat with Charlotte and Nella, talking with local reporters. Eric glanced at them, caught Cathy's eye and smiled, then looked at the door of the anteroom where John waited with Chris. The door was opened slightly, and he saw John nodding to him, as if to say, "Let's get started." Eric turned back to the noisy, restless audience. They had waited long enough, he decided. Now it was show time.

He stepped up to the podium, tested the mike, and said: "Good morning, ladies and gentlemen."

An immediate silence ensued, and he went on with a brief prepared statement, apologizing for the delay in having the conference and asking their indulgence with Chris, reminding them that this was his first meeting with any members of the media. Then he signaled John and Chris to come in.

Heads turned and necks craned as the two men walked up to the podium. At Eric's suggestion, Chris was dressed much the same way he had been on the program—a white pullover sweater, soft shirt, and lightweight slacks. His hair was slightly tousled, his tanned face flushed with excitement. He looked at once sincere, unaffected, and boyishly romantic, a quality that did not go unnoticed by many women in the audience.

Following Eric's idea that his status in broadcasting circles would set the proper tone for the meeting, John made a few opening remarks before introducing Chris. He spoke of the events that had taken place, the subsequent endowment of the Christopher Foundation by Charlotte Stanwyck, and his own participation in it. Then he presented Chris.

There was polite, restrained applause, as if the audience was uncertain how to react to Chris's disarmingly casual appearance and manner. Remembering Eric's caution to take his time, Chris waited for a moment before speaking.

"Good morning," he said quietly, a little nervous at the focus of attention on himself.

When no one spoke, he glanced quickly at Nella. She smiled encouragingly, and he turned back to the room.

"Well—I know why I'm here," he said, grinning. "The rest is up to you."

A murmur of laughter went up, and Eric, sitting with John and Catherine, smiled. "This may be easier than I thought," he whispered to them.

The first question came from *The New York Times*.

"Why did you wait until the Ridgeway factory explosion to demonstrate publicly your power to heal?"

"It was just circumstance, that's all. I happened to be close by and saw that I had to help," Chris replied calmly.

An editor of a scientific periodical identified himself and asked: "The scientific community is curious about the biological origins of your powers. When can we expect some hard data about the nature of those powers?"

Chris smiled. "I think that scientists have been curious about people like me for a long time. I wish I knew more about it myself, and that's the reason for the foundation. Dr. Marlowe will be working with other doctors, researchers, and physicists to try to understand and learn more about where my healing and sighting powers come from. But there is no telling how long it will take."

Chris looked at Catherine, who nodded her approval of his answer. Eric threw him a cautionary glance when he saw who the next speaker was: a clergyman, conspicuous in clerical collar and dark suit, who represented a religious newsweekly.

He spoke slowly, emphasizing his question with a from-the-pulpit tone of voice.

"Mr. McKenzie, it is generally acknowledged by the Church, and by many individual healers, that the power to cure diseases and heal wounds comes from God. But you have made no mention thus far in any of your responses that God is the only possible source of your ability. May I ask why?"

The audience grew quiet as Chris lowered his head for a moment, remembering what Eric had said to him about answering this expected question: "There are thousands of people who will come out against you if you offend anyone with your answer. It has to be stated sincerely, and still be oblique enough to let anyone read into it whatever he wishes."

Chris looked up at the clergyman and said: "I believe there is, within all of us, a power that is part of a universal life force, the life force that exists in and animates all living things. I don't know the true nature of that source of power, or where it comes from. We have so much to learn before we can make absolutes of what is still unknown to us. That is one of the goals of the foundation, to determine if this power can be developed in everyone."

Catherine turned to Eric and whispered: "Where the hell did he get *that* rhetoric? I've never heard him speak like that before!"

Eric patted her hand and grinned. "He's got a great teacher—me! Didn't he handle that beautifully? I had a feeling he'd be a natural when it came to all this crap!"

Catherine leaned back and remarked: "Now I know the real meaning of the term 'public relations.'"

"Just tell the people what they want to hear, only not too clearly," Eric murmured, watching Chris.

A question was asked by one of the network people about the possibility of his appearing on television. Chris replied that any TV appearances he made would be handled through the foundation. Other questions followed quickly, and through all of them, Chris remained politely noncommittal where necessary, and answered more fully when he could. Asked to comment on the current Administration, he declined, pleading ignorance of the workings of government— "Like so many Americans, I just don't understand it!" On his interests or hobbies, he said: "I've been very successful as a gardener. Some people think I have a green thumb with ailing plants." The response brought a burst of warm laughter.

Eric smiled with undisguised delight. "Christ, he's terrific! They love him!"

John nodded, looking pleased. "The boy is simply wonderful."

A woman editor of one of the major women's magazines asked Chris about his relationship with Nella Stanwyck: ". . . and will an engagement be announced in the near future?" She smiled slyly, glancing at Nella.

"Nella and I have been friends since we were children," he answered. "Being able to make her walk again has made me very happy."

To further evade the question, he gestured to Nella to join him on the podium. Flustered, but pleased by the unexpected request, she rose and went to his side as a round of applause broke out.

"He's beginning to ad lib on the script," Eric said, frowning. "I'd better bring this thing to a close."

He started to rise from his seat when suddenly Chris held up his hands for silence and said: "I have an announcement to make that may be important to you."

The news people quieted down. Catherine gave Eric a questioning look and he shrugged, nodding his head negatively.

Holding Nella's hand, Chris looked out over the room and said: "Hundreds of letters have come in from people requesting my help. I want to answer them now by saying that a public healing will take place in the very near future, here in Philadelphia. As soon as the time and location have been determined, they will be announced."

An excited buzz went through the audience. Eric looked astonished, and Catherine asked under her breath: "Did you know about this?"

Charlotte, looking bewildered, leaned forward to hear his answer.

"No, I didn't," Eric replied, anger darkening his face. "Chris was in the studio the other day and asked to see the letters. I had no idea that he had this in mind, or that he would announce it like this!"

"He must have been very moved by what he read," Charlotte said.

Eric got to his feet and started toward the podium, giving Chris a sign to close the conference.

"Okay, that's enough!" he muttered to him under his breath as he smiled at the news people getting to their feet and leaving.

"Did I do it right?" Chris asked anxiously. "Was I good?"

"I'll give you a critique later. Just follow John and get out of here, and try keeping your mouth closed!"

A few minutes later they were all together in the anteroom. Eric closed the door and turned to Chris.

"I don't know whether to hug you or hit you!" he snapped. "What the hell was all that nonsense about a public healing?"

Chris paled before Eric's attack and Nella came to his defense.

"I thought he was wonderful," she said, "and the healing is a beautiful idea!"

"I agree, Eric," Charlotte said in a milder tone. "Those people can't simply be ignored."

"Perhaps we should calm down before we discuss this further," John suggested. "The last hour has been trying for all of us."

Eric faced Chris, silent for a moment. Then he threw his arm around him in a rough embrace. "I'm sorry, kid, you just took me by surprise. You really were terrific."

"I tried to remember everything you told me." Chris laughed, relieved. "God, now I'm nervous! Look, my hands are shaking!"

Catherine went up to him and hugged him. "I'm very proud of you," she said. "You handled yourself just beautifully."

"You're not angry about my announcement, are you?" he asked. "Once I read those letters, I knew I had to do it."

"No, I'm not angry," Catherine answered. "I just don't understand why you didn't discuss it with the rest of us first."

"It was something I wanted to do on my own," Chris explained.

"Like running off to the explosion?" Catherine questioned.

"I suppose so," Chris said defensively. "I can't keep following orders for the rest of my life!" he added sharply.

"No, of course not," Catherine agreed quietly. "Well, it's done now, isn't it?"

Chris smiled at her slowly. "Yes, it is."

◆

A few evenings later Chris lounged on the floor of the playroom with Nella. At every opportunity that they had to be alone, they came here, as if to re-establish the bond of years they shared. Once the door was closed and locked, the room became their private world, filled with memories and secrets known only to them.

Tonight stacks of newspapers lay spread open on the floor, some thrown casually over the games and toys they had played with as children. The only light in the room came from a lamp whose base was a music box, a merry-go-round that automatically turned when the lamp was on. Distorted shadows of the tiny horses pranced across the walls in a slow dance, accompanied by the tinkling sound of calliope music.

Chris was smiling with amusement as Nella read to him.

". . . apparently unaffected by his astonishing gifts, McKenzie presented a picture of a sincere and rather modest young man. Articulate and charming, he captured the affection of the large group."

"Stop!" he cried, laughing. "That's enough! Any more and I shall proclaim myself king!"

He swept the paper from her hands and pulled her into his arms.

Nella rested her head against his chest and said: "I think it's wonderful! I'm going to start a scrapbook!"

He tilted her head back and kissed her softly. "Can you put that in your scrapbook?" he asked teasingly.

"Yes," she said, smiling. "I have a very special scrapbook for that."

They were quiet for a while, content to lie in each other's arms and watch the dancing shadows of the lamp play across the walls.

"What are you thinking about?" Nella asked dreamily.

Chris sighed deeply. "How everything has changed. It's all happened so fast I still don't quite believe it. You must feel the same way."

"Yes," she answered. "When I get out of bed in the morning, I find myself reaching for my crutches." She looked up at him and laughed. "Isn't that strange? All these years I wanted to walk without them, and now that I can, I still look for them."

He smiled and stroked her hair.

She sat up to face him and said: "Do you realize what you've done for all of us?"

"No." He grinned lazily. "Tell me."

"I've never seen Mother so excited about anything as she is about the foundation. And Eric and Catherine, too! Mother told me that Catherine is moving into a suite of offices in her building until they find a place that's, as Mother put it, 'suitable for so important a project'! And did you know that several doctors from Drexel University have called to ask if you'd work with them in their psi programs?"

"Yes, I know," Chris said. "My life is going to become a series of conferences and meetings and tests. And do you know what?" he asked with mock seriousness.

"What?"

"The garden will go to rack and ruin!"

Nella threw her arms around him. "Didn't you know? You've been replaced! You're no longer the Stanwyck gardener."

"I'm not? Who am I, then?" he asked, holding her face between his hands.

Nella looked at him with dark, shining eyes. "I think you're going to be a very famous man," she said slowly. Then, smiling mischievously: "You're the golden prince of ancient legends, come to cure the world of its ills and fears."

He stared at her for a few minutes, his hands moving over her hair and down her back, drawing her closer to him. A slight nervousness came over him as his fingertips slid down her arm to her hand, bringing it to his lips to kiss. Nella shifted her body to sit more comfortably between his legs, and when he kissed her, she pressed against him, feeling his tongue slip into her mouth, his hands cover her breasts. They drew apart, not speaking, searching each other's eyes for the question and the answer. Then she stood up and unhooked her skirt, letting it drop silently to the floor, pulled her sweater over her head, and faced him clad only in a pair of pale-yellow panties. In the soft light her slender body was as white as ivory, her small breasts firm, girlish, tipped with light-pink buds.

Chris's eyes moved over her slowly; he saw the softly rounded hips and thin legs, the pulse beating in her throat, and her long, dark hair fanned out in thin strands along the curve of her shoulders. He got to his knees and buried his face against her thighs, his hands moving to her small buttocks. He slid his fingers under the silky material covering them and tugged the panties down her legs, pressing his mouth against the soft curl of hair that was revealed.

Nella gasped at the touch of his lips. She reached down and

brought him to his feet. Hesitantly at first, then more eagerly, she helped him take off his clothes and let her hands discover the warm, firm flesh of his back and his hips.

Chris's legs trembled as he lifted her in his arms and carried her to the center of the room, then lowered her to the thick, soft rug. Nella's mouth was open, moist, and he covered it with his own. His hands moved up between her thighs, spreading them wide to his gentle, teasing touch. She clung to his lips, feeling him shift his body over hers, aware of the slow, uncertain prod of his erection. With a quick, impatient movement, she lifted her legs around his back, bringing him into her. A low moan of pain escaped her lips at the sudden flash of pain. He paused and remained absolutely still. Nella opened her eyes for a moment and saw the shadows of the merry-go-round horses moving slowly over the walls in time to the jingle of music. She thought of Chris and herself as children here in this room, heads bent close together, whispering secrets to each other. The memory was illuminated as if by a bright light. Then he began to move within her, and as she was slowly overwhelmed with sensations of pleasure, the memory dimmed, replaced by the reality of an unexpected ecstasy.

30

Within two weeks following the press conference, Eric and John had formed a production company to film the public healing Chris had announced. Catherine and Amanda began to set up the research and studies program, while letters asking for Chris's help continued to pour in as more stories about him appeared in newspapers and magazines. Requests for him to be a guest on programs about psychic investigation came in from major universities and colleges, and a cross-country tour began to take shape.

Television network reps called almost daily asking when Chris would be available, but Eric side-stepped them with smooth public relations agility.

He told Catherine in her office one morning: "I want him to have absolute legitimacy before he sets foot inside a network studio. The AMA and church groups have already begun to publish statements claiming he's a fraud. We've got to have documentation from researchers and doctors and more proof of what he can do to offset that kind of publicity. Too many people are saying that the tape of

Nella's healing and the explosion footage were inconclusive evidence."

"What shall I do about these bids from publishing companies and literary agents who want his life story?" Catherine asked. "Four of them have offered advances that are pretty dazzling."

"It's too soon for that. After Chris does the tour, those advances will be doubled! Then Charlotte's lawyers can take over; everything should come through the foundation. Otherwise we'll all be accused of cashing in on his abilities."

"Speaking of cashing in," Catherine said, "I have about fifty requests for product endorsements on my desk. Everything from razor blades to breakfast cereals."

"A polite 'no' to all of them," Eric replied. "Once he starts getting into the muck of commercial advertising, we're finished with any claims to dignity."

Catherine couldn't help grinning at him.

"What are you looking so sly about?" he asked.

"I was just remembering how afraid I was that Chris might be exploited by all this sudden fame and fortune. I like the way you do your job. I've never seen you in action before."

He pulled her close to him. "What was that line again?"

She kissed him lightly. "I haven't seen any of that action lately, either."

He smiled. "Put yourself down on my schedule for dinner and a long evening."

She kissed him hard, slipping her hands inside his jacket and running them over his back. "I didn't know I had to make an appointment," she said.

"Make that a very long evening—in bed," he whispered, kissing her again.

The phone rang and they pulled apart. Catherine caught her breath before answering: "Hello? . . . Yes, I'll be there in a minute, Amanda. . . . What? Yes, Eric's here. . . . No, dear, you didn't interrupt anything, sorry." She laughed and hung up.

"How's it going with the research program?" Eric asked.

"Slowly," Catherine said. "We've been too busy being receptionists and secretaries. Amanda's in the process of interviewing girls right now."

Eric looked at his watch. "I've got to run. I'm meeting John in a few minutes to check out a hall, and later this afternoon we're having a production meeting with the crew."

"Eric, wait," Catherine called as he started for the door. "I wanted to ask you about the tour. Charlotte said it looks as if it's going to be a long one."

"Just a couple of weeks—we'll talk about it at dinner. There's nothing definite yet. I want to wait until we see what happens at the healing." He blew her a kiss and then was gone.

Catherine looked after him for a moment, frowning. Then the phone began to ring again.

"Oh, for Christ's sake, Amanda, I'm coming!" she muttered.

◆

It was Charlotte's idea that they all spend Sunday together. The public healing was scheduled to take place the following Wednesday night, and everyone agreed that a breather was an absolute necessity before, as Amanda said, "total madness set in."

It was late September, and the weather began to promise a crisp and splendorous fall. The sky was blue and filled with drifting clouds. The first hint of autumn color had seeped into green, leafy boughs of trees, speckling them with dashes of red and gold, and the gardens around the Stanwyck house were a colorful profusion of the last of the summer flowers.

It was still warm enough to eat outdoors; a buffet table was set up on the terrace and was covered with plates of cold cuts, salads, rolls, eggs, pâtés, desserts, and drinks. Silver and glassware sparkled against white linen, and a dazzling sun touched a gleam to freshly washed fruits in cut-glass bowls.

Almost everyone arrived early: John and Margaret, proudly escorting their grandson, who was appropriately dressed in a white suit, followed by Eric and Catherine, their arms loaded with a variety of toys and David's favorite blanket.

Amanda arrived a few minutes later with a large basket of fruit and flowers. She took one look at the buffet table and the gardens and grumbled something about "carrying coals to Newcastle." Charlotte laughed and made a special display of the flowers on the table set up for lunch. Nella was everywhere at once, greeting them all as if they hadn't seen one another in weeks, instead of just days. The bright sound of their laughter echoed over the lawns, and when

Chris drove up, tooting the horn of a new Mercedes sports car that Charlotte had given him, everyone burst into a round of applause.

Later in the day, after lunch, Eric and Catherine took a walk with Chris and Nella. Chris was carrying David on his shoulders and pretending to be a great bear on the prowl. The little boy giggled and yelled "Go! Go!" encouraging Chris to a gallop. Nella ran after them, shouting gleefully as Eric and Catherine watched.

"What a wonderful day," Catherine sighed.

"Yes, it's perfect." Eric smiled and put his arm around her. They walked across an open grassy area to a grove of maple trees and sat down. At the far end of the grounds they could see Chris and Nella playing with David, the sound of "London Bridge" drifting through the still air. Eric lit a cigarette and lay back contentedly.

"We may not have another day like this for a long time," Catherine said, almost to herself.

"The voice of doom," Eric kidded her.

Catherine smiled and slipped down beside him. "No, really. I mean all together like this. It's a lovely moment, one to be treasured."

Eric nodded, took her hand, and kissed it softly.

"I wish Susan had joined us," Catherine said.

"Chris said she simply refused to come. He told me that she didn't feel comfortable with everyone, that she was still just a dressmaker and didn't 'fit in,' as she put it."

Catherine looked unhappy. "That's not true—she was just trying to spare his feelings. She's against all this, has been from the beginning." She paused, and then added: "I'm worried about her. And I feel guilty. We've broken every promise we made to her about Chris."

Eric sat up, frowning. "Cathy, there was nothing else we could do. You can't keep someone like him hidden away from the world. Eventually what he's capable of doing would have come out."

"I know," she agreed. "And if I haven't mentioned it before, thank you for being so careful with him, so considerate of his future. I wish Susan understood the efforts you're making."

Eric took her in his arms. "I owe Chris a lot, and not only for finding my son. In a way, he brought us together. And that's something I'll always be grateful for."

That evening, after dinner, the party moved into the library. The weather had turned cloudy and cool, and a fire was started in the fireplace. Amanda began a game of gin rummy with John, Margaret, and Charlotte, while Eric and Catherine joined Chris and Nella by the fire. Murmurs of laughter came from the game table, and around the fireplace, conversation was idle, reflective.

". . . and the list of psychics throughout history is endless," Catherine was saying in answer to Nella's question about other men like Chris. "And they always faced the same problem," she went on, "that of being accepted by the world. When someone comes along who is able to disregard the ordinary physical laws that hamper the rest of us, we get very nervous."

"Why?" Eric asked.

"Because we have no easy explanations," Catherine answered. "These people are a threat to our security; they make us realize that we don't know everything. We look for the trick, the deception, the proof that no one is that much more capable than the rest of us. And yet, we're fascinated by their unexplained gifts."

Chris looked up from staring at the fire, his face flushed rosy with warmth, the flickering light sparkling in his large green eyes. "What happened to those men in the past, the ones with powers like mine?" he asked.

Catherine hesitated. "Well—many of them came to rather unpleasant ends." She laughed at the look of dismay on his face. "We're talking about the past, Chris. Not today."

"What did happen to them?" Eric asked.

"Oh, let's see," Catherine mused. "There was Cornelius Agrippa. He was born in 1486, I believe. He was a sensitive, with the gifts of precognition, telepathy, and an ability to use his mind to influence events." She glanced at Chris, uncertain whether she should go on.

"What happened to him?" Nella asked.

"He was a rash, tactless man, and angered his colleagues many times. Once he was thrown into prison and tortured. He died in 1535, his health broken, cursing his gifts."

"And the others?" Chris questioned. "How did their lives go?" He looked at her steadily, his face expressing only curiosity.

"Paracelsus lived in the fifteen hundreds. He was a doctor with extraordinary gifts of healing, thought to be magical powers. But he had a violent temper and drank heavily. He made many enemies who eventually ruined him financially. He died of injuries from a fall taken while he was drunk."

"Good Lord!" Eric exclaimed. "Chris, do you drink?"

"Not a drop."

Nella shivered, and Chris put his arm around her. "Don't worry," he said, smiling. "I won't fall down drunk, and I promise not to die in prison."

"We've been talking about ancient history," Catherine said. "Today, all over the world, there are many people with extraordinary gifts who are leading quiet, simple lives, doing what they can to help others."

"I guess that's what my mother wanted for me," Chris said thoughtfully. "Maybe, if things had been different . . ." He frowned, and for a moment his eyes clouded with a look of concern.

"But I think what's happening to you is good—it's right," Eric stated. "You'll be able to help more than just a few people; you'll contribute something valuable to many. Isn't that true, Cathy?" he asked.

She looked at him affectionately. "There speaks the positive voice of today," she said. "I have to agree. You do have a chance to do something valuable, Chris, and not just with healing and sighting, but for all the efforts being made to learn more about those areas of human capabilities that still mystify us."

Chris had been listening to her intently, but at the back of his mind a memory was taking shape, intruding into the warm, cozy scene, blurring the sound of her voice. He saw himself as a child, standing at the doorway of the room, *this room*. And in the flickering light of the fire the image of Tom Stanwyck appeared. He saw the pleading, terrified look in his eyes and then the vicious battering of his head against the oak beam framing the bookcase, streams of blood covering the man's face. And he could hear the distant echo of his mother screaming: "Stop it! Chris, for God's sake, stop!"

◆

On the night of the public healing, scores of police were out in the street trying to clear traffic in front of the auditorium. Newscasters, followed by cameramen carrying porta-packs, were interviewing the lame and the crippled, men and women with children in their arms, elderly people sitting in wheelchairs. Many of them had been in line and waiting all afternoon.

By eight o'clock everyone was inside, filling the seats, standing in the back of the hall, spilling out into the lobby. Three cameramen were busily manning video tape recorders: one in the audience, another on the stage, and the third near the ramp leading from the center aisle to the stage.

Eric came out and made a brief introduction, then Chris walked onstage. A hush fell over the hall. He looked out over the auditorium and saw a blur of faces peering up at him, silent and hopeful. Standing under the bright lights, he felt uncomfortably warm, and trickles of sweat ran from under his arms down his body. He was dressed in what had become his public-appearance clothes: a soft white shirt under a white pullover sweater, white slacks, and white shoes. In the glare he seemed to radiate a glow of youth and energy; his blond hair looked almost as white as his clothes, creating an aura around his deeply tanned face and emphasizing the color of his eyes.

He stepped forward to the microphone, cleared his throat, and began to speak.

"Good evening. Before we begin, I want to thank all of you for coming here, for showing so much faith in me."

He stopped and glanced up at the control booth where Catherine sat with Eric. They smiled and Eric waved him on. He continued, his voice becoming more assured.

"I don't know how many of you I can help, but I'll do my best."

There was a murmur of approval from the crowd, a little sound of applause.

Chris looked toward the light booth. "Could you turn on the houselights, please? I want to see everyone." The hall lit up and Chris walked to the edge of the ramp. "That's better," he said, looking out at the audience.

The front rows were filled with people holding crutches and many whose legs were covered with blankets, their wheelchairs out in the lobby with attendants and ushers.

Chris stared at them, frowning, his face grave with concern. "You can't come to me," he said quietly, "so I shall come to you."

The onstage cameraman followed him down the ramp to a small open space by the first rows of seats.

And then it began.

For the next three hours people walking or held up by friends and relatives passed before him. He touched their bodies, ran his fingers over paralyzed legs and withered arms, placed his hands on those struck down by cancer, asthma, arthritis, restored the power of speech to one man who had suffered brain damage in an accident, and cured a victim of psychosomatic blindness. There were moans of pain, then gasps of joy, outcries of relief and gratitude that rose and swelled through the steady flow that came to him more and more eagerly. Tears streamed down faces of young and old. They swore their belief in him, praised the miracle of his gift. Others begged him to find a lost one, a child missing, a brother who had disappeared. Chris clutched sweaters and rings, watches and caps, his eyes squeezed shut, face strained with concentration as he haltingly tried to locate the missing.

"Eric, that's enough!" Catherine said tensely. "He can't do any more. Signal him to stop!"

Eric had the houselights brought down. A groan went up from those who had not yet been with Chris. He staggered back up the ramp and onto the lighted stage, holding up his arms. The sounds of disappointment quieted, and he said in a weak and trembling voice: "I promise you that I'll come back." He stopped and swallowed, tried to speak again but couldn't. Bowing his head to them once, he turned and began to leave the stage. A cry of "God bless you!" rang out and was taken up by other voices that rose and became a roar of gratitude, augmented by applause and weeping.

Backstage Eric and Catherine were waiting. They led him to a small dressing room.

"Was it all right?" Chris asked weakly, sitting on a chair.

"You were fine," Eric said. Catherine handed him a cup of hot coffee, and he held it while Chris took a sip. "Drink some more, then catch your breath. We won't leave until the hall is cleared."

Eric left the room to check with the crew. Catherine sat down beside Chris and held his hand tightly. "Are you feeling all right?" she asked.

"Yes, but God, I'm tired."

"You did it for too long. You've used up an enormous amount of energy. I don't think you should do this again."

"I've got to," he said slowly. "Didn't you see those people, their faces?"

"But, Chris, you can't! There's no way you can cure everyone who comes to you. We don't even know how many people you cured tonight!"

"But *I* know," he said, shaking his head. "There were some I couldn't do anything for—I could feel that. But the others . . ." He looked at her and smiled. "There were so many others I—I cured, I healed!"

He closed his eyes and leaned back in the chair. Catherine covered him with his topcoat. "Just rest now, then we'll take you home," she said.

A few minutes later Eric came in and they roused Chris, slipped him into his coat, and started to leave the hall through the empty auditorium.

Eric had parked his car by a side exit, and as they approached the door, Gary called out from the back of the darkened hall: "Eric, before you leave, I think you and Chris ought to take a look in the lobby."

"What's the matter?" Catherine asked as they went up the center aisle.

"I don't know. Some vandalism, maybe . . ." Eric muttered.

Chris remained silent, walking between them slowly.

They pushed through the swinging doors into the lobby. The main lights had been turned off, but small yellow wall lamps shaped like candlesticks were still on, casting a pale, ghostly light over the marble floor and oatmeal-colored walls.

Gary was standing by the door of the ticket booth, and the other members of the crew stood around the lobby, staring silently.

"Oh, my God!" Catherine breathed in a low whisper.

Stacked against the walls and lying on the floor were dozens of crutches and canes, left like a scattering of kindling wood. Near them, standing empty and discarded, were wheelchairs. One had been pushed over on its side and a wheel was still spinning, making a light whirring sound in the silence of the room.

Chris slept on the way home, and Catherine and Eric were silent, afraid of waking him. Susan was waiting at the door when they drove up to the house. She took Chris by the arm, thanked them for bringing him home, led him inside, and closed the door without asking what had happened. In his room, she helped Chris out of his clothes, turned down his bed, and went to get him some hot milk. By the time she returned, he was under the covers and sound asleep. She tucked in the blankets, opened a window from the top for air, turned off his night lamp, and left the room. They had not exchanged a single word.

Chris opened his eyes and stared into the darkness. He glanced at the illuminated clock beside him, wondering how long he'd been asleep. It was almost three in the morning. He closed his eyes and tried to go back to sleep, but a strange restlessness overcame him. After turning and tossing for a while, he got up and paced the room. He didn't understand the sudden surge of energy flowing through him when just a few hours ago he'd been almost completely exhausted. Unsettled by the demanding wakefulness, he slipped on his clothes, pulled a heavy jacket from the closet, and, carrying his shoes so as not to wake Susan, went through the house to the back door and outside. He put on his shoes, thinking he would walk for a while to calm himself. Then he caught sight of his car parked in the driveway and changed his mind. He opened the door and got in and released the brake so he could coast down the slight incline to the road without turning on the motor, knowing his mother would be up at the slightest sound. Once on the road, he switched on the ignition, threw the car in gear, and took off.

He drove aimlessly through the countryside, not caring where he was going, but driving only to find relief from the agitation that churned within him. He had a vague memory of having felt this way once before. When was it? After the explosion? Yes, that was the time, late that night in the Stanwyck house. And he'd gone to Janet, seeking release. But she had left her job to go to New York. And it was too late to see Nella.

He turned the car in the direction of Philadelphia. He might find a girl in some club or all-night restaurant or coffee shop, or even on the street. He didn't care where. He just wanted to get laid. He began to fantasize what he'd do when he found a girl, and the thoughts aroused him. He gave vent to his imagination and drove faster.

The twisting roads were dark, but the night was clear, the moon bright. An inexplicable anger came over him, somehow making his sexual excitement more intense, and he drove with increasing speed, tires squealing around treacherous curves, the car tipping dangerously. Suddenly headlights of an approaching car appeared. They weaved sloppily across the road, rushing at him with a blinding glare. Chris hit the brake and felt the car pull to one side as the other car was almost upon him. His front fender was sideswiped in a shriek of tearing metal, and he slammed his car off the road into a ditch.

The other car stopped with a screech and a man got out, cursing loudly.

Chris opened his door and sprang from the car, yelling: "You stupid son of a bitch!"

The man turned, surprised. Then he howled: "What? Why you fucker, you were driving like a maniac!"

Chris felt his anger erupting. "You dumb shithead farmer! You drunken prick!" he shouted hoarsely, starting toward him.

In the glare of his headlights the man's figure swayed and tottered. He searched the ground wildly, then reached down, picked up a rock, and rushed at Chris, screaming: "I'll bust your fuckin' head, you bastard!"

Chris's eyes opened wide, stopping him in mid-flight. The man stood frozen, his body half crouched, head snapped up, staring in shock. Chris walked toward him slowly, eyes blazing as the man sank to his knees, his headlights shining directly on his face.

He began to gasp. A hoarse cough tore through his throat and was choked off. Chris stood over him, not moving, an enraged expression distorting his features. The man's eyes bulged, and he wheezed, struggling for air, unable to move his arms, to use his hands to tear at the invisible fingers tightening around his throat. His face was as gray as a dirty sheet, his lips pulled back in a grimace over his teeth. His eyelids began to flutter wildly, and his tongue shot out of his mouth, dribbling spit.

Suddenly Chris's body shook violently. He gave a loud cry and tore his eyes from the man's face. The figure before him collapsed, rolling to the ground like a sponge, his chest shuddering as he gulped for air.

Chris ran to his car and fell into the front seat, breathing heavily. His body was damp with sweat and he felt light-headed, faint. He looked back at the man lying in the road and saw him turn groggily, trying to sit up. Relief swept through him, knowing that the man was still alive. He turned the key in the ignition and started the car; he had to get away before he was seen, recognized. By the time the man was on his feet he would remember nothing except being sideswiped by a passing car. Chris reached for the handle of the door to pull it closed. At the same time he glanced up into the rearview mirror and saw his face, pale and shadowy in the overhead light of the car.

What was that on his cheek? He leaned closer to the mirror. Was it blood? But he hadn't been touched. Then he sat absolutely still, his eyes opened wide, staring at the scarlet tear. It was blood. A shock of fear went through him like a volt of electricity, making him gasp for breath.

In a quick, fearful gesture, he smashed his hand against it, leaving a thin smear of red on the side of his face.

31

Eric had agreed to let the networks pool their coverage of the healing in order to feed the program simultaneously to their affiliates. The three-hour event was seen across the country on newscasts, and during the weeks that followed, diligent reporters sought out for interviews those people who had attended and been cured. There were almost nightly reports about Chris and his powers; the medical profession continued to be vague about the results, even though some family doctors confessed that their patients did, in fact, appear to be remarkably improved or altogether well.

The foundation was deluged with more letters from people seeking help, psychics claiming even greater powers than Chris's, cranks who swore he was a fraud, and promoters with a variety of schemes to make him world-famous and rich.

The most surprising requests came from thousands of young people reacting to his youth and appearance as they might to a film or recording idol. They asked for autographed pictures, volunteered to form fan clubs, and begged Chris to make personal appearances in their cities.

Charlotte cleared an entire floor in her building so that Eric could set up a staff to handle the details of what became known around the office as the "Christopher Movement." A newsman picked up the expression and used it as a headline for his column.

Catherine's office was flooded with mail from psychic organizations all over the country wanting to know more about her studies with Chris and asking her to participate in their research programs.

John announced the formation of the Christopher Company in ads that appeared in *Variety, Broadcasting, Advertising Age,* and other trade papers. The announcement stated that the company would produce and syndicate tapes of healing and sighting events to independent stations nationwide. Advertisers responded in a rush to buy time from the stations, and a tour of major cities throughout the country was scheduled. Eric would accompany Chris, direct the tapings, then send the tapes to John, who would supervise the editing and get the shows out to the stations.

"The networks are howling!" Eric laughed as he told Catherine. "They all wanted the program, but with total control. Now we've got them by the short hairs!"

"I have a feeling you enjoy being the head of a production company," Catherine said, smiling at his enthusiasm.

"It's something I've always wanted, but I never dreamed it would happen like this!"

"How long will you be on tour?"

"All together, about two months. Are you sure you can't come with us? I hate the idea of us being separated for so long."

"I wish I could, but you wouldn't believe the load of work on my desk. Answering the correspondence alone will take months! And organizing the research program, ordering equipment, supervising the staff—my God, life was so simple just a few short months ago!"

"But it's what you always wanted, isn't it?" Eric reminded her.

Catherine laughed. "My mother once very wisely said, 'Be careful what you wish for—you're liable to get it!' I'm beginning to think she was right."

Eric saw the anxious expression in her eyes and took her in his arms. "What are you worried about?" he asked.

"Chris, mostly. He's so young and inexperienced. What will all this do to him?"

"Don't forget, I'll be with him," Eric said reassuringly. "We've become great friends. I'll take care of him, I promise."

◆

In the fitting room in Susan's house, Charlotte stepped back from the mirrors and examined the lines of the simply cut black gown she was wearing.

"You don't think it's too severe?" she asked, turning to Susan.

"Not at all. The slight drape at the hip softens it just enough."

Charlotte looked back at her reflection, turned to see the side view, and nodded her head in agreement. "You're right, as always. Now get me out of this and let's have some tea. It's been ages since we've talked."

"Oh, Charlotte, I'd love to, but I have so much to do," Susan said hurriedly. "Perhaps another time?"

"Susan, don't try to put me off," Charlotte replied with a trace of exasperation in her voice. "I haven't seen you or talked with you about anything that's happened since Chris healed Nella." She saw Susan's reluctance, and added: "We've been friends for too many years for me not to know when you're upset about something. Please, can't we discuss it?"

"There's really nothing to discuss," Susan said sharply. At the look of dismay on Charlotte's face, she relented and said: "Oh, all right. I'll go put on the kettle."

A few minutes later they sat facing each other in the living room. Charlotte looked around and smiled as Susan served the tea.

"I remember the first day I brought you and Chris here. God, that was more than fourteen years ago!"

"Yes, I remember it too," Susan said quietly.

"Oh, my dear, so much has happened, so many good things!" Charlotte said. "And especially now! I still can't believe what Chris has done—Nella walking again, and all those people he's helped. You must be so proud!"

"Yes," Susan agreed, "I'm very proud of him for that."

"Then why have you kept away from all of us?" Charlotte asked. "You haven't accepted any of our invitations to be part of the foundation. You haven't even come to visit the offices."

Susan looked at her calmly. "You believe in all of this, don't you, Charlotte? The healing and sighting, the work that Dr. Marlowe is doing, the tour Chris is going to make. You believe in it and you approve of it, don't you?"

"After what he's done for me? Of course I believe in what Chris is doing."

"Well, I do not," Susan said firmly.

Charlotte stared at her, shocked. "But why? How can you not believe in all the good he's accomplished?"

"And what good will it do for him?" Susan raised her voice. "I'm concerned about my son!"

"But we're all concerned for his welfare," Charlotte argued. "You know how much I care about him. Since that first moment when he walked into the placement office in London—such a darling little boy, so serious and grown-up—you know how deep my affection has been for him." She laughed, recalling the incident. "Why, if it hadn't been for him, I might never have brought you to the United States, to my home—remember?"

Susan nodded, thinking to herself how Christopher had made Charlotte change her mind about hiring her, just as he had made her rescue him from drowning . . . forced Tom Stanwyck to injure himself . . . Johnny Stark to leap from the fire escape . . .

The frightening chain of her thoughts was interrupted by Charlotte saying: ". . . and there's something else that I'm sure you're aware of; Nella and Chris are very much in love. I wouldn't be at all surprised if soon you and I were bound by more than just years of friendship."

"What?" Susan sat up tensely. "You think they'll marry?"

"Yes, I do," Charlotte said, smiling.

"You can't mean that!" Susan cried out, incredulous.

Charlotte stared at her, confused. "Why not?" she demanded. "Nella loves him, and I think Chris is one of the finest young men I've ever—"

"And would you think he was so fine if he was just your gardener?" Susan asked scornfully. "What is he without his gifts? No more than his father was—a simple, ordinary man! He has no trade, he doesn't know anything about the world, he's—"

Charlotte stood up, her face pale, voice trembling. "Susan, I don't understand how you can talk that way about your own son!"

"There are so many things you don't understand!" Susan said furiously.

Charlotte picked up her bag and started to leave. "I can't talk with you when you're like this. It makes no sense to me at all."

Susan was frantic; how could she explain the fear, the terror she had lived with all these years, the dread that he might hurt others as he had Stanwyck and the Stark boy?

"Charlotte, please," Susan pleaded, "I'm not some domineering mother trying to keep her son! You must believe me when I tell you that he cannot go on with what he's doing—that he must stop!"

"How can he?" Charlotte replied. "There's too much at stake! The hundreds of people he can help, the important research Dr. Marlowe is doing—"

"And what about Chris?" Susan shouted. "His whole future is at stake—his life! Everything you're doing can only hurt him!"

"You're wrong!" Charlotte said fiercely, her eyes blazing. "I believe in Chris as I've never believed in anything or anyone in my whole life! What he's done for me can never be repaid except by making it possible for him to do the same thing for others. And I fully intend to make that happen with all the resources at my command!"

The two women faced each other, suddenly silent, aware of the awful chasm that had opened between them. Shaken and embarrassed, Charlotte went to the door. She turned and looked back at Susan.

"I'm sorry this has happened," she said, her voice trembling. "When you've had time to think, to understand, please call me. I would hate to think that after all these years, particularly now, when we share so much, our friendship should suffer in any way."

Susan stood still, her body rigid, face drawn and white. She heard the door close behind Charlotte, the sound of her car starting and driving off. Then, as if some vital strand of her being had been stretched to the breaking point and then suddenly snapped, her body sagged with defeat, her head slumped forward, and tears began streaming down her cheeks.

She walked slowly, aimlessly through the house, staring dully at rooms that were strangely unfamiliar. A feeling of alienation from everything she had known came over her, the sense of being completely lost and set adrift in some foreign place where she would perish.

Then she was in Chris's room, looking blankly at his bed, a shirt tossed carelessly over a chair, his shoes lying on the floor as if he'd just stepped out of them. Her eyes fell on the row of model planes he had made with Michael when he was a child. And she saw once more the man with his bright-red hair and sparkling blue eyes so filled with love for her and Chris. She remembered the night he died, and Chris's terrified whimpers as he clutched Michael's shirt and described his death.

With a howl of rage and torment, Susan swept the planes to the floor, watching the fragile painted wood splinter and crack.

◆

Nella looked out the window as Chris pulled the car up to a shabby building standing beneath the blinking red neon sign.

"Chris, this isn't a motel," she said, giggling. "It's the set left over from the movie *Psycho!* The manager will come in and kill us both while we're in the shower!"

"I'm sorry, honey." Chris laughed. "But I just couldn't risk going someplace where either one of us might be recognized. Do you want to skip it? We could try to get a few hours alone at the house. . . ."

"No chance! I've always fantasized spending a night in a place like this with my lover; it's so clandestine."

He pulled her to him and kissed her. "I like hearing you call me your lover," he murmured. "It gets me excited."

She pressed against him and laughed. "Let's check in before we get to the point where we don't need a room. Besides, it's freezing out here!"

A few minutes later he hurried out of the manager's office, got back in the car, and drove down to the last cabin in the court. Nella pulled her overnight case from the back seat and they went in. Chris switched on the overhead light, revealing a plain square room furnished with a double bed, night tables and lamps, a side chair, and a magazine rack spilling the torn pages of back issues. A door scarred with peeling paint led to a tiny bathroom.

"Oh, it's awful!" Nella cried, laughing. "For God's sake, turn off the light and put on the lamps—anything would help!"

"Christ, it's the pits," Chris grumbled. "I shouldn't have brought you here."

Nella put her arms around him and said softly: "As long as I'm with you, it doesn't make any difference where we are."

In the dim yellow light of the room they took off their clothes and stared at each other with a sense of wonder. They drew closer and reached out with tentative fingers to touch, to feel the perfection of flesh, to marvel at the response and the excitement of being together. Like dancers moving to a slow but insistent rhythm, they came together in an embrace of lips and hands, bodies touching lightly at first, then pressing firmly, turning to move to the bed, clinging to each other as they lay down. In a silently understood exchange of pleasure, they took turns in caresses and kisses, startled, then pleased at the other's arousal. Chris trailed his fingertips along the soft curve of Nella's loins, down to the warmth between her legs. Her thighs opened at his touch, and she gasped softly, moving his face to her breasts, directing his lips and tongue to her nipples. She stretched her arms along the length of his back, trying to embrace his entire body. Her hands clasped his buttocks, drawing him between her legs, and she urged him into her with low, whispered commands. He slipped his hands under her hips, bringing her body up to meet his more tightly, heard her quick intake of breath as he moved in long, steady strokes. She half rose from the bed and threw her arms around his neck. Pulling her with him, he sat up so that she was in his lap, her legs clamped around his waist. For a long, breathless moment, they were still, not moving, like children trying to prolong an instant of exquisite pleasure. Then their lips met feverishly and in a rush of excitement Chris lowered her to the bed.

"Ah, Chris! Chris!" Nella cried out. "I love you!"

"It's late; we must leave soon," Chris murmured.

"No, not yet," Nella said, her face buried against his throat.

He smiled and kissed the top of her head. "Then you have to move," he said. "My arm is getting numb."

She shifted her shoulders with a sigh and sat up beside him. The thin gray light of dawn was coming through the worn shades and curtains at the windows, lightening the shadows and dark corners of the room.

They rested comfortably in each other's arms for a while. Then Nella asked: "Will you call me? Whenever you can? I don't care how late it is."

"Of course I will. If we can work it out, we'll even fly home for a day or two."

Nella smiled and moved into the circle of his arms to be closer to him. "But you will be home for Christmas, won't you? I have so many things planned for us."

"Yes, the schedule was worked out so that we'll be home about the middle of December."

Nella sat up and turned to face him, brushing her hair back with her hands. "Chris?" she said hesitantly, wondering how to frame her question. Then she went on. "How do you feel when you're healing people? I mean, what do you think of while you're doing it? And afterward, when you know you've made them well."

A puzzled frown creased his brow. "How do I feel? Well, I'm not sure I can put it into words. It isn't something I really understand, you know. I'm concentrating very hard on them, just as I did with you. I'm not thinking about myself at all. And while it's happening, I feel—well, I guess it's larger than I really am. I feel very strong and calm. And very big, as though I'd doubled in size. I'm not really thinking at all," he repeated. "I'm just—doing, I guess, doing what's necessary."

"And after. What do you feel after you've healed someone?"

"I feel tired," he said. "As if I'd drained myself of all energy." He grinned and touched her face. "Like last night, with you."

"Is it like that?" she asked. "Like making love?"

He nodded slowly. "In a way—yes, it's like making love, only different. I can't describe how."

"But it makes you feel good, doesn't it?"

"Oh, yes. I feel wonderful. . . ."

He stopped, suddenly remembering how he woke up after the mass healing, the restlessness and unaccountable feelings of anger and frustration, the wild drive he took through the dark, and the other car on the road, the drunken man coming at him, threatening and cursing. For a moment he saw the doughy face in the glare of headlights, eyes bulging with fear, choking and gasping for air.

"Chris, what is it? You're so pale!" Nella said anxiously.

"What?" he asked her, startled.

The face disappeared like a nightmare vanishing in the instant of waking. Chris shivered and tried to laugh.

"I'm cold, that's all." He swept her into his arms. "Come and warm me."

32

For the first few weeks of the tour Chris followed Eric like a child clinging to its parent's coattail in a crowd. Each day was a phantasmagoria, a dreamlike rush of hotel rooms, and lunches and dinners with men and women who questioned him suspiciously or greeted him with excitement. There were interviews with skeptical reporters and meetings with the heads of psychic research institutes. Crowds gathered for every healing, filling the halls to overflowing and waiting on the streets afterward to catch a glimpse of him. Chris felt surrounded by a constant wave of people, blessed by those he healed and damned by others for refusing to credit his powers to God.

Eric kept things moving smoothly, using his position as director and personal manager to help Chris maneuver out of the grasp of aggressive interviewers and to ignore the organizations that spoke out publicly against him. The video tapes of each event were sent to John, and within a week independent stations began to receive them. As they were aired, the controversy about his powers grew. Late at night in their hotel rooms, Eric and Chris listened to newscasts on the radio and watched commentators on TV discuss the sweep and ramifications of the Christopher Movement with a solemnity befitting international politics. Eric would laugh, make notes, and outline a plan to offset every negative opinion. More and more Chris admired Eric's positive ability to deal with setbacks and problems. He saw in Eric an image of success and confidence that elicited respect from everyone they came in contact with, and unconsciously he began to pattern himself after that image. He became bolder at meetings with the press, more relaxed during interviews on local TV programs, and generated a mature charm that, combined with his youthful handsomeness, captivated an even larger audience.

The number of his younger followers grew larger. Crowds of teenagers were on hand at airports to greet him, holding aloft banners and posters with his picture on them. In Chicago a cheering demonstration broke out as he stepped off the plane.

"Jesus, I'm beginning to feel like a movie star!" Chris exclaimed.

Eric smiled. "We had to work fast to get your pictures here so that the posters could be printed in time, but we made it. They look good, don't they?"

Chris turned to him, taken aback by what he had said. "You mean all this was arranged?"

"Well, not so much arranged as helped along a little." Eric laughed. "I'll explain it later. Get ready, here they come!"

The next half hour was spent trying to get through the crowd. Chris signed autographs and shook hands while Eric pressed him along. Chris saw members of the crew following them with minicams, recording the welcome.

"What are they taping this for?" Chris asked as they got out onto the street.

"Just some action footage to cut into the tape of tonight's show—fills it out," Eric replied briefly. "There's the car. Make a sprint for it," he said as another eager crowd closed in on them.

Later, in their hotel, Chris said: "I don't understand about those kids with the posters and the crew filming all of it. Haven't all the demonstrations for me been spontaneous?"

"Not since Cincinnati," Eric explained. "Oh, they have been, to some degree, but I found it expedient to work with APRC, that's Associated Public Relations Company. They've sent out an advance man to help set up the interviews, distribute releases, and get the artwork done for posters and newspaper ads. There are a thousand details to be handled on a tour like this. I can't do it alone, you know."

Chris shook his head. "No, I didn't know. I didn't realize it was such a—business." He stared at Eric, confused.

"Well, in a way, that's exactly what it is. It doesn't affect how people feel about you. It's just a means of letting them know you're here, generating more excitement about you, creating an image that gets their attention."

Chris sat down on the bed, trying to absorb what Eric had said. "But, Eric, aren't the healing and sighting enough?"

"Not altogether. Try to understand, Chris. The foundation is paying for this tour, and there are a hell of a lot of expenses. There has to be a profit from the admissions charged for each event in order to reimburse the foundation and have a little left over. Charlotte can't foot the bill for all of this. So we add a hype to the show, and people get curious, want to see you—not necessarily people who are ill or crippled, just people who are curious. And in that way we sell out the house for a week instead of a night or two. You see what I mean?"

"Yes, I think so," Chris said slowly.

Eric grinned and slapped him on the back. "I know all this advertising and promotion is difficult to understand—"

"No, it's not really. It's just good merchandising, isn't it?"

"Hey, you *are* learning!" Eric laughed. "But you don't have to worry about any of that. That's my job."

"And you do it well," Chris said with a touch of sarcasm.

Eric bristled with anger. "You're damn right I do! If it weren't for me, you'd be traveling in a bus and doing your number in tents and high-school auditoriums!"

Chris reddened with embarrassment. "I'm sorry. I didn't mean to sound critical. I guess I have a lot to learn." He paused, and then, smiling a little, added: "But I will; I'll learn it all. I've got the best teacher around."

"You bet your sweet ass you do!" Eric said, laughing. "Now get some rest while I check everything out. These next couple of days will be a bitch!"

To conserve Chris's energy, the shows (as he had come to think of them) were limited to an hour and a half. This gave John enough coverage to edit the tapes down to an hour for their broadcast time slots. White-jacketed attendants were stationed throughout the audience to help the infirm, and the front rows were taken by those people whose requests were most urgent. A format was established: Eric introduced Chris with a brief statement, and then Chris would come onstage to a thunderous round of applause. Always dressed in the white pullover sweater and slacks that had become his uniform, he stood in a dramatically arranged design of lights, head slightly bowed as he waited for quiet before welcoming the audience. To the worshiping and hopeful, he appeared, as one columnist had enthusiastically stated: ". . . standing in the lights like one of the mystical figures in a Blake painting, graceful and handsome, glowing with an inner radiance."

Then Chris would ask for the houselights and walk down a ramp into a large area left open for the healings and sightings. The pitiful parade of lame and crippled, ill and afflicted, passed before him, and afterward the response was the same: gratitude, tears, blessings, and applause. Often he was left surrounded by gifts and tokens of love and adoration; always were the lobbies of the hall scattered with crutches, canes, and wheelchairs.

Eric saw to it that the publicity man he worked with had pictures taken of Chris during the healings and later, standing in the midst of the discarded crutches. These were sent out with news releases and began to appear in papers around the country. The ratings on the weekly show kept rising, and young people all over the nation began to band together in groups called the "Christopher People," revering him with the same idolatry they would a rock star, and with just as little purpose.

One night, in Detroit, Eric, on his way to attend a late dinner with officials of the local TV stations, left Chris in the hotel lobby.

"I begged off for you," Eric said. "It's just business, and you need some rest. You look washed out."

"Yeah, I'm bushed," Chris agreed tiredly. "I'll give Nella a call and then crash. See you in the morning."

"Give her my love and have her tell Cathy I'll call her tomorrow."

In his room, Chris stripped off his clothes, ran a hot tub, and soaked for half an hour, letting the strain of the evening ease out of him. He closed his eyes and tried to relax. He was worried. In the last couple of weeks, after his acts of healing, he had been experiencing the same troubled state that had occurred before: first he was exhausted and would sleep for a few hours, then suddenly awake, filled with an unaccountable energy that was always accompanied by feelings of anger and frustration. The memory of his encounter with the drunk on the road was still vivid in his mind, and he made every effort to control himself until the mood passed, afraid of what might happen if he left the hotel. Having Eric in the adjoining room helped; they had notes to go over, the PR man to talk with, the news reports to watch on TV.

But lately the feelings had grown more persistent, his sleep more restless and troubled. Sometimes talking with Nella helped, but often the sound of her voice and the memories of their lovemaking only increased his agitation. Mobbed by devoted followers after each show, he was more and more aware of the many young girls staring at him adoringly, asking for his picture or if they could write to him. A few had pressed close enough to whisper invitations for a later meeting, and some had made overt sexual suggestions. He'd mentioned the incidents to Eric and had received a stern warning to be careful of doing anything that might smear his image.

"You can't start fucking your way around the country," Eric had said. "It would be bound to get out to the press, and there are enough people who are against you as it is. Any kind of scandal could wreck the tour, your work, even the foundation."

"What the hell am I supposed to do—jerk off every night?" Chris had exploded angrily. "I'm not a fucking saint!"

Eric couldn't help laughing. "That's one image we don't need for you. But listen, I understand how it is. I'll talk with Phil and see if we can arrange something for you."

But Phil Conners, the public relations man, had advised against it. A rock group he had worked with recently had enraged the management of hotels they had stayed in with all-night parties that had ended in drunken vandalism, and legal action had been taken by the parents of a teen-age girl who had been raped. Chris was counseled, advised, and offered sedatives.

Getting out of the tub, he dried himself wearily, trying to set his mind on a full night's sleep. He slipped on his robe and walked into the bedroom, only to stop and stare in surprise at the sight of two girls sitting on the small couch by the windows.

"Who are you? How did you get in here?" he demanded.

"Oh, please," one of the girls cried, getting up, "don't throw us out! One of the bellboys is a friend of ours and he let us in. We're both writing for our school paper, and we just want to talk with you for a minute, that's all!"

"If you call the manager, our friend will lose his job," the other girl pleaded.

Chris hesitated, unsure of what to do. Eric probably wouldn't be back for an hour or so, and the bellboy could slip them out of the hotel without anyone knowing they'd been here; perhaps it would be all right.

"Okay," Chris said, "but just for a few minutes. I'm pretty tired."

"Oh, we know. We were at the healing tonight. You were wonderful," one of the girls said breathlessly.

"What's your name?" Chris asked, sitting down across from them.

"I'm Darlene Gorman and this is Sally Foster."

"How'd you get the idea to do this?" Chris asked. "I mean to get in here, to my room."

"It was my mother's idea," Darlene said. "Oh, I don't mean it was her idea to come here to see you," she said, giggling. "I mean, she told me how she got in to see Frank Sinatra once, when she was a girl. She wanted to interview him for her school paper, too. So she bribed the bellboy like we did—" She stopped, realizing what she had said, and turned red with embarrassment.

"How much did it cost you?" Chris asked, grinning at her confusion.

"Twenty dollars," Darlene said under her breath.

"I'll give it back to you before you leave," Chris said. "You don't have to pay to interview me."

The girls exchanged surprised and delighted looks, thanking him effusively. Chris sat back, beginning to enjoy himself. They were about sixteen, he thought, not exceptionally pretty, but cute in the way they were flustered in his presence and trying to act grown up.

"Do you mind if I smoke?" Sally asked.

"No, go ahead," Chris replied. Then, just to tease her, he asked: "You nervous?"

She smiled at him brightly. "No, should I be?"

Darlene threw her a look that said "Stop flirting!" and Chris laughed.

"Well?" Sally tilted her head to one side coquettishly. "Should I be nervous?" She stared at him frankly.

He stared back and grinned, enjoying the teen-age game he hadn't played since he was in high school. "You never can tell," he said lightly.

Darlene dug into her large shoulder bag and pulled out a notebook and pen. In a deliberately prim and businesslike manner, she began to ask him questions, nudging Sally to do the same.

While Chris answered them, his eyes moved back and forth over the girls. They had both dressed for the occasion, forgoing jeans and T-shirts for neat skirts and blouses, a little too much junk jewelry, and heavy eye liner. Darlene had wide blue eyes and long brown hair, and her complexion was good. Sally's hair was blond, and she had mischievous brown eyes. Both girls were braless, and Chris decided that Sally's tits were better, fuller; but Darlene had nicer legs. He wondered what they would do if he came on to them. He was sure that Sally was a tease, all pose and no action, and Darlene would probably make some excuse to leave. They were just kids, like the girls he'd known at school, probably virgins, but then again . . .

Darlene put on a pair of large-framed glasses, and he was suddenly reminded of Catherine's student, the girl named Sarah. She had been a buttoned-up little thing like Darlene, but he had mind-pressured her to change, get loose and sexy. Could he do it with these girls, with both of them? He'd done it with the woman he'd picked up on the street in Wynnewood, and with Janet, but he'd never tried to mind-pressure two people at once. He was titillated by the idea and slightly aroused; if anything did happen, they'd never remember it. . . .

Both girls were talking at once, firing questions at him about his home, his hobbies, his favorite movie star or rock singer. Chris continued to answer, but concentrated on his idea, his mind directing them to make a sexual overture to him.

Darlene made the first move. In the middle of a question about his favorite food, her face suddenly went blank, her eyes half closed. She put down her pen and notebook, slowly stood up, and began to unbutton her blouse. Sally was caught, too, he could tell. She sat perfectly still, but her breathing had grown rapid, and she was playing with the zipper on her skirt.

Chris smiled, elated; he was in perfect control of both of them! Darlene was nude to the waist. She slipped out of her shoes and walked a few steps to where he sat, her hands playing over her breasts. They were small and firm, with tiny pink nipples. Chris felt himself getting hard. He opened his robe a little so she could see him. Darlene moved closer, and he spread his legs so she could stand between them. He leaned forward and ran his hand up under her skirt, feeling her thighs and closing his fingers around her small buttocks, barely covered by nylon panties. She sank into his lap, and he cradled her with one arm. Then he looked up at Sally. She had taken off all her clothes and was standing perfectly still, waiting. He glanced toward the bed, and she walked to it slowly and lay down with her legs spread slightly. Chris reached out and turned off the lamp by his chair. One lamp in the far corner of the room was still on, casting pale light across the ceiling. He stood up, lifting Darlene in his arms, and walked to the bed. As he passed the large mirror hanging above the chest of drawers, he glanced at his reflection and stopped. In the semidarkness he could see the half-naked body of the young girl in his arms. For a few seconds he was overtaken by a feeling of remorse for what he was about to do. He could stop now, make them dress, send them home; they'd never know what happened.

Darlene shifted in his arms, and his hand closed over her breast. A small shock of excitement went through his body, and his moment of indecision was overcome by a sudden intense desire to finish what he'd started. He'd never been with two girls at the same time, but now he could do whatever he wanted to—and no one would ever know!

He glanced back at the mirror, exhilarated by the thought of his own power. Then he saw the dark-red tear at the corner of his left eye. He stared at it calmly, not frightened as he had been that night on the road with the drunk, but now only curious. Had they seen it? The girls, and the drunk, and the others: Johnny Stark and the boy who had thrown coffee in his own face? Tom Stanwyck? Was it the physical sign of his power to command, appearing like stigmata? No one had ever mentioned seeing it; but then, no one had ever remembered what he had done.

He looked down at Darlene, and she responded to his thought by lifting her hand and gently wiping the tear away.

◆

In Cleveland, Chris insisted on having a room that didn't adjoin Eric's, one that was in another part of the hotel.

"I've got to have some privacy," he argued. "When I'm with you, there are meetings, phone calls, people dropping in—I'm on top of this thing all the time. I have to be alone for at least a little while!"

Eric agreed and Chris took a room on a different floor and in another wing of the hotel. That night, after the event was over, Chris went back to his room, showered, and shaved. An hour later there was a light tap at the door, and he opened it to admit a young woman who had slipped a note into his hand while getting his autograph. She had requested a private meeting for personal reasons. Chris had whispered the name of his hotel and the room number before they were separated by the crowd.

She walked into the room, clutching her purse, and looked around uncertainly. "I can't thank you enough for seeing me," she said. "I know you must be very tired and—"

"No, I'm not tired," Chris said, smiling at her.

He took her coat and gestured to a chair. She sat down, legs pressed together primly, her hands clasped in her lap. She glanced at him nervously and tried to smile.

She is pretty, he thought. Her ash-blond hair was shoulder length, and her face was small, delicate, with large blue eyes and a generous mouth. She wore a simple gray suit that almost disguised the curves of a good figure, but not quite. He guessed that she was about twenty-eight.

"Why did you want to see me?" Chris asked softly.

She began to say something, cleared her throat, and laughed shyly. "I'm a little nervous, and embarrassed," she said. Then, taking a deep breath, she went on. "My name is Louise Gaynor. A few weeks ago I went to a doctor for some minor surgery and he discovered that—" she faltered, and finished in a low voice. "—I had ovarian cysts." She stopped and swallowed hard. "May I have a glass of water?" she asked. "I didn't think this would be so difficult."

Chris brought it to her and she drank deeply. "Thank you," she murmured. "Do you mind if I smoke?"

"No, not at all," he replied. He was a little disappointed; she had come to him for help, not games.

"What can I do for you?" he asked as she lit a cigarette.

"Well, my doctor made some tests, and he told me I needed a hysterectomy. I'm married, just over a year, and it would mean we couldn't have any children, and my husband wants a family."

She began to cry, and Chris went to her, knelt by her chair, and took her hands.

"Don't cry, Louise. I can help you," he said gently.

"Can you? Really? I was afraid to tell my husband what the doctor said, and then, when I read about you being in town, I thought maybe—at least it was worth trying to see you. I didn't tell Ted I was coming here. I mean, he doesn't know anything about it at all."

Tears rolled down her cheeks and she stared at Chris imploringly.

"I can help you, Louise," he repeated. "Now dry your tears."

"Are you going to do it now?" she asked hopefully.

"Yes. It will only take a few minutes."

Chris stood up and went to his closet. He came back with a terry-cloth robe and handed it to her. "Go into the bathroom and take off your clothes. Put this on, and then we can start."

While she was changing, Chris paced restlessly. This wasn't what he'd expected. He felt a surge of irritation, almost anger, at her, as if in some way she had tricked him.

The bathroom door opened and Louise came into the room. She looked like a little girl wrapped in her father's robe. Her hair was slightly mussed and her face was flushed. She smiled at him uneasily.

"It's a little big for me," she said huskily, her fingers tugging at the belt nervously.

Chris smiled reassuringly. "You look fine," he said. "Don't be afraid. I promise I won't hurt you."

"Oh, I know that. I saw what you did tonight. All those people you helped."

"And now I'm going to help you," he said, taking her arm and leading her to the center of the room. "Just trust me."

She looked up at him and smiled. "I do trust you. Completely."

Chris stood close to her, slowly undid the belt, and opened the robe. She gave a nervous start, but remained quiet. He put his hands on her waist and waited for a moment.

"Your hands are so warm," she whispered, closing her eyes.

He stared at her full breasts moving with her rapid breathing. Her nipples were erect, and he smiled. It had happened before; other women had become aroused by his touch while he was healing them.

He kept one hand on her waist and moved the other slowly to her stomach and down to her mound, his fingers moving through the soft brush of pubic hair. Her body stiffened and swayed closer to him so that they were almost in an embrace. She threw her head back, and her lips parted in a deep sigh. He moved his hand between her legs, and she spread them slightly so that his fingers could close over her crotch.

"Oh, God!" she gasped. "Your hand is like fire! I'm burning!"

He held her tightly, moving his hand over her stomach and back to her vagina.

"It's burning me!" she cried, tears streaming down her face.

A moment later he moved his hand back to her waist, holding her quietly until she had recovered.

"Are you all right?" he asked quietly.

"Yes," she answered huskily. "The burning sensation is gone now."

"How do you feel?"

"I—I can't describe it. Warm and relaxed—better than I've ever felt before."

She lifted her head. Her eyes were bright and filled with adoration. "How can I ever thank you?" she whispered. "You'll be in my prayers for the rest of my life."

She started to pull away from him, but he held her fast. "Louise, don't go yet," he said.

She looked up at him, a little surprised, and saw in his eyes what he was thinking, what he wanted. She smiled almost sadly and touched his face lightly with her hand.

"I can never repay you for what you've done for me," she said softly. "But I can't stay with you. I love my husband very much, and we shall always be grateful."

Chris kept one arm around her waist, holding her tightly. He moved his other hand to her breasts and caressed them.

"Louise, please," he insisted.

"No, I can't. Don't . . ." Louise pushed his hand away and tried to get out of his grasp, frightened by the expression on his face.

"Yes!" he said firmly.

A few seconds later she took off the robe and dropped to her knees before him. Her hands reached out to unclasp the belt buckle and open his pants, responding to his thoughts with all the feverish sexuality his mind could imagine.

A few days later, in Atlanta, they answered a special request and went to a private clinic where Chris conducted a healing session under the watchful and amazed eyes of the director and his staff. Patients suffering from blood clots, bleeding ulcers, leukemia, and tumors were cured; a woman with inoperable cataracts was able to see a few minutes after Chris had touched her.

While the doctors, astonished by what they had witnessed, hurried to examine their patients, the director took Chris and Eric into his office and said: "I've been in touch with Dr. Marlowe in Philadelphia, and at her request, I'm sending her a complete report of our findings after we've examined the men and women you were with this morning."

"Catherine is making a study of the people Chris has healed on this tour," Eric said. "We appreciate your cooperation, Dr. Gainer."

"How do you feel, Christopher?" the doctor asked, turning to him. "When you've finished a healing session, are you depressed or elated? Do you feel tired?"

"I used to experience great exhaustion when I was finished," Chris replied. "But with each healing I find that lessening. It's almost as if by doing it, I revitalize myself. Actually, I'm beginning to feel stronger every time."

Dr. Gainer nodded and made some notes. Chris looked at Eric and said: "Don't you think we'd better get going? There's a lot to do this afternoon."

The request took Eric by surprise; they had planned to have lunch with the director and his staff. But Chris's mouth was set in a tense line, and his eyes were nervously signaling Eric to leave. Making apologies and excuses, they rose and were escorted to the front entrance by Dr. Gainer and a few of his associates. Chris replied to their questions with a forced smile and brisk answers.

When they were finally on the street, walking toward the car Eric had rented, Chris said: "Sorry about the lunch, but I really wasn't up to it."

"Are you feeling all right?" Eric asked.

"Yeah, just a little restless and keyed up. Why don't you drop me off downtown and I'll do some shopping; I still have Christmas gifts to buy. I'll meet you back at the hotel later this afternoon."

"Well . . ." Eric hesitated, a little worried by Chris's nervousness. "Why don't I come with you? I have some things I want to get for David, and then we—"

"Eric, for Christ's sake, stop mothering me!" Chris snapped. "I'll be all right, and I'd really rather be alone."

"Sure, okay—I understand," Eric said soothingly. "We have been living a little out of each other's pockets these last weeks."

A few minutes later Eric dropped him off in the main downtown area of the city, and Chris began to walk. The day was overcast, with a leaden sky threatening rain. The sidewalks were crowded with shoppers bundled up in topcoats and scarves, hurrying from one store to another, nose tips turning red and eyes tearing from the cold. Several people recognized Chris and stopped him for autographs or just to talk with him. He was polite, if somewhat brusque, and finally most of them moved off, staring at him and whispering among themselves.

Chris moved quickly, trying to quiet the agitation that had come over him when he had finished the healing at the clinic. It was beginning to alarm him; in previous sessions, this unrest had not been evident until hours later. But with the last few events, he had found himself nervous and uneasy almost immediately after. He tried to rationalize that it was simply a reaction to the energy he was using when he healed, that eventually he would be able to control it.

He entered a department store that was lavishly decorated with Christmas trappings. Recorded carols were being played over loudspeakers throughout the store, and the aisles were jammed with people carrying packages. He maneuvered his way to the perfume counter and squeezed in beside an overweight, red-faced man arguing with his wife. She was thin and anxious-looking, her blond hair streaked with gray, her face tense and lined. The man looked up and recognized Chris.

"Hey, I know you!" he exclaimed. His breath smelled of whiskey, and his small eyes were bloodshot and blinked continuously. "You're —what's his name—that healer kid, ain't you?" he demanded.

"Yes, I am," Chris replied without looking at him. He began to examine the labels on an assortment of bottles set out on the counter.

"Yeah, you're the one," the man went on. "I saw your picture in the paper." He turned to the woman and said loudly: "Hey, Tess, this is that kid you said you wanted to see tonight. He's right here!"

Chris nodded to the woman. She broke into a wide-eyed, surprised smile and mumbled something he couldn't hear, then turned nervously back to the counter.

Chris started to move away when the man took his arm and said: "You really do all those things? Make cripples walk and heal the blind and all that crap?"

A few people close by looked up at them, but the din in the store was too loud to hear what was being said.

Chris pulled his arm away from the man and answered irritably: "Why don't you come tonight? Then you can see for yourself."

"Shit, I wouldn't fork out eight bucks for that kinda bull!" The man laughed. "I think you're a goddamned phony, that's what I think!"

Chris shrugged and began to move away, but the man followed him closely. "I read where you don't believe in God. Is that true?"

"Listen, I've got some shopping to do, if you don't mind," Chris answered between clenched teeth.

"Do you believe in Jesus?" the man demanded in a rasping voice.

The woman caught up with them and tried to quiet her husband as Chris walked toward the front doors. A little girl got in his way, and then they were beside him, the man raising his voice.

"I asked you a question: Do you believe in Christ? Answer me, punk! Who the hell do you think you are?"

Chris turned on him angrily. "Why don't you go home and sleep it off, mister?" He shoved through a group near the doors and left the store.

The man pushed his wife aside and followed him, shouting: "You're phony trash, that's all you are!"

The woman came after him and grabbed his arm, pleading with him to calm down, to come home. He thrust her aside and she almost fell. A few people passing by ignored them. As the man started after Chris, the woman recovered herself and tried to grab the man's arms. They grappled for a few seconds, then he shouted something obscene and slapped her across the face. She let out a howl of pain and cursed him. Someone nearby said to get the police, but she cried out "No." Chris had turned around, and the man was almost on him when the woman tried once more to take his arm. He hit her again, this time knocking her to the pavement. At the sight of the woman, bleeding from the nose and mouth, Chris's anger turned to rage. He focused on the man, making him spin around to face him for an instant. The bloodshot eyes widened in surprise and the brutal face went pale. Then the man staggered back and suddenly darted into the street in front of oncoming traffic. A van hit its brakes, but too late; it smashed into the man and flipped him over. Another car screeched to a stop, but not before running over his legs. The crowd on the sidewalks gasped, and the woman struggled to her knees, screaming. A police car came around the corner and stopped. Traffic jammed and motorists blew their horns and shouted furiously.

Chris saw an alley between two buildings that cut through to the next street. He ducked into it and began to run, automatically wiping away the tear he felt on his cheek near his left eye.

Back in his hotel room he stripped off his clothes, went into the bathroom, and turned on the shower. He let the water stream over him full force to ease the tremors that still shook through his body. He closed his eyes, wanting to forget what had just happened.

I didn't do it on purpose, he whispered to himself. I didn't mean to hurt him. I just did it—I just did it!

The image of the man's body lying in the street was vivid in his mind. He groaned aloud and began to cry, his body shuddering under the flow of water.

"Oh, Christ!" he said, weeping. "I didn't even wait to see if he was alive or dead!"

◆

In the first week of December they were in Miami. It was the last city on the tour and an unexpected relief from the wintry weather they had just left. Temperatures were high during the day, with intermittent rains making the nights stiflingly humid. Chris's nerves were ragged, and the muggy climate only added to his irritation. They were booked for three events and had sold out the hall. When Eric told him that they could do two extra nights because of the demand for tickets, he refused.

"We're turning away a lot of people," Eric argued.

"You mean we're losing a lot of money, don't you?" Chris snapped. "Well, forget it! I'm tired; I need some rest."

"Okay, okay," Eric said, trying not to get angry. "It was just a thought."

Ashamed of his outburst, Chris relented. "Sorry, Eric. I'm just a little on edge. If you think we should do the extra nights, I'll do them."

"Are you sure? I know I'm pushing you, but the requests for tickets were a hell of a lot more than we anticipated."

"I think this whole tour has been more than either of us anticipated," Chris said with a touch of bitterness.

Oblivious to the tone of his voice, Eric smiled at him and replied: "Listen, when we get home you can loaf straight through the holidays, I promise. No meetings, no interviews. Nothing but fun and games."

"Sure, sure," Chris sighed, knowing he was being pacified.

"Hey, I mean it!" Eric laughed. "We'll eat home-cooked meals and sleep until noon."

The phone rang and he picked it up. "Cathy! How are you, darling? . . . Yes, just fine. I miss you. . . . What? . . . No, he's fine too. . . . No, I'm not running him ragged."

He laughed and winked at Chris, signaling him to talk with Catherine, but Chris shook his head no.

"What? . . . You're kidding!" Eric went on. "No, hold it until we get home. . . . Just another week. . . . Yes, I know, but the demand has been more than we expected." He paused, listening, and a serious look came over his face. He whistled softly and said: "Well, well—how about that! . . . No, we'll discuss it when we get home. . . . Right. Kiss David for me. Call you tomorrow night, darling."

Eric hung up the phone and turned to Chris. "Cathy sends her love. She said that Charlotte received a letter from the Pentagon requesting an interview with you."

"What for?" Chris asked.

"They were a little mysterious about it, but I think they're interested in your sighting abilities."

"Why?"

Eric narrowed his eyes and assumed a Bogart voice. "Secret mission for the CIA. You're the only man who can sight the enemy's hidden missile bases. Will you do it, McKenzie? Will you serve your flag and country and save the world from certain death?"

Chris did a ho-hum yawn and answered with feigned disdain: "If I have time—I'm terribly busy. I'll talk with my manager and see if we can squeeze saving the world into my schedule!"

"Terrific!" Eric laughed. "Now get some rest. Tonight you have to save Miami!"

"Seriously, though, do you think I should do it? Work with the government, I mean, if that's what they want?"

"Hell, no!" Eric exclaimed flippantly. "There'd be foreign agents all over the place trying to gun you down! Besides, we may be doing a tour of the West Coast after the first of the year."

"Are you kidding?"

Eric chuckled. "Don't panic. We haven't agreed to it yet. But think of it—Seattle, San Francisco, Los Angeles. Think of all the really sick people you could save in Hollywood!"

"Oh, Christ!" Chris groaned.

"We go where we're needed, when we're needed," Eric intoned solemnly.

"The hell we do," Chris muttered.

By the time they reached the auditorium that night, it had begun to rain. It was a moderate but steady downpour that didn't seem to affect the lines of people waiting to get in. Or a group of demonstrators who had driven up in a bus painted with signs reading: "JESUS SAVES—CHRISTOPHER DOESN'T."

They were marching in a weaving line, arguing with the waiting people, and shouting that Chris did not believe in Jesus, that his power was a fraud or the work of Satan and would damn them forever.

Eric took Chris into the auditorium through a side entrance, assuring him that the police would disperse the unruly mob. From inside the lobby they watched the angry protesters waving their signs and yelling at the crowd in line to leave. A fight broke out and someone screamed. In moments there was a tumult of flying fists and people slipping and falling on the wet sidewalks. Several patrol cars drove up, and when the police rushed the demonstrators, there was a furious scuffle. The demonstrators locked arms and wedged themselves into a tight knot to resist being arrested. Local network reporters and cameramen arrived on the scene and began covering the incident with porta-packs and minicams. It started to rain harder, adding to the confusion and turmoil. Men and women on crutches and in wheelchairs tried to dodge the press of bodies and skidded on the pavement and fell.

"I'm going out there and break it up," Chris said to Eric.

"Don't be a damned fool! The police can handle it. You'll only get hurt!"

Chris shoved past him, opened one of the doors, and ran out onto the wide steps fronting the building. Over the din he began to shout for attention. Someone in line saw him and cried out his name, and everyone looked up at him. The throng of protesters, still clinging together, called out for him to repent, to admit his belief in Jesus, and to accept Him as the Savior.

Through the driving rain Chris saw that there were about thirty of them, mostly young people dressed in jeans and T-shirts. He walked down a few steps so that he was closer to them and raised his arms, crying out: "What difference does it make what I believe? Isn't what

I do more important? You call yourselves Christians, but you behave like a street gang!"

A roar of anger and abuse went up. Eric rushed to Chris's side and grabbed his arm. "Get the hell out of there before they start throwing rocks at you!"

"Goddamnit, leave me alone—I can handle it!" Chris said defiantly.

He pushed Eric aside and stepped forward, staring at the wedge of young people intently. The rain had soaked his clothes and plastered his hair across his forehead. Water ran down his face and neck, but he stood unblinking, his eyes hard. Once more he raised his arms and shouted: "Go home! Let me do what I can to help these people! Behave like the followers of Christ you claim to be!"

Their jeers and cries abruptly lessened, then ceased. An uneasy silence fell over them, and they stood quietly, their attention fastened on Chris. The police looked at one another questioningly, as if they expected a sudden flare-up of violence. The men and women in line stared, confused and bewildered by the quiet.

Then the young protesters silently let go of one another and began to walk slowly through the crowd toward their bus. A few officers, confounded by what was happening, started to make some arrests, but Chris waved them off, saying to let the demonstrators go. A cheer went up from his followers as the young people filed into the bus and drove away.

"Christ, you were terrific!" Eric said in amazement.

Chris turned to him and smiled. "I told you I could handle it," he said. "Now get me some dry clothes and let's get this show on the road."

"That's my boy!" Eric exclaimed as they hurried backstage. "Do you realize that this little display of leadership and courage will make every newspaper in the country?"

Chris threw him a wry glance and laughed. "I had a feeling you'd say that."

33

Catherine tested the roast with a fork, closed the oven door, and glanced at the clock hanging on the kitchen wall. It was almost eight; Eric would arrive in a few minutes. She went into the dining room and glanced at the table, moved the flower-filled centerpiece slightly, and smiled with satisfaction.

In the bathroom she checked her make-up and ran a brush through her dark hair, thinking about the television coverage of Eric and Chris's arrival that morning. The scene at the airport had reminded her of their return from Omaha. Only this time Chris was the center of attention, hugging Nella to him and beaming at local reporters and TV newsmen. She had caught a quick glimpse of Eric in the background as Chris said a few words to the crowd, flashed a handsome smile for the cameras, and then waved the reporters away before they could talk to Eric.

A little upstaging there, she mused to herself. He went out a boy and came back a star.

The doorbell rang and she hurried to answer it.

"Is this the place?" Eric asked.

"You're damned right it is," she answered, going into his arms and kissing him.

A few moments later she pulled away from him. "You keep that up and we'll never get to dinner," she said, trying to catch her breath.

"To hell with dinner," he muttered, kissing her again.

"Okay, you win," she said, weakening under the touch of his hands and lips. "To hell with dinner."

Catherine turned on the bathroom light and began to repair her make-up. In the mirror she caught sight of Eric through the open door of the bedroom. She watched as he slipped into his clothes and for a brief moment felt a flush of anger at herself for what had happened. You've got more libido than good sense, she chided herself. Then, glancing back at his reflection, a strange feeling came over her; for a few seconds Eric seemed to exist only in the mirror, a distant image rather than an intimate presence. It's the months of separation, she thought. Somehow we've lost something that will take time to regain. She wondered if he had noticed it too.

A few minutes later they were at the dining-room table and Eric was laughing. "I like well-done lukewarm roast! It's my favorite, really."

"You obviously need a rest—you've been working too hard; your mind is going."

"What's for dessert?"

"You've already had it."

"Don't I get second helpings?"

"Like all men who come home from the war, you're crazed with lust."

" 'War' is right," he agreed, "and so is the 'crazed with lust.' God, I missed you! Why weren't you at the airport?"

"I didn't feel like another homecoming scene," she answered quietly. "I watched it on television. Chris looked very well. He handles himself with the poise of an international celebrity. But you look awful. You're thin and you have hollows under your eyes." She shoved a plate of potatoes at him. "Eat."

"Jewish mother," he murmured. "Next you'll be giving me chicken soup."

"No, that got cold while we were having dessert," she said with a half smile. "Tell me about the war."

"It wasn't that bad, not really. A rough schedule, too many interviews with writers holding hatchets between their teeth, but we managed. Chris was sensational."

"So I read, and saw. The pictures of him surrounded by canes and crutches got a little boring. You'll have to think of something new. Like maybe a crowd of worshipers on their knees around him?"

"Do I detect a note of sarcasm?"

"Unless you're deaf," she answered. " 'Sensational' is exactly what I thought when I saw those pictures. Oh, I know that publicity is necessary, Eric, but I really felt you went too far."

"If we could appeal to the public in any other way and succeed, we'd do it," Eric replied, a little annoyed by her criticism. "What's bothering you, anyway?"

"Just about everything," she flared. "The shows looked like Hollywood productions with Chris as the leading man. John added that banal quasi-religious music; Chris was lighted to look as though he'd just floated in from a quick visit with God—"

"Wait a minute! I worked hard on that lighting, and with good reason. People respond to drama and theatricality. If we're going to draw an audience of two thousand to an auditorium in the dead of winter, we have to give them a show. They expect it, and so do the advertisers. They're clamoring to buy time on the program. And the profits go to the foundation—to further your work. Isn't that the point of the whole project?" He smiled confidently.

"You're changing the subject," Catherine said, irritated by his smug self-assurance. "I was talking about the way Chris is being promoted."

"Don't you understand that it's all one and the same? I thought we did a hell of a job."

"A job on what? Making Chris look like a performing seal? You've turned him into a star! He has fan clubs all over the country. Teenage girls are having wet dreams about him! We've received requests for locks of his hair, his socks, and his jockey shorts!"

Eric began to laugh and Catherine grew furious.

"It's not funny! It wasn't supposed to be like this!" she exploded. "We talked about dignity, about presenting him in a serious, legitimate context—not marketing him like a 'hot property'!"

There was an ugly silence between them for a moment. Eric tried to control his anger before answering her.

"Cathy, I'm not infallible, I know that. But aren't you forgetting the reports that were sent to you from the clinics and hospitals we visited? We had the cooperation of every doctor and head of research we talked to. Hasn't their material been of some benefit to your studies?"

"Yes, of course—"

"And what about the people themselves—the sick, the blind, the crippled? What the hell difference are fan clubs or teen-age girls with the hots or publicity devices to them? He saved their lives!"

"I'm not ignoring that part of it," she protested.

"Then what the hell are you upset about?"

"Chris! He's become an attraction; he has the status of an entertainer. His gifts have been cheapened by every promotional gimmick your feverish little agency imagination could conceive!"

"My feverish little agency imagination has turned a profit for the foundation so that you can continue your work and more people can be helped!" Eric said heatedly.

"But at what price? Chris is beginning to imagine himself as some kind of savior bringing the word to the masses. I've watched the shows, read the interviews. He's become brash and arrogant; he's made attacks on the church and the medical association—"

"I admit he's made some rash statements, but he's only a kid! I can't put a tape on his mouth! Even Charlotte has said that what he's doing is right, that the only way people can learn is to shake them up and make them think."

"Charlotte is his most fanatic follower! As far as she's concerned he can do no wrong. And don't think that doesn't worry me too!"

"What are we really arguing about?" Eric asked abruptly. "I don't think it's Chris or Charlotte or any of this, is it?"

Catherine stared at him angrily, then turned away. "I thought I was supposed to be the psychologist," she said caustically.

"I'm not trying to play games," Eric bristled. "Tell me what's really bothering you."

She looked back at him and nodded her head. "All right. It's what's happening to you—and to us. You've been gone for two months, and now there's talk of a West Coast tour. John told me it's almost definite, and that you engineered it. What about your son? What happens to David? John and Margaret are too old to raise him —he needs a father. He was better off with the Harkins!"

"That's a cheap shot, Cathy," Eric said in a tight voice.

"But true, nevertheless." Her eyes softened as she looked at him.

"I love you, Eric. Before all this happened we had begun to talk about a life together."

"Do you think I've forgotten any of that?"

"I think you've tabled it," she said harshly.

"That's right, I have," he admitted. "I thought you understood that. I don't mind admitting that this is an opportunity for me to get somewhere after years of futzing around in the business. And that doesn't alter my feeling that I've done the best job possible for Chris and the foundation, either. I think the work I've done has been prestigious and in good taste, despite your objections!"

"So now we have your ego to deal with as well as Chris's!"

"Goddamnit, let's cut all this crap! It certainly isn't what I expected from you!"

"What did you expect?" Cathy cried. "For me to *approve* of what you're doing to Chris, for devoting all your time to bigger and better promotional schemes, hopping around the country and running yourself ragged? Did you expect me to just be here when you breezed in for a quick lay and a hot meal?"

"The meal was cold!"

Tears had started in her eyes, and suddenly she began to laugh and cry at the same time. Eric got up from the table and pulled her into his arms.

"Cathy, I'm sorry, I'm sorry," he murmured. "What the hell are we doing?"

"Having a fight, you dummy."

They held each other, afraid, and confused by what had happened, feeling the sense of something lost between them, mingled with the urge to overcome the pain they had caused. Eric kissed her urgently and lifted her in his arms, and Catherine clung to him as he carried her into the bedroom.

They lay side by side, slightly apart, not touching, staring into the dark. She could see the tiny tip of his cigarette glowing as he drew on it, hear the sigh of his breath as he let the smoke out in thin, curling wisps. It hadn't changed anything, Catherine thought; it never does. What they had done was so patterned, so typical: throwing themselves into a frenzy of sex to forget the accusations and bury the fear that they had torn something vital in the fabric of their relationship. The knowledge filled her with regret. Now they would be careful of every word, every gesture. They would tread cautiously on the thin shell of each other's emotions.

"Would you like some coffee?" Catherine asked, breaking the silence between them.

Eric sat up and reached for his clothes. "No, thanks, Cathy. I promised to be home for breakfast with David. Then I'm having a meeting with John and Chris."

"About what?"

"There was a lot of reaction to that incident in Miami with the demonstrators, and Chris has been asked to appear on *The Tonight Show*. I think it might be too soon; we have to talk about it."

Cathy stood up and slipped on a robe. "Just exactly what did happen in Miami?" she asked cautiously. "The news reports were a bit confused."

"Well, it was a little frightening at first. A bunch of kids showed up in front of the hall carrying signs and yelling abuse at Chris and at the people waiting to get in. There were a couple of fights and the cops came to break it up. But Chris went out and talked to the protesters and they quieted down, then left."

"Just like that? He talked to them and they left?"

"Just like that," Eric answered, putting on his jacket. He turned to her and saw that she was frowning. "Why do you ask?"

"He stood up in front of an angry mob of fanatics, told them to go in peace, and they did," she said thoughtfully. "Just like in the movies."

"What are you getting at?"

"Do you remember the tests I told you about at the university? Where Chris used mind-pressure to make my students do what he wanted them to? And the incident with Frank Pearson, the boy he made scald himself with hot coffee?"

"No, I don't remember that," Eric said slowly.

"It's understandable; we both got caught up in the sighting tests and finding David. I never did have a chance to do any further studies with Chris."

Eric started to laugh, then stopped. "You're not seriously telling me that he mind-pressured those people?"

"I don't know that much about it," Catherine admitted, "but I think it's possible."

"Cathy, I'd be the last person in the world to scoff at anything Chris is capable of. But making a group of twenty or thirty people obey him with *mind commands?* Don't you think that's a bit much?"

He turned and went into the living room to get his topcoat.

Cathy followed him, saying: "I suppose you're right. As soon as the holidays are over I'll do some tests with him. There's so much I still don't know."

Eric slipped on his coat and looked at her with a worried frown. "You may not get a chance to do those tests right away. The West Coast tour *is* definite. We'll probably be leaving soon after the first of the year."

Her face was expressionless, her voice even, as she asked: "How long will you be gone?"

"About two and a half, maybe three months."

"And after that, will there be another tour? Canada, Mexico, South America?" She spoke quietly, with no rancor or anger.

"Cathy, it's late, and we're both tired," Eric sighed. "Let's talk about it later, please?"

"Of course." She went up to him and kissed him lightly. "Get some rest. I'll call you in the morning."

Eric held her, his eyes searching her face. "I don't think I like it when you're being quietly noble."

"Next time I'll try to be noisy about it. Now go home before I lose my poise."

When he was gone she stood for a few minutes in the living room and looked around absently, too confused to think. The dining table was still covered with the dinner dishes, and she automatically began to stack and carry them into the kitchen. After she had washed and dried them, she wiped her hands on a towel and went into the living room to her desk. From a bottom drawer she took out a thick folder neatly labeled "McKENZIE," sat down on the couch, and carefully began to read all the notes she had made since her first meeting with Christopher.

34

Pale winter sunlight flowed into the apartment through wide windows that reached from floor to ceiling. The cool light gave a frosty color to the spacious living room that was artfully arranged with glass and chrome tables, ceramic lamps, and long, low couches made of huge oversized pillows. At the far corner of the room was a dining area that led to a cheerful kitchen of built-ins and natural wood cabinets.

"Well, how do you like it?" Chris asked proudly.

"It's absolutely beautiful!" Nella exclaimed, looking around. "So this is what you've been so secretive about! When did you rent it?"

"Two days ago. Wait until you see the bedroom!" Chris said eagerly, taking her hand.

He led her down a short hallway and into a master suite that included a large dressing room and bathroom. Sliding glass doors opened onto a terrace overlooking the city.

"Oh, Chris, I love it!" Nella said. "But can you afford it?"

His face darkened. "I'm not the gardener anymore, Nella," he said flatly.

Nella flushed, embarrassed. "Oh, darling, I didn't mean—"

"The foundation takes care of all my expenses," he stated brusquely. "You know I can't live at home anymore, and this is what I wanted."

She went into his arms and kissed him. "It's wonderful. And much nicer than seedy motels."

He grinned and held her close. "Did you notice the mirrored sliding doors on the closet? They face the bed."

"I noticed," she replied archly. "I can't imagine why the designer did that."

"I can—and you'll find out soon enough," Chris said, and kissed her hard.

She wiggled out of his grasp, laughing. "Wait—I want to see the rest of the place!"

"There's only a small guest room through there," he said, pointing to a door. "And it has its own bathroom too. Wanna move in?" he teased.

"Not into a small guest room, I don't! It's the master suite with the master in it or nothing at all!"

He pulled her back into his arms. "God, I missed you," he whispered huskily.

"You've been home almost a week and we've been together every day," she said, smiling. "How can you still miss me?"

"I'm making up for all those weeks away from you." He kissed her again, his hands running over her body hungrily. They sank down on the bed, and he moved his leg between her thighs, shifting her skirt up to her waist.

"Chris, wait—" she said breathlessly. "It's broad daylight and the drapes are open."

"And we're on the twentieth floor where nobody can see us."

"Except them." She laughed self-consciously, pointing to their reflections on the mirrored doors.

Chris sat up and pulled her into his lap so that they both faced themselves in the mirrors.

"They're two beautiful people," he said, slowly unbuttoning her blouse and cupping her breasts in his hands. "Why don't we watch them and see what they do?"

A light snowfall had started by the time Chris drove Nella home. The small flakes fluttered in front of the headlights like a spill of fine white powder dusting the road before them. Chris turned on the radio and tuned in a soft rock station, humming along with the music.

Nella said suddenly: "I don't want to go home yet. Let's go dancing! Do you know I've never danced with you? I don't even know if you *can* dance!"

"Of course I can dance! But where can we go this time of night? It's almost one o'clock."

"There's a new disco in Wynnewood called the Dance Machine, and it's open until two. Oh, Chris, let's go!"

"Lead the way and I'll dance your feet off!"

A rainbow of neon lights spelling out "Dance Machine" in splashy colors hung over the narrow doorway of the club. From inside came a raucous blast of music and noisy customers. Chris paid their admission at the door and they went in. Multicolored lights swung wildly over the large room filled with young people twisting and jerking their bodies to the frantic beat of the music. They found a table, ordered some beer, then joined the throng on the floor.

"You're terrific!" Nella cried, snapping her fingers.

"So are you!" Chris yelled happily over the noise.

When the tape was finished they fell into each other's arms, laughing, and began to make their way back to the table. The room lights had dimmed to a low rose color, and as they pushed past a young couple to get to their seats, the boy turned to Chris angrily and said: "Stop shoving, creep!"

"Sorry," Chris said, ignoring him and helping Nella.

"Hey!" the girl exclaimed, looking at Chris. "You're that guy I saw on television! He's Christopher!" she said to the boy.

"So? Who gives a shit? The fucker shoved me!"

"I said I was sorry." Chris's voice was sharp. "Now bug off!"

"C'mon, Teddy," the girl pleaded, "you've had too much beer. Let's go." She turned to Chris and smiled. "I saw that show you did. The one in Chicago? God, it was crazy, the way you healed all those people. I thought it was some kind of trick."

The boy suddenly pushed her aside and grabbed at Chris's jacket. He was in his early twenties, with a puffy, sallow face half covered by a thick black mustache and a scraggly beard.

"Yeah, I saw it too. And I think you're a fake!"

"I don't give a shit what you think!" Chris burst out angrily. "Now get your hands off me!"

He grabbed the boy and thrust him away, making him stumble and knock over a chair. He recovered his footing and lunged at Chris, hitting him in the face with his fist. Chris ducked back and came in low to punch him in the stomach. Another tape of disco music began to blare out, and only a few people nearby paid any attention to the fight.

The boy gasped from Chris's blow, then yelled: "You son of a bitch!" He threw himself on Chris, fists pounding. Enraged, Chris slammed him with a solid punch to the jaw. Nella cried out and the girl screamed as the boy staggered back cursing, reached into his leather jacket, and suddenly flashed a knife.

In that instant, Chris felt a savage impulse sweep over him to mind-pressure the boy into killing himself. Seething with fury, Chris faced him with almost uncontrollable rage, only seconds away from giving vent to his murderous urge.

Suddenly the boy was grabbed from behind by a burly figure who spun him around, sent the knife flying, and dealt him a punishing blow to the head. He snapped to one side as the man jabbed him sharply in the crotch with his knee and finished him off with a punch in the kidneys. The boy grunted and fell forward into the man's arms, bleeding from the nose and mouth.

"Okay, you little prick, let's get outta here," the man muttered, half dragging the limp body away. "You, too, cunt," he said over his shoulder to the girl.

Chris sank into a chair, breathing heavily and trembling.

"Oh, darling, your face is all bruised!" Nella said, on the verge of tears.

"It's okay—I'm all right," he said, trying to catch his breath. He was still reeling dizzily from the violence he'd almost committed.

Nella's face was white, her eyes large with fright. He took her hand and tried to smile. "So much for a fun evening of dancing, huh?"

"I've never been that close to a fight before," she said shakily. "It was awful. Let's get out of here."

Chris looked around. "I wonder who the guy was who broke it up and took that bastard out? Jesus, he really gave him a going-over."

"He was vicious, the way he beat him and talked to the girl!"

Yeah, but he saved my ass, and in more ways than one, Chris thought. Aloud, he said: "He must be the manager or the bouncer. I'd like to thank him."

"I'm the bouncer," a rough voice behind him said. "Sorry you folks were disturbed like that—we get a lot of drunks in here." The man moved around the table so that Chris could see him. "The manager put me on to keep the peace," he continued. "We've had too many busts in here because of shitheads like that."

Chris stared at him closely as he spoke, examining the tough, brutal face. The man's eyes were dark and narrow. He had full lips and a short, bumpy nose, as if it had been broken, and his hair was black and shiny, slicked back in a fifties style. A pale ragged scar ran from his hairline down his right temple, cutting into his eyebrow and drawing down the eyelid. He had the look of a battered ex-boxer, and yet, Chris guessed, he couldn't be more than a year or two older than himself.

"You okay, miss?" the man asked, giving Nella's shoulder a nudge.

"Yes, thank you," she replied, looking away from him.

He grinned at her disdain and shrugged, as if he had encountered that reaction from girls before. He turned to leave, and the multicolored lights began to swing across the room again. One of them hit Chris for a moment like a spotlight, and the man stopped, his eyes wide, staring in surprise.

"For Christ's sake!" he roared. "You're Chris McKenzie!"

"Yes, I am," Chris said hesitantly, hearing something in the way his name was pronounced that startled him.

"Don't you remember me?" the young man asked excitedly. "I'm Stark—Johnny Stark!"

Nella looked up at him sharply and Chris stared, numb with surprise. "Johnny," he said almost in a whisper. "I don't believe it!" Chris stood up and took his hand, making an effort to be calm. "Stark! I haven't seen you since—"

"Since that day we had the fight in the school yard!"

Chris let go of his hand slowly and nodded, searching Johnny's face and wondering if he remembered anything about that day.

"Hey, sit down and tell me what's been happening to you," he said.

Nella moved her chair to make room, too surprised to speak. Johnny gave her a wink and shoved in beside her.

"Christ, I just don't believe it!" he exclaimed, beaming at Chris. "You know, I seen you on television. I mean, I've watched every one of them shows, you healin' all those people—my old schoolmate! Jesus!"

"Tell me what happened to you. Did you move away?"

"Naw, I just dropped out of school. I was in the hospital for a few weeks—you know, I never did figure out why I did that, why I jumped off the fire escape that day. I remember I was beatin' the shit outta you, and suddenly—bam—I wake up in the hospital!" He grinned, showing bad teeth, and shook his head. "I musta seen that teacher—what's his name?—Mr. Strathmore—remember him? That old fairy! I musta seen him comin' at us and got scared." He paused, looking confused, and then went on: "That's how I got this," he said, running a thick finger along the scar.

"Christ, I'm sorry," Chris murmured.

"Aw, hell, it wasn't your fault. Hey, you coulda healed me if you'd known then what you could do," he said, laughing. Then his face grew serious. "That's really fantastic, the way you help people. It really is. Do you heal everybody?"

Chris smiled. "No, not everybody."

Johnny nodded his head, as if he understood, then turned and glanced at Nella. He raised his eyebrows questioningly to Chris.

"Oh, I'm sorry. I didn't introduce you. I guess you don't remember her, but she's the reason we had the fight. This is Nella Stanwyck."

Johnny's jaw dropped, giving him an idiot look. "Oh, shit! Sure, sure I remember. The little girl that was crippled! I saw that program where you healed her!"

He stared at Nella openly, his dark eyes growing insolent. "You turned out just great," he said, lowering his voice intimately. "Sorry I was such a meathead about your bein' crip—"

"Thanks," Nella interrupted him coldly. She turned to Chris and said: "It's getting late. Don't you think we should go?"

"In a minute," he answered. "Johnny, what have you been doing with yourself? Why are you working here?"

"Well, I wasn't much for school, and my old man didn't give a damn if I went or not. I was too old for school, anyway," he said, laughing. "Shit, I was sixteen and still in junior high! So I got a job haulin' bricks for a construction company, and did a lot of different things. I picked this up for night work to get some extra bread."

"Chris, I'd really like to go," Nella said impatiently.

"Sure, in a minute," Chris answered, looking at Johnny. "How are you doing now?" he asked him. "This place pay well?"

"Are you kiddin'? They pay shit! But I need the dough. But you must be doin' great! Travelin' around the country, bein' on TV. You ever need somebody to work for you, just let me know!" He laughed and stood up. "I got to get back to work. It was great seein' you again, man." Then, in a formal, solemn voice, he added: "I'm really proud to know you."

Chris shook his hand, and Johnny looked flustered for a moment. Then he laughed loudly. "I just can't get over it! Runnin' into you like this!" He gave Nella a quick bow of his head. "Good to see you, too, Nell," he said, then moved off into the crowd.

As they drove away from the club, Chris stared ahead moodily.

"That was quite a surprise, wasn't it?" Nella said.

"Yes, it was."

He lapsed into silence, and they drove for a few minutes without speaking.

Then Nella asked: "What are you thinking about?"

"I'm thinking of offering Johnny a job," he answered distantly.

"A job? Are you kidding?"

"No, I'm not. I think I should do something to help him."

"But why? And doing what? I don't understand. He's terrible; loud, cheap, and foulmouthed. And he's vicious, the way he talked to that girl."

"He's had a tough time," Chris said quietly.

"But that's no reason to offer him a job! Besides, what could he do for you?"

"Oh, be around—maybe a bodyguard." Chris smiled. "Look what happened tonight!"

"Chris, that's ridiculous! Something like that doesn't happen every time you go out."

"It happens," Chris said, thinking about the man on the street in Atlanta. "Besides," he went on, almost to himself, "I owe Johnny a favor."

After he dropped Nella off at home, Chris started back to Philadelphia. Nella had continued to argue with him about hiring Johnny, and he was abrupt with her, irritated by her caustic remarks and a social snobbery he'd never suspected. Now he felt depressed and a little angry. He had to admit that Stark was rough and ill-mannered, but he was strangely taken with the idea of having him close by, fascinated by the thought that there was a reason they had met again. The power he had felt with large audiences had always seemed distant, somehow remote. But for the few minutes he had talked with Stark, it had been sharply immediate and satisfying. Acting on impulse, he turned the car in the direction of the disco.

Johnny was just leaving when he drove up. Chris called out and invited him to his apartment for a couple of beers and to talk over old times. Stark agreed and followed him back to the city in his own car.

"It's simple, really," Chris was saying an hour later. "If you want the job, you can move in here. There's an extra bedroom with its own bath. You'll get a good salary, travel with me, and make sure I don't get into any trouble, like what happened tonight."

"Christ, man, I don't believe it!" Johnny said in astonishment. "This place is a fuckin' palace! And you want me to live here with you?"

"I think you'd enjoy it," Chris said, smiling.

"Enjoy it! You kiddin'?" He threw his head back and laughed, burrowing his body into the deep pillows of the couch and running his hands over the soft, luxurious fabric. "It's a goddamned dream come true!" Then he sat up, his dark face suddenly anxious. "You sure they'll go for it—the foundation, I mean—all those people you work with?"

"I'll see to it that they do," Chris said calmly.

"What about your girl—Nella? She didn't like me much, did she?" He ran his fingers over the scar on his face in a nervous gesture. "A lot of chicks get turned off to me," he muttered.

"I won't have any problems with her," Chris replied confidently.

Johnny grinned, wrinkling the scar and giving his face a distorted look. "Shit, I guess not. After all, you made her walk!" he exclaimed. Then, more soberly, he said: "You know, that's a little scary to me, you bein' able to do stuff like that. I watched all them shows and, Christ, I got chills seein' all them people healed." He stared at Chris uneasily, his black brows drawn together in a frown. "Doesn't it make you feel—well, funny, knowin' you can do things like that?"

"No, not at all," Chris answered, stretching out lazily on the couch opposite him. "I'm used to it, I guess. It's just something I can do." He thought about what he'd said and added: "I think we're all used to it, in a way. Eric and Catherine, Charlotte, even Nella." He paused, then grinned at Stark. "Everybody but you."

"How the hell do you get used to a thing like that?" Johnny asked with a sound of awe in his voice. "Jesus, it's like a fuckin' miracle!"

Chris laughed and sat up, suddenly struck by an idea. "Would you like to see me do it?"

Stark looked confused. "What? You mean now?"

Chris stood up and walked over to him. Johnny looked up, his face pale. "What are you goin' to do?" he asked hoarsely, a strange timidity in his voice.

Chris reached out and touched the scar with his fingertips. "You got this because of me. It's only fair I heal it for you."

Stark pulled away nervously from Chris's touch. "No, listen—you don't have to. I mean—"

"Don't be afraid, Johnny," Chris said quietly, staring at him. The sense of power he had experienced earlier in the evening with Stark was surging through him; he felt dynamic and omnipotent.

Stark watched Chris's hand descend to his face, felt it covering the scar. He sat, afraid to move, struggling to understand what was happening to him. Chris's eyes were burning into his with a blinding force, and for a moment he saw the school yard where they had fought, felt the heat of the summer afternoon and the pounding in his chest as he ran to escape those eyes, heard the sound of rushing wind in his ears before he leaped into space.

"Oh, God!" he cried out. "Your hand is like fire! You're burnin' me!"

Chris stepped away and Johnny fell back against the pillows, dazed.

"Are you all right?" Chris asked softly.

"Yes," he answered dully. "The burnin' is gone now."

Chris smiled. "Get up and go look in the mirror."

The next day Stark collected his things from his rented room in Wynnewood and moved into Chris's apartment.

35

Amanda was quick to note the rift that had taken place between Eric and Catherine. She tried to offer some friendly counsel, but Catherine cut her off sharply.

"When I need advice on my love life, I'll ask for it!" she snapped.

"If you don't ask for it soon, you may not have a love life!" Amanda retorted.

"I'm not so sure I have one now," Catherine said under her breath. "How are you doing with your request for a government grant?" she asked, changing the subject.

"Lousy. Chris made some very damaging remarks about organized religion after the incident in Miami with the demonstrators, remarks of which our current Administration took a very dim view. He's a wonderful boy and I adore him, but I wish he'd keep his mouth shut."

Catherine gave her a cynical smile and said: "Funny, isn't it, how hero worship wears a bit thin when you're close to the subject."

"That's a hell of a thing to say!" Amanda responded in surprise. "I wasn't criticizing Chris. After all, he's just a kid. I'm sure this sudden notoriety and acclaim are very hard for him to adjust to." She looked at Catherine with a shrewd smile. "He's not mature enough to handle changes in his life—like the rest of us."

"I love the way you attack, defend, and give subtle insights into living all in the same breath," Catherine said acidly. "But much as I hate to admit it, you're probably right—"

"Of course I am!"

"—about Chris, that is," Catherine finished. "I think we've all jumped into this thing too quickly. None of us understands what Chris's powers are all about, particularly Chris. He's being adored for his gifts and his youth, both of which are being merchandised out of all proportion."

"And that's where you think Eric's influence is undermining him?"

Catherine nodded. "I guess so. He doesn't understand the possible harm all of this could do."

"And not just to Chris," Amanda added softly.

Catherine's eyes narrowed. "You're about to sneak up on me with your good intentions and lousy advice," she said sternly.

"Okay, okay." Amanda shrugged in defeat. "I was just trying to be a friend and help you understand—"

"Stop trying! I'm the one with a degree in psychology!"

"So—use your education and stop letting your emotions confuse you!" Amanda shot back. "And try to get to the bottom of whatever is bothering you about Chris."

Later in the morning, still rankled by Amanda's remarks about Chris, Catherine decided to call him for lunch. In the ten days he'd been home, she had seen him only twice, and in the company of other people. She'd had the feeling that he was trying to avoid being alone with her. She dialed his apartment and was surprised to hear a strange voice answer.

"Mr. McKenzie's residence."

"What? Who is this? Is Chris there?"

"Who's callin' please?" the rough, gravelly voice asked.

"Do I have the right number?" she asked, confused. "Is Christopher McKenzie there?"

"Yes, ma'am. Who's callin' please?"

In the background she could hear a burst of laughter. "Catherine Marlowe," she answered crisply. "May I speak to Mr. McKenzie?"

"Just a moment, please. I'll see if he's in," the voice said, speaking the lines as if they had been painstakingly rehearsed. There was another burst of laughter, then Chris was on the phone.

"Hello, Catherine," he said, still chuckling.

"Chris, who was that? Am I interrupting a party?"

"No, that's a friend of mine who's staying with me."

"Staying with you?"

"Well, he's working for me, really. I hired him a couple of days ago."

"You hired him?" she asked, puzzled. "What for?"

Chris's voice grew evasive. "Oh, to be around—chauffeur, bodyguard, that sort of thing."

"Are you kidding?" She smiled, thinking he was joking with her.

"No, I'm not kidding," he said flatly. "Listen, I'm pretty busy right now. Was there something you wanted?" he asked brusquely.

Startled by his tone of voice, she stammered: "Well, I thought we might have lunch together. We haven't had a chance to talk since you came home, and I—"

"Gee, I'd really like that, but I have a lot of things to take care of. You know, Christmas shopping . . ."

He is putting me off, Catherine thought, confused. What the hell was going on? Why was he being so rude?

After a moment's pause, she said: "Yes, of course. I understand."

"Thanks, I knew you would. I'll see you at the Bradfords' on Christmas Eve. We can talk then, okay?"

"Yes, sure, Chris. By the way, what's your friend's name—the one you hired?"

There was a long silence before he answered: "Stark. John Stark. We went to school together."

"Well, I'll remember that the next time I call," she said, trying to sound pleasant. "Have fun with your shopping."

She hung up and sat back in her chair, bewildered. I suppose it had to happen, she thought. A penthouse apartment and a bodyguard: the Star Syndrome in full swing! But, as Amanda had pointed out, he was only a kid and bound to act immaturely.

Foolishly would be more apt, she muttered to herself. Hiring a bodyguard! Next he'll have an entourage trailing after him.

Then what Chris had told her resounded in her mind with a sudden, distinct clarity. She felt every muscle in her body tense, her breathing stop short as if she had been struck.

She remembered who John Stark was.

◆

A few days before Christmas, Eric finalized the plans for Chris's second tour and presented them at a meeting with Charlotte, John, and Catherine. The itinerary included Denver, Dallas, Phoenix, Seattle, Portland, San Francisco, and Los Angeles, with stopovers in a number of smaller cities. The ten weeks of travel and appearances would take them into late March and produce enough segments for syndication to meet the demands of advertisers as well as make a projected profit for the foundation.

Charlotte immediately gave the plans her wholehearted approval, and John agreed. Catherine only nodded and handed Eric a list of institutes and clinics in each city requesting conferences with Chris. Eric was annoyed by her quiet acceptance and lack of enthusiasm, and when he spoke of it to her later there was a quick flare-up of the tensions that had grown between them. He realized that they were becoming more estranged, and he felt caught in a trap of contradictory emotions. When he defended himself to her, he was aware that what he said had the hollow ring of advertising slogans, but the cutting tone of her rebukes and questionings of his judgment only made him more defensive. On the other hand, he was more and more aware that she was correct in her growing fears for Chris. Eric began to find him more difficult to work with than during the early months of the tour. His unpredictable changes of mood and bursts of arrogance reminded him of temperamental clients he had dealt with in the past. He saw the megalomania of success taking Chris over, and while he tried to rationalize that feeling out of existence, every meeting with Chris only gave it more substance.

John brought the point home more sharply in an early-morning conference in his office on the day before Christmas.

"The publicity is double-edged, Eric. It's helped to sell the program in some markets, but we catch the backlash in other ways."

"What do you mean?"

"There is an alliance of business and church leaders who believe Christopher's use of his powers is sacrilegious. They've put pressure on several stations in California, Louisiana, and Tennessee to drop the program. Even though we can sustain the loss, the impact is going to be immediate and widespread."

"And his remarks about religious street gangs in that incident in Miami don't help any," Eric added wearily.

"He's also dismissed the requests of the Pentagon to discuss a sighting program the military wants to start, making irrational claims that the brass simply want to exploit his powers for further world domination."

"Oh, Christ!" Eric groaned. "He heard Amanda say that the other day at the foundation, but she was only joking! She was upset about the problems she's been having getting a grant authorized."

"Well, knowing how close the church and business are with government, that's probably why she's having problems. And Chris's attitude doesn't help."

"Okay, okay," Eric sighed. "I'll talk with him and see what I can do."

John looked at his watch and stood up. "I'd better get going. I have some errands to do for Margaret and she wants me home early." He smiled at Eric. "Do you realize that this is our first Christmas with David? My God, what a year it's been."

"Yes, I know," Eric replied quietly, suddenly thinking of Jenny. He looked up at his father-in-law and saw that they were sharing the same thought. "I miss her too," he said softly.

"Why don't you take the rest of the day off and go home and play with David?" John suggested gently.

"I can't. Some people from *Time* are coming in to discuss a cover story on Chris."

John saw the look of pain that crossed Eric's face and put his arm around his shoulders. "Ah, well, business first. Try to get away early. Are you picking Catherine up to bring her to the dinner?"

"No, I'm not," Eric sighed. "She said she'd drive herself out to the house."

"I see," John said, refraining from making any comment. "Well, I must go."

They left the office with the uneasy knowledge that the events they had set in motion were no longer entirely in their control.

◆

Chris finished combing his hair and went back into the bedroom. He slipped on his jacket and turned to the mirrors covering the closet doors, staring at himself with satisfaction. His face was glowing with health, and his blond hair caught shimmers of light like threads of gold. He stroked the soft fabric of the cashmere jacket and checked the shine on his expensive alligator shoes. He smiled at his reflection, enjoying the way the clothes molded to his broad shoulders and slim hips, the knife crease of his slacks, and the deep-chocolate color of his turtleneck sweater.

"You look terrific," Johnny said from the doorway.

"I think so too." Chris grinned.

He walked past Johnny into the living room and began to gather up an armload of presents stacked on a table.

"I'll be at my mother's place all afternoon," he said as Johnny followed him. "Then I'm going to the Bradfords' for dinner."

"What time do you think you'll be back?" Stark asked.

"I'm not sure." Chris glanced up at him and saw a sly smile on the boy's face. "You have something planned for the evening?"

"I thought we might have a little late Christmas Eve party," Johnny replied, his smile growing wider.

Chris laughed. "Okay, whatta you got cooking?"

"A couple of chicks, really dyin' to meet you."

"You know, you're a fuckin' sex maniac! We just threw two of your broads out of here this morning!"

"And you had 'em both before you even got outta bed to take a leak!" Johnny chuckled. "But these two tonight—" He made a kissing sound with his lips.

"Okay, you convinced me," Chris said. "I'll get back early."

Catherine drove slowly along the icy suburban roads. The late-afternoon sun reflected on the snow-covered hillsides and bathed the countryside in a pale, crystalline light. Bare trees cast stark shadows on the white snow, like an endless row of etchings, and the air was sharp with the tang of wood burning in fireplaces. She moved the high fur collar of her coat more closely around her face and let her thoughts drift, trying to separate them from the tangled confusion of her feelings.

Her love for Eric had obscured the clarity of her thinking about Chris, and now she wanted to recapture the objectivity she had lost in the last year, come to a better understanding of the changes he had made in their lives. But she needed time; there was too much to sort out, she realized. Perhaps after this tour was over, she and Eric might regain what they had lost.

Wishful thinking? she questioned herself. She hoped not. At the moment they were treating each other like polite friends. She was seeing him through too-critical eyes, and what she perceived filled her with anguish; a man being victimized by his own ambition. And Chris, what was he doing?

Responding to his success like any other normal, not terribly bright young man being exploited for an extraordinary gift, she answered herself. But was he exploited? Or *doing* the exploiting?

"Oh, shit!" she exclaimed aloud. "I should have done what Mother wanted and majored in home economics!"

The sun began to die and dusk fell quickly. She switched on her headlights, and a few minutes later a light swirl of snowflakes began to fall as she pulled into the Bradfords' driveway.

Catherine found Margaret in the kitchen. The handsome, aristocratic-looking woman was busily stirring ingredients into a big bowl. A large white apron covered her pale-blue gown, and small diamond earrings bobbed and flashed in the bright light as she checked a recipe. A thin scarf was tied around her head to protect the careful set of her hair, and there was a smudge of flour across her cheek.

"What a picture you are," Catherine said, laughing.

"Oh, I must be a wreck! Come, sit down and keep me company. I decided at the last minute to make this bread pudding. It's absolutely delicious and the one thing I do really well in the kitchen. Besides, I was restless. John was late getting home and I insisted he take a nap, and Eric just got in a little while ago and is playing with David upstairs. Shall I call him and tell him you're here?"

"No, don't bother. Let him stay with David for a while. Is John feeling all right?"

"Yes, he's just a little tired. I don't think he anticipated the amount of work involved with the production company. We missed going to Europe this fall, but I can't begrudge him the satisfaction he gets from what he's doing."

Catherine was quick to detect a note of bitterness in her voice, but remained silent, nodding her head in understanding.

"Do you know who gave me this recipe for the pudding?" Margaret asked. "Chris's mother, Susan; maybe ten or twelve years ago. We were very close. She did this dress for me. Isn't it lovely?" she said, taking off the apron and turning around.

"It's beautiful. She is going to be here tonight, isn't she?"

"No. As usual, she refused. There was nothing I could say to persuade her. I simply don't understand what's happened to her. Susan used to be one of the most vibrant women I've ever known. But in the last year she's become brusque and cold. There are times when I feel we are like strangers. Charlotte's noticed it too. Ever since this thing with Chris began—"

"Susan is very deeply attached to Chris. I think she feels she's lost him in some way," Catherine suggested.

"I can understand that. After Jenny died, there was a time when I didn't think I could go on living," Margaret said, her voice sinking to a whisper. She stared ahead emptily for a few seconds, then looked at Catherine with a smile. "But Chris is very much alive, and doing such important work. And John and I have so much to be grateful to him for, bringing our grandson back to us. I did so want Susan here to share that with us."

Margaret finished making the pudding and put it in the oven. She gestured to Catherine to follow her, and the two women went through the dining room and across the foyer to the living room, where a cheerful fire blazed in the white-marble-faced and manteled fireplace. An enormous Christmas tree stood near the bay windows, surrounded by gaily wrapped presents and scarlet poinsettias, adding a splash of vivid color to the room.

Margaret called for a maid to bring them some sherry and was about to go repair her make-up when Charlotte and Nella arrived, their arms loaded with gifts. There was a confusion of greetings and embraces, then Charlotte went off with Margaret and Nella joined Catherine.

"You look lovely," Catherine said, "but I'm not used to seeing you alone. Where's Chris?"

"He spent the afternoon with Susan. He said he'd be here before dinner," Nella answered absently.

She walked around the room, making a pretense of examining the tree and the packages around its base. Her dark eyes were melancholy, and there was a tense, anxious expression around her mouth. She seemed nervous and preoccupied. Catherine watched her for a few minutes, then the maid walked in with a tray of sherry and glasses.

"Nella, have some wine?" Catherine offered.

"What? Oh, yes, thanks."

When they were alone again, Catherine asked: "Is anything wrong? You seem a little edgy."

Nella smiled brightly. "Oh, no, nothing is wrong." She sipped from her glass and turned away from Catherine's inquiring glance.

"Is it Chris?" Catherine asked gently.

Nella remained very still for a moment, her eyes staring ahead worriedly.

"Is there anything I can do to help?" Catherine asked.

"He's changed," Nella answered without looking at her. "He's different now."

"How?"

Nella looked at her. "I'm not sure," she answered slowly. "Harder, more self-assured, but in an unpleasant way. And he's become secretive."

"Secretive?"

"I have the feeling he's keeping things from me. Oh, not that I have to know everything that's happening to him, but we seem to have lost that shared confidence we always had."

"A great deal has happened to Chris in the last few months," Catherine said earnestly. "And to you. Don't you think changes are inevitable?"

"Oh, yes, I understand that, but—" She paused, seeming unable to go on.

Catherine looked at her intently and suddenly thought: She's frightened.

"Nella, what is it? Please let me help you if I can."

"I feel as if I just don't know him anymore," Nella said in a dead tone of voice. "And it all seems to have happened so quickly. Ever since we ran into that boy he hired."

"Johnny Stark?"

"Have you met him?"

Catherine nodded no, and Nella said scornfully: "He's awful! Mean and tough. I think he's dangerous. I just don't understand why Chris wanted to hire him."

"I'm afraid I don't understand that myself."

"Oh, Catherine," Nella burst out, her eyes filling with tears, "I love Chris so much! And we're becoming like strangers!"

Join the club, Catherine thought to herself. She put her arm around the girl's shoulders and comforted her. "Nella, you have to understand how difficult it is for Chris. This life is so new to him; he has so many adjustments to make."

"Yes, I know that. But he's going away again, and he's taking Johnny with him, and it frightens me."

"He's taking Johnny on the tour?" Catherine said slowly. "I didn't know that."

"He said he needed him for protection. Protection against what? What does Chris have to be afraid of?"

There was a sound of voices in the foyer, and Nella turned away, dabbing at her eyes.

Catherine said to her quickly: "Let's get together and talk about this later, okay?"

Charlotte came into the room with Margaret, and behind them Catherine saw Eric coming down the stairs carrying David on his shoulders. John was a few steps behind.

As Eric put David down and started across the room to her, Catherine noticed the tense set of his shoulders and a strained, uneasy expression in his eyes. He gave her a smile at once so tender and pleading that she felt a sting of guilt. She went to him and kissed him lightly on the cheek, one thought emerging out of the scramble of her confusion and questions about the impact Chris was having on their lives: she loved him.

"You look tired," she murmured. "Bad day?"

"A little trying," he agreed. "Chris made an unexpected appearance at my meeting with a journalist from *Time*. She made a few comments of a slightly critical nature about his sudden rise to fame and his somewhat—shall we say 'careless'?—statements about the church and the efforts of the AMA to dismiss his healing power."

"What happened?"

Eric sighed and shook his head. "He lost his temper, flew off the handle and became abusive. If I didn't know him better, I'd have thought he was drunk."

John and Margaret were standing nearby with Charlotte, and John said: "You must keep a tighter rein on him, Eric. The boy has no judgment where these things are concerned."

"I agree," Margaret chimed in. "He doesn't seem to understand the harm he can do to himself and the foundation by such a lack of diplomacy."

"I don't seem to be able to shut him up." Eric laughed weakly, as if trying to make a joke.

Catherine saw how troubled and bewildered he was beneath his attempted humor. And she saw, too, Margaret's anxious glance at the gloomy expression on John's face.

"Chris is just feeling his oats, as we used to say," Charlotte interjected mildly. "He's young and perhaps a bit impetuous, but he'll learn."

Nella flashed her mother a look of annoyance and said: "That's no excuse for his being rude, especially after all the effort Eric has made on his behalf."

"I think it's a bit unfair to call him rude," Charlotte rejoined. "Inexperienced, perhaps, but certainly not rude!" Her voice grew sharp.

Nella paled before her mother's harsh tone and turned her attention to David, who was playing happily among the gifts near the tree.

Margaret murmured something about everyone having a drink, and John went to the bar to mix them. Eric put David on his lap and began to tell him a story, while Catherine sat nearby. For several moments no one spoke. Catherine had the uncomfortable feeling that choked thoughts and unuttered words had separated everyone in the room, that they were together but somehow alone in a private, personal response to what was happening. The atmosphere was tense, almost mysterious, with a subtle sense of alienation.

Then the doorbell chimed, and seconds later Chris burst into the room with a cheery cry, snowflakes clinging to his hair and clothes, and sprinkled over the gifts he carried. He looked vital and iridescent, glistening with self-assurance.

While the others sat, hesitant, as though his appearance had come as a surprise, an intrusion into their thoughts, Charlotte rose with a smile to greet him.

36

Eric and Chris left Philadelphia on a dismal wintry morning in the second week of January. A pall of frosty air lay over the city like a gray veil, muting all color to the dull, shadowy tones of a crypt. The cold was icy and aggressive, and people on the streets had a harsh, washed-out look, their faces pinched and white, as if they were ill. Traffic moved in a sluggish crawl, helpless in the grip of the freezing weather.

The group gathered at the airport was tense and restless, waiting impatiently to board the plane, like victims about to be rescued from some near-fatal captivity. They stood near one another, yet separated in small clusters, chatting in muttered tones. Eric was with Gary and Shelly; because of the overwhelming amount of business details to be taken care of, he had hired Gary to direct the tapings and Shelly to be his personal secretary. Phil Conners, the PR man Eric had worked with on the first tour, had been added to the company on a permanent basis, and he was checking out last-minute instructions from Eric on the publicity coverage of each city they would be appearing in. Nearby, the camera crew of four men stood talking among themselves, while a few feet away John was saying to Charlotte: "We're growing into quite an impressive group, aren't we? But where's Chris? He hasn't arrived yet."

"He'll be along in a moment, I'm sure. Nella was on the phone with him when I left the house. Poor darling, she wanted so to be here to see him off, but her cold is much worse and I insisted she stay in bed."

John glanced at his watch and looked around the terminal nervously. He caught Eric's worried eyes and nodded to him reassuringly.

"Eric doesn't look well," Charlotte said. "I wonder why Catherine isn't here."

"Eric said she had an appointment with a doctor from Drexel University that couldn't be rescheduled," John told her.

Charlotte looked disdainful. "I doubt that. They've had a spat, or something equally silly. I could tell something was wrong between them Christmas Eve at your house."

"Well, Eric has been devoting a lot of time to this whole project, and Catherine may resent it," John murmured.

"But that's nonsense! Surely she, of all people, must realize how important Chris's work is?"

John couldn't help smiling. "Well, where her life with Eric is concerned, she may not have your single-minded devotion to Chris," he said mildly.

"I am devoted to Chris, and I don't mind admitting it," Charlotte said passionately. "For the first time in my life, I feel involved in something really worthwhile. When Tom was alive I felt useless; I was just something decorative in his life. After he died and I took over the business, there wasn't that much for me to do; it practically ran itself. But this! The foundation and what it can accomplish has given me a feeling of real achievement!"

"I know it has, my dear," John said fondly. "Without you, none of this might ever have happened." He looked toward the entrance of the terminal. "Ah, here's Chris. And what perfect timing. The press is right behind him."

Chris swept into the airport talking with a reporter and looking up to smile at a cameraman trailing alongside with a minicam. Behind him were a half-dozen or more newsmen calling out questions. Chris came to Charlotte and John, and in moments they were surrounded by the reporters. Just then a noisy throng of teen-agers burst into the terminal waving signs and banners.

"Ah, the star and his fan club." Gary laughed cynically.

"Can it, Gary," Eric said tersely. "This is going to be rough enough without your jokes." He looked at his watch and turned to Shelly. "We still have a few minutes before takeoff. I have a call to make."

"Okay. I'll come get you when the flight is called."

Eric went to a phone booth and dialed the foundation, waiting impatiently until Catherine answered.

"I wish you were here," he said to her in a low voice.

"It's probably just as well that I'm not. I get very emotional at train stations and airports."

Her voice quivered a little, and Eric could hear the effort she was making to control it.

"I don't like leaving you this way—with so many things left unsaid."

"Eric, it's all right. Don't worry about it. Maybe the time apart will do us both some good, give us a chance to think."

"If this separation does as much good as the last one, we may never speak to each other again," he said with forced humor.

She was silent for a few seconds. They both started to speak at the same time, laughed, and then paused, not able to bridge the painful gap of unexpressed feelings.

"Well, I'd better go," Eric said at last. "Shelly's signaling to me that the passengers are boarding."

"Eric, take care of yourself."

"Yes, I will, I'll call you as soon as I can."

"Yes, please do."

He thought she sounded on the verge of tears, and he began to say something else, but she suddenly hung up.

Eric put the phone back in the cradle and stared at it blankly, unable to collect his thoughts. Then he heard Shelly calling him and hurried to join the group. Chris was shaking hands with John and kissing Charlotte goodbye. Johnny Stark, wearing an expensive black topcoat, stood close by. The collar was turned up, framing his dark, swarthy face, and Eric had a momentary impression of him as Chris's shadow. Eric disliked the boy's coarse manners, and his houndlike devotion to Chris made him uneasy. But Chris had coldly insisted that Johnny was going with them on the tour.

After saying goodbye to John and Charlotte, Eric was the last one to start down the ramp to the entrance of the plane. An inexplicable nervousness seized him, and the length of the passageway suddenly stretched ahead like an unknown road, ominous and threatening.

◆

Dissension broke out almost immediately.

Small disturbances at first, no more than minor irritations. Johnny was obnoxious with the flight attendants and made obscene jokes. Chris was only mildly reproving, seeming to enjoy his adolescent behavior. When Eric got upset, Shelly made excuses for them, claiming they were just kids having a good time, and told Eric not to take any notice. Chris turned on all his charm and began to flirt with her outrageously until she blushed with embarrassment.

In Dallas, Chris took a separate suite for himself and Johnny. At the end of their stay in the city, Eric was surprised by their bill for room service, but when he talked to Chris about it, he was dismissed with the terse reply that the foundation could afford it.

In Denver, Phil Conners complained that Chris was too often late for interviews and local TV guest appearances, in one case missing a show altogether.

"Has there been a drop in ticket sales?" Eric asked.

"Well, no. Instead of being at the station for the show, he went out to the high schools and colleges unannounced and talked with the kids in his fan clubs. Broke up the school day and had more than five hundred kids walking him around one campus."

"Okay, get all the details and send it out as a news release," Eric said, grinning in spite of his irritation. "The kid just did some one-upmanship on you in the PR department."

Phil scowled. "He's getting out of hand, and you know it," he declared.

"What do you want me to do, use a whip and a chair?" Eric snapped.

In Albuquerque everything went more or less smoothly until the last night. An enormous crowd had turned out for the program, shouting and cheering Chris with so much enthusiasm that he went on healing and sighting after the program was officially over. When Eric tried to stop him, Chris waved him aside with a dazzling smile and made a gesture that embraced the entire auditorium, bringing the crowd to its feet with a roar of approval.

"If he could sing and play a guitar, he'd rule the world," Gary snorted, signaling the crew to continue taping.

"Why don't you take your cynicism and shove it!" Shelly said impatiently. "For the rest of your life, you'll never do as much good as he has tonight!"

"And exactly how much good is that? From some of the articles I've read, his batting average in healing is way below what his publicity makes it out to be," Gary shot back.

"That's bullshit and you know it!" Shelly flared. "You're just so goddamned jealous of him all you can do is bitch!"

"Hey, hey, listen to the mouth run wild! Our golden boy getting to you? Or are you trying to get to him?"

"You son of a bitch!" Shelly cried, tears stinging her eyes.

Backstage Eric watched anxiously as Chris clutched a man's shirt in his hands, trying to sight the location of its owner for a woman who stood before him. The large house was silent as he moved the shirt through his fingers, his head thrown back, eyes closed, rocking slightly on the balls of his feet. The woman stared at him transfixed, her careworn face harsh under the bright lights. Suddenly Chris stopped moving and lowered his head to look at her. He put his arms around her shoulders and leaned close to whisper in her ear. The woman nodded and began to cry softly. Chris led her to her seat, then returned to the center of the lights.

Johnny Stark came up behind Eric and asked: "What the hell was that all about?"

"Whoever she was looking for is dead," Eric said flatly.

"You're kiddin'! You mean Chris can see that?" he asked wonderingly.

Eric nodded. "It's happened before. He'll probably stop now. Something like that usually leaves the audience ready to fall on its knees." Eric's voice was tinged with sarcasm.

"Christ, he's fuckin' fantastic!" Johnny breathed softly.

"Yes, he sure is," Eric answered grimly. "I was right; he's finishing up." He turned to Stark and said intently: "See to it that he gets some rest tonight—cancel the party."

"Whattaya mean? What party?" Johnny asked with feigned innocence.

"Knock it off, Johnny. I know about the girls you've been getting for Chris and the sessions in your suite."

Stark's eyes narrowed. "You got your spies, huh?"

"No," Eric answered angrily. "Just conscientious hotel managers who don't want any trouble. In Denver one of your parties caused more than four hundred dollars in damages to the room. Now I'm warning you—cool it!"

Johnny's face broke into a wide, mocking grin. "Why don'tcha tell Chris to cool it, Mr. Manager? Or has he already told you to fuck off?"

Eric grabbed his collar and slammed him up against the wall. "You do what I say, you little prick, or I'll ship your ass back to Philadelphia so fast you'll get a nosebleed!"

Stark's voice was softly threatening. "I do whatever Chris says, Mr. Manager, and only what Chris says. Now let me go before I waste you."

Shelly suddenly appeared and rushed up to them. "Eric, stop it! Let him go!"

The two men separated just as Chris walked off the stage. He looked at Eric, then at Stark. "What's going on?" he asked quietly.

"Nothing, Chris," Shelly said hastily. "Eric just lost his temper for a minute. You look bushed. There's a mob out front. Why don't you duck out the back entrance and get back to the hotel?"

She took Johnny's arm. "Get him out of here," she muttered.

As soon as they were gone, she said to Eric: "Are you okay?"

"Yeah, sure. Thanks, Shelly. Just nerves, I guess." He looked away from her concerned expression, trying to control the anger still trembling through him. "I'll go check with Gary and the crew. Talk to you later," he said.

She started to say something, thought better of it, and simply nodded as he walked off.

Later, back in her room at the hotel, Shelly was getting ready for bed when the phone rang. It was Chris.

"Johnny told me what happened earlier this evening," he said. "I want to thank you for getting the situation under control. How 'bout coming up to my room for a drink?" Shelly hesitated, and Chris went on: "I think we ought to talk about Eric. Maybe get some things straightened out? I'd really appreciate it." His voice was warm, almost caressing.

"Yes," she said finally. "I'll be there in a few minutes."

In the darkened bedroom Shelly's body moved feverishly under Chris's, her legs clamped around his waist, head snapping from side to side on the pillow as his hips moved in rhythmic precision. The door opened for a moment, casting a ray of light over their bodies. Johnny stood watching them for a few seconds until Chris looked up at him and nodded. Johnny closed the door and came up to the bed, quickly slipping off his robe and stroking his erection.

"You can have her in a minute, buddy," Chris whispered, his breath ragged.

"Sure she won't mind?" Johnny whispered back.

Chris smiled. "She'll never know what happened."

◆

In Portland, after the last program was over, Gary rushed up to Eric exploding with anger.

"Where the hell have you been for the last half hour?" he asked furiously.

"In the box office with the manager, going over the receipts. Why, what happened?"

"Chris decided to end the show with a lecture on how the church has failed to promote 'man's abilities within himself,' as he put it! He left the healing spot and went back onto the stage. I had the crew scrambling like a bunch of clowns to keep him in frame!"

"Is there enough footage of his arrival at the hall to cover if we take it out?"

"Christ only knows!"

"Do the best you—"

"You gotta talk to that pompous little bastard, Eric! If you don't knock some sense—"

"Goddamnit, I'm doing the best I can!" Eric said sharply. "I can't do anything with him! It's out of my hands!" He paused and looked at Gary pleadingly. "We've got only two more cities to play: a week in San Francisco and a week in Los Angeles."

Gary was silent for a few seconds, then he said quietly: "Eric, we've worked together for a long time. I think I know you pretty well, and I think I know why you're holding off belting Chris in the mouth. But you can't let your gratitude for his finding your kid make a pile of shit out of this tour! Phil is breaking his back to cover up every rotten brawl he's had in every hotel we've stayed at, and Shelly's ready to drop her pants every time he comes near her!"

"I know, I know," Eric said wearily. "He's become a raving ego-maniac, and no matter what I say—"

Phil Conners came up to them excitedly. "Jesus, I don't see how he does it!" he exclaimed. "Tonight's house topped every audience we've had, and I talked with San Francisco and Los Angeles, and they're sold out and want to know if we can stay over at least an extra night or two because of the demand for tickets!" Gary groaned and Eric began to laugh as Phil continued. "They want him for the *Dinah!* show; Merv Griffin's people called, they want to devote a whole show to him; and *The Tonight Show* will put him on when-ever he's free for a half-hour taping with Carson!"

Eric's laughter grew loud and hoarse. "Oh, Christ!" he gasped. "Now we're really in trouble! You can't argue with success!"

By the time the company reached Los Angeles, Eric and Chris were communicating through Shelly. The frantic schedule of inter-views and guest appearances on television, visits to clinics and psy-chic research institutes, and conferences with station managers was managed with a warm cordiality between them that ceased as soon as they were alone. Eric's phone calls to Catherine had become less frequent as the tour had progressed, and now he was afraid to call her at all. There had been a few sharp conversations with John about Chris's erratic behavior on camera, but Eric refused to comment, pointing out instead the increased take at the box office and the rise in donations to the foundation, plus the good ratings the show was receiving in various polls.

"Have you seen the stories that are appearing in some of those su-permarket tabloids?" John thundered angrily. "And the insinuations about Chris in the gossip columns?"

"John, that sort of thing is inevitable, and you know it," Eric ex-plained tiredly. "All it does is make more people want to see him and read about him."

"What the hell has happened to that boy?" John asked.

"I really don't want to discuss it now, John. I have a meeting to get to in a few minutes."

"Eric, are you all right?"

"Frankly, no, I'm not," Eric replied. "But we'll talk about that when I get home. Kiss David for me."

"Shall I tell Catherine I've spoken to you?"

"No, don't," he said brusquely and hung up.

A few nights later Eric was awakened by the insistent ringing of the phone on the night table by his bed. He turned on the lamp and looked at his watch; it was a little after three. The phone rang again and he picked it up. It was the hotel manager. There were complaints from other guests about the noise in Chris's suite. He had called several times, but no one answered. Rather than make a disturbance, would Eric take care of it?

Slipping on some clothes and running his hands through his tousled hair, Eric took the elevator to the top floor and started down the hallway to Chris's rooms. He heard the raucous sounds of music and laughter, punctuated by shrieks and cries, as if someone was in pain. He knocked on the door, but there was no answer. He knocked again, loudly, and suddenly the door was flung open by Johnny Stark. He was naked, his stocky body wet and reeking of alcohol, his eyes glazed and bloodshot.

"Goddamn, it's Mr. Manager come to join the party!" he cried, an idiot grin breaking across his face. A half-naked girl staggered up to him and flung her arms around his neck.

"I just had a whiskey shower," he said to Eric. "And little Cindy here is goin' to lick me clean." He buried his face in the girl's neck and mumbled: "You goin' to lick me clean, honey?"

"Where's Chris?" Eric demanded.

Stark laughed and wagged a finger in Eric's face. "Nope, can't see Chris. Can't disturb our leader."

Eric shoved them out of his way and stepped into the room. Stark began to protest, then he fell weakly back against the wall to let the girl's mouth move ravenously over him. There were a dozen or more young people in the room, some of them dancing to the blast of rock, others sprawled on the chairs or lying on the floor. Most of them were naked or half dressed. Someone had thrown thin scarves over the table lamps and the lights were dimmed to deep reds and greens, giving the bodies in the room a sickly cast. The air was thick with the smell of whiskey and pot and other odors: semen and urine.

Eric looked about in disgust. A nude couple was lying on some pillows in the corner. The girl was moaning loudly as the boy's body hammered against her. A scrawny kid with long hair and vacant eyes sat near them, punching his arm with a syringe. Stark came up to Eric, dragging his girl with him.

"Some party, huh?" he grinned, weaving drunkenly.

"Who the hell are these people?" Eric asked thickly.

"Celebrities, man—all celebrities. Some band we picked up at the Whisky . . ." He shook his head and squinted at a reed-thin youth who was dancing with a bizarrely made-up girl. "Who are you guys?" he asked in a bleary voice.

The boy looked at him with savage eyes, his black hair hanging in thick strands across his sallow face. "We're The Clap, man, The Clap," he answered in a thin whisper.

"Shit, that's funny." Stark laughed.

"Listen, asshole, we just got signed to a three-album contract. We're not funny, man, we're a disease."

A scream came from the bedroom, followed by muffled cries and the sound of a body falling heavily to the floor. Eric went for the door, but Stark grabbed him by the shoulder.

"Stay out of it, Mr. Manager!" he grunted.

Eric spun around and punched him in the stomach, then hit him in the face. Stark fell, crying out in pain. Eric shoved the door open and burst into the room. He stopped and caught his breath, too astonished to move.

A girl was lying on the floor. Her body was covered with cuts and bruises, blood trickling in thin streams from each wound. Clutched in her hand was a knife. Chris was on his knees beside her, and clustered around them were four or five young people, watching with dulled eyes.

"Fix her, man, before she bleeds to death," a boy said in a hollow voice.

Chris laughed and began touching her, his fingers smearing the blood from one cut to another. The girl moaned and twitched under his hands until he was finished; then she sat up, her breath coming in short gasps. Her body was blotchy with dried blood.

"Chris!" Eric cried out.

Chris looked up and saw him in the doorway. His face went hard and his eyes blazed. Drops of blood were scattered across his chest and stomach, and when he stood up Eric saw that he had an erection.

"Get out of here, Eric," Chris said softly.

The girl who had been bleeding dropped the knife she was holding and threw her arms around Chris's legs and took him in her mouth. Chris glanced down at her and then back at Eric.

"I said get out of here," he repeated quietly.

Eric lunged back into the other room and out the door into the hallway, the nightmarish scene burning before his eyes. He broke out in a cold sweat and tried to choke back the nausea rising in his throat. Once back in his room he stumbled into the bathroom, fell heavily to the floor beside the toilet, and began to vomit.

37

Catherine went into the kitchen and poured herself a cup of coffee during a commercial break in the late-night television newscast. She came back into the living room and settled into a corner of the couch as a Special Report on Christopher began. On the screen, the network commentator in Los Angeles was saying:

". . . this amazing young man, whose tour across the United States has become a national phenomenon, has drawn one of the largest crowds ever gathered in Los Angeles, the final stop of the tour.

"It is difficult to find an appropriate predecessor to Christopher McKenzie, his approach is so unlike that of any other evangelist or faith healer. His programs have been presented without the background of a choir or guest appearances of famous entertainers; he doesn't exhort his audience to religious fervor with rhetoric or bombast. He has attracted his followers with his extraordinary gifts to heal and sight, and a unique view of the source of those gifts. In his most controversial statements to his audiences and the press, he has accused government leaders, the church, and members of the

American Medical Association of a kind of conspiracy to prevent the American people from investigating and developing their own psychic abilities. Although plagued by opposition from an alliance of Christian clergy and the 'back-to-God' movement that has swept the country in the last few years, he has steadfastly refused to align himself with any religious order.

"Some commentators have labeled Christopher a 'pop star,' claiming that the publicity used to promote his tour is primarily responsible for the overwhelming response he has received from the nation. We attempted to contact his personal manager, Eric Wynters, for an interview on that accusation, but our staff learned that Mr. Wynters has left Los Angeles unexpectedly to return to Philadelphia, the headquarters of the Christopher Foundation. . . ."

Catherine sat up, startled. She leaned forward and listened intently as the commentator continued.

". . . Phillip Conners, publicity director for the tour, has agreed to appear in the studio this evening to answer a few questions about Christopher and the manner in which his tour has been conducted."

She reached out and turned off the television set. The broadcast was a replay of an earlier newscast she had missed, which meant that Eric had left Los Angeles earlier in the day. But why? she wondered. It had been weeks since she had talked to him, and when she questioned John, he had reluctantly admitted that Eric had not wished to call her. But John had also said how worried he was about Eric, that when they had talked, Eric had sounded tense and overwrought. Catherine had dismissed the tabloid stories of Chris's drunken parties as so much nonsense created to sell papers. Now she wondered if any of it was true. Was that why Eric had left the tour? Or was he ill? She paced her living room, then decided to call John at home, even though it was late. He might have heard from Eric, or know why he'd left the tour.

The doorbell rang as she was dialing, and she knew who it was.

Eric stood in the doorway, pale and haggard. When she led him into the room, he held her close in a bruising embrace.

"I had to come here first," he whispered. "I couldn't go home; not yet. Oh, God, Cathy, you were so right and I was so wrong."

Without asking any questions, Catherine helped him stretch out on the couch. She propped some pillows under his head, loosened his tie, and then went into the bathroom to run a hot tub. Later, after he had bathed and was in bed, she brought in a tray of fresh coffee and sat beside him. He smiled up at her gratefully and drank from his cup. Then he pushed the tray aside and took her in his arms. Through the long hours of the night, he told her what had happened.

◆

John accepted a drink from Margaret and turned to face Eric and Catherine. They were sitting on the terrace as the unusually warm March day began to fade into a lilac-and-rose-colored twilight. The fragrance of early spring flowers drifted like the light scent of perfume on the still air, and dark-green shadows lengthened across the grounds. Eric glanced down at his son dozing in his lap and smiled at the slightly scabby knees and soiled T-shirt on the small but sturdy three-year-old. Catherine leaned over and gently brushed back the unruly tumble of dark hair over the boy's brow.

John was telling them about a long phone call he had received from Chris. He paused to sip his drink and then went on.

"He's staying on in Los Angeles for a few more days to complete his negotiations with the William Morris Agency for personal management, and he assured me that all proceeds from the programs we've completed will continue to go to the foundation and that a major percentage of his future income will also be transferred directly to the foundation."

"That's very generous of him," Eric murmured absently.

"I spoke to Charlotte and explained that the strain of handling the tour and managing all the business details had become too much of a burden for you, Eric. She seemed to understand. She hopes that you will continue to work with the foundation. She was a little surprised that you left the tour before it was over, but I told her that the work had taken its toll of your health and you thought it better to come home, that Phil Conners was carrying on in your place for the few remaining days. The explanation seemed to satisfy her."

"Thank you, John," Eric said, smiling. "You're still the smoothest man I know in the business."

Margaret looked at Eric, perplexed. "But I don't understand, Eric. Why did you leave Chris so suddenly? It's not like you to quit before a job is over."

"It just got to be too much for me, Margaret," Eric lied quietly. "Chris and I had a few differences of opinion that couldn't be resolved, and, as I told John, the pace was beginning to wreck me. I was very tired and wanted to come home. There were only a few days left; I didn't think it mattered." He looked down at the boy in his lap. "And I missed my son and"—he glanced at Catherine—"my girl."

Margaret nodded, accepting his story. Then her eyes grew anxious and she said: "Charlotte has called me several times. She is terribly worried about the stories that have been appearing about Chris, those parties and girls in his hotel rooms."

Eric looked at her steadily. "There is no truth in any of those stories, Margaret. They appear when anyone becomes a celebrity. The public can easily be fed a diet of lies and scandal about their idols; everyone would like to think that famous people roll in the mud, just the way they do." He laughed. "Devouring that kind of gossip is a national pastime."

"What do you want to do now, Eric?" John questioned him.

"Rest for a few days, play games with my son, take long walks with my fiancée, and plan a wedding and a life for my family." He turned to Catherine. "If that suits you, darling?"

Catherine smiled. "That suits me just fine."

John and Margaret smiled at each other and stood up. Margaret took the sleeping boy from Eric's arms and murmured something about dinner being served in a little while and that she would call them when it was ready.

When they were alone, Catherine moved into Eric's arms and leaned her head on his shoulder. For a few minutes they watched the last of the sunset fade into a silvery dusk touched with dying traces of pink and gold. A warm breeze stirred through the trees, and only the trilling call of birds broke the soft silence.

Finally, Catherine said: "You're a very kind man, darling, a very considerate man."

"I couldn't tell them what was really happening to Chris, what I saw. It wouldn't have been fair—to them or Chris. It's the last of my debt to him, keeping silent about what I know. With the William Morris people handling him, there's a good possibility that no one will ever know; they have a lot of clout with the media."

"But Chris knows," Catherine said sadly. "Despite what is happening to him, what he's doing to himself and to others, he knows. And it must be terrifying for him."

Eric sat up and turned to her, his eyes troubled. "I hear the sound of a psychologist and a mother rolled into one. I don't want you to see him when he comes back, Catherine," he said bluntly. "I don't think you or anyone else can do anything for Chris at this point."

"But, darling, I've worked with him; I know him. He's still just a boy, and he needs—"

"No," Eric said firmly. "I mean it, Cathy. I don't want you to see him. As far as I'm concerned, we're finished with whatever we can do for Chris. It's out of our control now."

"All right, dear," she said soothingly, trying to placate him. "I won't see him."

But it couldn't rest there—she knew that. They were all tied to one another in a bond they had forged together, an intricate web of feelings and alliances, debts paid and debts owed.

No, Catherine thought to herself, it isn't over yet. Chris's hold on them was too strong to be dismissed. If anything, it was growing stronger.

One morning, two weeks later, Catherine's secretary buzzed her on the intercom and said that Susan McKenzie was calling.

Susan's voice was low and tense, and she began to speak as soon as Catherine picked up the phone.

"Dr. Marlowe? Forgive me for bothering you. I know how busy you are, but—"

"Not at all, Mrs. McKenzie. It's been ages since I've spoken to—"

"Please, you must help me," Susan interrupted, her voice trembling on the verge of tears. "I couldn't think of anyone else to call."

"Mrs. McKenzie, what is it? What's wrong?"

"It's Chris—he's been home for more than a week and I haven't seen or heard from him. I tried calling his apartment and some man answered. I know Chris was there; I could hear him in the background. But he wouldn't talk to me." She began to cry. "Please, would you call him or see him? I know there's something wrong, that he's sick or—"

"Of course I'll call him, Mrs. McKenzie," Catherine said. "Please don't worry. I'm sure that Chris is fine. He's probably been so busy since he got back. . . ." Her voice trailed off lamely.

Susan made an effort to control herself, and after a moment's pause, said: "Chris and I have had our differences, I know. But I was only trying to protect him; you understood that. I've watched the shows, and—he's changed. I could see that."

"Well, of course, his whole life is so different now—"

"No, no—I don't mean that," Susan said quickly. "There's something wrong. I know my son." Her voice rose. "I know him better than all of you, and there's something wrong with him. He's afraid of something! I could see it in his eyes! Oh, please, call him, see him!"

"I will, I promise," Catherine said gently. "And I'll get back to you as soon as I have."

Catherine put down the phone and frowned, thinking briefly of her promise to Eric not to see Chris again. But she had to; surely he would understand that. Not only because of Susan's request, but for herself as well. Something had to be done to help Chris, and as his friend, and a psychologist, she was convinced that she could bring him to his senses.

She dialed his number and Stark answered.

"Sorry, Dr. Marlowe. He's busy. He said he'll call you back later."

"I want to talk to him now," Catherine said sharply.

"Sorry," the rough voice cut her off and hung up.

Catherine slammed the phone down angrily, picked up her purse, and left the office.

The security guard in the lobby of the building squinted at her through thick steel-rimmed glasses.

"Mr. McKenzie expecting you?" he questioned in a wheezing voice.

"Yes," Catherine lied. "I'm Dr. Catherine Marlowe."

"I'll have to check," the guard grunted, picking up the housephone. He mumbled into the receiver, nodded his head, and hung up. "He's sending somebody down to get you."

"Why? I can push elevator buttons by myself," Catherine retorted.

The guard shrugged. "Lots of people come here with all kinds of stories trying to get to see him," he offered as an explanation.

Catherine walked to the wide plate-glass windows overlooking the well-kept grounds of the apartment-house complex. The spring morning had turned overcast; rain threatened, and dark-gray clouds scudded across the skies. She shivered, feeling suddenly nervous. The sound of footsteps rang across the marble floor behind her, and she turned to face a young man coming toward her. He was dressed in a sweat shirt and jeans and moved with a cocky, arrogant swagger.

"You Dr. Marlowe?" he asked. His voice had a flat, metallic sound.

"Yes."

"Follow me." He led her to the last of a row of elevator doors. "This goes right to the penthouse," he explained.

They stepped in, and he pressed the button on the wall panel, staring straight ahead as the doors closed with a soft whooshing sound. Catherine watched him out of the corner of her eye, wondering who he was. He caught her glance, and his eyes flickered over her in a cold appraisal.

"What do you do for Chris?" she asked uncomfortably.

"Anything he tells me to," he replied tonelessly.

The elevator doors opened, and they stepped into a small foyer. Another man was standing by the apartment door. He knocked twice, and it was opened by Johnny Stark. This was the first time Catherine had ever seen him, and her curious stare brought a scowl of anger to his face. He ushered her into the living room with a mocking flourish and told her to wait. He went into another room and she sat down.

Half a dozen people were lounging around, talking and having drinks at the bar. Their dress and attitudes made them easy for her to identify. Two men in Cardin suits and deep tans were probably agents from Hollywood. A couple of girls wearing the latest radical fashions had the bored expressions that came of having too much money and too little imagination; they were here for the thrill of being with a new celebrity. The other two appeared to be hangers-on, kept around to fill out the party.

Fifteen minutes passed, and Catherine grew impatient and uneasy. The air in the room was stale and overwarm. One of the girls was staring at her with contempt and whispered something to the boy sitting next to her that made him laugh derisively. The two agency men were busy conferring at the bar and ignored her.

Finally Stark opened the door and signaled her to come in. She got up and walked past him into Chris's bedroom. He closed the door after her, whispering something to the people in the living room that made them laugh.

Everything around her was in disarray: clothes strewn over the bed and floor, suitcases lying open, half unpacked, the bedcovers twisted and unmade. Chris was on the terrace with his back to her, standing at the railing and looking out over the city.

"You should have made an appointment," he said without turning around.

"Since when do I need an appointment?" Catherine asked, stepping out onto the terrace and approaching him. "I'm not someone you do business with; I'm a friend. You've been home for more than a week without calling me or anyone. Your mother is very worried about you. She thinks you're ill." When he didn't answer, she added with a touch of sarcasm: "Or are you just too busy with your new friends to be concerned?"

He whirled around to face her and said coldly: "I don't need that shit from you."

Catherine stared at him, shocked by his appearance. His face was drawn and gaunt, his eyes as lifeless as glass.

"You look like hell," she said softly.

"So what? If I'd wanted surf and sun, I'd have stayed in L.A." He looked away from her impatiently. "Why don't you leave me alone? I'll deal with my mother by myself. I don't need you for a conscience!"

"From what Eric told me, a conscience is exactly what you do need," she flared, then regretted having said it so bluntly.

"I don't have to make excuses to you or anybody else for what I've done," Chris said angrily. "I don't need your advice on how to conduct my life!" The outburst flushed his pallid cheeks with blotchy color.

Catherine waited for a moment before speaking. If there is any way to reach him, she thought, it will demand all my skill to do it. He was obviously so tense that one wrong word would alienate them completely.

"Chris, we've always been able to talk to each other," she began gently. "Won't you let me try to help you now? Please?"

"I don't think there's anything you can do," he replied sullenly.

"Perhaps not, but there is something you can do. You look exhausted, worn out from the tour. Why don't you give yourself a chance to get some rest. Maybe we could talk once in a while, do a few tests together. There's still so much neither of us understands."

"What are you talking about? What do you want from me, anyway? To be your guinea pig for the rest of my life?"

"Chris, you're being unreasonable. All the energy you've expended to heal has helped only a few hundred people. But there are so many more who could benefit from further studies of your powers."

He gave a short, ugly laugh and shook his head. "You and my mother want the same thing—to hide me someplace like the freak you think I am, put me under glass to study me and protect me from the big, rotten world. Well, I like the way I'm living and I won't change it for anything!" His eyes grew hard and a calculating smile played at the corners of his mouth. "Eric told you about me," he said softly. "I'm no better than the rest of the world. I hurt people —and sometimes I enjoy it."

"Chris, that's not true, no matter what you've done. You're basically a decent human being who has—"

"No." He shook his head from side to side like an insistent child. "I'm not a decent human being. You remember what I did to Frank Pearson when he insulted you? I enjoyed making him scald himself! And there were others. A man who almost crashed into me on a road in Wynnewood. I nearly killed the stupid bastard! With my mind, not my hands! I forced a man in Atlanta to run into the street and get hit by a car—I don't even know if he lived or died!"

"Chris, stop it. You don't have to tell me this—"

"Why not? You can add it to your notes, make it part of your research!" His voice rose and began to crack. "You don't understand. I'm not even conscious of what I'm doing when these things happen! I can't always stop it! If I get angry, or right after I do a session of healing or sighting, it begins, it takes over! That's why I hired Stark. To get people away from me if I get too violent, and sometimes even he can't do it fast enough to prevent me from injuring somebody! So I heal them afterward and nobody's the wiser."

"Oh, Chris, my God, you're ill!" Catherine cried. "Send those people in there away and let me help you."

"You can't help me." He laughed shrilly. "I can't even help myself!"

"Then you can't do any more healings or sightings until we've found a way to stop this from happening again."

Chris choked back his laughter and stared at her. "Are you kidding? I can't stop now. I'm scheduled for the rest of the year. There's talk of a world tour. I couldn't stop now if I wanted to!"

"But you must! You can't go on like this. Eventually someone will find out, expose you to the media, and then everything will be destroyed; you, the foundation, people's belief in you—everything!"

His face blazed with a sudden, violent anger and his voice shook. "No one knows the truth about me except you, Eric, and my mother. Stark doesn't understand; he just does what I tell him. And none of you would expose me; you all have too much at stake. You all *owe* me!"

His burst of fury frightened her; she saw an underlying threat in his eyes, like the repressed violence she had seen in the eyes of psychotics. For a moment she wanted to leave, but despite his anger and bravado, she sensed a desperate pleading and knew that she couldn't abandon him.

Catherine faced him as calmly as she could and said: "It's true—we're all in your debt, but not at the cost of your health, possibly your sanity."

A savage light glinted in his eyes as he stared at her. "I don't need your sympathy and concern," he said in a guttural voice filled with rage.

Catherine started to speak, then stopped, silenced by the intensity of his eyes. The light on the terrace seemed to fade, as if darkness were suddenly falling, and a cold, rushing wind began to moan in her ears, rising to the sound of a shriek.

Chris's voice rose above the roaring in her head: "You can't help me and you can't stop me! No one can!"

She felt her will slipping away from her, evaporating into the wind, leaving her helpless before the brilliant flames of his eyes. The terrace beneath her feet slipped and tilted. She staggered, trying to fight off the weakness enveloping her, struggling to maintain her control. Her vision blurred and she saw only his eyes burning into hers . . . and in the corner of his left eye, shimmering in fading light, a red tear, bright as the color of blood! With a tremendous effort of will, she tried to reach out to him, heard her voice crying his name. He backed away from her touch, his face ashen. A scream tore from his throat: "Stark! Stark!"

Johnny Stark burst through the door and caught Catherine as she crumpled to the terrace.

Someone was holding her arm tightly, walking her into a small space, then standing still. She felt a soft movement and blinked her eyes, trying to focus on where she was. The elevator; a man beside her, his hand a tight grip on her arm. Then the lobby, doors pushed open and a chill of air against her face. She swallowed hard several times to relieve the dryness in her throat. Her head began to clear.

"Where's your car?" the man beside her asked.

"In the lot," she replied painfully, her voice raw. "I can find it. I don't need you."

"Whatever you say," he murmured and walked back into the lobby.

She moved slowly; her legs and arms felt stiff, aching; her back was a searing pain of tensed muscles. In her car, she slumped behind the wheel, waiting for the shock of what had happened to wear off, for the bewilderment and confusion to abate.

She had seen it now, experienced the full force of Chris's power. And she had seen the manifestation of that force in the tear of blood. Had it been there when he scalded Frank Pearson? Yes, she remembered, thinking then that she had imagined it. She gripped herself tightly to keep from shuddering. What could she do? Chris had said that there was too much at stake for anyone to expose him —and he was right. The work of the foundation and the trust of thousands of people would be lost. A mockery would be made of all the good he had accomplished.

Her head began to ache and tears of frustration filled her eyes. She needed time to think, to reason out a way to help him.

Driving home, she knew that she would have to see him again, talk to him, make him realize the danger of what he was doing. And for the moment, no one else must know—not Eric, not anyone.

One thought sustained her resolve to help him, gave her a slight measure of hope: Chris had stopped himself before harming her.

Hours later Catherine lay in bed wide-eyed, staring into the dark. She went over and over in her mind what had happened, what Chris had told her about himself. She understood now why Susan had been so fearful, what she meant when she had said that Christopher was frightened and why he had avoided calling or seeing her. He was terrified of what was happening to him, and perhaps that was the key to helping him. . . .

The phone rang, jarring her thoughts. She picked it up and heard Chris's voice.

"Catherine, just listen to me, please. And don't speak." His voice was low and shaky. "I'm sorry for what happened. You've always been good to me, tried to help me. There's nothing you can do now, so please don't try. I have to work this out by myself. I'm leaving tomorrow morning for New York to do some interviews. And from there I'm going to make a tour of veterans hospitals that the agency has arranged. I don't know how long I'll be gone. Call my mother and Nella. Tell them—" He paused and for a moment she thought he was crying.

"Chris, listen to me," Catherine said urgently.

"No, let me finish," he interrupted. "Tell them I love them, but that I can't see them, not for a while, anyway. Make up something, some explanation—please? And, please, oh, God, please forgive me for what I did to you."

"Chris, I know you didn't mean it. You're ill. You've got to let me—"

The line went dead and there was silence. Catherine hung up, then dialed his number frantically. A busy signal sounded in her ear. Throughout the night she called him again and again, finally falling asleep from exhaustion, the phone clutched in her hand, the busy signal a strange, monotonous sound in the darkness of her room.

38

Catherine did as Chris requested and called Susan and Nella. She tried to explain to each of them that Chris needed time to adjust to the phenomenal success he was having, that he cared for them both, but felt that his life had changed and that he had to find his way without their influence, sort out what was happening to him by himself. She knew how feeble her excuses for him sounded and was grateful when Susan accepted them with no comment. But Nella burst into tears and hung up before she was finished. A few days later Catherine heard that she had gone to visit relatives in London. Charlotte, too caught up in her work with the foundation to recognize anything but Chris's continued success, dismissed their separation as a lovers' quarrel.

In the weeks that followed, Catherine saw Chris only by way of the media: he appeared on *The Tonight Show* and in a special interview with Barbara Walters. His picture was carried on the covers of *Time* and *Newsweek*; and for the first time in its publishing history, the cover of *Reader's Digest* bore a photograph—that of Christopher McKenzie. Controversy still raged around him, but that only increased the public's fervor and interest. Reports from doctors and directors of clinics and hospitals continued to come in, but no further stories appeared in the scandal sheets. In those moments when she was alone, Catherine wondered if somehow Chris had managed to overcome the dreadful seizures that afflicted him, if in some way he had found a means of healing himself. There were times when she thought of him as lost in a strange and foreign world, traveling like an emigrant without a passport and finding no place to rest.

While she continued to work at her research, Eric kept busy managing the syndication of the shows that had been taped on the tour and handling the public relations for the foundation. Their evenings were occupied with plans for the wedding, and weekends were spent looking for a house. Chris was spoken of only in passing.

In the first week of June they received word from the Morris Agency that Chris would be returning to New York for a rally to be held in Madison Square Garden. He had made a special request that Eric be retained as consultant for the rally, which was going to be telecast on NBC as a special event. Eric refused. A few nights later Eric told Catherine that Chris had called him.

"He begged me to be there, to work on the show. He said he couldn't do it without me."

"How did he sound?" Catherine asked.

"Tired, anxious, like a kid who is worn-out," Eric replied.

"He probably is," she said. "He's been all over the country in the last few weeks. Why are they having the rally now? Why don't they give him a chance to rest?"

"The agency planned it months ago to capitalize on all the publicity he's been getting. He told me that next month he's going to Europe and they wanted to do this before he left."

"What did you tell him?"

"That I didn't want to do it. He understood why, but pleaded with me to help him this one last time."

They were silent for a few minutes, then Catherine asked softly: "Are you going to do it?"

Eric sighed uncomfortably. "Do you think I should?"

She hesitated for a moment, and then said: "Yes, I think you should. For the very reason that you yourself want to—because you feel you owe it to him."

Eric smiled and took her hand. "I'll never be able to put anything past you, will I?"

Catherine laughed and kissed him. "Not much," she answered. "But don't ever worry about it—I'll love you just the same."

"Will you come with me? Will you be there the night of the rally? Chris told me to ask you; he wants you there too."

"Yes," she said slowly. "I'll be there."

When the public announcement of the rally was made, press coverage followed every detail of the preparations as if it were an important political event. Chris appeared nightly in taped segments from cities he was still visiting, performing healings and sightings at an incredible expenditure of his energy.

A few nights before the rally was to take place, Catherine watched him do an interview. He appeared haggard, exhausted, and looked almost like a stranger compared to the boy she had met only a little more than a year ago. Listening to the host introduce him, she thought of his rise to fame as a particularly American phenomenon. From the first tests in her lab to the swelling Christopher Movement was a distance measured in hundreds of newspaper stories and interviews, countless hours of TV time, months of traveling on tours, culminating in the nationwide adoration of a hero who possessed all the fantasy qualities of dreams: youth, beauty, and almost Godlike gifts.

The interview was like so many others he had given, and she was about to turn it off when he said something that captured her complete attention.

". . . yes, the rally promises to be the highlight of all my work," he was saying. "And an event will take place unlike any other you've seen so far."

When pressed for information concerning the event, he smiled and offered the interviewer two press box tickets.

The next morning Catherine received a call from Nella.

"I thought you were going to stay in England for a few more weeks," Catherine said, surprised that she was home.

"I was," Nella replied. "But I received a cablegram from Chris telling me about the rally. He asked me if I could come home to see it."

"Oh, Nella, that's wonderful news! I'm sure that whatever has been disturbing Chris is better now. Eric is going into New York today—he's a consultant on the show. And I'm driving in the morning of the rally. Would you like to go with me?"

"No, I can't. Chris called me at home last night and asked me to be with Susan, to watch it on television with her."

"Oh? Well, I can understand that. It's a big night for him, and I guess he doesn't want her to see it alone. As usual, she refused to be part of the program."

"I don't think she refused," Nella said, sounding puzzled. "I think he asked her not to be there. Catherine, when he talked to me, he sounded so tired. . . ."

"I know. He's been all over the country these last weeks. Maybe you can convince him to take a rest when this is over."

"I'll do my best," she said. Then, after a moment's pause, she added: "You know how much I love him."

"Yes, dear. And I think he needs your love very much."

After they hung up, Catherine sat staring at the phone thoughtfully, remembering what she had heard Chris say about a special event that would take place at the rally.

Was it possible, she wondered, that he would do as she had asked? Would he give one last healing and then announce that he was going to stop to devote himself to further research of his gifts?

At eleven o'clock on the morning of the rally, traffic on the New Jersey Turnpike between Newark and Manhattan was at a standstill. People were pouring into New York in everything from battered wrecks of cars to sleek new Cadillacs, flatbed trucks crowded with youngsters, and gaily painted vans with "CHRISTOPHER" lettered on the sides. Signs and banners floated from the open trucks and out the windows of old buses pressed into service, while bumper stickers and decals identified the drivers of more conservative vehicles as Followers.

Catherine swore softly at herself for not taking the train and closed the windows against the smell of auto exhaust and the noise of blaring horns. She shrugged out of the jacket of her beige linen suit and reached for a tissue to blot the light film of perspiration forming on her brow. The bright June morning was beginning to grow warm and muggy, and she wished she had dressed more comfortably for the drive into the city.

She glanced around at the cars closest to her, seeing the lure of the rally wherever she looked: wheelchairs folded and strapped to the roofs, the tops of crutches showing through windows. In the car beside her a child lay on the back seat, the lower part of his body in a brace. Up front a man sat behind the wheel, waiting impassively for traffic to move, while the woman next to him knitted methodically, stopping every so often to glance back at the child and smile, her face anxious but her eyes full of hope.

That's what Chris has done for all these people, Catherine thought; more than anything else, he's given them hope. He stands alone outside the confines of religion and politics and makes things happen before their eyes like a divine magician. How could church or government leaders possibly compete with him?

The traffic ahead of her began to move. Catherine started the motor and joined the swollen throng of cars that crept slowly toward the city. She emerged from the Lincoln Tunnel into a dense jungle of movement. Sunlight hovered above the crowded sidewalks as if it were unable to penetrate the roar of noise from people and machines. Out-of-state drivers, confused by Manhattan streets, blocked impatient motorists and shouted for directions from stony-faced pedestrians, while shoppers and office workers hurried on their way, seemingly oblivious to the snarl of cars and angry cries.

Evidence of the rally was everywhere: groups of musicians, jugglers, and mimes were performing skits and singing songs about Christopher on street corners, and mammoth posters featuring Chris's face were plastered on the sides of buildings, giving Catherine the eerie impression that he was looking down on them, urging them to acclaim him.

She parked her car in an all-day garage on 34th Street and started to walk to Madison Square Garden. Troops of bright-eyed, clean-faced boys and girls wearing Christopher T-shirts that identified their fan clubs strolled along the pavements, mingling with flashily dressed hookers and pimps in white suits. Hustlers lounged in doorways of porno bookstores and grinned with hard-eyed amusement at the youngsters. Dotted throughout the crowd were businessmen and students, housewives and clerks, heedless of the swirling action around them.

Catherine worked her way around the outside of the Garden to the VIP entrance on Penn Plaza. A guard checked her name on his list and directed her to a corridor that led to the broadcasting area under the floor of the arena. She found Eric in the control booth conferring with the public relations director of the Garden. As soon as he was free, she went up to him. There were dark shadows under his eyes, and a day's growth of beard scratched her face as they embraced.

"Darling, you look exhausted. Did you get any sleep?" she asked.

"Maybe two or three hours. More like blacking out than sleep. We've been at this since early yesterday morning, and it isn't finished yet."

An assistant producer called out to him, waving a sheaf of papers clutched in his hand, a thinly concealed expression of panic on his face.

"Oh, Christ, let's get out of here," Eric muttered. "It's been nonstop chaos and I need some rest. C'mon, I have a room across the street at the Statler."

Catherine closed the windows and drew the drapes, dimming the noise from the street to a distant murmur of sound. She slipped out of her clothes and folded back the spread and blankets on the bed, then lay down against the cool sheets, one arm behind her head. Eric came out of the shower and stood in the doorway toweling his hair.

"There's a vision of beauty to brighten a man's heart and quicken his pulse," he said, smiling at her.

She looked up at him with a lazy grin. "The bellboy sent me up. My name's Trixie and I get fifty bucks a shot."

"And undoubtedly worth every penny." Eric laughed, lying down beside her.

"I thought you were exhausted," she murmured as he took her in his arms.

"Only a part of me," Eric answered, kissing her breasts. "Not all of me."

They lay quietly in each other's arms, breathing together in measured unison and listening to the muffled sounds of the streets.

"Did you have a chance to see David before you left?" Eric asked.

"Yes. I had dinner with John and Margaret last night. David read me a story. He's so bright, Eric."

"I know." Eric smiled. "The other day he told me he wanted a little sister. Think we can arrange that for him?" he asked in a teasing voice.

"I think we just did," Catherine chuckled, kissing his lips lightly.

They were quiet for a few minutes, then Eric asked: "Did you have any trouble getting into the city?"

"The traffic was unbelievable. And the streets are jammed."

"It's going to be a mess tonight. Tickets are already sold out, and there are still lines forming. Christ, I'll be glad when this whole thing is over. I still don't know why I agreed to do it, but Chris sounded so desperate on the phone."

"I can only imagine what he must be going through right now," Catherine said almost to herself.

Eric lit a cigarette and stared ahead thoughtfully. "When I think back on what Chris was like when I first met him, the times we've had together—the *good* times—I just can't help feeling responsible for what's happened to him."

Catherine sat up and looked at Eric seriously. "No, you can't do that. You can't go on feeling that way. However it turned out, you did your best for Chris, what you thought was right."

Eric smiled and reached out to touch her face. "You know, I like you. Not too long ago you were telling me that I was hurting him, and now you're defending me. You're like a lioness with her cub, giving it a cuff when you're angry and then licking the bruise to make it better."

"You've just learned something very important about women, dear," Catherine said tenderly.

"Yes; now if I could just figure out what it means," he said, laughing. Then, glancing at his watch, he groaned: "Oh, God, it's late. I've got to get back." He scrambled to his feet and began to dress quickly. "Will you be all right until the broadcast?"

"Of course. I'll get something to eat and be along later. What about you? Shall I bring you a sandwich and some coffee?"

"No, we can have a late supper when the program is over."

He knotted his tie and slipped on his jacket, then bent over the bed and kissed her.

"I'll give the bellboy a tip on my way out, Trixie," he said huskily. "You were just great."

"So were you. Next time you get it for free."

A few hours later Catherine left the hotel and started toward the Garden. Crowds were assembled along the sidewalks and overflowing into the streets. Mounted police struggled to keep vehicle traffic moving, while evening commuters tried to push through the lines to get to Penn Station. Angered by the delays, they exchanged jeers with the Christopher followers and several fights broke out. A picket line of young people marched doggedly amidst the confusion, waving their signs and yelling anti-Christopher protests. A man stood on the broad concrete plaza yelling through a megaphone, urging people to abandon Christopher and go back to God, to Jesus. Newscasters and camera crews from all three networks scurried to cover the outbursts of anger and the fights, stopping for on-the-spot interviews.

Catherine heard one woman exclaim to a reporter: "This is really terrific! I mean, it's really wonderful! It's like the beginning of something new—you know what I mean? I wouldn't miss it for the world!"

The newscaster shook his head dumbly and turned to a couple helping a young boy on crutches. Their voices got lost in a shriek of sirens as an ambulance screeched to a stop near the steps on Seventh Avenue and attendants raced to help someone who had collapsed.

Catherine made her way cautiously to the Penn Plaza entrance and was stopped by a guard. She gave him her name, and he called another guard over to escort her to the control booth.

"Is there something wrong?" she asked. "I can find my own way."

"Just precautions, ma'am. We had a bomb scare earlier—a couple of kids trying to break up the show," he explained briefly.

Eric was in the corridor outside the booth talking with an assistant. He gestured Catherine to his side, and the guard went back to his station.

"This place is like a madhouse," Eric said to her hurriedly. "Just stay by my side so I don't lose you."

He turned back to the man he was talking to and they finished their notes. Then Eric took her aside. "If any of this falls into place, it'll be a miracle. We're going to run overtime, I'm sure." He glanced toward the control booth. "The director is going bonkers trying to trim out excess marching bands and testimonials."

"Are we going to be out front?"

"No, we'll watch it on the monitors in the booth. But that reminds me—Charlotte sent word with one of the guards that she and Amanda are here. They're in a special section up front for members of the foundation. She said they would see us after the show was over. What about Nella—isn't she coming?"

"No, she said that Chris asked her to watch it with Susan."

"The William Morris people were upset about Susan refusing to be here; they'd planned a whole segment around her."

The hallway was suddenly filled with people, and someone called out to Eric. He looked at his watch and sighed: "Well, here we go—it's show time!"

Inside the Garden the audience was scarcely able to contain its excitement. Seated in sections representing individual states or regions of the country, they waved banners and chanted Christopher slogans. Giant photo blowups of Chris decorated the walls and the stage, which was flanked by flags of every state and enormous banks of flowers. Four-sided TV monitors hung from the ceiling to insure everyone's being able to see what was happening, and spotlights blazed down on the arena stage. Nurses and white-jacketed attendants were stationed throughout the hall to aid the lame and the infirm, and security guards were posted at every entrance.

On the streets surrounding the Garden, hundreds of people crowded together in front of gigantic TV monitors that had been set up by the network. Crews and reporters threaded their way among them, asking questions, getting interviews, while police troops stood by, watchful of any disturbance.

At nine o'clock the houselights in the Garden dimmed to a roar of approval from the massive audience and the throngs watching from the streets. A collection of high-school bands marched in formation into the arena area and grouped alongside the stage to begin the national anthem. A beautiful young singer, well known for her recordings and TV appearances, walked onto the stage and led the assembly in the anthem. Patriotism, absolute belief in Christopher, and sweat glistened on every face.

Then, through loudspeakers directly overhead, the host for the program, an internationally recognized film star whom Chris had cured of arthritis, was introduced. After a burst of applause, he made an opening statement, referred to the foundation, and asked Charlotte to say a few words.

"I didn't know she was going to speak," Catherine whispered to Eric.

"Neither did she until a few hours ago. Chris requested it, and, of course, Charlotte agreed."

Catherine smiled. "She'll always be his number-one fan. In a way, I think he did more for her than he did for Nella."

A series of testimonials followed, each speaker telling of his or her affliction and of how Christopher had cured it. A young girl shyly described her life in a wheelchair until she had been healed, and her dream of becoming a dancer. Then, to the accompaniment of an orchestra that had assembled on one side of the stage, she did a specially prepared number with awkward but fervent grace.

Short films of famous moments from the tours were shown, and many of the healed were in the audience, bowing to cheers and shouts as the cameras picked them out. A new rock group called The Threat came on to sing their hit single "Christopher."

"Why are they on the show?" Catherine asked.

"Part of a campaign by the Morris Agency. It handles them too," Eric answered with a wry grin. "Everybody's just doing business."

Another group of testimonials followed, recited in halting fashion by a group of elderly people whose lives had been extended by Chris's power. Several of them broke down in tears, moving the audience to sympathetic murmurs and reverent applause.

Catherine stared numbly at the monitors, watching the spectacle being made of the guests. Eric sat beside her, his arms folded, face grim, as the procession went on.

"I don't think I can stand much more of this," Catherine said under her breath.

"Chris is on in a minute, and that will wind it up," Eric replied. "Then we can get out of here and put this whole thing behind us."

Just then the houselights were dimmed even further, and a single spotlight was focused on the door leading to the backstage area. A hush fell over the audience; anticipation of Chris's appearance was almost palpable. After a few seconds, the door opened and he walked out of the darkness and into the light. Dressed as always in a white sweater and slacks, his blond hair like an aura around his head, Christopher seemed to be bathed in celestial light. Everyone was awestruck and, for a few moments, remained silent. Then, as he stepped to the center of the stage, a chorus of unanimous acclamation rose from every throat. Chris stood with his head bowed as the thunderous ovation washed over him. When he raised his eyes to his followers and held up his arms, their frenzy increased, until he finally waved them to silence.

In the control booth Catherine stared at his face on the monitors, aware of the skillful make-up that had been applied to disguise his wasted features. He was thinner than she remembered and appeared to tremble as he spoke.

". . . you've demonstrated your belief in me and in yourselves by being here tonight," he was saying. "There are others here, and others watching from their homes, to whom we all owe a great debt —especially myself."

He paused, and the director signaled for a close-up. Catherine watched his face closely. He looks ill, she thought, and suddenly felt apprehensive. Chris looked directly into the camera, and for a moment she had the sensation that he was staring at her.

"I owe more than I can ever repay to Dr. Catherine Marlowe and Eric Wynters," Chris said quietly, "and to Mrs. Charlotte Stanwyck, who has made it possible for thousands to be helped by further studies and research, and who has unselfishly championed my work." He stopped and swallowed nervously. "And to her daughter, Nella, whom I've loved since I was a child." He paused again, then said: "And last, but certainly most important of all, to my mother, Susan McKenzie, who has always understood me better than anyone else."

His voice had dropped almost to a whisper as he finished. There was sustained applause that seemed to be a surging outpouring of love from every member of the audience.

Catherine's attention was riveted to Chris's face. There was an expression in his eyes that filled her with dread.

Chris looked slowly around the arena and, in a voice filled with emotion, continued: "Now I want to do something for all of you." He hesitated, taking a deep breath before going on: "It will be my ultimate act of kindness to you, and proof of my gratitude for what you have all given to me—your faith and your love."

Eric stood up and went to the director. "What the hell is he doing?" he demanded. "None of that is in the script!"

"How the hell should I know? He refused to tell me what he was going to say or do!"

Chris was staring at his audience intently, as if he were looking directly at each man, woman, and child there before him.

In a low voice he asked: "May I please have a moment of complete silence?"

Catherine got to her feet, her hands clenched together nervously, watching the monitors with frightened eyes.

After a few seconds of restless murmuring and puzzled whispers, the house grew quiet, expectant. Every face was turned to Chris, every eye intent on him. The silence in the hall was ominous, foreboding, and Catherine felt herself grow pale.

Chris's face filled the bank of monitors in extreme close-up, his features turning harsh with the effort he was making. Suddenly a tear formed in the corner of his left eye, tiny at first, then swelling, clinging to his lashes, fully formed, like a blazing red jewel.

Catherine made a strangled cry in her throat and moaned: "No! Oh, God, no!"

"What is it?" Eric asked, shocked. "What's happening?"

At that instant the thousands of people gathered in the hall rose to their feet as a single body in perfect, robot precision. They stood straight and silent, row upon row, absolutely motionless.

An astonished gasp went up in the control booth. White-faced and shaken by the awesome sight, the director struggled to cue his crew. The cameramen, apparently unaffected by the immensity of Chris's act, panned across the vast sea of silent, expressionless faces.

Then, as if on command, the audience moved again, slowly sinking to its knees in a terrifying gesture of supplication. Even the lame and crippled moved as if they had never been afflicted, twisted limbs bent under them, withered arms hanging by their sides.

Catherine tore her eyes from the horrific sight and rushed out of the booth to the corridor. Eric ran to catch her as she staggered dizzily.

"I feel sick," she gasped. "I need some air."

Eric put his arm around her shoulders, and they hurried down the hallway to a side exit. He pushed open the door, and they stepped outside, only to stop frozen with shock.

Hundreds of people stood before the huge screens set up around the building. Silent, dazed by what they saw, they stared blankly at the enormous image of Christopher on each screen, their figures bathed in the silvery light from the monitors. They stood motionless, crowded together on the plaza and along the sidewalks, spilling out onto the streets like closely placed tombstones in a cemetery.

"Oh, my God!" Eric breathed hoarsely. "What has he done?"

Catherine slowly turned to the screen nearest them. Eric followed her gaze, and they looked at Christopher's face.

Tears of blood were overflowing his eyes, running down his cheeks like scarlet streams, coursing over his chin and neck, and spreading into a wide stain on his shirt collar.

Catherine collapsed against Eric and screamed: "He's killing himself!"

For an endless, terrifying moment they watched, horror-struck, as blood drenched Chris's face, bursting in angry spurts from his eyes until he staggered and with a tortured howl of pain fell to the stage.

The crowd on the street shuddered like a great beast suddenly waking. A shocked outcry rumbled through the throng as people stared at one another in bewilderment. Eric grabbed Catherine's hand, and they ran back down the hallway toward the arena. When they reached the auditorium, they raced past rows of people groggily becoming conscious of what they were doing, their faces filled with confusion, dumbfounded to find themselves on their knees.

Charlotte and Amanda were struggling to their feet as Eric and Cathy reached the open area near the stage. The two women looked dazed and incredulous at the growing chaos around them.

"Catherine! Eric!" Charlotte cried out when she saw them. "What in God's name is happening?"

Catherine shook her head dumbly, running with Eric up the steps to the center of the stage where Chris lay crumpled in a pool of blood, his body sprawled like a broken doll. The stage manager was kneeling beside him. Johnny Stark burst from the backstage door, shoving people out of his way to get to Chris. A doctor and one of the attending nurses hurried across the stage as Stark fell to his knees and pulled Chris into his lap, tears running down his face.

The doctor looked up from the lifeless body clutched in Johnny's arms and shook his head. "He's dead," he said softly.

Charlotte had reached the group gathered on the stage and let out a scream of anguish at the sight of Chris's bloody face. She turned away, sobbing, and Catherine reached out to hold her.

Shaken and trembling, Eric stepped to the front of the stage and faced the audience, holding up his arms for their attention. Then, barely able to speak, he announced that Christopher was dead.

For a moment there was stunned silence in the huge arena. Then a woman screamed and a man began to weep. A wail of sorrow rose up, and people turned to one another, crying out their grief. Like lost children, they clung together, confused, hysterical, afraid.

With all the strength and authority he could summon, Eric asked them to leave, to return to their homes. Still unable to grasp what had happened, they stood, not moving.

"Please," Eric cried out. "You must leave, as quietly as possible. The guards and attendants will help you."

The security guards flung open the exit doors, and in an eerie, funereal silence, the people began to file out, afraid now to turn and look back at the body lying on the stage.

Catherine and Eric stood to one side as Chris was lifted onto a stretcher. Someone wiped his face clean of blood and closed his eyes. As a sheet was pulled over him, Catherine wept, seeing the handsome features, composed now in an expression of calm and peace, disappear under the white cloth.

The Garden looked like the aftermath of a terrible battle, desolate and quiet, a wasteland. Agency men and women, police officers, and TV crews and newscasters wandered about in a daze. The telecast had gone on, recording every terrifying moment of what had happened. The doctor had announced that based on his brief examination, Chris appeared to have died of a massive cerebral hemorrhage. Members of the foundation were approached by reporters, but they waved aside all attempts at an explanation of what had taken place during those few mysterious moments before Chris's death. None of them clearly remembered what they had done. All they wanted to do was leave as quickly as possible, as if they knew some hidden, vulnerable part of themselves had been suddenly and shockingly exposed, and they wanted to forget it. Charlotte had been taken home by Amanda, and Johnny Stark had vanished.

A newsman found Catherine sitting with Eric on some seats near the stage. Still shaking with nerves, he asked: "Dr. Marlowe, you were the first person to discover Christopher's extraordinary gifts and make studies of them. Is there anything you can tell us about what happened here tonight?"

Catherine looked up at him dully and shook her head.

"Please, Dr. Marlowe," the newsman persisted, "surely you can give us some explanation of this awful tragedy."

How can I explain? she thought wearily. No one would ever understand. No one knew of the dark compulsions that overtook Chris with each act he performed. To tell them and destroy their belief in him would be to destroy a part of their selves.

Eric started to ask the man to leave them alone, but Catherine stopped him and said quietly: "I can offer you no explanation of the events that took place here tonight. Christopher McKenzie is dead, but I know that the good he accomplished will not die. Those he healed have been blessed with new lives, new hope. And others have learned more about themselves and their own potential."

She stopped and turned to Eric, her face wet with tears. The reporter moved off, and Eric held her in his arms.

"Darling, let's go home," he said softly.

As they walked out of the building and through the crowds, they heard the sounds of weeping, the mourning for a fallen leader. Catherine knew that investigations of tonight's tragedy would be started, that conjecture and controversy would fill newspapers and magazines. But the truth of Christopher's death would never be known.

◆

In the small brick-and-white-frame Colonial house on the Main Line, where Christopher had grown up, Susan comforted the sobbing girl in her arms.

"Don't cry, Nella," she whispered, rocking her slowly.

Susan stared dry-eyed at the television set and watched her son's body being carried off the stage. She heard Eric make the announcement of his death and saw the shocked and grieving faces in the audience.

"He died like the hero of his childhood dreams," she said almost to herself.

The centuries-old sorrow of Irishwomen who had seen their men perish in battle was etched into the fine lines of her face. But she had finally found peace from the fears that had haunted her for so many years. She smiled and gathered Nella closer to her.

"Christopher was like Cu Chulainn," Susan told her. "Cu Chulainn, the invincible hero to whom fate ordained a short life with lasting glory. He was the most courageous hero in the land of the Tuatha De Danann. And it was said that a warrior's light arose from the crown of his head during battle."

She paused and stared into space, remembering the gray misty clouds floating across the skies of Inverness, the great Moray Firth, and the golden-haired boy running across the fields. Then, in a soft voice, she went on.

"But the gods decreed certain absolute laws which no one could transgress and live, and Cu Chulainn deliberately violated those laws. And so he was wounded by treachery and yet remained heroic until his death, defending his people, chained to a stone pillar so that he might die standing, as his final act of courage."